THE

RAMADI

AFFAIR

THE
RAMADI
AFFAIR

Barry Schaller

QP BOOKS
New Orleans, Louisiana

Published in 2016 by QP Books, an imprint of Quid Pro Books.

ISBN 978-1-61027-332-9 (pbk.)
ISBN 978-1-61027-344-2 (hbk.)
ISBN 978-1-61027-330-5 (ebk.)

QUID PRO BOOKS
5860 Citrus Blvd., suite D-101
New Orleans, Louisiana 70123
www.qpbooks.com

This is a work of fiction. The characters, names, events, dialogue, and circumstances are imaginary or are used fictionally. Any resemblance to real
persons or actual events is purely coincidental, fictitious, or imaginary.

Cataloging-in-Publication Data

Schaller, Barry.

    The Ramadi affair / Barry Schaller.

        p. cm.

    ISBN 978-1-61027-332-9 (pbk.)

    1. Veterans—Fiction. 2. Trials—United States—Fiction. 3. Iraq War, 2003–2011—Fiction.
I. Title.

PS3613.I5783.S1 2016

813' .41.8—dc22
2016421980
CIP

Cover image is original artwork provided courtesy of Donna Colburn, copyright
© 2015, used by permission. Author photograph on back cover inset courtesy of
Connecticut Law Tribune, an ALM publication.

THE
RAMADI
AFFAIR

PART ONE

"I found Him in the shining of the stars,
I marked Him in the flowering of His fields,
But in His ways with men I find Him not.
I waged His wars, and now I pass and die.
O me! for why is all around us here
As if some lesser god had made the world,
But had not force to shape it as he would,
Till the High God behold it from beyond,
And enter it, and make it beautiful?"

—Alfred Lord Tennyson, *Idylls of the King*, 1859-1885

1

I n March 2008, the following post appeared on the news website *Gawker*:

AL QAEDA REPORTEDLY EXECUTES "U.S. SPY," GUTS HER BODY
By Albert Stern
Filed to: DRONE WARS 3/6/08 4:50PM

Al Qaeda operatives in Iraq reportedly shot, then stabbed to death and gutted, the body of the daughter of a local sheikh, after accusing her of collaborating with American troops. Her body was found hung from a soccer goalpost near a site where American troops conducted a raid earlier this year.

A report on the woman's death was first published in English, along with a photo of her body, by the *Long War Journal*, a terrorism discussion website sponsored by the Council for the Preservation of Democracy. The full photo is at the bottom of this post.

An Iraqi journalist with deep contacts in Al Qaeda in Iraq (AQI) has claimed in an Arabic-language Facebook post that the woman in the photo is Jasmine, the daughter of Sheikh Abdul Abdull Farad, who led a coalition of tribes under the name of the Anbar Awakening in 2007. The coalition assisted American troops against insurgent forces. The woman had been publicly accused by AQI sources of consorting with American soldiers and operating a prostitution ring.

The *Long War Journal*'s report read:

Arabic-language news reports have confirmed that the woman was shot in the head before being stabbed and her body gutted from her neck to her pelvic area and then hanged for all to see. The local media said the location where the corpse was found was near the site of an American raid carried out in January of 2008 that killed five Iraqis.

The woman was apparently killed because it was suspected that she was working with the Americans. An AQI flag and black banners were found beside her body reading, "American collaborator and traitor" and "whoever fights with the government or cooperates with it is not an Iraqi, but a traitor." Arabic reports

3

also note that AQI sources charged the woman with planting microphones in AQI vehicles and meeting places in order to guide American troops.

This is not the first time such an attack has occurred. In 2007, AQI militants allegedly crucified a man they believed to be assisting the U.S. with its surveillance and attack programs in the country. (Warning: video at the link is extremely graphic.)

On the same day, a graphic six-minute video was posted that showed a sparsely furnished room in which three men, their faces covered, stabbed a screaming young woman, who was bleeding profusely, until she was motionless. At that point, one of the men, who appeared to be in charge, gutted her with his knife from her pelvic area to her neck. There was a great deal of blood visible. Screaming and wailing female voices could be heard outside of the room. The men then dragged the body outdoors and suspended it by the ankles to the crossbar of a soccer goalpost. The video closed on the image of the body hanging under the goalpost. Written across the video was Arabic lettering roughly translated as "Justice to traitors." The posting was taken down three days later with the simple notation that it had been removed.

One week later, the following news item appeared on the BBC World Service news website:

In an apparent retaliatory strike against Al Qaeda, in the city of Ramadi, in Iraq, allied soldiers carried out an attack in the northern quarter of the city. The strike was the third of three strikes that, according to a reliable source, were a reprisal for the murder of an Iraqi woman from the family of a local sheikh known to be cooperative with American forces. No further information is available at this time.

The news item was carried the next day by Al Jazeera. No follow-up appeared.

* * *

In the late summer of 2009, the *Philadelphia Guardian* carried under local news a story about a hero's return from Iraq: "Sgt. Nicholas Serrano, of Philadelphia, was welcomed home after 14 months in Iraq during the final stage of the surge in Anbar Province. Sgt. Serrano has been reassigned to Fort Benning."

* * *

In the latter part of August 2024, the *Philadelphia Guardian* carried a report that "Sgt. Nicholas Serrano, a native of Philadelphia, has been arrested for the murder of Harold Wickes and the attempted murder of Dolores 'Dee' Hamilton. Serrano, a well-known hero of the Iraq war, served in Ramadi for 14 months in 2007-2008 during the surge."

2

The rasping sound of the alarm startled David Lawson awake from another of his recurring nightmares of a bloody rampage in what appeared to be a village bordering a desert. He bolted upright in bed, straining to get his bearings in the pre-dawn darkness. The nightmare was beginning to fade as he struggled, as always, to fit its shards into a sequence that made sense. Although he could not compose a coherent story, he recognized familiar elements. In the nightmare, he appeared as aggressor and defender, killer and savior, armed with two M16 rifles, one on each shoulder. Although David followed an evening ritual of touching the gold cross given to him by his grandfather—a veteran of the bloody fighting in Northern Ireland—to ward off nightmares, his sleep was rarely undisturbed.

Despite the elusive nature of the nightmare, he was able to grasp its meaning when he awoke. He could identify some of the people and events from his combat tour in Iraq and some from his present life. It was as though his sleeping brain had a story to tell and set about recruiting actors and settings from his daily thoughts and experiences.

This time he was running in slow motion down a dusty, littered street in what he sensed was the Iraqi city of Ramadi, desperately struggling to reach a ramshackle house made of cement blocks and a poorly tiled roof on a street corner. When he reached the house, he peered through a window. He saw a tangle of bodies—men, women and children—body upon body, limb upon limb, literally afloat in a river of blood that rushed across the entire floor of the large room. He felt certain that he had caused the deaths and he had a powerful urge to add his own corpse to the heap. He was abandoned and alone, unable to utter a sound or to move.

As the insistent sound of the alarm ripped through the silence again, he shuddered, and stuffed the fading remnants of the dream back into his subconscious. Sitting on the edge of the bed, drenched with sweat, breathing heavily, he was on the verge of drowning in despair. A wave of fear washed over him that his wife, Lucille, had awakened in the next room and that she would find him in this desperate state. They had not slept together for years, mainly, she said, because of his nightly terrors. Regaining the moment, he staggered uneasily toward the bathroom, where he turned on the shower and stood under its merciful, redeeming coolness. He resisted giving in to the sense of despair that threatened to overtake him—the despair that welcomes death, even death at one's own hand. He had put that to rest in his waking life long ago. But he usually awoke from these dreams knowing that despair was close at hand, lying in wait.

Two hours later, David was in his office at the Supreme Court in the Old State House in Hartford, prepared to enter the courtroom for a morning of arguments. As usual when he'd had a disturbing experience, he had fortified himself with medication to help ward off further intrusive thoughts and images of horror that his mind had replayed over and over since their origin in Iraqi villages more than fifteen years ago.

As he followed the other six black-robed justices from the formal, wood-paneled conference room down the narrow hallway to the dimly lit, elegant chamber of the highest court of the state, David was distracted by two disturbing feelings. He felt like an imposter, an alien, in his judicial robe despite having been a member of the court for nearly six years. He attributed his lack of belonging to the tension between himself and the Chief Justice, Ernest Burkhardt, who never missed an opportunity to display his hostility toward David. But feeling like an alien was nothing new. He'd felt the lack of connection most of his life, going back his childhood.

Added to that, David still dreaded his sense of confinement when he was in the courtroom. Whenever he felt trapped, he was driven to find an escape route. His service was long over. By now, he should have recovered from this distress. But he'd never done anything about it. Long ago, he decided to live with the condition rather than risk telling anyone about it. He had to prevent the stigma of mental illness from appearing on his record.

His discomfort was worse on bad days like today when painful memories intruded on him, escalating his anxiety. As the justices lined up in seniority before the ten-foot high doorway to the courtroom, he heard the court officer bang her gavel and announce: "All rise." He followed the others onto the high bench to his seat, after closing the door behind him, a task reserved for the junior member of the court. After the justices' arrival was announced with sufficient gravity, the seven took their seats. The lawyers, litigants, and spectators followed suit.

With his graying chestnut hair, piercing blue eyes and erect posture, David had a quality that made him the natural focal point in any room that he entered, including a courtroom. His internal struggles had not detracted from his external image. Since his direct appointment from law practice to the Supreme Court, he had often been the center of attention at judicial and bar gatherings. His combat service, highlighted by several media reports of heroism and his academic accomplishments—a United States Supreme Court clerkship, a staff position for a U.S. Senator, two books, and numerous media interviews—gave him special status throughout the state and beyond.

The reports of his courageous action in exposing himself to danger while thwarting the capture of two soldiers in his platoon had been nationally publicized at a time when the public, eight years into the conflicts, was war-weary and desperate for encouraging news. Any news of heroic action, real or contrived, was welcomed. The luster of his war record, embellished by the

Pentagon, had temporarily succeeded in shielding from public attention what he felt were his moral failures.

David still carried himself with military bearing. Now at age 43, he prided himself on a rigorous exercise regimen. He was, in the public view, a model of success and promise for the future. Before accepting the high court seat, he had been widely mentioned as a leading candidate for a gubernatorial nomination or a Congressional seat. Now that rumors had circulated within the legal community that he had political support in Washington as a candidate for the unexpected vacancy on the U.S. Supreme Court, he was star quality material. Many politicians, lawyers, and judges privately resented his speedy rise to prominence.

The morning's docket had three appeals assigned for argument during the three-hour session. Each side had a half hour to argue, with the party appealing having the privilege of reserving time for rebuttal. Two cases would follow in the afternoon session, standard scheduling during the one week per month when the Court heard cases. Argument before this court, as in most appellate courts, was a vigorous interactive experience for the lawyers. Virtually all the justices made it a practice to read the briefs and trial record, preparing themselves to question the lawyers aggressively, interrupting whenever they chose—some politely and some rudely. The noisy and crude Chief Justice did not hesitate to trample on any of the lawyers' answers or, for that matter, on questions asked by the other justices.

Some members of the court were armed with memos prepared by their law clerks. David insisted on doing his own preparation for argument, preferring to have his law clerks concentrate on research and editing. He generally was prominent in questioning the lawyers, always courteously and often with humor, but recently several of his colleagues had noticed that he was subdued. He admitted to Jeffrey Webster, a Vietnam veteran and his only true friend on the court, that he had been preoccupied with the federal appointment rumors as well as what he called "family problems." Jeffrey knew enough not to probe the latter issue but he readily offered advice on the political situation.

David had read the briefs for today's session, but concentrating was difficult and his focus had slipped a few times. He knew it was risky to question the lawyers at such times. Asking an irrelevant question or repeating one that had already been answered was an embarrassment that appellate judges struggled to avoid.

3

David Lawson had returned home in June of 2009 after an extended deployment of fifteen months in Iraq, followed by short leave and then six months in Djibouti. He had reentered law school to complete his second and third years. The three-year break from school had given him perspective as well as a renewed energy to excel. The second year of law school had passed quickly. His impulsive marriage to Lucille just before his third year began was still a mystery to him. His abortive first marriage after college had ended with minimal turmoil; his wife had filed for an annulment of the marriage during his deployment.

In the summer before his third year, David had applied for a judicial clerkship with the U.S. Court of Appeals for the D.C. Circuit. Getting an introduction to the judge who hired him through one of his law school professors didn't hurt, but David probably would have gotten a clerkship anyway. During his year on the D.C. Circuit, he had been hired by the Chief Justice of the United States for a U.S. Supreme Court clerkship without even applying. Once again, he had an advantage since his circuit judge was a close friend of the Chief. After that, he had stayed in Washington for another two years as a special assistant to a U.S. Senator from Massachusetts, who happened to be a Vietnam vet.

David had turned down numerous offers to practice law in Washington, choosing instead to return to Connecticut to practice in the Hartford office of a large national firm. He got into Democratic politics and was immediately identified as a rising star, displaying early the undefinable charisma that all politicians long to have. He drew people to him with nearly unshakable loyalty. His notable war record, an asset in the wake of the long wars, added luster to his image. Casual observers would say that he had everything going for him.

Not only did his loyal core of close friends from college and law school band around him, but party leaders began to see him as the only person capable of defeating the two-term Republican governor. It was not a huge surprise when word leaked out that Governor George Rawlings, being the beneficiary of an unexpected vacancy to fill on the state Supreme Court, offered the seat to David. Direct appointments of lawyers without judicial experience were rare. At the time of his appointment, David figured that he didn't have to make a lifetime career of this position. He could use it as a steppingstone to a federal judicial career, or he could resume his political career. After a short period of soul-searching, he gave up his immediate goal of pursuing political office and accepted the appointment.

4

Burkhardt called a fifteen-minute recess between arguments, giving David a chance to return to his chambers. His mind was on the morning's disturbing argument with Lucille, in which her hostility had spilled into new territory.

David had been in the kitchen having coffee and reading the *Times* when Lucille came downstairs. She had appeared washed out and weary and as though she had not slept well for some time. Perhaps her drinking was sapping more of her strength than he had imagined. He had not spent much time with her during the past few months although he had observed the number of empty wine bottles that went out with the recycling bin twice a week. Heavy alcohol use had been a pattern in her family. She had grown up with it and the excesses of college years had never diminished, as it did with most people. She had gained weight and seemed to go out of her way these days to choose unflattering clothes.

Whatever qualities she had exhibited that had once interested him no longer existed. Not that he had ever been in love with her. He had backed into the marriage because the relationship existed and she wanted desperately to get married. Of course, he admitted to himself, to be fair, the inner turmoil that was left over from his combat experience had been a contributing factor in the deterioration of the relationship. He had not shared his innermost feelings with her, never trusting her with his vulnerability and emotional pain given the lack of intimacy in their relationship. He had never explained his frequent flashbacks or the insomnia and nightmares that were part of his life. When pressed, he attributed the anxiety that plagued him to the stress of work. He never mentioned the oppressive weight of moral guilt that he carried on his shoulders day and night.

David had hidden the full meaning of his mental anguish from himself as well as from others. He knew what it was on some level but had stuffed it somewhere in the labyrinths of his mind. He was afraid to think about it for fear it would make more demands on him. He had some control over it by keeping it hidden. That was the solution and the problem. He couldn't talk to anyone about it except Willard Coleman, David's old friend and spiritual advisor, a term both humorous and serious. Willard, the former university chaplain, knew nearly everything about David's life. They had begun their lifelong friendship during David's undergraduate years. "Nearly" did leave quite a gap, come to think of it. Someday he would tell him all the excruciating

10

details. When he permitted himself a glimpse at the underlying causes, David began agonizing over how he ever allowed the massacre to happen. There were no answers. That was worse than keeping the lid on. He couldn't afford to acknowledge the dark secrets. And so he was trapped somewhere between heaven and hell, the way war was fought somewhere between life and death. Death in life; life in death.

David believed his mental condition was due to PTSD but hadn't shared his belief with anyone. How could he do that without answering questions about trauma? So he would go on managing his memories and deepest feelings by controlling his mind, and by plugging the gaps with anti-anxiety meds. The list was long—Xanax, Atavan, Paxil, Zoloft, Prozac. Who could remember them all? Perhaps he would die without anyone knowing the depths of his damaged soul. That was his hope and his fear. Sometimes, despite himself, he was unable to prevent vivid scenes from forcing their way into his consciousness, the girl hanging upside down, gutted like a slaughtered pig, and the gruesome bloodbath in the house with Nick Serrano and his troops circling like beasts caught up in a killing craze. The images had lives of their own and they reappeared like popups on a computer screen when he least expected them.

The scene of this morning's disheartening argument was vivid in his mind.

"Morning, Lucille," he had ventured in an effort to keep the relationship cordial. "Today may be when I find out more about my chances for the nomination. My old friend Bradley Thompson is supposed to call me to let me know about his conversation with both senators."

"What's that to me?" she snapped crossly, scowling at him from across the kitchen. "Do you think that'll make you happy? It certainly isn't going to make me happy. Where were you that kept you so late last night?"

"I was at Bradley's house. There were a lot of people there," he said trying not to sound defensive.

"You could have let me know. Who else was there? Why did you have to stay so late?" She was relentless.

His irritation began to rise but he kept the tone light. "Hey, what is this, cross-examination?" Laughing, he said, "Your father was a good cross-examiner too."

Her face did not reflect his attempt at humor directed at her father, who had been a lawyer.

He went on, "What good would that've done? I had things to talk over. They're helping me." He could feel the bile of swelling anger rising in his throat, like the old days after he'd gotten back. He had worked on it to slow it down, bury it, but lately the tension caused it to rise on its own.

"It would have been thoughtful and anyway the kids were asking. Why is this damned appointment so important to you? Isn't it enough to just do your job? If you didn't want it, why did you take the appointment to the Connecticut court? You are so driven and tense, so wrapped up in yourself. What's going on with you? You don't reveal anything. Why are you so secretive about where you are and what you're doing?"

He felt the sting of the barrage. "You're certainly no help. You keep me on edge, badgering me like this all the time," David barked, despite his determination not to let it get out of hand. The anger bubbled over the top unchecked, venting itself. "I never know whether that's you or alcohol doing the talking—"

"I keep *you* on edge," she interrupted sharply. "That's a cheap shot. I didn't expect that from you despite the way you feel about me. I could say plenty too."

"Why do you always interrupt? Yes, this means more money and a lot more prestige and a lifetime appointment. Lawyers and judges would give anything to be on the U.S. Supreme Court."

"Thanks. I've had enough," Lucille said as she got up and headed toward the stairs. "Let me know when you're leaving so I can come back downstairs in peace."

"Figure it out for yourself. I won't be home tonight. It's Friday and after work I'll be going to the lodge in New Hampshire for the weekend to meet with the group and sort all this out."

Lucille looked furious at this remark. "Nice. Very nice. Suppose I have plans? Suit yourself, right? Maybe I'll just take off too. The boys have games, both of them, but that isn't important for you, is it?"

"You're always on the attack. You'll have to stay with the kids. This is important."

"We'll see."

David felt in jeopardy after surrendering to the acrimony. She could do anything, anything crazy. She could damage his career. He recovered with an effort to be conciliatory. "Lucille, I know we've had problems for a while but this is a critical time and I need your support. I have within reach what a lot of lawyers and judges would die for."

"Oh, would you give anything for it? And what happens if you get it? What's next on your agenda?"

"I'll have more time, and we can make our family a priority."

"Oh, really. Does that include your marriage, not that I'm sure at all that I want to hold onto it any longer, frankly," she said with rising anger of her own and an undercurrent of resolve that was unsettling.

"I have to get to court," David said. "We'll talk about this when I get back but let's work to hold things together."

"That would be nice for you, wouldn't it, but what's in it for me? If you do get it, I have no interest in living in Washington. And don't expect to interrupt the boys' lives either. They have friends here. We're staying here. Nice arrangement, right? Just what you want, I suppose."

"Please, Lucille, can we keep this civil? Will you please back me up in this?"

"Sounds like a one-way street to me, David," she tossed off sarcastically as she headed up the stairs.

5

After he got back from Washington, Lucille and David had settled into a routine and within a couple of years had produced two children, providing a common interest and bringing life to the house. The marriage relationship settled into a truce of sorts, the acrimony buffered by the children's presence. David confided only in Willard and, to a lesser extent, Jeffrey Webster, about the unhappy marriage. He wanted more from life, and he suspected that Lucille probably felt the same way. His fifteen-month tour in Iraq had gone by quickly but the damages seemed endless. He told no one but Willard how much his soul had been shattered along with some bones and ligaments.

David had been skilled since childhood at forgetting—or at least stuffing painful memories into a secret compartment. Lucille had never expressed the slightest interest in what had happened in Iraq. Willard was the first and, so far, the only person he had ever trusted completely in his life. He often wondered if he would be the last.

David was afraid to seek treatment within or outside the service. If his silence about combat experiences meant conforming to the prevailing code of silence of soldiers and veterans, that is, refusing to discuss them with civilians, so be it. He did not support the frequent practice of veterans shutting out civilians from the details of combat but he did not want to risk being stigmatized. Establishing PTSD might produce disability benefits but it certainly wouldn't help a military or civilian career, especially in public service or politics, where every blemish was subject to penetrating inspection. So he kept everything to himself, following the practice of a long line of military veterans.

Willard had warned David about relying on his military experience to promote his career and said he thought it was disingenuous, not to mention risky, to exploit his combat service. David had even made a trip, a pilgrimage of sorts, to Ramadi to meet with the survivors during the period that he had worked as a special assistant to the U.S. Senator from Massachusetts.

This opportunity arose about midway through his two-year stint with the senator after completing his Supreme Court clerkship. His fixation on a pilgrimage to Ramadi had been brewing in David's mind for months, starting when he learned about a fact-finding mission to Iraq that the senator was scheduled to make. David became obsessed with finding a way to get to Ramadi from the Green Zone in Baghdad to see who was living in the house where the killings had taken place while he stood outside transfixed, frozen in time and space. He'd thought of that moment many times. It was as though he was an actor in a movie reel that was stuck on one frame, stuttering over and over. Each time he reimagined the scene, he saw himself unable to move. His immobility reminded himself of a lecture he once attended. A law professor was speaking at a judicial conference about some subject now forgotten. Suddenly, the audience gasped audibly as though it were a single organism, aware that the speaker was frozen, a statue, motionless, a ghastly shade of gray, leaning slightly forward, his right arm poised in the air, as if making an important point. The audience stared for two minutes in growing astonishment until the moderator moved forward and said calmly that they would take a break. Still no one moved, gaping at the spectacle, as the moderator approached the man saying "Professor," taking him by the arm until he awoke with a start, surprised, from his trance, oblivious to what had happened.

David had felt that way precisely. He had been a living statue motionless in a trance seeing mayhem before his eyes, bodies trying to flee desperately, dropping like flies with an army of fly-swatting marauders. Blood was spraying, spurting, flowing like a river toward the front door. The wailing, screaming, was awful and he was crouched furtively now, afraid to move, afraid to enter, afraid to leave until Flaherty and Cronin lunged through the door shouting. More shots, then silence. Deadly silence.

Now he had to make his own visit to the scene of the crime. Or was it more his journey to Golgotha, the place of the crucifixion, or perhaps his pilgrimage to Makkah? He should have known there was no good in it and that the only thing he'd accomplish would be to rip apart the barely healing wounds of the survivors and fuel the hatred they felt.

6

David remembered recounting for Willard, months later, the details of his abortive pilgrimage to attempt a reconciliation with the surviving family members. He had been depressed to the point of being immobilized after returning to the States. He had met Willard at his Boston apartment.

"It went back to my failure to stop the slaughter," David said. "I felt that I had to atone in some way, talk with survivors of all the victims, to show them my remorse and to ask forgiveness. I knew that as many as thirty people had been killed. It was sickening, worse than anything else I saw the whole time in Iraq. Evil is the only word I can think of. It was truly evil."

Willard slowly nodded his head. "I know how it made you feel but you can't blame yourself for what other people do. Sure, you could have ordered someone else to do the mission, to target the people responsible, but the outcome might have been the same; the revenge might have happened anyway."

"I understand that, but I had to see what was left of the family, to find out what happened. I used to search the Web for stories about what my unit, Fox Company, had done, looking for any mention of this incident. Nothing. I didn't want to make any official inquiries of course because I was afraid of stirring something up, something that was already forgotten or ignored. Then one day I found an AP story about the Ramadi incident by one of the journalists who had been embedded in my company at the time—Frank Caruso, a reporter at the *Washington Post*. I still have the newspaper. I couldn't believe it. He wrote it about four or five years after returning to the States. He obviously investigated the story at the time but held onto it until his assignment was over. He must have been worried about keeping his embedded status. He had some of the facts but obviously not all. He wrote about the killing of the woman and the retaliatory raids. He knew there had been three of those, and he put the death total at over thirty civilians."

"Is Caruso still in the business? Is he still a journalist?" Willard asked.

"Yes, I've seen his name on stories in major newspapers and magazines. Actually that is one of my worst fears, that if I ever do or say anything about what happened in Ramadi, he'll pick up on it immediately. I'm sure he hasn't forgotten. He had some missing facts but he identified the right area section of the city. He didn't mention names, as though he didn't know them all. He treated it as though the retaliation had been officially sanctioned, ordered—

not what it was, an unofficial, personal vendetta on the part of one man. He had gone back to interview the people who lived there now, all family members. They were bitter and hated the Americans. I was stunned. After not finding anything for so long, I wasn't expecting to find this story. I felt encouraged that I could make contact but worried about the family's reaction. I became even more interested in seeing them, but also fearful that I could open up something that seemed to be a closed book by this time. What if I made contact with these people and they let Caruso know? He might do more digging or come after me."

"It hasn't happened, though, right?" Willard asked.

"Right. Anyway, my opportunity to try and meet the survivors came about when I accompanied my Senator on a fact-finding mission to Iraq last year. We stayed in the Green Zone, as all visitors did, because it was the safest place. We had handed it over to the Iraqi military back in 2009, but it was still available for visitors and private contractors. I had some free time while meetings were going on. It was quite a distance to Ramadi and a dangerous trip, but I managed to make the arrangements. I told the Senator I wanted to visit some people I knew. He helped arrange the vehicles, drivers and the whole crew. I could tell that the Senator didn't appreciate the danger. This was insurgent-held territory, although there was a strong Iraqi government force in the area. It was possible to slip in and out but risky. I didn't care if I got shot. That's how driven I was to do this. It was crazy, really, but we set out early that morning with three Humvees and nine men. The military insisted on that.

During the surge, Ramadi was a very dangerous place, more violent than Fallujah. It was the capital of Anbar and 30 miles closer to the Syrian border. It was and is mostly Sunni and those people have reason to distrust the Shiite majority and the government, once Saddam was toppled."

"Ramadi is still a hot spot," Willard remarked.

"It is," David said, "for a lot of reasons. That isn't likely to change. It was October when we arrived in Iraq and we set out for Ramadi very early one morning. Ramadi was only a hundred and twenty miles from Baghdad but we had to figure on three or four hours to get there, with diversions and having to deal with insurgents. After basically wasting three days in the Green Zone, where I was not much help to the senator, I was actually glad to be on the road and heading for Ramadi. I was not glad to be breathing in the fine dust that was everywhere, what people who haven't experienced it would call 'sand.' It goes deeply into your lungs and makes you cough like crazy. Someday veterans will be having respiratory cancer like mesothelioma. When the rains come, the dust turns to mud that is as thick as peanut butter. When it's dry, you sink into it like light new-fallen snow; when it's wet, it's more like quicksand."

"I would have urged you not to go there at all," Willard said. "It doesn't pay to talk with survivors. You have to leave the past alone. You can't obsess about what happened when you were in combat. It's a different world. It'll drive you crazy. You can't undo the horrors that have been committed."

"You're right. I know that now," David said, "but one reason I joined up in the first place was to put myself to the test. I knew my weaknesses and I wanted to force them out into the open, like driving all the ghosts out. You know what I mean, into the broad daylight. I remembered that the house wasn't far from the OP, the small operational observation post that we used most of the time when we weren't stationed in our COP, the combat operation post. That COP was about the farthest away of any from our FOB, the forward operating base, and the small OP was way out in the middle of hostile territory. That was effective during the surge, and afterward I enjoyed being out there.

"It was really how I got to know the local sheikh, the one whose daughter got murdered, which started off the whole revenge for revenge business. It wasn't just what his daughter did, which they said was consorting with Americans. It was that he was a leader in the Al Anbar Awakening, the movement of Sunni sheikhs who were recruited—and paid handsomely I might add—to resist Al Qaeda and diminish its influence in the western part of Iraq. It was successful on the whole, although it cost the U.S. 400 million dollars to recruit and pay them. We shouldn't be under any illusion that they did it purely to regain control of the country and establish a moderate Sunni government in the province. They were bound to feel the retaliation pain when Al Qaeda got the upper hand again."

"I've heard that over and over," Willard said. "We need moderates to oust the militant jihadists but paying them to do it goes only so far. We've heard that war cry during the past decade too, as a way of rolling back the jihadist takeover of the western provinces. We've been through that routine several times. It might help us temporarily to save face and leave but then, before you know it, we're back in there again and again. It's different from Southeast Asia where we pretty much have stayed out. But this is the Middle East, the land of oil and Israel. We'll never be out of there. But go on with your story. You know how I feel about your doing this but I want to hear how it went."

David continued. "After the incident, the killing, happened, the house was unoccupied. Anyone who survived or maybe happened to be out that night wouldn't dare come back or perhaps couldn't stand to. It was in a broken down section of Ramadi. The house had once been quite grand, I think, a large masonry house with at least two floors. It towered over everything else in the section, probably had seven or eight rooms or more, and I imagine probably close to twenty people lived there. That's what we would call in Iraq an extended family. Most of the people were supporters of AQI in that area, not openly, but they harbored insurgents and gave them help. I can't say that Serrano had the wrong target but there were probably only one or two young AQI members, maybe cousins or friends, who were involved in the killing of the girl. The rest were just ordinary people living ordinary lives."

"We drove through the streets kicking up the moon dust," David said. "The place looked more desolate than before. I directed the driver as best I could, knowing I'd recognize the house if it was still standing. I didn't know much about the people living there, just what Caruso had uncovered. Each family had so many extended members that houses tended to stay in the same family for generations. If one family group had a problem, they'd move in with their relatives. They had extra blankets around for sleeping. It was no surprise if one day there were eight people in a house and the next, twenty or more. It was bad luck that there were probably thirty people in the house when Serrano and his storm troopers showed up and they all paid the price, the ultimate price."

Willard said, "I can't imagine you taking that risk, venturing into the ISIS territory. It was changing hands every week or so. It's still volatile."

"Sure enough, I recognized it when we got to the square. It was more rundown than I recall but still grand in a way and I could see signs of life, a couple of motor scooters, old bikes, laundry visible in the backyard. I was excited but very nervous. I had no idea what kind of reception I'd get. I was prepared for anything and when I saw all the men hanging around the square, I got nervous that there were so few of us. I don't know what the others were thinking except to make this quick. This wasn't part of their job description that's for sure. The usual burnt haze was in the air and the whole area looked more rundown than I remembered. I could sense the tension. I got out of my Humvee and the entire team stood by the vehicles. I went to the open door. I could see two women sitting in the front room. The door was wide open. That was the custom.

"I greeted them in my limited Arabic. I said, 'Good afternoon madam, ladies.' The older woman motioned to the younger one to come to the door. 'Good afternoon, my name is David Lawson. I'm an American. I was stationed in Ramadi a few years ago. I knew the family who lived here. I'm back in the country for a few days. I came here hoping to talk to the family members of the people who lived here, the people who were killed in a raid. Are you their relatives?'

"They said nothing, just stared at me but the young one left the room and she came back with a half dozen people, four men and two women. They all looked solemn, curious but grim. I tried to explain why I was there in simple terms. 'I'm here hoping to talk to someone in the family who lived here. I knew them and know that some terrible things happened. I realize it was Americans who did some of the bad things.' They started talking quietly to each other. I couldn't pick up all they were saying.

"The men stood by, looking pretty hostile, I'd say, but the older woman said slowly enough for me to pick up, 'Why do you come here. You killed my whole family, my sisters, their children, and my parents, my whole family.' I guess these people were aunts and uncles, cousins and so on. I suppose the whole immediate family had been killed.

"'I did not kill them,' I said. 'I fired no weapon here and did not come inside. These were men under my command who disobeyed my orders. They had no authority,' I said, which wasn't quite true, of course, 'to come here and to do this terrible thing. They were angered because of the murder of the young woman of another family who did no harm to anyone but who was murdered brutally. Her name was Jasmine.'

"Some of the women started to weep but the old woman said, 'she deserved to die. She was a plaything of your soldiers and disobeyed the holy law.' The men, they just stood there. I said, 'I am truly sorry for your loss. It was not right. I did not order it and those American soldiers killed two of their own brothers and sisters in this place.'

"'Why do you come here today?' the old woman asked again. She became very agitated and the men nodded. 'What good can this do? You are American. You are responsible. You can do nothing to remedy the situation. There was no excuse, no reason to kill my family, the children too. It wasn't the first time. Why did you kill them? They did not harm anyone. They were innocent.'

"I didn't want to get into an accusation that they had harbored AQI members or that the murder of Jasmine was cruel and unjust. I could see there was no point in arguing. They did not understand or they did not want to understand. I did say: 'I come to ask your forgiveness. I come to atone for the wrong that my men did to your family.'

"One of the men, a middle-aged man, spoke up at this point in English. 'We cannot forgive you. For what was done there is no forgiveness on this earth. We do not want Americans here. Most Americans have left. You are not welcome here. We did not invite you. There are some who would want to kill you and your men outside. Are you here to do us more harm?'

"'No,' I said. I will leave but I came to tell you I am sorry and that I will do all I can to make sure it doesn't happen again.' They just stared at me.

"I was looking for absolution, and I didn't find any," David said. "They listened but were not moved. I reopened wounds that had not even begun to heal, judging by their bitterness. Now, so many years later, we have troops there again. We're trapped in the spider's web. We can't undo all the harm we did and yet we continue to do harm."

"You know how I feel about this country's dependence on war," Willard said.

"I do. I apologized for intruding and made my exit carefully. I could tell my team was getting itchy. Quite a few Iraqi men had gathered and were standing around, even some with weapons, an assortment of AK-47s and Russian SKS rifles. It was nerve-racking and I wondered what I'd gotten us into. I wasn't sure we'd get out of there alive. But we did drive away without anyone shooting at us or even approaching us. Maybe they respected the mission after all. I don't know. Overall, it was a foolish thing to do, selfish, but I'm glad I tried at least. I feel the incident and the people are somehow more real to me. I'll remember what happened for the rest of my life. I'll never forget the faces I saw during the massacre, suffering, beyond explanation, enduring something that no human being should endure.

"Unfortunately," David said, "someone got to the reporter at some point or he got to them. My visit must have stirred things up, and Caruso got wind of it. He must have wondered why I would do that. I remember, come to think of it, getting a phone call or two from the *Post* out of the blue. Whoever it was, probably Caruso, left a message about wanting to talk to me about Ramadi. I never called back and he never followed up. But when my name was mentioned in the Washington press, I heard that he was making phone calls around. I'm sure he's tracking me. I'll probably get a call one of these days."

"I was afraid of that," Willard said. "I hope it never gets to the point where it hurts you. Problems like this rarely go away for good. Secrets remain secrets for a while but eventually they escape. Just be prepared and think about how you'll handle it when it happens."

7

David was startled into attention by the telephone. His secretary was calling to alert him that court was about to resume. He took a few minutes to orient himself and walked to the conference room. He knew Burkhardt would make a sarcastic remark about his being late. He was right. The justices headed for the courtroom to resume the session. In the next case, the strident voices of the lawyers, two of the most aggressive advocates, prevented David from drifting into his thoughts. He wondered for a moment how long he had lapsed before the recess and, worse, whether anyone had noticed. He glanced at Jeffrey Webster and caught his eye. He felt sure that Jeffrey had noticed his earlier mental lapse.

Back in the present now, David felt annoyed with the lawyers, both of whom talked so fast and so loudly that it was hard to get a question in. It was necessary to stop them in their tracks, although that did not prevent them from trying to trample on his questions. Oral argument was supposed to be a time for the judges to get answers to questions that were important to them, although some judges also liked to dominate. Most lawyers welcomed questions because it gave them a chance to address what the justices wanted to know. That was the point.

David kept his annoyance in check, realizing how vulnerable he was now that he had to cope with mounting personal problems. Attempts to cover up momentary lapses were transparent to experienced observers. David was thankful that he had found the time and the concentration to absorb the basics of the three cases that were being argued this morning. He thought his questions were not bad, considering everything.

After a stretch of two hours without a recess, the morning arguments were over and, after a short break when each justice went to chambers briefly, the justices returned to the conference room and took their assigned seats by seniority around the long conference table. Discussion and preliminary voting took forty-five minutes and then they were on their own until 2:00.

Burkhardt was abrupt with David as usual and made a few stabs at putting him down, which David ignored. He hurried back to his chambers and conferred with his law clerks about the afternoon cases. Once he was alone, he called Bradley to make sure arrangements were set for the weekend. They were. He could count on Bradley.

8

Following his undergraduate days at Dartmouth, Bradley Thompson had been David's law school roommate before David left for the Army. After graduating, Bradley had done a Second Circuit clerkship before working for the Justice Department for three years. He eventually returned to Hartford and joined the national law firm that David joined later on.

Bradley transferred to the Washington office before long and continued to juggle law and politics since then. He had risen to the pinnacle of the elite group of most powerful Washington lawyers and had already been a key figure in several administrations. He had not only vetted candidates for Presidential appointments, but had represented a number of prominent political figures on both civil and criminal matters. His expansive network, influential friends, and wise judgment made him one of the most important Democratic lawyers in the country. He was a shrewd politician who knew how to manage the information he gathered with resourcefulness and, just as importantly, had an instinct about information that was missing. Based on his recommendation, one of his associates had been hired as Chief of Staff for Senator Timothy O'Leary, a law school classmate of both Bradley and David. That helped to solidify the relationship among the friends.

Bradley had great respect for David, not only for his natural leadership and charisma but for his combat reputation. He had never had any reason to probe deeply into David's war record, but David knew that would not hold for long if the Supreme Court campaign went forward. They had talked at length last night. The conversation was still fresh in David's mind and he reviewed it now that he was alone in his office.

Bradley had begun the conversation by saying: "You got a good report out of the Senators' screening committee. Of course, they're mostly academics who provide an evaluation for the Senators. It's more than window-dressing but they don't do any serious vetting. That comes later. O'Leary found out about your competition though. There are some serious contenders."

"I suppose they all got cleared by the screening committee?" David asked.

"That's my understanding," Bradley said.

"Any idea which way the President is leaning or is this even on her agenda yet? It sounds like she has her hands full with the Middle East and North Africa coming apart at the seams again thanks to the latest Islamic State resurgence and with China getting hostile and more openly in the Pacific."

"She knows. She pays attention to these things and she's aware of your background. She's not a veteran but her father was a General who made it to the Joint Chiefs."

"But what does that have to do with Supreme Court appointments?" David asked.

"I think the idea of nominating a distinguished veteran who is also a political progressive has a lot of appeal for her," Bradley said. That makes up for your being a Caucasian, Euro-Centric male. You're a minority these days, you know. She sees the Court in trouble. It's still in the throes of the changes that Roberts had on his agenda—cutting back on individual rights while expanding rights of corporations, especially in the political campaign area. The majority stranglehold is still with the neo-cons. No one has been able to make a dent in that since Kennedy swung that way once O'Connor's influence was gone. She's hoping to start the process of de-polarizing the Court. You'd be a great start, and I think she'll understand that. Incidentally, O'Leary made sure she got a copy of your memoir on the war and she liked it," Bradley said.

"Does she see herself as a war president like her predecessors?" David asked.

"Yes, and that influences what she wants in a candidate. The way she sees it, privately, is that we've been in a continuous war since 2001. There was a brief respite, when it seemed that Iraq and Afghanistan were finished and Al Qaeda was damaged. Any illusion that we would enjoy a peaceful interlude ended when the Islamic State in all its various forms emerged all over the globe. I can't foresee peace and stability in that part of the world. You know everybody was predicting an endless war back a dozen years ago. It's true. We're on the brink of getting involved in two or three countries, and that's been a continuum for the last ten years. She doesn't adopt that stance as an excuse to curtail civil liberties. She doesn't want to encourage the hawks to fatten the military budget. But she realizes that the world is full of threats."

Bradley continued. "She sees herself as the logical successor to the Obama-Kerry strategy of avoiding military engagements unless we get backed into a corner on an issue where our national interest is directly involved. She's taken heat from the hawks just as Obama did but it's worked since Iraq and Afghanistan, not perfectly but it's kept us out of a dozen situations that could have tied us up in knots for the second decade of the century if we weren't careful. She does wish that Obama had resisted jumping in with war against the Islamic State. It does no good in the long run and doesn't accomplish any more than could have been done under cover. We know that every hostile act on our part has only stimulated their recruiting. The President believes that we have to expect setbacks with her non-involvement strategy. We can't just give up on it every time there's an adverse development. It has to be a long-range view. The tide ebbs and flows. The drones haven't been the miracle solution some people thought. We're still using them but we're as vulnerable as the terrorists are. They have them too and the collateral damage keeps upping the ante. Using drone strikes is not cost-free for our own operators either. The Middle East and North Africa haven't been stable since before 2001."

"The President likes what she knows about you. Her White House counsel, Arthur Lehman, is an old friend from my Justice days. He's spoken to her about you . . . but he hasn't committed to you or anyone yet. But we've got to give him a lot more information about you. You know, some parts of your file are sealed, classified, and they tell me that even you can't authorize opening them up."

David was surprised. "I didn't know that. What parts?"

"Can't tell until we see them," Bradley said, "but there's something about an investigation I think. That's what I picked up. We can have White House counsel dig into it or I can handle that myself through O'Leary. You can count on Tim. He's in your corner you know. But Lehman was leaning toward Noreen Grady, the Ninth Circuit judge, until O'Leary started to work on him. I think we can turn him around unless the President moves strongly in a different direction."

"Great," David said, feeling apprehension that he hoped wasn't revealed on his face. He hated to keep secrets from Bradley but the idea of digging deeply into the war records hit him in the pit of his stomach. He knew that Bradley had his own secrets and his own agenda but he owed him a duty of loyalty nonetheless. "Let's keep it under control ourselves. I don't know. I'll see what I can find out but it's been a long time. My contacts are not fresh."

"I know. Do you have any idea what it's all about? Was there an investigation?" Bradley asked, looking for David's reaction.

"I don't remember at this point," David said. "Not that I knew about. Do you know the time period? I don't think it'll amount to much. Can we find some other way of satisfying the White House?"

"No," Bradley said quickly. "The Justice Department and the FBI, if you get that far, will need to vet you thoroughly . . . but, of course, a lot of the vetting is pro forma, just pushing paper around. They do talk to a lot of people, guys you served with, and just about everybody you have had contact with since that time. They'll ask you to give them a list of names. That makes it easier for them and gives you some control. But they make their own list too. Presidents have been burned in this process by what they didn't know. There have been lots of close calls that the media never heard about. One good thing is that your name and picture along with two of the others floated two weeks ago in the Washington press and the reaction among lawyers and veterans groups, of course, was terrific. They like you. They admire you. You're a folk hero to a lot of people."

David nodded. "That's good to hear."

"Next weekend," Bradley said, "when we're in New Hampshire, we'll go over a lot of things and see if you can figure out what all this classified crap is. We've got to clear that away so it doesn't get to be a big issue."

"Sounds good," David said. "It's good that you were able to get us into the

Conference Center for the weekend. I've been there for a couple of MacArthur Foundation programs before it went private as the Lochland. It's a perfect spot with privacy, peaceful surroundings and easy to reach."

Bradley hesitated, then spoke quietly. "I'm going to tell you something absolutely confidential so you'll understand a key factor in how we're going to run this campaign. Lehman's not going to be in his present position forever, not at all, if you get me. We have to move quickly because the likely successor will not be easy to deal with. Keep that to yourself."

9

After a quick walk and a sandwich from one of the food trucks in the fleet that lined the streets bordering the park, David returned to the courthouse to talk with his law clerks about their progress on the assigned cases. He had trouble concentrating. Too many issues were swirling around in his head, too much distraction and too much conflict. He found it easy to solve other people's conflicts but, when it came to his own, he easily became immobilized. That had always been a problem, almost pathological at some points in his life. Something in him froze when too much was at stake. He would lose his confidence.

His mind went to the conversation with Bradley. He knew exactly what had been in the official files. He knew it was the brigade commander's investigation into complaints about the civilian deaths in Ramadi caused by Americans after the brutal slaying of Nick's girlfriend, Jasmine. That entire incident took place on his watch as commanding officer of his platoon.

The call two weeks ago at home from Larry Cutter was fresh in his mind. Larry was one of the men he had liked and trusted the most. Larry had been a sergeant, one of the non-commissioned officers serving under Nick Serrano. But Nick had never been a friend, rather an aggressive competitor. Larry had stuck with David through it all, never wavering in his loyalty. It was disturbing to learn that Larry had gotten a threatening call from Nick, whom they both called that son of a bitch platoon sergeant. Larry reported nervously that Nick had been arrested in New Jersey for murder. He also said that Nick had been in a lot of trouble before that. He'd done prison time and had only been out three years since the last incarceration. Nick was facing big time if he got convicted. Larry had heard from another member of the platoon, Mike, that Nick had called him and asked him to testify.

Thinking about this made David feel apprehensive. He allowed his mind to replay Larry's call.

"Hey Lieutenant. How you doin', buddy?"

"Larry. For God's sake, how are you?"

"I'm okay. I had a rough time for quite a while but I got it together finally. I'm clean and sober now and working at the VA here in Providence."

"I'm sorry to hear you had problems. I'm glad you're on top of that now. What's up? We haven't talked in a while."

"Yeah, I know. I was wondering if you got a call from Nick Serrano. I thought I'd give you a heads up if you didn't. We always had each other's back, you know."

"We sure did . . . but Nick? No, why would I get a call from him? We didn't part on very good terms if you remember."

"I know, I know, but I got a call," Larry said.

David interrupted, sensing trouble, "About what?"

"Seems he's in big trouble, arrested for murder. The papers say he's charged with attempted murder of his common law wife and murder of some guy she was with. His trial is coming up pretty soon and he wants me to testify."

"Testify!" David blurted out. "About what? Do you know anything about what happened?"

"No, no, not that, but he wants me to testify that he was, like the shrinks call it, traumatized like all the vets these days are claiming trauma, you know, PTSD. That's going to be his defense. His lawyer says he needs a defense, like he felt threatened by some guy. He reacted without knowing what he was doing. He thought he was in combat and being shot at and having to kill people."

"What crap," David said angrily. "What did you tell him?"

"I said I'd think about it."

"And?" David had asked.

"And he like threatened me. That's what."

"What do you mean, he threatened you?"

"I'll tell you exactly what he said. It was, 'You fuckin' better think real hard then because you're in this shit too. If I go down because you and the other guys don't fuckin' back me up, I'll bring you down too. I was carrying out orders, and all of you are responsible for the results. You're conspirators. That's what my lawyer says.' That's exactly what Serrano said, practically word for word."

"What did you say, Larry?"

"I said, 'Nick, you took it on yourself to do that and you caused the whole thing in the first place.' He said, 'don't you know the law, asshole? You're in it just as deep.' I think he's going to call you. I just wanted you to know if you didn't already," Larry said nervously.

"I appreciate that. Have you heard from anyone else in the platoon?"

"Just Mike. Nick had called him too and asked him the same thing—to testify. Also, Serrano said he had tried to reach Karl and Malvin, but he says they're dead."

"I knew about Karl, but Malvin? Dead? When? How?"

"He said they both committed suicide."

"No shit," David said, realizing that he had lapsed into vernacular that was second nature when he was in the service. "I thought this was all behind us."

"I know. Me too," Larry said reflecting David's obvious distress at the news.

"What else did he say?"

"He said he tried to reach Doug and Albert too but they're in prison."

"No kidding. For what?"

"Not sure. He didn't say but I heard that a while ago."

"What else?" David pressed.

"He didn't mention Mike or the other guys . . . but I'm sure he'll contact everyone. I think he's a little close to the edge. We always felt he could explode any minute especially after he started screwing that Iraqi broad. I don't think he's changed. He'll do anything. Now he killed some guy and shot up his own girlfriend."

"Thanks for telling me," David said.

"All right, Lieutenant. I gotta go. I just wanted to warn you. I don't have a lot to lose, not much at all, but I hear that you do."

"What do you mean?" David asked.

"Serrano just said he heard you were doing great. He actually said, 'I hear our boy is living up to his potential, if you know what I mean.'"

David felt sick to his stomach. "Well, thanks for calling. I can't say I'm surprised that Nick has been in and out of trouble or that he's charged with murder. But this has nothing to do with us."

"Yeah, right," Larry agreed quickly, "except he's a fucking psycho and you never know what he's capable of. He's trouble. He'll stop at nothing and I hate to say this, but he's got stuff that we wouldn't want him to bring out. I wouldn't put anything past him."

"Larry, will you let me know what you're going to do and what's happening? Let's stick together on this but don't tell Nick you called me, all right? I need to think about this, how to handle it, this is a real rough time for me."

"How's that? What do you mean?" Larry asked.

"I can't go into detail. I'll tell you later. Hey, how's everything with you otherwise these days?" David had asked, wanting to leave off on good terms with Larry. "So, you're in Rhode Island, right? How do I reach you?"

"I'm calling from my cell phone. Best to use that. Take it easy, David. I'll let you know when I hear something," Larry said.

10

David had trouble sleeping for three nights after the conversation with Larry. He had no one around to talk to about it. He couldn't talk to Lucille. It was difficult enough holding the tenuous relationship together. He'd get in touch with Willard. They hadn't talked in a while. He'd be in his Boston apartment or perhaps on Nantucket, although it was early in the season. He'd set something up the weekend after next.

Nightmares and fragmented scenes from Iraq, some invading his mind with the intensity of flashbacks, continued to break through the wall of defenses that David had built. At night, he lay awake tossing and turning, drifting off before waking in a cold sweat. Several times, he'd had trouble convincing himself to get out of bed in the morning. He was afraid that a phone call from Nick would come any moment during the day. The pressure of the nomination time drawing closer was enough to make him tense. The thought that the horror and the anguish of war might derail his campaign was too much to bear.

On the bench one day, he experienced a moment of panic. He felt lightheaded and dizzy and a chill swept over him from his gut to his brain. He felt shaky and had a desperate urge to escape from the courtroom. He managed to distract himself by focusing tightly on a portrait in the back of the courtroom while he breathed deeply, controlling the wave of panic until it subsided. He removed a Xanax tablet from a pill container and gulped it down with water, trying not to draw attention to himself. He was relieved when the Chief Justice called a short recess after the second argument. David wondered as he followed Jeffrey off the bench and through the doorway whether anyone had noticed. He felt under control now but knew that he'd feel groggy for the rest of the morning. At least he got through the moment. He vowed to take precautions. He would take a pill before each court session. The fear of passing out gathered its own force and accelerated the anxiety reaction. When the other justices were out of the conference room, Jeffrey came over and asked quietly whether he was feeling okay. David appreciated the concern but was dismayed that his reaction had not gone unnoticed.

David wondered whether he actually had PTSD or whether it was just a recurring anxiety reaction. Maybe Nick wouldn't call or, if he did, he'd back off if David came up with a good reason why he couldn't comply. He could hint that his testimony wouldn't help Nick. If he got to the High Court, he'd never have to worry again. He would be safe, untouchable, with a lifetime appointment.

That was just a dream, a long shot, at this point.

He knew a lot about PTSD. He'd been to wellness sessions with a VA psychiatrist and a small group of veterans right after getting back from Iraq. One time he'd purposefully stayed behind until the others had left. He approached the psychiatrist, who was staring oddly at him.

"Doctor, may I ask you a question?"

"I have a group coming in ten minutes. Why didn't you ask it during the session?"

"This is a personal matter. I prefer to keep it private."

"Go ahead briefly," the psychiatrist said, pausing, "but if you want personal counseling, you have to get that on your own. I'm here to work with groups. I don't have the time. This is not one on one therapy."

"Okay. Forget it then," David said with rising anger, "I wouldn't want to ask you to do something outside your job description."

"No. Go ahead. One question. Then I have to move on."

"I'll be returning to law school in the fall and hope to have a career in public service. I'm having symptoms that I recognize as PTSD. I can't afford—not a question of money, just risk—to engage in mental health counseling. I don't want a diagnosis and I don't want disability benefits. But I need some professional answers, very limited. I thought perhaps if I keep coming to this group, you might be willing to talk with me for a few minutes after the group sessions and. . . ."

"No, I can't do that. Ask what you want in the group but I'm not here to give individual therapy. Go get help when you get discharged. It's all confidential. You'll be protected."

"Bullshit. That's not true," David said. "Records are kept. Disclosure requirements can infringe on confidentiality. I can't afford to do that."

"Well, then, it's your problem, and I wish you good luck with it."

David left abruptly, disappointed and angry at the lack of cooperation or even concern. He never again broached the subject of mental health problems with anyone connected with the military or the VA. He certainly would not create an official record at the VA.

He got a prescription from his own doctor, avoiding any contact with a psychiatrist. He would never risk public exposure . . . so he lived with it, kept it under control, avoiding what he had to, using mind control and medication. He convinced himself that he could manage it himself although he worried about becoming addicted to the medication. So far it had worked.

11

David was on edge all the time. He and Lucille had more arguments, several of which ended in shouting matches. He struggled to control his rising anger, even rage, at her hostility. He felt disgust too in a way that hadn't struck him so vividly before. He knew that he had to accept some blame for the disintegration of the marriage. After all, he had agreed to turn their poor relationship into a marriage and then added to the damage by having children. Children were always the victims or, in military jargon, the collateral damage. His mind had flirted, over the years, with imagining life without her. How convenient if she just disappeared or died. He was repulsed at having such thoughts.

Fantasizing was dangerous because he knew only too well how good people easily become killers once they cross the moral boundary between good and evil. Evil, David thought to himself. It's interesting that I use that word even to myself. It's a religious concept, not a moral one. We never used it in the military although we all committed acts that would be considered evil if religion were a guide. Almost every soldier he knew had been perfectly law-abiding one day and on the next, when deployed, that same person could kill any number of human beings on demand or on suspicion or even on a hunch.

He wondered about the charge against Serrano. Had he just stepped over the line in the wrong place at the wrong time? What had provoked him to try to kill his girlfriend? Did he let himself go out of control because it was so easy, because he'd done it so many times during the war? Nick had always seemed a little too enthusiastic about fighting and killing. Did he have the ruthlessness of a psychopath? He never showed remorse or even regret. But that was not so different from most soldiers in combat zones. There wasn't time to make moral decisions, and giving way to regret or remorse was dangerous. A second's hesitation in reacting to a threat could mean the difference between your own life and death. David knew that he hesitated in those situations and that had almost cost him his life a few times. It cost others their lives, too.

David had never confided in any of his friends except for Willard. He was the most highly moral person David had ever known. He hadn't come close to confiding in anybody in the tight group of loyal friends who were managing his campaign for the Supreme Court now. He didn't dare shock them at this precarious time with disturbing information. Tomorrow he'd see Bradley, Jake and Dana, and Richard Sellers. The guys were the oldest, closest friends, going back to college and law school. Dana Nolan came on the scene later with Jake Whelan. He'd shared plenty during college and law school. They all had but he couldn't imagine telling them what was on his mind now.

Was it safe to talk freely to Dana? She was so easy to be with. He felt an attraction that made it pleasant to be with her. He had trusted her with a few personal observations but he'd never come close to revealing anything like the problems he faced now. Sometimes he was struck by the painful realization that he had no real friends, just allies for this or that purpose.

He'd learned a long time ago to seek refuge in himself. That was the way he'd coped years ago with the death of his brother. He fought to suppress the memory. This was not the time to revisit that, for God's sake. But after the incident with his brother—*incident*, a good, safe word—he felt he was a pariah, and that love was withdrawn from him by everyone even though no one actually knew what had really happened. His father blamed him although he tried to conceal it. He could see that his parents never stopped suffering. His father carried on and eventually took it to the grave. But his mother continued to feel the pain of his brother's death even in the dementia that consumed her for a full decade before her death. He suspected that she had brooded help-lessly and endlessly about it, blaming him for the death . . . believing the worst? He sensed that. Maybe that was why he couldn't stand to visit her more than once every couple of months. Her gaze at him, when she wasn't averting her eyes, was vacant and loveless. He had to shut out these thoughts, these jagged shards of memory. He had learned to do that well enough although he had to be on guard all the time.

After a week had passed with no call from Nick, he persuaded himself that nothing was going to happen. His anxiety subsided but his mind and body were exhausted from the tension. He was relieved that he had not panicked and told anyone about his fears. Maybe Nick had decided against calling him or found some other way out or his lawyer had discouraged him. Maybe the past will stay buried where it belongs.

12

At the end of the week following Larry's call, David spent the day in his New Haven office, thinking about the weekend ahead in New Hampshire. The afternoon went without incident. He finished talking with his clerks on the telephone by 4:00. He was scheduled to have arguments every day during the next week and bench memos were ready for the first two days. His law clerks would be working on the rest of the memos. He took the briefs for Monday's cases with him. Arguments would start at 11:00 on Monday morning. He'd have to return from New Hampshire on Sunday night. He'd prefer to stay away as long as possible to avoid more confrontations with Lucille, but he had no choice. He couldn't risk waiting until Monday morning to drive back.

He called Lucille's cell phone, hoping to mollify her about his absence this weekend. No answer. He was relieved. Voicemail would do.

"Hey Lucille," he said awkwardly, attempting to be casual. "We finished for the day and I'm heading for New Hampshire in a half hour. I wanted to touch base and I was hoping to talk. Sorry to be away. It's no vacation, that's for sure. We need to have the team together to plan our strategy for getting Cramer, the other Connecticut Senator, on board and making our approach to the Attorney General and the President. I need this time with them. Bradley has invited the White House counsel, the President's lawyer."

She wouldn't want to be there under any circumstances but she would resent his being away. He continued. "The lawyer is an old friend of Bradley's from his D.C. days. He's a key player. If we can get him on board, it makes—" Voicemail cut off and he had to redial. "Sorry. It makes it more likely that he can get the President to agree. I'll try to check in on you and the kids. Give them my love. Take care." He neglected to mention that he'd be giving Dana a ride to New Hampshire.

David wondered where Lucille was. Luke and Marcus too. At fifteen and twelve, they were old enough to be out on their own, probably at spring soccer practice. He seldom thought of the boys these days. They were left to fend for themselves much of the time although he assumed that Lucille was taking care of things at home. When he saw Luke and Marcus in passing these days, they seemed fine although distant and subdued. He suspected that they took in more than he would like about the marriage disharmony. Children always know when something's wrong at home and they have an instinct about how serious it is, although they may not acknowledge it even to themselves. They struggle to keep control of their lives and turn more and more to their friends. They separate themselves from their parents, both parents, it seems. Children don't usually try to find fault with one or the other and, when they do, they're not good at it.

He remembered how, after the incident with his brother, he separated himself from his parents, both of them, and they separated from him. They had the right side on that one although he didn't admit that to himself until years later. He'd take that secret to his grave. Modern society did not invent unhappy marriages. What was that saying about all happy families and all unhappy families? No matter. He hadn't ever seen a happy family or a happy marriage. Did they exist?

David had always thought he wanted children but it wasn't long before the luster wore off and he felt impatient about the amount of time he was expected to devote to being a father. During the past four or five years, even when he was with the boys, his mind was somewhere else, plotting career moves or wrestling with his demons. He had no illusions that he was a good parent. He vowed to remedy the situation with the boys as soon as the crisis was over. But he had to focus now on the political goal.

13

David had promised to pick up Dana since Jake would be coming to New Hampshire from a meeting in Boston. That way they could avoid having two cars when it came time to drive back to New Haven.

Ordinarily David valued his time alone but Dana was good company. She seemed wise and insightful for her years, mid-thirties he believed. She was vastly different from anyone he'd ever known. He found himself actually looking forward to being with her for the three-hour trip to the former Dartmouth conference center on Squam Lake in Holderness, where Bradley had arranged for them all to meet.

As David contemplated the weekend and the drive, he wondered whether he would ever experience being in love. He'd cared deeply about a few women in his life and had felt sexually attracted to others but those qualities had never coalesced. He surprised himself with the realization that the only woman in his life at the moment who had that potential was Dana. He knew that Jake wanted to marry her but he had intimated once, in an out-of-character moment of candor, that she wasn't ready to make the commitment.

She was pleasing to look at, not pretty, but attractive. She was tall, maybe 5′9″, slender, and moved confidently without compromising her femininity. Her Syrian and Irish background gave her unusually thick black hair and penetrating green eyes. She gave the impression of being open and transparent but with an air of mystery. She approached everyone with evident caring that bordered on intimacy. David's loyalty to Jake had so far kept him from acknowledging that he was attracted to her. Had his recent vulnerability broken down the barrier?

She always had something insightful to add to a conversation, something that had been overlooked to that point. He felt that she looked at him in a special way. At the same time, he was aware how deceptive that observation was since everyone she spoke to brightened in the warm light of her gaze. Something about the way she could meet your eyes, have direct contact, and yet not diminish herself at all was unique. She was comfortable with everyone. She could be judgmental yet accepting at the same time. He had the feeling that it would be easy to fall into a relationship with her if the circumstances were ripe. He'd be willing to bet she'd left a lot of disappointed males in her wake. He caught himself up short. This was not only treacherous but risky. He had too much at stake to throw it away in the heat of passion or curiosity, whatever it was.

David dismissed these thoughts before he pulled up in front of the red, brick front townhouse on Olive Street, just bordering the famous Wooster Square area of New Haven, where Jake and Dana lived. She had moved in with him six months ago. She came out, overnight bag in hand, wearing designer jeans and a pullover. David was dressed more formally in a gray suit, having come directly from the courthouse. They greeted each other with a simple "Hey, David," and "Dana, Good to see you. You look great," surprising himself that he blurted out his admiration so impulsively. He got out to open the hatchback of his compact wagon and then opened her door after loading the bag. Dana looked pleased and gave him one of her intense, searching looks, as if she were able to see through him with benevolent curiosity to understand what he was thinking and feeling. He smiled warmly and a little awkwardly, trying to conceal his feelings. Next to her, he felt like a clumsy adolescent. Her gaze was direct and steady but not uncomfortable. After they got underway in the light rain that had begun to fall, he relaxed and anticipated with a glow of pleasure the three hour trip ahead of them.

"When will Jake get there?" David asked.

"I'm not sure. He may not get away today. He called a few minutes ago. He said he might have to stay on for a meeting tomorrow morning in Boston. He's trouble-shooting for the management of a military high-tech supplier, you know, and apparently there's a crisis in the home office. He didn't think it would be later than noon though."

"Oh, okay," David said quietly, feeling a twinge of excitement that startled him. "Sorry not to have him there the whole time though. I rely a lot on his judgment. Do you know if Lehman is coming for certain?"

"I think he is and his wife, Marilyn, too last I heard. But I understand he's on the fence about the appointment. It seems as though he has some history with one of the other candidates. I forget which one, someone he knew in law school I think. I don't think he'd have agreed to come if he wasn't willing to listen. His wife is a player too, I hear. She's a lawyer and was with a big D.C. firm, a lobbyist. That's how she met Lehman in the first place. Her reaction could count for something. I can be on the lookout there and I may have opportunities that the rest of you won't have. How're you feeling about this whole thing? Are you holding up all right? It's a lot of pressure and a lot like being on a roller coaster."

"I'm okay, I guess," David said, tension creeping into his voice. "I learned to cope a long time ago and retreat inside myself to escape from the pressure, not to feel it so much. No matter what happened to me from outside, I was in charge inside my head. No one could reach me there. I learned that when I was really young. But enough about me. How about you? What was your growing up like? How do you deal with pressure and things that blow up in your face?"

"My childhood was pretty happy," Dana began without hesitation, "and I didn't have any real problems with either of my parents. They're still alive and in love with each other. I think I learned that if a situation was too bad, I'd change it, get out of it, rather than just retreating. But of course I was never in combat where I couldn't escape. I could always walk away from problems."

"When was the last time you walked away?" David asked, aware that his interest might show.

"A couple of years ago, before I met Jake, I ended a relationship that was turning sour. I could see it was going downhill fast and getting worse, giving me nothing, and he was trying to control everything. I don't like to be controlled. I might give in to something, give in to someone, but I won't be controlled. I left.

"Maybe I shouldn't say this," Dana added, "but I'm starting to feel that way with Jake. He wants us to get married now. He's getting impatient but I'm not there yet, if I ever will be. I'm not sure it would last and I can see the control starting to escalate. I don't do well with that."

"I'm sorry to hear that, Dana," he said, feeling that he wasn't sorry at all. "I didn't know. Jake doesn't talk about it. I'm surprised. I think Jake would be crushed if he knew what he's risking," David said, feeling a slight ripple of pleasure course through his body.

She looked straight at him, her words tinged with sadness and her eyes moist, as she said simply "I know," and then continued, "I care about him so much . . . and I feel badly about that, but I can't stay with him for that reason alone. I can't stand weak women. I can't even stand to read a novel about a helpless woman. I'm not saying it's definite but it hasn't been going well. But don't say anything, okay?"

"Of course not," he said quickly. She glanced at David, looking to see his reaction. He felt an impulse to say that he cared for her too, that his marriage was falling apart and that he hoped for something better. He couldn't figure out how to put it without appearing to be coming on to her. He knew that was unsafe territory to step into, not to mention that it was disloyal to Jake. How could he harbor such thoughts? He let his mind drift away, relieved that he had exercised this minimal restraint against a powerful impulse. He detected a reserve on her part, and he understood. She was still committed to Jake even if the relationship was shaky and, on the other hand, she would not leap into another relationship with someone as complicated as he was. Perhaps all he was feeling was the need for a release valve, something to dream about, to long for, to relieve the pressure and the pain he felt.

14

They rode in comfortable silence for a long time. Dana had curled up on the passenger seat, sipping a cup of coffee that she had picked up at the rest stop a half hour ago. David wondered why she had told him about the relationship with Jake; he sensed that she had decided to do that beforehand. He was confused about his feelings, distressed for Jake's sake, but pleased—even excited—about her revelation. Who could tell what the future held for his marriage? He'd heard it said that there was nothing like a long car ride to get to know someone. It made sense that a certain intimacy, an intimacy created by proximity, was created.

She smiled as though she could read his thoughts, looking straight at him but not speaking. In what seemed an amazingly short time, they were pulling off the main road down a long dirt road toward the conference center. The structure consisted of a rambling series of cabins, one main building with meeting rooms and a dining room large enough for twenty-five or thirty people, a dozen or so bedrooms, and several outbuildings. They would use only the main building since there would be no more than a dozen people. The gathering was more than he could comprehend at the moment and he wanted to talk more with Dana. If Jake did come in the morning, there'd be no further opportunity. He found himself hoping that Jake did not come tomorrow.

They pulled up, unloaded their overnight bags, and David went on to park the car, leaving Dana to go inside. He saw Bradley Thompson's car and Richard Sellers getting out of his but didn't recognize the others. He was happy to see Richard. They had become close friends during law school. He was the first African American whom David had gotten to know on a highly personal basis. They hadn't seen a lot of each other since law school but they had kept in touch regularly and had collaborated on a few cases when David was practicing. He was glad that Richard had joined the planning group. Even though he was with a New York firm now, he had maintained strong ties to key people in Washington. They greeted each other warmly and walked into the lodge together. He knew everyone would already have asked Dana where Jake was. He was glad to have missed that scene.

The greetings were over when he got inside. Nearly his whole group was there: Bradley, Tim O'Leary, his wife Beth, who planned a long weekend of reading by the lake, Richard, and Herb Gerson, another law school friend. Herb was active in the American Bar Association, a vital element in the nomination process. David did not overlook the fact that Herb was a divorce lawyer of considerable stature. David might need him later. Bradley and Tim O'Leary would be running the show this weekend.

With Dana—who had worked with Elizabeth Madison, before she became President, for a year near the end of her tenure at the Global Crisis Network—the group numbered seven at this point. The President's tenure at GCN came just before her surprisingly successful run for the presidency and followed a partnership in a Boston law firm along with a faculty position at Harvard Law School. Arthur Lehman and his wife would arrive tomorrow morning. Despite the fact that both women, Beth O'Leary and Marilyn Lehman, had legal and political experience in their own right, they would not be participating in this meeting. The main focus would be to make progress in bringing Lehman on board to support David's candidacy. He was a pivotal figure because of his close relationship with the President: he had been one of her major strategists during the presidential campaign.

By the time the greetings were completed, and drinks and light food shared, the time was close to 10:00 p.m. David said he'd turn in at that point and helped Dana bring her bag upstairs. Her room was at the opposite end of the hall from David's. David said goodnight even though he would have been glad for a chance to continue their earlier conversation. He sensed that she shared a similar reluctance to separate. In a few moments, however, he was by himself and became absorbed in thinking of the encounter with Lehman the next morning.

15

Alone in his room, David did the bare minimum of organizing before letting his mind drift over the events of the day. He struggled to make sense of where he stood. He felt buffeted by events over which he had little control. His last thought before drifting into deep and, thankfully, uninterrupted sleep was whether Jake Whelan would show up on Saturday. He knew that when Jake was on a trouble-shooting mission, it became his sole priority. Jake thrived on intense challenges as he had thrived on his special forces assignments. During his days with the CIA after his career with the Navy SEALs, he was in another world. He'd drop in to see David once in a while, always without warning, and then he'd be gone for weeks, months, even a year at a time, before resurfacing.

One conversation with Jake was etched in David's memory. One weekend when David was working for the Senator, Jake came to the city from the SEAL base in Virginia. They spent most of the weekend catching up on their war experiences as well as their personal lives. They had quite a bit to drink as they went from bar to bar. David hardly ever did that but Jake seemed to need the release that alcohol provided. At that point, both of them were suffocating in bad marriages. David was free at the moment since Lucille had chosen not to accompany him to Washington. Jake was in the midst of a bitter divorce back in Connecticut. Jake was hardly ever at home and, when he was, he never knew when he would be summoned on an emergency mission for an indeterminate length of time. He had spoken before about not trusting in his wife's loyalty. He hardly knew her when they decided to get married during one of his brief times at home.

As a SEAL, Jake had been a key figure in more than two dozen secret missions, but he focused on one in particular that had been a high point for him. David had never forgotten Jake's chilling remarks, spoken while considerably drunk as he recounted a particular rescue of hostages in an American embassy somewhere in North Africa. A half dozen SEALs assaulted the embassy from the air at night, apparently similar to the way Bin Laden's compound had been assaulted.

David recalled vividly the way Jake described the mission. "The six of us were dropped into the embassy compound and we rushed the place. I think I killed seven or eight insurgents myself. We knew there were a large number of people, hostages and guards, in the compound. We had no casualties and had only one guy injured, until we were withdrawing, that is. We got the hostages into the bird, which is why we had to do this with only six. We knew they had at least a dozen embassy employees, including the Ambassador, held prisoner."

"Sounds like it went smoothly, then," David said, "but what do you mean until you were withdrawing?"

"One of our men got shot on the way out," Jake said, a slight smile curling across his face. "You see, I discovered that one of the guys assigned to this mission was the guy who was fooling around with my wife while I was away. I barely knew the guy, name was Foster, and probably never would have known about what was going down. Sometimes on these missions, with all the tension, guys say things to keep themselves calm without thinking. I've probably done that too. It's a way of blowing steam off and keeping cool. The guy didn't know who was listening."

"Oh my God," David said. "So what happened? Did you confront the guy?"

"I guess you could say that," Jake said with a smirk. "I worked with the team for the mission until it was over, but I decided early that guy would not fool around with her again. I was just ahead of him as we left the building. I made sure the others were already outside near the copter in the dark. I turned on that son of a bitch and he never knew what cut him down. Took him by surprise in the dark and...." Jake paused and made a cutting motion across his throat. "No traces. No evidence. Got outside, lifted off, and then I said, 'hey where's Foster?' No one had noticed him and AQI reinforcements were pulling into the compound by now, five or six vehicles. We couldn't go back. The other guys were pissed at themselves for not noticing. I said he was behind me but lost track of him, thought he had taken a different route out. No one ever knew. They assumed one of the insurgents had survived long enough to take him out. The guy who was paired off with him blamed himself. I felt bad for that guy but that son of a bitch Foster got what he deserved. When I told my wife I heard he hadn't survived a mission, she cried and cried. I pretended not to understand."

David was stunned into silence. Jake was the last person he thought would ever violate the code of honor or the code of silence for that matter. He figured Jake rationalized that, with the mission accomplished, Foster was fair game for him. David never saw Jake in the same light again. He handled Jake with kid gloves after that.

Despite what David knew, they remained fairly close, trying to pick up where they left off in their college days. But sometimes Jake looked as though he was war-weary. There was something forbidding, even frightening, about Jake's eyes, enough to make David shiver. Crossing Jake would be no small matter.

David slept more soundly than usual until 5:30. He awoke to voices downstairs. He was groggy but didn't want to miss a chance for a morning run before breakfast and before others arrived. He dressed hurriedly in his running clothes. Bradley and Dana were both in running clothes and, after coffee, all three went out to the dirt road that circled the lake, jogging for an hour and talking intermittently in the warm sunshine cooled by an early spring breeze. They returned sweaty but refreshed and had just enough time to shower and change before Lehman and O'Leary arrived.

One by one, the others filtered into the dining room. Bradley had arranged for staff people to be on duty to take care of their mealtime needs. Lehman knew only Bradley and O'Leary, who insisted on telling his version of how their group came to be together. At some point in their careers after law school at Yale, they all ended up in the New York-New Haven metropolitan area and met once a month for lunch at the Yale Club in New York. The standing joke was that they were the 12:47 Club because that was the time they first met in the Grill Room. Everyone in the close-knit group had a Yale College or Yale Law School degree or both. Despite their educational experience in common, the political philosophies of the members, some of whom were not present, ranged across the spectrum. Jake was the most conservative and the most adamant about the role of the military, O'Leary the most liberal, with everyone else on a political spectrum between those points. Despite their occasional heated arguments, everyone put friendship first and, typically, no one pushed arguments to the point of rancor.

David sat next to Dana at the table and was constantly drawn to glance at her. It was not her looks so much as the magnetism that she radiated. He felt fairly sure that he concealed his interest, but he also knew the dangers of self-deception when chemistry prevailed. This was not the time to stir up animosity; everyone here was loyal to Jake as well as David. Besides, most of the group assumed that David was settled in his marriage. Midway through the meal, David stepped outside to take a call from Jake, who was still in Boston. He would not be able to join the group after all. David made the announcement in a disappointed voice, concealing his true feelings. He recognized that danger lay ahead in the renewed opportunity to be alone with Dana. A personal conflict could ruin not only the relationships among them all but his chances for support. He resolved not to forget that fact.

The rest of the breakfast was uneventful. The group gathered in the spacious living room, looking out over the expanse of the lake, shimmering in the bright sunshine, bordered by dense pines extending the length of the opposite shore. A serious tone replaced the light conversation. Bradley offered preliminary remarks and then asked Tim O'Leary to talk about his assessment of the present political climate of the Senate. When O'Leary finished summing up, he asked Lehman to tell the group how he saw the situation and what guidance he could offer.

16

Arthur Lehman's demeanor and remarks were not designed to please anyone in the room. David instinctively did not like him. It was difficult not to see him as anything but a predatory creature like a fox, always on the lookout for prey. He knew he would have to work to conceal his antipathy. With a humorless delivery and contentious attitude, Lehman presented a discouraging picture of the nomination prospects for David. Although O'Leary had made it clear that Lehman was not committed to David and would speak frankly, the atmosphere in the room clouded over at his remarks.

"I've had several conversations with the President," Lehman said, "but I can't disclose the details, of course. Your candidate, whom I've just met and barely had a chance to talk to, is one of many. There are at least a half dozen other serious candidates. It's a complex process but I can assure that he," nodding slightly in David's direction, "will get fair consideration. President Madison is not a military person, herself, although she grew up in a military family. She sees herself as a reluctant war President, similar to her immediate predecessors. It is endless war with the terrorists and has been that way for two decades. Beyond that, we all know that several major countries continue to pose acute threats of a more traditional nature. The President inherited those situations. She doesn't overplay that hand as an excuse to expand executive authority or to cut back on civil liberties. The President is adamant on that score despite the apparent willingness of the American people to accept encroachments on liberties so long as they do not feel directly affected by them."

Lehman continued without a pause in the same tedious style. "The President doesn't endorse the endless war mentality as justification for expanding our military operations all over the globe. She's made practical choices but she's keenly aware of the harm that's been caused by our supplying arms to various factions in the Middle East and by our bombing and drone attacks. We've inspired Islamist recruiting on a large scale. The President is especially concerned about the growing number of Islamist recruits from the Western world including the U.S. That's a new phenomenon . . . but, of course, the make-up of the Western world, and our own country, has changed radically in the past decade or two."

Lehman wasn't through. "You may be wondering whether all this has anything to do with the President's choice of a Supreme Court nominee. I assure

43

you that it does. The posture of the U.S. in the global environment, with the nation involved in multiple military ventures and with the prospect of American citizens and Western Europeans being on the enemy side in some of them, raises legal issues that will have to be decided by the Supreme Court. Dozens of issues are at stake such as domestic and foreign policy legal issues. The issues with international implications are endless. That's in addition to the social justice and economic issues that normally are on the Court's docket.

"This legal environment may work to the advantage of some candidates on the President's short list." Looking at David, he added: "You combine veteran status with progressive views much like the President's own. The President trusts people who have a sophisticated and nuanced view of the world we live in. We live in a very complex global society. These are revolutionary times. The President wants people in government—every branch—who share her global outlook. We can't afford to have a Court that cowers in the face of bold and dramatic issues. The days of tolerating a Court whose approach is outdated and ineffective are past. We need a Court that can function in the real world. This is the first opportunity in years to break the stranglehold of the majority that resists change."

Finally, Lehman got personal. "We've discovered a serious problem in our background checking so far. Bradley is aware of this. We've gotten an early start on vetting multiple candidates to avoid getting caught short by eleventh hour disclosures. I won't let the President be blindsided. She needs to know more about you, David. Every time we try to track down the details of your service record, we run into a firewall, something about an investigation. We need to know every last detail of what happened in Iraq during your fifteen months there, especially during the last six months. We need your cooperation in accessing all the records and sealed files."

David maintained his outward composure despite the reference to the sealed records. His instinct was to assure Lehman and he began to speak, not knowing exactly how to frame his response. Lehman looked his way and snapped, "Wait, let me finish," in a harsh tone that stunned David. "Assurances aren't enough. We need to see the files. We know there was an investigation at some point and then it ended without a hearing and apparently without a public report. We know who you served with, who was in your platoon, your company, and all the way up. We know that some of those people are dead, some were suicides, some are in prison, and some we haven't tracked down yet. If you want consideration, you have to help. You must know about all this."

David replied quickly, "Yes, of course I will. I'll do everything I can to get the information released. It's been a long time though and I haven't seen anyone since we got out. It's been years."

"Have you had any recent contact at all with anyone that you served with?" Lehman pressed.

"No," David said, unable to control a slight stammer on his part, recalling Larry's recent contact. He wasn't about to give that information out and reveal a pathway directly to Nick Serrano and the threat he represented. He wondered what had led Lehman and his staff to start digging behind the scenes at this stage. Were there any other veterans among the candidates? Could he satisfy Lehman without opening Pandora's box of evils?

Lehman pressed further. "Have you ever tried to get hold of the records?"

"No, I had no reason," David replied.

"When you got the medal from Obama, there must have been a lot of information available. Did the White House staff look into the investigation?"

"I don't know," David quickly responded. He knew nothing about a background check.

Lehman spoke over David again. "What was the investigation? What was it all about?"

David felt as though he was wading into quicksand, but he had to respond. He regretted that this conversation was taking place in front of everyone. He suddenly felt alone on a stage, with bright lights blinding his eyes as he stared into a blackness that concealed his audience. Choosing his words with care, he said, "I didn't know much about it actually. There were questions about what happened on a few occasions in Fallujah and Ramadi, which, you recall, was a nest of Al Qaeda activity. There were constant attacks on our forces. I was deployed there in March of 2007. We started deploying extra troops in January but the surge is usually considered to run from March to September of 2008. That didn't end the hostilities. I came back stateside after fifteen months and then had a short deployment to Djibouti before my active commitment was up.

"My platoon was right in the middle of the fighting in Ramadi," he continued. "Sure, there was controversy and complaints about some of the insurgents who were killed. That's no secret. Everybody in the squad was questioned, maybe the whole platoon, I'm not sure. I was, too. Then nothing happened for a couple of months and one day I was ordered to tell my platoon the investigation was closed. Frankly, I haven't thought about it for a long time, years really."

"Well," Lehman said, "we're going to have to know what went on and what the investigation was all about if you're going to be a viable candidate, someone I could recommend to the President. Why did the investigation take place at all? Was there a problem? What did the investigation consist of?"

Lehman was waiting for a response and no one, not even Bradley, was stepping up to bail him out. After an uncomfortable silence, David spoke. "My platoon was ordered to search and destroy insurgent elements throughout Anwar province, my brigade's area of operations, especially Fallujah and Ramadi. This was part of the surge that got so much publicity back home. Brigade command had information that some locals were creating hiding places for AQI operatives, which they were. They were conducting raids and could be a bigger problem if they weren't stopped."

David went on, aware that he could dig a hole for himself by giving up too much information without considering the implications. "Our platoon was bigger than any other in the country. I divided it up into three, four, and sometimes five squads and sent them out every day. We had dozens of small communities and villages to cover and this had to be done fast. Command wanted our Iraq headquarters, and our embassies in Yemen and Djibouti, to be secure. Some squads encountered militants in a few villages. Other communities were clean. All in all, I'd say at least half of the villages had close ties with the insurgents. Some of the squads ran into hostile fire from insurgents and from villagers. It was hard to tell the difference usually. There was no way of distinguishing them from each other. I can't tell you how many suicide bombers we encountered. It was a daily event during that period."

"Why is all this relevant?" Lehman interrupted.

"Because it's the context for everything our troops did in Iraq," David said. "Al Qaeda was pretty well integrated with the locals in Iraq. So there were some deaths in some villages and headquarters wanted to know the details, who got killed and why. We took quite a few losses too. I haven't thought about this for a long time," David explained. "I can't remember all the details."

Lehman refused to back off. "Who headed up the squads?"

David replied, feeling that he was being forced to go into far too much detail without weighing the consequences, "My platoon sergeant, Nick Serrano, took most of them. He was tough. He didn't mess around, Larry, my other non-com, took some along with a few others, and I took the rest, nearly a quarter of them. Sometimes we went out together and then split up in smaller squads."

"So," Lehman demanded, "What was the big deal? Why the investigation?"

"Because there were complaints by local sheikhs when some family members of AQI insurgents got killed when we were retaliating for an attack on some civilians who were very friendly with our troops."

"A lot of deaths?"

"I don't remember exactly. It's too long ago. I don't know at this point," David argued quietly.

"You mean you have no recollection of how many were killed? That's hard to believe," Lehman said. "Women and children too?"

"Yes, sometimes, in one strike particularly. There was one time when there were quite a few deaths reported, and two of our own, a male and a female, got killed and it wasn't clear who killed them."

Lehman wasn't through pressing. "Who did the investigation focus on? Anyone in particular?"

"Yes," David said, "my platoon sergeant."

"And did you testify? What did you say?"

"It's difficult to remember. The upshot of the investigation was that the sergeant got very little punishment. Of course, there was a need on the part of the military not to let it blow up. Whether I might have handled things differently is another question, but I can't answer that off the top of my head," David replied quietly, knowing that he had been pressed to disclose far more than he had anticipated.

"All right," Lehman said finally. "You'll cooperate in getting access to the investigation reports, right?"

"Of course, whatever I can do." David tried to conceal his distress. When other conversation resumed, he excused himself to go the bathroom to regain his composure. He knew that his answers, while technically correct, were misleading. He had been evasive and had understated his role. The version he had just recited was only remotely the whole truth, and the investigation, little more than a whitewash, was barely described. He hadn't been any more eager than anyone at Headquarters to open up this mess, and he had felt the powerful pressure to minimize the incident to avoid disastrous publicity about the company and the conduct of American troops. It was at a time when they were trying desperately to win over the people while at the same time trying to control the violence. Very few people knew about the details aside from the squad members and they had a stake in not having it blow up, too. What happened was done. Nothing would change it.

He felt helpless because he had no control over the records. Back then, events had spiraled out of hand, and he hadn't wanted to be the one to force the hand of the brigade commander to dig it all out. What was the point? It could only hurt everyone. With the embedded journalists nosing around all the time, it was bound to explode if it wasn't carefully controlled. He'd been through years of nightmares about this. He hoped this was the end of the questioning this weekend. The feeling of panic subsided but did not go away at once. He couldn't stay away any longer.

He entered the room, trying to pick up what they were talking about. Dana glanced anxiously at him. He was uncertain whether it was wise to tell her what this was about. She seemed to have good judgment, but if she and Jake stayed together, she might reveal it. Everyone was capable of giving up confidences under the right circumstances. He'd decide later how to handle this.

17

The afternoon passed quickly without further skirmishes concerning David's military record. Lehman appeared detached after lunch. O'Leary and Bradley were unsuccessful in drawing him into the conversation about strategy. David assumed that he would leave before long. O'Leary spoke, dismissing concerns about the investigation. The subject of military service had come up at the time of David's appointment to the Connecticut Supreme Court. Nothing controversial had surfaced. He added that David had led a group of public figures calling for a national study of the aftermath of the Iraq and Afghanistan wars, similar to the National Vietnam Veterans Readjustment Study.

When O'Leary paused, Lehman said, "Look, Tim, I have no quarrel with what you say about your candidate's qualifications. The point is, aside from political realities, he's got a black hole in his resume. I won't support any candidate who has the potential to embarrass the President. I have strong reservations about your candidate. I'll advise the President of that when I see her tomorrow." Stunned silence greeted his harsh assessment.

Lehman and his wife departed shortly thereafter. David saw it as slightly hopeful that Lehman initiated a brief conversation in the front hallway with him before departing. "I don't want you to feel that you won't get a fair shake from me," Lehman said. "My loyalty is to the President. To be candid, she's open at this point but she's in a difficult spot politically. She's under fire from the right to be more aggressive militarily and from the left to curtail domestic surveillance. There are big cases on their way to the Court involving these issues of national security and privacy and challenges under the War Powers Act. Our handling of terrorist detainees continues to be a sore point, especially with the repeated demands to trade them for hostages."

"This seat on the Court could be pivotal," he continued. "The President needs a Court that is capable of acting with wisdom and foresight on the major issues. But for you to be a viable candidate, she needs to know everything."

"You can count on me," David said, although he had no misgivings about the tightrope he would be walking.

18

David listened quietly when the meeting resumed. Knowing the risks involved in exposing the investigation as well as his role in Serrano's trial, he searched for ways to avoid the problem. He did not know what the report contained specifically or how to locate it. He adopted a diversionary strategy by asking O'Leary to spell out what Lehman had alluded to as the President's position and what that meant for his chances.

"Let me give you the short version, guys," said O'Leary. "The President is not a pacifist. She just thinks that war should be the last resort after every other option has been tried. Sooner or later, we have to find a way to reduce the need to resort to war. There'll always be extremists who refuse to respect the world order. When the President was a political science professor, before she headed up GCN, her expertise was on wars of choice in the Middle East—Iraq and Afghanistan and all that followed. She worked for John Kerry when he was Secretary of State. She supported much stricter limitations on sales of arms by U.S. manufacturers in view of the evidence that they always come back to haunt us. She understands the value of using the special forces rather than boots on the ground but she's insistent on keeping them under tight civilian control and accountability.

"She's under fire for being too slow to react to crises that we used to jump right into, the way Obama took the heat on Syria and the Ukraine ten years ago. She's been avoiding military confrontation all over the globe, but what goes unnoticed is that she has people working to resolve the crises behind the scenes, very successfully, I might add. The point is to get the people who are directly affected to resolve the crises and let them get the credit. She refuses to get involved in the ongoing disputes between China and its neighbors even though she realizes that China's aggression is not going to go away overnight. She thinks eventually its aggression will give way to deepening concerns about internal problems, like pollution and inability to cut off the population from connection with the world through social media. She doesn't think war with China is inevitable any more than with Iran, and a decade ago we witnessed a turnaround in Iran. A slender majority in the Senate adamantly opposes her position."

"I don't see what this has to do with the Supreme Court, Tim. What's the connection?" Richard Sellers asked.

"It's the political context in which the President and the Senate exist right now." O'Leary said. "The midterms are coming up and she's got to get more popular support from independents if she wants to recapture the Senate. It's going to be close. We lost that a long time ago to the right wing. She needs to show some muscle. After all, she's the first woman President to be elected solely on her own and she sees herself as a stakeholder for women in general in an unprecedented way. If she were to appoint David to the Court, it could help her position with the voters who don't support her views on war as well as those who do."

David and Bradley listened attentively without interrupting. "Why is the Court so important in this political context?" O'Leary asked with rhetorical flourish. "This vacancy was unexpected. Everyone thought Scalia's conservative replacement would go on forever but his unexpected resignation opened up the first chance in two decades to tip the balance of the Court back to the center. All the leading candidates are people like yourself who look moderate, no left-wingers in the bunch, but they're open-minded enough to be their own people when the chips are down. That's good enough for the President. I know you well enough to have a sense of what you think about the important issues. There's no question about your views being acceptable to her."

"I've held back since I stepped out of politics," David said. "I saw there wasn't going to be any lasting change in the way this country approaches war. I didn't want to get aligned with the anti-war people. They don't have credibility with the average person. They may be morally right but if they sound too idealistic in a naïve way, they aren't persuasive. I didn't want to be marginalized. But I feel for the unprivileged youth of the country. They took the heat when the draft was on and they still take the heat with the volunteer system. But are you saying that I have to present myself as something I'm not? I have enough problems satisfying Lehman on the investigation business."

"You don't have to be anyone other than yourself. I'm saying that your war record will be a big selling point to the current Senate majority, as long as nothing tarnishes that, of course. I'm also saying that your nomination before the election would help the President retake the Senate because it would change her image with the middle ground voters."

"There's the problem, Tim," David said. "I don't know whether I can satisfy them that there isn't some hidden scandal. What if I can't get hold of anything that clears it up? Do I have to bring in witnesses?"

"No, I don't think so." O'Leary said. "You should realize that there's a lot at stake here. It's not widely known that the Chief Justice hasn't been well in several years. The President thinks that, if she wins a second term, he may step down, which means that whoever gets this seat is in a perfect position to be the new Chief. Everyone thought he'd never leave with a liberal in the White House, but he respects her, and I think he's ready to go. Only a few people know about this. Except for the fact that you're a white male, you're an ideal candidate. You're untouchable. No one dares criticize you because of your record. You can see that Lehman is gun shy about a candidate who might have a skeleton in the closet. I can't blame him for not wanting to let the

President get blindsided. It would ruin any chance she has of doing something constructive."

David wondered if he was untouchable, remembering vividly the death of his brother, Ronnie, so long ago and what he had let happen in Iraq. He didn't know how he could contain information about the killings in Ramadi but what he had done to Ronnie was another story, an old story that he relived every day of his life and would take to his grave. Would he ever be put in a position of explaining the death? He doubted it. It was his biggest source of shame. David knew he needed to keep his wits about him or he would lose control over the group. He couldn't afford to be distracted with all that had happened in the past. It seemed that the worse the situation became, the more his mind made its way to the darkest, most disturbing, memories.

Ramadi is bound to surface. It's inescapable, he thought. But maybe he could avoid it turning into a disaster. Next week might be crucial. He said nothing of this to O'Leary or Bradley. He had to bide his time. He doubted whether he could count on anyone's support if the truth were to spill out.

19

Dana divided her time between sitting in on the group meeting and talking with Beth O'Leary and Marilyn Lehman. She wanted to get their reaction to the current Supreme Court nomination prospects. They were well informed and candid about their views. They were impatient with the political aspects and preferred to focus on the merits of the candidates. Dana did not underestimate the private but significant role that spouses played in these matters. Both women were frustrated with the polarized positions that had dominated Congress for the past two decades and the obsession on the part of the opposition with preventing at any cost "that woman in the White House" from gaining a second term. The stubborn opposition that sought to block her initiatives and undermine her at every point was reminiscent of the opposition to President Obama.

These women were, as Dana expected, seasoned observers of the political scene and they followed assiduously the periodic shifting of national priorities. Both women shared frustration at what seemed to them the distinct absence, up to now, of a moral compass to guide U.S. policy. Since the Bill Clinton era, national politics had been an invidious game in which tactical moves and claims counted for more than substance. Washington politicians were now into their fourth decade of ferocious competition for wealth and power that allowed little room for constructive bipartisan thinking or concerted action in the national interest. Short-term thinking geared solely to the next election dominated. Long-term thinking, always scarce in American political affairs, had become even more outmoded than ever. The advent of a woman in the White House standing on her own credentials had not altered the poisonous partisanship that had become endemic in the country.

As the afternoon was drawing to a close, Richard asked, "What's our next move?"

"Let's stay in touch by phone and use the encrypted system that I set up for any emails we need to send," Bradley said. "David, can you make a contact to get to the bottom of Lehman's concern?"

David cringed visibly at this suggestion. "I don't know," he said, "but I'll make some phone calls to see who can figure out what to do. I used to have contacts at Fort Benning. I suspect that's where the records were initially located, although they may have ended up somewhere else. It's possible they ended up in the Pentagon. I'll let you know what I find out."

David had a premonition that he was going to hear from Nick soon and that Nick already knew what had happened to the files. He was a master at manipulating the system. There was always someone he'd done a favor for, covering something up or taking care of an enemy, or filling a need, illicit or otherwise. Bradley appeared to notice the slight change that came over David, and a momentary look of concern crossed his face. Dana noticed as well but no one else paid attention. They parted. Bradley asked Dana if she needed a ride. She said without hesitating, "No, I think I'm all set. I'm pretty sure David will drop me back in New Haven."

Dana pulled Bradley aside in the foyer and said quietly: "I had long talks with Marilyn and Beth. They feel frustrated with the obsession to dig into old files. They both think David is the choice the President should make. She wouldn't be selling out to any interest group. He's capable, honest and open-minded. It's a no brainer that his nomination would make a lot of important groups happy, like veterans, and probably the whole legal community too," she added.

"Good," Bradley replied quickly. "The more we can downplay this record business and get Lehman's mind off it, the better. If he doesn't make a big deal of it with the President, she may not pay a lot of attention to it. Dana, do you think there's anything to worry about?"

"I don't know really. The subject seems to be very upsetting to David. I can't figure it out. But maybe he will talk more about it on the way home." It was obvious that she would be faced with the pressure of divided loyalty—to David, to Bradley, to the President and, not the least, to Jake. "Okay, take care," Bradley said, "and let me know what you find out." She nodded.

20

As the group of supporters headed for their cars, David stayed behind to take a final walk out to the lakefront. He had no wish to rush back to the contentious atmosphere at home, and he needed a few minutes to make sense of what had happened at the meeting. It felt good to walk to the end of the long dock extending into the lake, breathing deeply and allowing tension to dissipate. Dana gave him time alone by talking with the women who had taken care of the food service and housekeeping. David savored his final look at the crystal clear lake water rippling in the light wind that had come up now that the sun was about to begin a slow descent in the sky. A solemn expression clouded his face. Dana left the women to finish up and approached David silently, surprising him gently with humor, "Are you taking me back or should I start hitchhiking?"

"Oh my God," he blurted out. "Of course! Of course! We can leave anytime you're ready. Sorry, I was lost in thought."

"I can see that," she said. "Is everything okay?"

"Oh, yeah, I'm fine," he said, before pausing and adding, "It's hard to leave here. It's such a beautiful spot, although I feel as though I had no time to notice that before now. I love this place. I've been here for several conferences, the last maybe ten years ago when Dartmouth still owned it. I took a boat ride around the lake, even had time to go swimming. I'm glad Bradley picked this for our meeting. It was worth the drive." He realized the awkwardness of his reference to the drive. He decided not to explain, which would entail confessing how much he enjoyed being with her and looked forward to the drive back.

She said, surprising him, "Do you want to take a walk before we leave? Or a swim? You don't look ready to get behind the wheel. Of course, I'd be glad to drive so you can relax."

"Sounds good," David said, mustering more enthusiasm than he thought possible after the demanding day. As an afterthought he added, "What about the women, the servers? Are they still here? Can we just lock up on our own, or do they have to wait for us?"

"They're finishing up in the kitchen. I think they'll be leaving shortly. As for swimming, I always have a bathing suit with me, just in case," she said cheerfully. "I actually have it on. I was hoping there might be a chance before we left when I saw how appealing the water looks."

"Okay," he said. "I'll get shorts on. Just be a minute. I'm not packed yet."

He returned in five minutes in shorts and a T-shirt. They took off down the dirt path and walked about a mile until they came to a small beach, which they had spotted that morning, bordered by a rustic picnic area and a gravel parking lot. The place was deserted. Dana removed her shorts and top, leaving her trim, athletic body in a modest one-piece tank suit. David could see that she kept herself in excellent condition. He knew that she was an avid dancer and a dedicated runner. David quickly removed his shirt and decided to wear his shorts into the water. They entered the shallow water tentatively, finding it bracing this early in the season. Finally, they dove in headfirst. The chilly water embraced their bodies, then melted into a warm glow as their skin adjusted to the crisp coldness. They swam vigorously for twenty minutes, stroking out several hundred yards into the pristine lake, and came out refreshed and invigorated. David could feel the cold water change his body chemistry as nothing else could. He observed that Dana was a proficient swimmer, gliding easily though the water far more gracefully and powerfully than he could think of doing regardless of the effort he put out.

Dana unfolded a beach towel for them to share as they sat on a bench feeling the glow of the warm sun on their bodies. David could sense how Dana's body responded to his closeness. He wondered if she sensed the same in him. The cold water and the sun's penetrating warmth directed at them from its perfect angle in the sky, plus sharing the towel, had a stimulating effect on him. He imagined that she wanted to ask him what was troubling him so much but was glad neither of them spoiled the magic of the moment. They sat close enough so that their arms brushed occasionally. His body's response was palpable. This was the first time they had ever been in a situation of such closeness and physical awareness. David was amazed at how his mental stress was fully relieved by the physical sensation of water and sunlight plus the intimacy of sitting closely together.

After what seemed a timeless stretch, David broke the silence and the moment by saying, "We should get back. I hate to spoil this, but we shouldn't stay longer. I'm concerned that the staff people might notice. It wouldn't look good even though there's nothing wrong. If Bradley calls Jake on the way back, Jake will know what time the meeting broke up. Am I paranoid? I just don't want to mess things up for you, for either of us." She agreed without hesitation although with regret. They headed back on the path. Reaching the lodge, they went inside through the screen door and up to their rooms.

When they reached her room, Dana asked, "Your room doesn't look out on the lake and the mountains, right?" He shook his head no.

"I have a gorgeous view. Do you want to take a look before we go? It's worth it."

David blushed slightly and took a deep breath. "Sure," he said, unable to resist the moment, sensing what might happen and feeling suddenly heedless, even excited by it. He followed her into the room and straight to the window that overlooked the full expanse of the lake and the forested mountains in the distance. They stood side by side for a moment, gazing at the sight, before David mustered his strength to say, his voice choking slightly, "Dana, if I don't get out of here now, I won't be able to." She nodded, obviously having the same thought. They were close enough to touch. She turned to look at him and, in an instant, some benevolent force drew them together and they embraced, kissing lightly, then more intensely. Each surrendered separately to the moment of delicious intimacy. David felt the tension of the past months give way and he felt a sense of peace and release that he had long missed. They glided effortlessly to the bed and allowed their passion to take over. After they had made love and remained wrapped in each other's arms for a half hour, they drifted lazily to sleep. Nearly an hour later, David came to his senses with alarm. He felt the deadening impact of reality pulse through his body. He said urgently, "We have to go," as anxiety overtook him again. They withdrew from their embrace slowly and he left the room to finish packing, saying, "Meet you downstairs."

When they met at the foot of the staircase, they could see down the hall to the kitchen that the two women were sitting at a table in animated conversation. David realized he hadn't seen or heard them when they came back from the lake. He wondered about his lack of attention to that detail. In any event, they were busily occupied with placing silverware in a chest. Concealed by the noise of the dishwasher, David and Dana made their departure without detection, or so they hoped. They hurried quietly up the dirt driveway to the parking lot.

In the course of a single hour, everything had changed. His fears and anxiety remained. But his mind and body had entered a different mode. He was amazed at what had happened, so quickly, so easily, despite his inhibitions and fears. How had it happened? He felt that Dana shared his growing attraction, an attraction that seemed to be more than physical. The fact that both had been willing to surrender to the pleasure of physical intimacy gave him additional confidence in the rightness of it despite his reservations and knowing how this had complicated their lives from one instant to the next.

What lay ahead was unknown. The options had changed. His mind was a muddle of mixed reactions. He recognized the familiar presence of lingering apprehension, but it was now suspended outside his being. Just an hour ago, it had been lodged in his inner core. He dreaded returning home to face strife with Lucille. He recognized the painful stress that had plagued him, although he had kept it in check by extreme acts of will, rather than professional treatment or spiritual redemption. Part of him recognized that he had just now shared himself spontaneously in a way that he had never before done in his life.

The future was uncertain, but he felt sure that Dana would be part of it. He knew that his longing for her had been incipient for many months now, escaping his detection. Perhaps he had suppressed those feelings, like a lifetime of so many other suppressed feelings. He had learned early in childhood to be expert at that and wondered whether he would explode if he ever unleashed all that was buried in his psyche. Someday he would have to let the demons out. He had an uneasy feeling that day was not far away.

21

As they drove out the long gravel drive, they had three hours together before reality set in. There were complications and questions needing answers.

After they had ridden in silence for a half hour, Dana asked, "What are you thinking?" He paused briefly, sighed, and said quietly, "I'm not sure I can put my thoughts and feelings in any kind of order. I'm glad for what happened between us. It was amazing. I don't know what this will mean for you and Jake. My relationship with Lucille is over and this may speed up the process, but I don't want it to hurt you. I think we had better guard this secret with our lives, don't you?"

She was quick to answer. "Absolutely. It could ruin your chance for the nomination. Jake and I go in different directions these days so we hardly talk. But he isn't ready to let go of the relationship. I'm getting close."

Dana paused. "I start my new job at the Global Crisis Network in New York in two weeks. Since I'll be deputy counsel, I'll be in the office most of the time. The chief counsel travels to the offices outside the U.S. We'll have to work that out. At some point, you and I will have to decide what all this means, but we're not close to that point. Don't make this into more than it is at the moment. That would be a mistake. I can tell you, I'm not ready to plunge into another commitment. That much I know."

His hurt reaction must have been plain to see. She apologized. "David, I'm sorry. That didn't come out the way I meant it." It was obvious that she regretted being so blunt. "It's just that it's true. I don't want commitment now to Jake or anyone else. Okay?" David nodded.

"I wish you'd tell me," she said, "what's going on about this secret file . . . this investigation report? It sounds important. I could see your reaction when we were talking about it. You were really upset. What's going to happen? Is there something damaging?"

"It has to do with something I've never talked about. I'm not sure this is a good time. I have memories from the war that have been buried for a long time. I want them to stay that way. It took me a long time, years, to recover. I finally got them under control. The surface may be healed but the wounds are deep, too deep to open up again unless I'm forced to."

"I'm not pressing you to talk about something you don't want to now, but if you ever want to, you can trust me," Dana said.

David's glance assured her of his trust but he added, "I know that. There's

57

only one other person who knows anything about what I went through in the war. You've heard me mention Willard Coleman? Does that name mean anything to you?"

"Of course. He's the university chaplain who led protests on civil rights, the Vietnam War, and the draft. He still speaks out about things like drone strikes and surveillance of citizens, data collection, and all that, right? I know he's your friend. You've mentioned him."

"Yes, all that and more," David said. "I got to know him during college and law school. He still is my best friend, my lifetime friend. I haven't spoken to him in person since the nomination came up. But we keep in contact with email and phone calls. Willard was in the CIA for three years after he graduated from college, so he isn't some ivory tower person who doesn't know what he's talking about."

"I'm not sure that I'm ready to go into the whole mess," David said. "I think there's a good chance that the issues may be raised very soon anyway outside any control on my part. I have no idea what these files consist of, what information is there or what the investigation report contained. I was interviewed along with most of my squad members, but I was never told the details. I didn't do anything bad, although I wish I'd done some things differently. Let's just say I have regrets and some guilt."

"I understand," Dana said. "If you don't want to go into that, can you tell me what you did in the service?"

"I joined up in June of 2006 after my first year of law school," David began. "I spent most of the first year training in the States. After Basic Training and Officer Candidate School, I got my commission as Second Lieutenant and was assigned to advanced officer training, then I was deployed to Iraq in March of 2007 and stayed for fifteen months during the surge. The most intense fighting was in Anbar Province. My platoon, with thirty to forty soldiers, was all male except for one woman."

"We were stationed primarily in the city of Ramadi, the capital of Anbar Province. We still read about it frequently. The two major cities in Anbar are Fallujah and Ramadi. Ramadi was a hotbed of Al Qaeda activity then. It was very hotly contested and very dangerous. Still is. My platoon was in a famous battle called the Battle of Donkey Island.

"I'll tell you about it someday," David added. "We were in deep shit all the time and I lost quite a few men and the only female. Women were still rare then and she had a really rough time. She was sexually assaulted once and harassed a lot. If platoons had any women at all, it was one or two, at most. We had just the one. I had to do a lot to protect her. It's not safe to isolate a single female like that but it happens all the time. She was killed, but that's another story. I was there a year and a quarter before I got home on leave."

"After a few months, I was promoted to first lieutenant. That was standard procedure. Unfortunately, I had the same platoon sergeant the whole time. This guy, Nick, was a sergeant first class, which meant he had more power than any of the other sergeants. He was very popular among the enlisted guys.

I respected him because he was a hard working guy and a capable sergeant, technically. Personally, I disliked him and didn't trust him completely. He took too much pleasure in killing, for my taste. To tell the truth, I was a little afraid of him. He was always competing with me for the platoon's loyalty. He'd undermine me whenever he got the chance. He was good to have at your back unless, of course, he didn't like you . . . in which case you were at risk. I think he came to respect me to some extent. But he hated me some of the time, mainly because of my so-called privileged background, and what that represented to him. But this is getting into a long story. It isn't over yet, unfortunately."

"I'm listening," Dana said.

David continued. "Anyway, the part of the story that will take a lot more time to tell you someday is the part I'd like to live over. This was a rough place to fight in. Almost everybody was potentially your enemy. I tried not to see things that way all the time but couldn't blame those who did. We were isolated and short on supplies. We felt surrounded by hostility and hatred. During the time I spent there we engaged in nearly daily fighting. Troops were beginning to be pulled out of other places then but not from Anbar. Troops were pouring in all the time, in fact.

"It was the worst period of my life. It was hell and it kept getting worse. I believed I was in charge of my platoon, but I think I was kidding myself. Nick was really in charge. Then an incident happened mainly because Nick had a relationship going with an Iraqi woman. She was just a girl really, maybe seventeen or eighteen. He got caught having sex with her a couple of times but I didn't put a stop to it. That was my responsibility and, as a result, people were killed, the girl, two of our guys, including our female, and a lot of civilians."

"Eventually, I got sent home, after the investigation you've heard about, and they sent me off again, first to Yemen and then to Djibouti for about four months until my active duty time was up. Part of my platoon stayed in Yemen and some went with me to Djibouti. We were just starting to be a presence there. We knew Al Qaeda of the Arabian Peninsula was beginning to put down roots there.

"Djibouti was on the North African side of the Gulf of Aden. You hear about it all the time now in the news. We were trying to bring things under control. It was fairly peaceful, relatively speaking. I got out in the late spring or early summer of 2009, went back to law school that fall. I was feeling wiped out but at least I had the summer to pull myself together."

22

They talked for the next hour, Dana questioning gently and David, behind the wheel, answering but holding back details that he wasn't ready to reveal. He had learned to deal day by day with nightmares, flashbacks, anxiety and occasional panic. The hardest part was the relentless moral pain that he inflicted on himself. He was barely aware of the extent to which his combat experience in Iraq so tightly intertwined with his role in his brother's death so long ago.

David glanced at Dana and resumed, "There's a term that psychologists and psychiatrists have been using for a while now: *moral injury*. I usually refuse to use military or psychiatric jargon, but it does express what I feel about the aftermath of killing. It's not just a mental health term. Writers and theologians, philosophers, too, have written about the concept. It's a very old idea, and it doesn't automatically mean a person has PTSD. You can suffer moral injury and not have PTSD. Conversely, you can have PTSD and not have suffered moral injury.

"When a soldier has to kill someone and is face to face so he can see what happens to the person, it's normal to feel wounded too. That is, unless the person is totally lacking in empathy, which I guess would make him a sociopath. Even if the soldier didn't do the killing personally but is responsible for it, by giving the order, it's almost the same. It's a strange concept. The person who commits an act that violates his moral code becomes a victim of moral injury. The perpetrator becomes the victim, and the real victim often gets lost in the shuffle. If the person is at all religious, in the broadest sense, he has to worry what it means for his soul. I'm skeptical about organized religion, but I feel that I am spiritual. I believe in God, someone or something that I call God. I have a deep sense that we'll pay a price for the bad things we do. Maybe that's left over from my childhood but I feel it anyway."

"I understand," Dana said. "It's because war forces you, or puts you in a position, to do things that are completely contrary to the morality we live by, not to mention it being criminalized by law. But I thought soldiers rationalized about this in a way that excuses them from wrongdoing, by convincing themselves that war is different, and they have no choice once they're in that spot."

"I can't help worry sometimes that my soul is permanently damaged. I've heard soldiers say they felt their souls had been wounded or killed, that they even visualized that happening. That means something to me. I feel worried at times, especially lying awake at night," David answered.

"I don't know, David. I understand perfectly the idea of moral injury, but I don't believe in a day of judgment, or eternal guilt, or original sin. I think it's an irrational fear, just childhood stuff we can't quite get rid of."

"Sometimes I feel the presence of something." David continued. "All I can say is sometimes I feel something dark in my body, my gut, but other times it's in my brain or my soul, whatever that is. I can't get rid of it. I've been lugging it around since childhood actually. You know what it's like? Maybe it's a fallen angel. I can't say for sure that I actually believe this literally, but some people do. Some very rational and convincing people do."

David continued. "When I was in college, I got to know another Protestant chaplain, got to know him very well, in fact. Jacques-Pierre and I continued that friendship, in fact, to this day, although we haven't seen each other for some years. He lives in Paris now. He was a French Catholic priest who left the church and converted to become an Episcopal priest. He was raised in the Roman Catholic Church to believe in angels. He believes in their presence in our lives. I would say I come close to believing in their existence at times. I would like to believe in them. But sometimes it seems too mystical for me, but sometimes real. It requires a leap of faith or trust. I think the presence I feel is similar to the presence of good angels that Jacques senses, but mine are not good. There is something malevolent about the presence I feel. When I first returned home, I thought the presence might be spirits of people who died because of me. Because of what I did or didn't do. I thought I was crazy but I didn't do anything about it and it gradually went away. I don't think about it much now. Does this seem bizarre to you?"

"Yes, it does. I have to say that," she said, suppressing a laugh. "I've never known or thought about angels, good or bad. But you said you've felt this dark presence since childhood and your combat experiences are intertwined with childhood experiences. Why? When did that start? You shouldn't have to carry a childhood burden into adulthood no matter what."

"I don't think it's that simple in my case," David said. "It started a long time ago way back in my childhood. It's not something I talk about or even think about, frankly. It's buried. I can't change the past but I've never found a way to put it to rest either. I'm sorry but I don't want to get into it now, maybe someday if we . . . if our relationship . . . you know what I mean." He allowed a little ironic laugh to escape.

Dana smiled. "I don't want you to talk about anything that you don't want to, but I will listen and not judge you. You know that, and I care about you very much so you can feel safe. You can trust me completely."

"I know that, Dana, and I care about you too. I think I have for a while, not just today. We've known each other for nearly a year now, but you have been Jake's girl and that's that."

"I do know all that," Dana said in a near whisper, moving closer to him and touching him on the shoulder. Seeing a highway rest stop ahead, David pulled into the exit lane.

"Shall we get coffee before we hit the home stretch? I could use a short break." They went inside and returned to the car with their coffee. They rode in silence for twenty minutes before Dana asked, "Would you tell me more about the war sometime? Not now. We don't have time and I know you're feeling wrung out telling me all that you have."

"Sure. There are a lot more memories buried there. We'll need some time. Are we going to be able to find time together? A lot has happened this weekend. We both have sorting out to do."

As they got closer to New Haven, David could feel his anxiety escalate. When they neared the Wooster Square area, he wondered with apprehension if Jake's car would be there. He finally mustered the courage to say, "Dana, my anxiety is getting the best of me. I don't know what to expect. How will we carry on? I don't know whether you'll feel the same way in a day or a week. Actually, I don't really know how you feel right now, but I'm not pressing you to say. We both know something has changed but we don't know what lies ahead."

Dana's silence conveyed to David that she felt as uncertain as he did. When they pulled up, Jake's car was in the driveway. David knew he had to go inside and greet him. Jake was astute in reading faces and body language. His life had depended on that ability, and he didn't miss a thing when it came to protecting himself. Despite their differences, he and Jake had remained friends since school. David cared deeply about Jake and had serious misgivings about getting involved with Dana. But it had happened. The physical attraction was there, actually not just physical, something emotional too. What was it anyway? It was hard to pin down.

Dana was clearly on edge too, although she controlled her nervousness more than David. "We need to be superb actors for now," she said.

"Okay, he said. I can do that. I'll tell Jake I'm feeling under stress about nomination problems and just needed to unburden myself, to talk it through on the way back and we stopped for coffee. The time got away."

"Sounds good," Dana agreed.

23

David got out of the car first and retrieved Dana's bag from the back seat. She headed up the short sidewalk to the brick townhouse with its tiny enclosed front yard filled with lush foliage, and the big white Greek-style portico shielding the entrance. David observed that the row of town houses displayed classic architectural style but some were slightly run down. They had lost the freshness and impressiveness they had when they were first renovated during the revival of Wooster Square thirty or more years ago. Jake opened the door and was standing on the top step. As Dana approached him, they kissed lightly, and she disappeared inside after giving a casual wave goodbye to David.

David greeted Jake with the biggest smile he could muster, and the two shook hands firmly, the ex-Navy SEAL enveloping David's hand in his powerful grip. Although David believed he was physically fit, he was no match for Jake in any physical competition. He'd been an outstanding athlete in high school and college, but Jake had been a level above everyone else on the football field, the wrestling mat, and the track. As a freshman, when they lived on the same floor but in different suites, Jake had been like a caged wild animal, driving roommates and floormates to their wits' ends with his constant physical challenges. His antics ranged from jumping around the room on the furniture to scaling down the dormitory wall from the third floor. Despite their different personalities, David and Jake ended up rooming together for the remaining three years. Jake gradually became tamed, channeling his unbounded physical energy and aggression on the playing field.

"Hey, Jake, you must have had a hell of a weekend. How'd it go anyway?"

"Okay," Jake said deliberately, "but it isn't over. The security system was badly hacked and a lot of data lost. I managed to stem the flow and stop the gaps but we still have work to do. This is a top security firm that does a lot of high level, classified national security work."

Jake went on, "How did the meeting go? How do things look for you?"

David hoped indecision and anxiety didn't show on his face. He was self-conscious about appearing weak or vulnerable in Jake's presence. "Not bad, but there are some potential problems," he managed. "O'Leary has our conservative senator, Neil Cramer, on board, but Lehman isn't committed yet. He's pressing for records of an investigation that took place near the end of my tour in Iraq."

"That's the report about the investigation into civilian deaths, right?" Jake interrupted, cutting him off sharply. "I knew that would be a problem. I've heard the rumors you know. What the fuck is that all about? What's Lehman going to do? Is he opposed to your candidacy?"

"I wouldn't say opposed," David countered, wondering how Jake knew about the investigation report. He didn't recall telling him about it. "Yes, he pressed that issue," David began, again cut off by Jake, whose agitation about the subject surprised him.

"What the fuck do you know about the report? You have to know something."

"Not much, really. I haven't thought of it for years," David stammered, surprised at what seemed almost hostility on Jake's part. Could he have picked up on some unseen clue about the changed chemistry in the relationship?

"We've got to put this to rest," Jake said. "Do you want me to look into that? I have some contacts still in the security area at Benning."

David hesitated, suddenly alarmed at the prospect of Jake getting involved. He anticipated that Jake could become an adversary, even an enemy. It would be awkward to turn him down though.

"Sure, Jake. It seems as though they've got to see the report or a summary to satisfy themselves there are no skeletons in the closet. You know the kind of stuff that happens in combat. You know that better than anyone."

"Yes, but stuff has to be handled, one way or another. You should know that," Jake said. "I'll get onto that."

"Great," David said, trying to appear grateful, although the thought of Jake accessing sensitive and possibly damaging information was disturbing. He wondered if Jake knew more than he revealed about the Ramadi incident. Jake had sources everywhere and he knew his way around the military as well as the civilian spy world. He had spent a career fighting, plotting and uncovering plots against the U.S. He was a SEAL team commander and a super spook too, an intimidating combination, not to mention a deadly one. Once in that business, always in that business, David thought. He wanted to say to Jake, "Sure, find out what it is, get something that will put it to rest and tell them to destroy the file or make it go missing." But he didn't dare for fear of alerting Jake to the importance of it. He could be a powerful ally but a dangerous adversary.

"Keep me posted on this," David said with as much force as he dared. "I'd like to take a look at the record myself."

"That may not be possible," Jake replied with finality, "but I'll see what I can find out. First we've got to locate it, if it still exists. I will need details. That will help me identify where it might be and who might get me access to it."

"All right," David said tentatively, cursing himself inwardly for crumbling in the face of Jake's persistence. "It was an investigation into some casualties, some of them probably collateral, in Ramadi during a cleanup operation. It had to do with a few guys who were dispatched to clean up the area. No one in the brass, all the way up, had any interest in looking into it and second-guessing what happened. We know Al Qaeda was active there. It was during the surge. Someone must have insisted that the investigation requirement be followed but no one had any stomach for it. CID never got involved. There were a couple of deaths on our side too and that's probably what got the thing going."

"When was it?" Jake snapped.

"As I recall, it was a long time ago now, possibly late 2007 or early 2008. I think It was 2008."

"So it was after the Bravo business with Green?" Jake asked, staring at David.

"Yeah, something like that. Hey, I have to get on home now. Sorry you couldn't be there this weekend. We missed you; I need you on this. Let's talk soon. Sorry to be late getting back. It's my fault, I needed to talk to somebody after the meeting to get things straight. We stopped for coffee and time got away. Dana is a good listener, really smart. Good feedback."

"Yeah, isn't she though. Take care of yourself."

"Sure. Tell Dana I appreciate her patience."

"Yeah, right," said Jake, turning to go into the house.

24

As David pulled his car into the garage and entered the house, he was prepared for a confrontation. He was already on edge. He assumed that Lucille would be hostile even without knowing what he and Dana had done. It had not been planned but he admitted it was wrong. He had expected only a tough strategy session. That hadn't turned out so well either. He had more problems now than before the weekend, but they were all going to surface sooner or later anyway. It was time to put his mind on other things, on the boys, for one. It was good that he'd have a little time with them now and tomorrow as well.

He called out in what he hoped was a normal tone. "Hello. Hey, I'm home." No answer. He could hear voices distantly, on the television perhaps? He headed for the family room of the stately, but modest, St. Ronan Street Federal that had once been owned by his favorite history professor.

"Lucille? Luke? Marcus?"

"Yes," he heard distantly. No greeting. "What is it," he heard Lucille's voice say in a monotone.

David went down the hall and entered the family room. "Oh hey Lu," trying to be casual, using a nickname from the past. How long had it been since he had used that? "How was the weekend?"

"Fabulous. What do you think? It was just what I was looking forward to after a week of work. I love driving, and entertaining the boys' friends." Her voice was dripping with resentment.

"I'm sorry," he said, feigning contrition. "It was work for me. Not fun. Was everything okay here?" Pause. No response. "Where are the boys?"

"At their friends' house down the street," she said with a sharp edge.

"I was hoping to spend a little time with them before bed," David said.

"Is that right? That's different," Lucille said sarcastically. "Actually, it's good they're gone because we need to talk."

"Oh. Sure. Let me just get something to drink, okay? I'm kind of beat. Do you want anything?"

"No," she said curtly, "but don't take long. The boys will be back soon." David returned with a glass of iced tea.

"I'll come right to the point," Lucille said in an even tone. "That's your style, right? When you want to, that is. I spoke with a lawyer on Saturday. I'm going to start divorce proceedings."

"You're what! Why? Just like that? Who's your lawyer?" Without waiting for a response, he added, "Thanks for the warning. What a great house to come back to," David said angrily, caught off guard. He had lost control of the situation. That's all he needed now, to deal with all that shit, with everything at stake. Bitch, he thought to himself.

"Give me a break, David. This shouldn't come as a big surprise. We've been strangers for nearly two years now. The past year has been a nightmare for me. I don't know where you are, what you do, who you're with, or what you're driving yourself for. Nothing satisfies you, and you're a train wreck to live with. I'm becoming a wreck, myself, living like this. I'm alone but without any freedom. I want a life, and I'm going to have one. In fact, I'm having one," she said with determination.

"What do you mean by that? You're having a life? What the hell does that mean?"

"You'll find out soon enough."

Desperation set in. "Lucille, please, you can't do this now. This will destroy what I have a real chance for."

She interrupted. "That's your concern. No surprise there. It's all about you. Always has been."

"That's not true but, even if it was, this is different." He wanted to point out her self-centeredness, her narcissism, but he knew he had to keep the lid on their quarrel. "Please, Lucille, wait. We can work out whatever it is."

"I don't think so," Lucille said firmly. "I'm tired of waiting. My life is slipping away."

"I know how you feel," he said with studied effort, although he knew it was bullshit.

"Really," she said, "I doubt that very much."

Again he resisted throwing the accusation back at her. "In a few months, by fall, this will be over, and we'll make our marriage work. I know I've been distracted." A divorce in process would kill any chance at the nomination. The President needed a clean candidate, not a controversial one embroiled in a divorce, along with other problems. Oh God, this on top of everything else.

"For all I know, you have another life going," Lucille asserted, searching his face.

"That's ridiculous. That's bullshit," he said. Yesterday, it certainly wasn't true but now? That was hard to say. He had to continue distracting her from the divorce issue. "I have a real chance at the Supreme Court. It's a once in a lifetime chance."

"Why should I care? What do you expect of me? Do you think I'll just move to Washington if that happens?"

"Of course not. You don't have to do that. When did you ever do that?" He could feel anger rising at this argument. "You didn't before, did you?"

"That's my fault? I'm supposed to uproot whenever you say the word? What marriage do we have left to save?" she asked sharply, barely containing her anger.

"We married too young," David said. "We weren't ready. But we can work it out at least for the boys' sake." He knew this wasn't what he wanted but he felt he had no choice but to forestall her move at this critical time.

"This is a hell of a life for the boys. They show all the signs of stress, thanks to you."

"That's cruel and you know it. One person doesn't cause relationship stress. You're an active cause of that. But I ask you again, don't rush this. What lawyer have you talked to?"

"John Morehead. Surprised?"

"Yes, I am. He's a friend of mine. I knew him long before you did. Did he say he'd represent you?"

"Not for sure. He wants to talk to you, to both of us to see if he should. If it's amicable he said."

Amicable, he thought. Fat chance. "Don't rush into this. There's a lot at stake and I don't mean just for me. For the boys. We've been through a lot together."

"Yes. Most of it bad. I can see what counts with you, everything and everyone but me."

"You count too, Lucille. Of course you do. But this is a unique time."

"We can talk to John, both of us, but I'm warning you that I'm serious. This is a pause, that's it. I have no illusion we can resurrect what we never had."

"Thank you, Lucille. I feel sometimes like I'm going crazy with all the pressure, but I want to try again." She rolled her eyes before looking away.

25

David's intention was to keep things stable for the moment. He had wished many times that Lucille was not in his life. He had married, out of weakness, at her insistence, her pleading, and her desperation. Worn down, he'd backed into it and had regretted it ever since.

When he'd been in the service, violence and killing was a way of life, every bit as natural as brushing your teeth. He'd had nightmares about bringing about her death. They were so real that it became difficult to separate fantasy from reality. My God, he had thought, is that my role in life? Am I a murderer, a sinister, secret murderer, or do normal people wrestle with these dark thoughts too? That was years ago and seemed a hazy memory that he didn't know was real or imagined. He thought of his brother, Ronnie, and the times before the lake incident when he had felt a similar powerful urge to be rid of him. He had resisted the urge but when the opportunity presented itself, it had happened. Where was the line between causing something and merely letting it happen?

During the war, everyone was welcome to kill. He knew firsthand stories about kill squads among the troops that targeted victims for the most arbitrary of reasons, or no reason, just because they could. He had never even contemplated it, but he felt that he probably was capable of going over the edge if circumstances were right. He shuddered at the thought. The familiar cold, dark presence was palpable. Maybe the lock on the dark place where he stored bad memories was wearing thin.

Did Nick get caught up in the killing on that awful day in Ramadi? At least there was a motive, a reason other than the thrill. The freedom to kill was powerful. It took on a life of its own. What about his own backing off when he came upon the scene of what else could you call it but a massacre? He had been overwhelmed with horror, rage, fascination, shame, fear, confusion. He had let it go on and even watched when the two of them, Walter Flaherty and Roxie Cronin, screamed in horror and outrage, and rushed into the house trying to stop the bloodbath. He had cowered outside, frozen, sick to his stomach, doing nothing to stop it. What was wrong with him? How could he not have stopped it?

He was startled back to reality by Lucille's harsh and insistent voice far away, then closer. "David. David!! Where are you? You disappeared. The boys just got back. I hear them in the kitchen. Wake up. For God's sake, what's wrong with you?" He shook his head and started for the kitchen.

26

The first part of the following week was uneventful. When Thursday came and no crisis had arisen, David allowed himself to relax. The Court was in recess following a two-week term of daily oral arguments, and the justices were free to spend time in chambers working on opinions. Three of them followed their usual routine of working in their home district offices when the Court wasn't in session. They appeared at the Court only on Wednesdays for the weekly conferences, when the Court as a whole took up motions, certification petitions, and approval of opinions for publication.

David had an office in the New Haven courthouse but preferred to be in Hartford where his law clerks were. Ordinarily, he made the trip every day. He was glad for the lack of pressure this week but relaxing did not come easily. At home, the atmosphere was chilly and tense but temporarily calm. Lucille did not mention the divorce or Morehead, and David was careful to avoid provoking her. He decided to contact Morehead if, for no other reason, to ensure that the lawyer, whom he had known for many years, would commit to fair treatment if David waived the conflict of interest, allowing him to represent Lucille. He ignored his inner voice that said to let the matter ride, but he made a call and left a voicemail. Morehead called back later.

"How are you anyway? We haven't talked in a long time," David said.

"David," Morehead said, "I'm glad to hear from you. When Lucille called, I was really surprised. I had no idea that you two were having problems. She didn't go into much detail though. I didn't commit to her that I would handle it. You know I wouldn't unless you gave the okay. I hope you can work things out but, if you can't, I hope you'll consent."

Although David doubted that Lucille had not gone into much detail, he left that issue alone. "I'd say we have things on hold. I don't know what's going to happen really, but it's a long story."

"Figured that," said John. "You don't need to explain. I won't file anything yet. You can have more time."

"That's not what I'm saying, John. I haven't decided whether to waive the conflict of interest. You've done a lot of work on personal matters that concern me as much if not more than Lucille. You know more about my personal affairs than any other lawyer. If it gets bitter, she would have an unfair advantage. So I don't want you to do anything until I, not Lucille, say to go ahead."

"Oh, if that's the way you feel, I have to follow that," Morehead said with an edge. "I'm shocked that you'd consider withholding consent. The implication that you don't trust me enough to consent is a bit offensive, frankly. I thought we had a better relationship than that."

"This is serious stuff, John. I have every right to be on a level playing field if the divorce goes forward. It could get nasty. I would expect you to be fair and consider my interests too even if I waived."

"You mean you wouldn't get your own lawyer?" Morehead asked.

"No, I definitely would."

"Then why would you expect me to consider your interests? Would you expect me to be your second lawyer? Is that fair to your wife?"

"Frankly, John, I don't like your attitude. Are you hungry for business? Sounds that way. If this is your attitude, I don't think I will consent. I expected more from you."

"I can say the same. If you trust me as a lawyer, you are obligated not to prevent your wife from having competent representation. It sounds as though you're trying to control everything," Morehead replied.

"I'm going to end this conversation," David said, recognizing that his temper was nearly out of hand.

"Fine with me. I'll wait to hear from you. In the meantime, if Lucille calls me, I'll give her minimal advice."

"You'll give her *no* advice unless you want a grievance to be filed against you. I insist on that. I will do that if you take any steps to represent her in the absence of a waiver."

"Fine," Morehead said, banging the telephone down abruptly.

David was left with feelings of uncertainty, vulnerability, and anger. He decided not to consent to Morehead representing Lucille, although he realized that she could seek out, perhaps with Morehead's encouragement, a lawyer far more hostile and dangerous to his interests, not to mention more expensive.

On the drive to Court on Friday morning, a text message came in for David from Jake marked urgent. It simply said "call me now." That was Jake's style. He decided to wait until he reached his office before contacting him. David insisted on preparing himself for any eventuality and his years in the service, especially in combat, had reinforced that natural quality. Jake, however, preferred the direct, aggressive, approach to everything, and actually preferred an unannounced contact in person to give him the advantage in any encounter.

David told his secretary he'd be on the phone for a while and she asked, "Do you want me to place the call?"

"No thanks," David said quickly. "I'll call him. He's an old friend."

David closed the door to his office, dialed the number, and waited. Jake picked up on the first ring. His voice had the usual controlling urgency, low key but commanding just the same.

It started as a typical Jake-type conversation. "What took you so long? Is this line secure? Do you want to call me back on a different phone? I left you a message on your cell phone."

"Hey, what's up? I saw the text come in but didn't check calls on the way up. I don't like to talk when I'm driving. This line is fine."

"You ought to have a phone that automatically encrypts numbers, conversations, everything. Can't be too careful these days. The feds have gotten more and more power during the past ten years to access just about anything and anybody they want. After the big protest and the Snowden fiasco, it didn't take long before everybody stopped paying attention again. FISA gives them free rein. No matter what their philosophy, presidents get addicted to the power and they're scared shitless about another 9-11 on their watch. Funny how all that goes down."

"Yeah, I know," David replied. "Not this president. She is trying to curtail it, but she hasn't gotten control of the agencies or the FISA court yet."

"That's the price we have to pay to be safe. But everyone is free to protect himself. That's my view," Jake rejoined. "I'll give you the short version. I made some inquiries at Benning. Got to the right guy right away. I told him what I was looking for and he said he'd get back to me today. He just called."

"Got it," David said. "What did he say?"

"He found the report of the investigation indexed and felt sure that was what we are looking for. It's marked sealed and stamped confidential, but not classified. All investigation files created after 2000 have been computerized. That means they're reduced to digital form by scanning. Some of the print versions apparently are stored too. Others were destroyed with no print duplicates retained. This file was digitized and my guy thinks the print file was probably not destroyed. He was able to examine the digital index to tell generally what the contents consist of—subject-matter, number of pages, disposition, all that but not the actual content.

"Anyway, he found that the contents of this digital file can't be accessed. In other words, the barebones skeleton is there and some kind of code. But whatever text was in the file can't be read. He says it was corrupted so that it's not accessible. He's sure from the description of what was there that this is the investigation report into incidents on various dates in the spring of 2008 in Ramadi, and it pertains to your company. He reported what he found to a superior who can look at confidential stuff. That guy verified that there is nothing that can be read in the file. His conclusion is the same, that it was corrupted, most likely intentionally. He doesn't know if somebody hacked in to do this or if someone on the inside did it. They are going to look into it. I know you probably don't want to lose control like that, but I had no choice."

"You're right about that," David said.

"Now, what happened to the print copy, the original, is another mystery," Jake said without breaking stride. "Those files were handled in different ways, some destroyed, some not. Who the hell knows about that is anybody's guess. My hunch is that, if someone went to the trouble of corrupting the digital version, but didn't wipe it out, that person probably got hold of the print file."

David gasped audibly. He wondered if this was a good development because the file was missing or a bad one, because it would raise suspicions and focus attention. If they found it, it would be scrutinized carefully.

David asked cautiously, "Did you ask whether they thought to determine whether any other files, especially in proximity to this one, had been corrupted too?"

"I did," Jake said quickly. "This was the only one they found after scouring the particular series of files, the ones that were chronologically close. They checked for files that had any relationship in subject matter, source, as well as time. Nothing else is missing."

David hesitated to comment because he had figured out instantly who was behind this. Nick, of course. He wasn't sure how much to let Jake in on this. Once Jake knew anything about it, there was no stopping him, and he couldn't predict what Jake would do with the information. Jake was his own man and he acted with ruthless persistence and honesty, no matter who got hurt. Not that his judgment was always the best. He could be impulsive, and he didn't think very far down the road in terms of consequences, that is, who would ultimately be hurt. David managed a cautious "this is disturbing," and let it go at that.

Jake wasn't listening. "I think they're right. It was hacked and stolen. Now we have to figure out when, why, and who did this little operation and whether the print file still exists." Jake said, with some respect, "This is a professional job. My question is why. We don't know how long ago all this was done. Can you think of any reason for doing this or any person who would do this?"

"This is ancient history to me," David said. "I haven't got a clue. I haven't given it a thought in so many years," he said in an effort to mislead Jake. His stomach churned with anger as he thought of Nick Serrano, that devious, pathological son-of-a-bitch. The guy always seemed to be able to pull anything off, to get to anybody, to get what he wanted. David couldn't reveal this but he had an ominous feeling that he'd hear from Nick soon.

"So," David grimaced, sounding as troubled as he could, "where do we go from here, Jake?"

"I'm going to follow up," Jake assured him. "This is my field too you know. I'll work with those guys and we'll figure out when this happened and how it happened. The why is harder because we don't know what's in there unless you do, David?"

"I don't. I was never told what the result was, just that it was all okay. Things went back to normal. I'd better let Bradley know. This is going to shake up Lehman and O'Leary too."

"If you think of anything call me," Jake said.

"Let me know what's going on. There's a lot at stake."

"That's for sure," Jake said after a pause.

27

Two weeks passed without any further word on the missing file. David told Bradley about Jake's comments, and Bradley notified Lehman. On Friday morning of the third week in June, David was in his Hartford office reviewing briefs for the morning arguments, the final arguments for the current court year. In less than six weeks, on August 1, the Court would begin a month-long recess prior to the September term. The rest of June and July would be devoted to finalizing as many cases as possible for publication before the recess. With dozens of complex cases in various stages of drafting and discussion, some lacking agreement, this was a high-pressure time of the year. Some cases would have to be carried over until fall because it was impossible to reach consensus and complete opinions in all cases. Separate opinions often held cases up for months after a majority opinion had been crafted.

The entire appellate system, including both the high court and the intermediate court, essentially closed down during August. All the justices and judges departed for their summer break. As far as they were concerned, work stopped on opinions that were in process, regardless of their status or their importance to the parties. The staff, including permanent law clerks, the ones who were not limited by one year, kept working through the summer. David was eagerly awaiting liberation from the daily obligation to be at court or in his New Haven chambers. He'd have the month of August to concentrate on keeping the nomination on track. He felt the urgent need for a break, hopefully to Nantucket, but that was uncertain given the domestic turmoil.

Lucille's family traditionally held a weeklong reunion every summer in Michigan at the sprawling lake house where the extended family members had vacationed during her childhood. The remaining weeks were divided up among the siblings. She never missed the opportunity to take the children to join her seven siblings and their families. Whether David went was a matter of indifference to her. He preferred not to go. He always felt like an outsider so he most often declined if she thought to mention it. He believed her siblings went out of their way to make him uncomfortable. They were a close-knit but contentious family whose main activities seemed to be competition—on the lake, on the tennis court, the golf course, or card playing. Most were heavy drinkers and smokers. Not only did the feeling of being trapped in the remote place give him the willies but being on a lake brought to mind the disturbing scenes from his own childhood. This summer, there was no chance that he would go and no chance that she would want him to. She'd have conversations with her sisters about the marriage problems, ensuring that he would be persona non grata to the family group, in which he was alien under the best of circumstances.

He found himself looking forward eagerly to the break when she would be away. He might need to go to Washington and meet with key people or he might help track down the missing information. He wondered what other opportunities would present themselves. Since the weekend in New Hampshire, he'd seen Dana only once, with Jake, but they had exchanged text messages and phone calls a few times. Given the sensitivity of the nomination process, they had agreed to minimize personal contacts. Anyway, she was busy adjusting to her new job, staying over in New York most of the time. David felt that his life was on hold.

He was weary of the tension involving the anticipated phone call from Nick Serrano. The fact that Nick had gone so far as to corrupt and steal official Army files, which David was convinced was the case, suggested that this was a serious matter not to be easily resolved.

Some days, he fantasized that it was simply a bad dream that would fade with time. Maybe Nick had settled his criminal problem without having to go to trial. David could imagine the relief that would pulsate through his body if that turned out to be the case. Despite reluctance to stir up trouble, he decided to check with Larry this afternoon to see what he knew. The issue of the missing file continued to cast a shadow over his spirits whenever he tried to grasp a moment of happiness.

Happiness for David had typically been the absence of pain or sadness. For as long as he could remember, he and his parents had existed in a dimly lit world after his brother's death. Happiness, laughter, and lightness were not only absent but forbidden. Because he had been used to that plane of existence, during college he had once labeled it "*the unavoidable burden of being*," a sardonic twist of the title of the Milan Kundera novel. He was reminded of other worlds when he was in the homes of some of his friends, those homes that sang with laughter, spontaneity, and palpable love. In later teenage years, life became even more intolerable in the house. He stopped even calling it a home. In those years, he kept to himself and avoided contact with his parents except for occasional bitter arguments. At least, arguments rarely got out of hand because the three of them were so disengaged that their relationships were not worth fighting over.

28

At two minutes to ten, the seven justices assembled and strolled to the courtroom door, each carrying an armload of briefs. The final three cases of the court year were criminal appeals having common issues related to claims of incompetence to stand trial because of mental health disorders. David scanned the spectators in the courtroom, as he often did. His attention was drawn to a familiar-looking figure seated in the back row on the opposite side of the courtroom. The man was watching the bench attentively with his gaze focused directly on David. Although that corner of the courtroom was dimly lit and in shadow, David realized with a sinking feeling that the man could well be Nick Serrano, a decade and a half older, heavier, with thick and hardened features.

"Damn," he thought to himself.

Sure enough, ten minutes after the court recessed, David's phone rang.

"Justice Lawson," the court officer said, "There's a man here who says he's an old Army friend of yours. He says he was in town and decided to drop by for a surprise visit. His name is Nick something. I didn't catch the last name."

"Okay, Darlene," David said, hoping his voice did not reveal the tension that tightened his throat. "I thought I recognized him in the courtroom. Sure, bring him up." David's chambers were on the second floor above the conference room and administrative offices. He prepared himself to appear confident by putting on his jacket. In a few moments, he could hear voices as they approached his door. "Thanks," he heard in coarse tones. "Much appreciated, sweetheart. What do you call Dave? Judge?"

"Justice," she said quickly, not pleased with the familiarity.

"He'll be real happy to see me. It's been a long time but we went through a lot together." David could tell that the old swagger and arrogance remained a part of Nick's personality.

David answered the firm rap on the door with a robust "come in," an invitation that was not necessary since the door swung open at the same moment with enough force to slam against the wall. Nick stood stolidly in the doorway, the footsteps of the court officer retreating down the hallway. He was overweight but still a powerful man of medium height.

"Davey-boy," Nick said with a mix of arrogance tinged with barely suppressed anger. David stood at least four inches taller and a good fifty pounds lighter. If David had the height and build of a Division II quarterback, a few inches over six feet, lean and athletic, Nick resembled a Division I linebacker.

He was no more than 5 feet, 10 inches tall but probably weighed 240 pounds, a good forty pounds heavier than his fighting weight a dozen or so years ago. David noticed the mocking grin, a signature feature of Nick years ago, that still dominated his face. "How are ya, buddy, long time. Glad to see me, aren't ya?"

"How're you doing, Nick. You still look like you could take on any ten men."

"You bet. Nice chambers, Davey, or should I call you Judge. I forgot. Justice, right? That's what you do, too, right, do justice?"

"I try," David said in a controlled voice. "No formalities necessary. What brings you to town, Nick?"

"Well, I wasn't exactly just hanging around Hartford. I came to see you."

"Oh," David said, not revealing that this visit was, if not expected, not a surprise.

"What can I do for you, Nick? Want to talk over old times?"

Nick ignored David's getting to the point so quickly. "Hey, how about a tour? Nice fucking place you have here, Your Honor," he said, in a mocking tone. "Great office. I like it. Bet you do too. I could be real comfortable here."

He seemed to know that he was in the driver's seat. He was as disrespectful as ever, and David could do nothing about it. No mistaking that Nick knew he had him in a vise. Nick, no doubt, suspected that David had been forewarned by Larry, or at least had heard about his problems from someone else in the unit.

"Hey Nick, not much to see but, sure, we can look around a bit. I can show you the historical society area or, well, you've seen the courtroom, right?"

"Yeah," Nick asserted boldly, "sure did. You were pretty quiet out there, buddy. Are you the Clarence Thomas of the Connecticut court or something? You see, I follow court stuff pretty closely. In fact, I've followed your career. You've moved up fast and I hear you're heading for the big time."

"I don't know about that. Long shot, about as long as they come."

"Well, maybe I can help. I've got real good contacts just about everywhere You know a career in the Army puts you in pretty good company. I spent a year at the Pentagon, computer stuff and administrative. I hooked up with a General and he took me along. I had a good life for a while. I just did everything he asked me to do. Generals leave lots of messes to clean up, if you know what I mean." David had a sudden sickening flash of insight as to how Nick could easily have gotten someone to corrupt the digital file and steal the print copy.

After a short tour, during which the only people they saw were David's two law clerks, they returned to his office. "So Nick, what's up?" David asked firmly as though he was pressed for time. He added, "I have an appointment at five o'clock in New Haven so I'll have to be going soon."

"Oh," Nick said, with a smirk that David recognized slowly creasing across his face, ending in a sneer. "We've got some things to talk about. I think maybe you'll be a little late for your appointment. Davey, I have a little problem and I think you can help me solve it."

"Oh," David said, "What's that?"

"My guess is you already know but, anyway, I've been living down in Philly with a woman I met when I was in D.C. Seems she and her boyfriend had a little accident and the police think I might have something to do with it."

"Accident?" David asked, pretending ignorance, not revealing that he had found several newspaper articles in just a few passes at Internet searches after Larry's call.

"Well, let's put it this way. She was shot, didn't die though. Very unfortunate. Her friend wasn't so lucky. It was a street thing, I guess. I had nothing to do with it so far as I remember. But, if somebody proves I did have something to do with it, and just don't remember, my lawyer and I figure that I had a blackout. They call it, you know all about this, a dissociative state," Nick said as if uttering an expletive.

"That's one of my PTSD symptoms," he said. "I'm a card-carrying PTSD victim. My lawyer, he's a top defense lawyer, the best and he owes me a couple of favors, thinks this is the kind of situation where PTSD would kick in. In fact, he's lined up a shrink who has been seeing me. We need to nail down the—what do you call it—the trauma, and that's where you come in. You know how I probably got it and, man, you've got credibility, if it comes to that of course. The jury and the judge would love you if we get to trial. The prosecutor will think, hey, a Supreme Court Justice? Why would I want to fuck around with that guy? I might just get a walk without a trial at all. Sound good, Davey?"

"I don't know anything about this, Nick. I can't get involved in a criminal trial. That would violate the Canons of Ethics. Sorry, this won't work. Maybe I can help in some other way."

"I don't think so, David. This is the way. I'm not just blowing smoke out my ass, you know. You'd be just a fact witness. I know all about that. You wouldn't be a reputation or opinion witness. A judge, even a Justice," he said drawing out the word again with his mocking voice, "can testify to facts. My lawyer explained all that to me. I know my way around the courts too even though I didn't go to college and law school like you, a fancy school and all that shit.

"There were a couple of other episodes where, I have to admit," Nick went on, bearing down now, "I lost my cool, and when that happens, you know, somebody is going to get hurt, but since I can't control myself because of my PTSD, I'm not responsible."

David was silent. Trapped, he thought. He wanted to redirect the conversation. "What are you doing, Nick, for work I mean?"

"I'm in the security business and, you might say, law enforcement. I started out working for a bail bondsman and then I started chasing down bail jumpers on the side, anywhere in the world. In fact, I was good at it, very persuasive. It got to be so lucrative I don't really need my bail business any more. Bounty hunting keeps me going.

"My lawyer and my shrink think my PTSD came from the incidents in Ramadi. You remember them, right, where we spent more than a year, where we had to clean out the insurgents from those villages? We did our job and it wasn't pretty, but we followed orders, right? Your orders. Remember that. We disposed of the troublemakers on your orders."

David nodded again, not knowing what to say and yet not wanting to remain silent. He wanted to avoid getting into an argument. The truth was irrelevant to Nick, as always. But David knew that he had been as anxious as anyone, the whole company included, to bury the investigation and the truth along with the bodies. David felt locked into silence, not knowing how to react. That was a familiar feeling, his downfall, his Achilles heel. He knew what was morally right and wrong, but it got so fucking complicated and he became immobilized, unable to act. He had to figure this out, this fatal flaw. But solving it would mean not giving priority to self-interest. Part of the problem was weighing the moral decision against the most expedient decision. He could not deceive himself on that score.

He managed to ask, "Where is this leading, Nick?"

Nick ignored the question. "By the way, Davey, did you talk to Larry recently? You and Larry were pretty close."

"No, I haven't talked to anyone from the old days in a long time," David lied, feeling as though his face was transparent. He felt he was blushing.

"Okay," Nick said, grinning and ready to pounce. "Don't fuck with me, David. Remember that. There are consequences. You know what they are. You've got as much, more actually, to lose than anyone." With that, Nick swung his feet to rest them on David's desk.

29

Put your feet down," David snapped as he struggled to maintain his composure. Nick took his time but complied.

David went on. "What is it you think I could say that would help you, Nick? I don't even know what you're charged with."

"Did you forget so soon? Don't you remember what it was like over there?" Nick asked aggressively, a wild look in his eyes, drowning out what David was about to say. "You just tell the jury what the fuck was going on there. Draw a picture for them of what it was like to walk around never knowing when an IED or an RPG would blow you into little pieces.

"Remember, every time we stepped into the street," Nick said, "we put our lives on the line. We took contact from snipers practically every time. They cost us a lot of casualties. And the IEDs and RPGs? How many guys did you see blown to bits? Remember the time when someone dropped a grenade into one of our Humvees. Two dead and one missing. Remember that? Missing? That was until we picked up enough pieces of his body and brains to report the third death? And there were ten people standing around, some in view and some not, who wanted to kill us. You must have a short memory."

"I remember perfectly well," David said, his voice rising to reflect the anger building inside him. "But what does that have to do with you now?"

"Plenty, you bet your ass. You know what I went through, even more than the rest of you. After Jasmine's murder, I had to go out and clean up the mess, the mess that you didn't clean up, the mess you didn't have the guts to clean up. You ordered us, me, to take care of the troublemakers, the ones who killed her. She was just a kid."

"You're claiming that I ordered you to do that? I told you not to do that. I told you I'd get another unit to take care of it."

"Bullshit," Nick proclaimed, edging closer to David until his face was less than a foot away and his spit was splattering on David's face. "You weren't about to do a fucking thing. You left it to me. My final words to you were, 'We'll take care of this.' What did you say? Nothing. And we did take care of it. We rooted out the terrorists so you could keep your hands clean, just the way I got you that medal for courage. Courage my ass. You fucking don't know what that is." Nick's voice was rising to a steady shout and David was aware that it probably was being heard in the chambers on both sides and in the hallway. "You think I wanted that job, to kill all those bastards? You authorized it and you don't have the guts to come clean about it."

Nick had worked himself up. He was seething with rage. "And, my friend," he spat out, "it seems to me from what I read that you played on your combat heroism to get where you are. Heroism. What bullshit that is. I heard you got a fucking medal for rescuing your men who were captured. You know fucking well that I'm the one who pulled that rescue off. Yeah, you were there but the media made a big deal out of the college boy being a hero. You kept your mouth shut and took all the credit and I didn't object, did I? I could still blow that one sky high and I fucking will if you turn your back on me now. You got your payoff and now you're fucking going to do what I tell you to do."

The crescendo of rising anger was stirring David to a peak of outrage. "Yes, you had a role in that rescue just as I did. I didn't have any control over how it got played in the media. The journalists did what they wanted to, and I said it wasn't just me. I haven't made a secret of my war experience, but I haven't played anybody," he asserted, "and I've never used PTSD, never exploited what happened over there, as apparently you have."

"You can do whatever you want about PTSD but I expect you to back me up," Nick said in a loud voice. "Just tell the story, how we had to eliminate the Al Qaeda operatives. We had to fight for our lives. We couldn't tell who was and who wasn't when we went into those houses. We took flak and we had to kill everybody before they killed us. 'Do what you need to make it right.' Those were your words to me. 'Show no mercy. No survivors. Those bastards don't deserve to live.' Remember saying that?" Nick shouted in his face. "And we did. We tracked them down, house by house, until they were gone. And things were better after that, weren't they?"

David was suddenly exhausted by the exchange. His anger spent, he mustered weakly, "That's not the way it was, Nick, and you know it. What about Walter and Roxie? They were good people who stepped inside to calm things down. What did you do to them? Why did they deserve that? You killed them just because they got in your way. Why reopen this? Do you want the investigation reopened? Is this the only way you know to defend yourself? I thought you said you had nothing to do with what happened to your girlfriend."

"Yeah, Davey boy, but I can't prove that."

"You don't have to," David said. "The prosecution has to prove that you did. You must know that."

"Of course I know that. Let's just say my lawyer says they have enough to get to the jury," Nick said with a sneer.

"Why reopen something that's dead and buried, like your innocent victims?" David asked.

"You're right in the middle of this, pal. You don't get to call the shots."

David was silent, weary of the scene.

Nick went on relentlessly, "Let's put it this way. If you don't, the others, the ones who are still alive, will do it. We might end up saying things in the courtroom that won't, shall we say, put you in the best light. Might not be good for your career."

"You're asking me to lie to save your goddam neck from a murder," David said with a clenched jaw.

"Careful, Davey. You're on shaky ground here. Lying? Seems to me you've done your share of that to get where you are now. You've used your inflated, exaggerated war record to get yourself into high places. There's a long way to fall, my friend."

"You son of a bitch," David said, raising his voice, starting to lose control again. "I'm not lying to save your neck. I'm not going to testify at your god-damn trial. Pennsylvania has no jurisdiction over me. What are you going to do about it?"

"Fuck off, Davey boy. You don't get to choose. Tell you what. I'll give you a little time to think this over, and I guess I don't have to warn you about talking to anyone do I? You're not likely to. Am I right? By the way, did you talk to Larry?"

David glared at Nick but didn't reply.

"You have an appointment, right? Guess you'll make it after all," Nick said with a mocking tone. "Take me back to the bitch who brought me here. I'll see myself out. If you recall, I was pretty good at navigating. Here's how to reach me but don't take too long. Get hold of my lawyer. He'll give you the story. The trial is scheduled for early September. I'm beating this charge, one way or the other. I could care less who goes down. Play ball with me, and you'll go on your way. Fuck with me and you'll lose everything."

David walked him silently to the office down the hall and waved to the court officer, who looked less than happy at the thought of seeing Nick again. David turned abruptly back toward his office. Reaching his door, he slammed it shut and began shaking, with rage and regret for exploding, and with apprehension about the future.

He was incredulous that Nick had reentered into his life at this moment. He did not doubt Nick's determination and ruthlessness. David knew that he had lost control of the situation and exacerbated it by reacting the way he did. But he couldn't control himself. In a sudden surge of rage, he wanted Nick dead. He knew he was capable of doing it under the right circumstances. Too bad they weren't back in Iraq where that option was always on the table, just another choice. Killing your own wasn't in the rulebook but it happened more than anyone acknowledged. Anything was possible in that desert wasteland. He was horrified at his own thoughts. The idea that killing was acceptable under any circumstances was sickening, and the most fearful part was that he could contemplate and relish the prospect.

David felt stricken, and immobilized. He had nowhere to turn, no one to talk to. A lawyer, yes. He would get a lawyer, his former partner, Richard. He would be bound by the attorney-client privilege, so his secret would be safe. As he sat there, unsure of what to do next, whether to leave or stay, a loud knock on the door startled him, causing him to jump.

It was Ernest Burkhardt. Without waiting for a response, he stormed in. The son of a bitch always did that, as though being Chief made him the proprietor of all the chambers. What gave him the right? David couldn't tolerate his overbearing nature. He was nothing more than another coarse, loud-mouthed bully, perhaps not the brutal killer that Nick was. Nick was unique in his capacity for violence, but Burkhardt was close, just lacking the physical violence. But if the circumstances were different, he could imagine Burkhardt in combat. Maybe he was a sociopath too.

"Lawson," Burkhardt bellowed, "Who the hell was that character? He came on to Darlene and gave the security guards a hard time. He said he was an old friend of yours. What's that all about? I don't want that shit in my courthouse. You keep that kind of company?"

"Lay off. It was a guy from my service days. Not a friend."

"Well, keep him out of here, understand? You've tried to take over this place since you've been here, but I'm still in charge. If you move on, good riddance to you. You won't be missed. By the way, you were quiet today. Did you read the cases? Is your mind already somewhere else these days?"

"Don't push me," David said angrily. "Of course I read them and, no, I'm not somewhere else. Don't count on it anyway. I'll be here for a long time, maybe longer than you."

Burkhardt stared at him with icy eyes brimming with venom, turned on his heel and went out, slamming the door, causing the framed pictures to rattle against the wall.

30

David slumped back in his chair. "Oh, my God, what next?" he said aloud. He felt trapped in the path of impending disaster. His world was disintegrating piece by piece. But his back had been up against the wall before and he had survived. He would see Willard Coleman. He should be on Nantucket now. He picked up the phone.

Willard was enthusiastic about a visit from David. David said he'd leave for Hyannis in an hour. Why delay until Saturday morning and run the gauntlet of a battle with Lucille? He was closer to the ferry if he left from Hartford instead of New Haven. It was only four o'clock. If he left now, he should make the six o'clock ferry despite the steady rain that was falling. Willard would have a change of clothes for him. He'd head back on Saturday or Sunday depending on how he felt. He'd call Lucille on the way.

The rain increased steadily during his drive until it became a torrential rainstorm as he approached Hyannis. He maneuvered the familiar, flooded streets with all the speed he dared, barely avoiding deep puddles that could derail his race for the ferry. He could already taste the release from stress that would come from being on the island. He and Willard might even borrow the Jensen brothers' workboat for the short trip to Tuckernuck Island tomorrow, if the weather was good. The old Coleman cottage near the tip of the offshore island represented the ultimate escape from the world.

He arrived at the landing with minutes to spare and found a parking place fifty yards from the gate for the fast ferry, which was still boarding. As he sprinted toward the gate, he breathed a sigh of relief that he had made it. The drive had been tedious with heavy traffic and minimal visibility all the way up the interstate, but the downpour tapered to a light rain as the ferry disembarked.

David had made many trips to the island over the years to spend time with Willard. Their friendship spanned all the way back to his undergraduate days when Willard was in his final years as university chaplain. He was an eternal optimist as well as a realist. He had no illusions about human failings, or his own, but never ceased to have faith in the capacity to change. David relied on him as his mentor, best friend and relentless critic. Given David's professed skepticism about organized religions, even in the face of Willard's strong faith, Willard did not overplay his role as spiritual advisor. David had to admit, though, that Willard's unyielding faith, as well as Jacque-Pierre's, gave him serious pause about his own skepticism. Maybe he was elevating intellectual understanding to the exclusion of spiritual understanding.

The challenge of making the ferry provided relief in itself. He'd been too busy to dwell on problems that were closing on him since his last trip out. So much had happened in the course of three months. He looked forward getting Willard's advice to help chart his course through these treacherous waters. The sailing image was perfect considering that Willard was still an avid sailor, although he didn't venture out into the Sound as often now. David shared neither the enthusiasm nor the skill for sailing, but he was in tune with its imagery.

During the last trip out, he had reflected that during every crisis in his life, since he was nineteen and a junior in college, he had sought Willard out, especially after Jacques-Pierre returned to France. He still remembered the first major identity crisis during his junior year. He was facing a moral decision about how to handle what he called a dilemma of betrayal involving romantic relationships. The dilemma immobilized him for weeks. He went to see Willard, whom he had met when Willard came to speak to David's Senior Society. The chaplain had a reputation for being fully accessible to students even though he was a prominent figure on the national stage as well as the religious leader of the university. Willard sat, relaxed, at ease and focused, as he listened to David's story before spending the next two hours talking through the issues. That was the beginning of a relationship that evolved into a lifetime friendship.

With only five minutes to departure, David was at the end of the boarding queue. To anyone observing him outside his professional mode, in this setting, David appeared younger than his forty-three years. His gaze and eye contact with everyone he encountered indicated a genuine interest in each person he encountered. He was an astute and interested observer of other people and his demeanor prompted an easy smile from strangers. He was drenched at this point, having been unprepared for the storm that began an hour into the drive and soaked him thoroughly at his stop at a rest area.

David customarily gravitated to the outside deck to enjoy the invigorating wind and sea spray. This time he was content to stay inside until he dried off. He observed that the seats on the outside deck were nearly fully occupied with passengers eager to experience the wind, even with the light rain. The interior seemed especially crowded today, and he had to settle for squeezing into a seat in a crowded booth with a group of people. They were obviously a family group, and their two golden retrievers straddled the aisle, making it difficult for passengers to walk by. David guessed that they were on their way to a long weekend at their vacation home. They did not seem pleased to have a stranger join them and offered no welcoming pleasantries. David didn't care. He was self-absorbed and glad to be able to let his mind drift to the events of the past few days.

There was no need to think about how to present them to Willard. The two of them would instantly renew their bond, and Willard would understand. His insights and advice would be tempered with insistence on David's ability to make the right decision. Willard did not always approve of David's decisions, especially when they lacked a strong moral foundation or courage to carry them out. Willard, who was now in his mid-eighties, refused to make a decision or take a position that lacked a moral basis, although his pragmatism allowed him to consider the long run, not just the short term implications.

The rain stopped halfway across Nantucket Sound, and David felt oppressed by the noise and still air inside the large cabin. He went out to the rear deck and found a vacant seat. The rush of wind was refreshing. The sight of the powerful, churning waves in the Sound caused a familiar tremor of excitement to run through his body. Seeing a few sailboats braving the weather this early in the season was fascinating, as they surged and listed in the powerful waves. David had always longed much more to be in the water rather than on it, however. At the outset of the trip, sitting inside, he felt overwhelmed by fatigue from the tension of the past month. Outside in the fresh air and sea spray, he could feel his energy returning.

He hardly noticed the other passengers except for a striking woman sitting opposite him, encased in raingear but with her hood flung back now that the sun had emerged from the storm clouds. She looked to be in her late forties or early fifties. She had a sense of serenity about her, along with the impression of strength and confidence. She was tall, slender, with well-tanned skin suggesting that she spent much of her life outdoors. Something about her bearing gave David the impression that she was a Nantucket native. Besides being attractive, in a traditional way, she had the inner beauty of what he could only think to call a natural woman, unpretentious and in tune with her surroundings.

David thought the woman looked familiar but he was unable to place her. Something about her fascinated him, and he felt disappointed not to know who she was. He kept glancing her way and their eyes met several times, both smiling spontaneously and innocently at the repeated encounters. In the course of one glance, she offered a pleasant, "Good morning," and he responded in kind, adding "Nice to see the sun, isn't it?" She nodded before turning her attention to a ferry passing in the opposite direction.

He separated himself with difficulty from his observations. He stood and leaned against the rail, eager to catch a glimpse of Nantucket through the lifting fog. The island had always seemed magical to him, ever since his first trip out as a child on one of those rare family weekend outings. They had also visited acquaintances on Tuckernuck, a small island west of Nantucket and part of the Town of Nantucket. David had been enchanted with Tuckernuck. Years later, he spent days and nights there with Willard, who had access to the Coleman family cottage, which dated back to the mid-eighteenth century. Tuckernuck had its own unique quality of remoteness and isolation. Although too barren for some tastes, it was reminiscent of the moors of Scotland and always brought to David's mind Thomas Hardy's *Return of the Native*, a novel that had gripped his imagination since first reading it in high school. An ancestor of Willard had bought Nantucket and Tuckernuck in the 1700s.

Nearly all old Nantucket families with roots on the islands had ancestral connections to the Colemans.

As a child, David had never stayed on Nantucket more than a weekend at a time, and visits had not necessarily been happy. What about his childhood was happy, actually? Regardless, he had always delighted in the air, the sparkling water, sunrises and sunsets and most of all, the night sky. He had always felt enchanted by the darkness, whether inside or outside the house. The night sky had a special quality for him, the profound darkness, accented by myriad stars that stimulated his awe at the immensity of time and space. He hoped he would find a sense of direction in this brief sojourn, as he had so many times before.

He was still standing, gazing at the town and trying to pick out Willard's street on the hill above the town, when the ferry landed with a heavy thud. He hurried through the crowd down the stairs to the lower deck and eased his way to the front of the line. He did not fail to look around several times to catch a glimpse of the woman, whose compelling presence remained in his thoughts. She was not in sight. How many times in the course of a life, David thought, do encounters like that happen? Some materialize and some merely slip away into faint memories. How many that never develop might be life-changing? What if I had acted on the chance encounter with that woman, David wondered. Maybe that will turn out to be a coincidence that means something. The thought drifted from his mind as he returned to surveying the scene before him.

Once he disembarked, he was glad not to be hampered by having to recover any luggage so he was able to walk quickly up Broad Street to Willard's house, the James Coleman House, a prominent landmark. The red brick Coleman ancestral home, which was impressive in size and beauty, was now operated by one of his cousins as a bed and breakfast, with the exception of modest personal quarters for Willard. He occupied a three-room apartment on the second floor for the entire summer as well as during regular visits in late spring and early fall plus occasional forays in the winter. He had rejected as unnecessary the idea of reserving more space.

When David reached the familiar house, admiring the perfect condition despite its vintage 1600s look, he approached the desk clerk, a relative of Willard's, who recognized him and rang Willard. He appeared on the stairs moments later and the men greeted each other with a hearty embrace with vigorous back slapping. Hugging was Willard's custom long before it became fashionable and acceptable in male company. As the two headed upstairs, David was happy to observe that Willard, despite his advancing years, moved with agility and strength. He was vigorous and healthy, still aging gracefully.

31

When they reached Willard's apartment, they went out to the front porch, carrying tall glasses of iced tea. David always looked forward to the spectacular view of the harbor reaching from the busy streets below to the far horizon.

"This is the strongest thing I drink now," Willard said in his distinctive resonant voice, with a hint of humor. "My drinking days are over for good. Remember when I could put them away with the best and still keep my wits about me, or so I thought anyway?"

"I remember that," David replied. "I did too in those days, but no more for me either. You never seemed to be affected by it. You were always the same, drinking or not, full of fire, and clear-headed, like your sermons. I still remember sitting in the chapel listening to them even though I was going through a period when I just about totally rejected religion. Actually, I'm still disillusioned with religious institutions, but I believe in the spiritual nature of each person. My preference is what Jacques-Pierre calls vertical religion, not horizontal, the direct relationship with God. I've always been amazed at the power of your faith in Christianity and what it tells you about right and wrong. I always longed for faith as strong as yours. But I do believe in Christianity modeled after Christ's actual words and actions, apart from theology. I'm not sure where I fit into the religious structure."

"I always felt sure of my beliefs," Willard replied. "I still do, actually, and, yes, I was intense all the time. I think I did my job through all the turmoil and controversy, and hard living in a way, but it took a toll on my marriages," Willard mused. "From the time I got involved in civil rights movements of all kinds, I was hardly ever home. Those were stressful years but the most satisfying I've ever had."

"I didn't realize then how much you sacrificed for all of us, myself included," David said. "I never thought of anything but myself when I went looking for you. You've never failed me and I guess I, like all the others who did that, should have realized that it had to take a heavy toll on your personal life," David said quietly with a note of regret in his voice.

"I never complained about it and I still don't. When I chose to become a pastor, I committed myself to people's spiritual and personal needs. I left behind every trace of my former cynical occupation with the CIA. I never regretted giving that up but it taught me a good deal about the way people think and act under pressure. I felt that my calling was to counsel anyone who came to me needing to talk. That was, for the most part, students. Most of the faculty steered clear of me. I was too controversial—liberal ahead of my time, let's say—and they were worried about guilt by association. They accused me of being a living contradiction—professing absolute faith in God's will but advocating human action to bring about change. I simply saw it as humans carrying out God's will. You could construe it as a paradox, though. The key to the paradox is that faith doesn't require suspending thinking or suspending action. It's the extending of trust and love unconditionally. Sorry, that sounds like a sermon."

"Your sermons have always fascinated me. I've come back to your definition of faith over and over. It's the only thing that made it possible for me to hold onto the idea that what I do matters. I can have faith of a sort, in something spiritual, something greater than we are that has nothing to do with religious dogma and institutions. Do you remember having this conversation when I came to see you when I was struggling with my dilemma and feeling like I wanted to escape from everything and everyone? Seems silly in retrospect."

"Of course I remember," Willard said with a laugh. "You said that you were at a crisis point of your own making, like so many other students. We talked for a long time. Your honesty and openness about your faults made it work for us. You felt that you were drowning in the maelstrom caused by a fight to the death between your desires and ambition on one hand, and your conscience on the other. You had two romantic relationships going but neither was going well. You wanted out of one relationship and in the other one, the girl wanted out. You felt rejected, betrayed even, by her. And you admitted that, whenever you had a crisis to deal with, you felt immobilized by the heavy burden of guilt that you had been lugging around since childhood, guilt that had to do with relationships within your family."

"Right," David agreed, "and we met three or four more times before the semester ended. I was amazed that you would spend so much time with a student when you were all over the country with organizing protests and speaking and writing too. Senior year was hectic but we got together for coffee at least once a week. I was in deep trouble, frankly, between trying to figure out what to do with my life and whether to break off the relationships. You were my only point of sanity."

"During your first year of law school," Willard responded, "before you joined up with the Army, you came to see me at least two dozen times. You were frustrated by law school, and, on top of that, your personal life and your relationship with your parents were both in turmoil. Although I felt the Army would be a waste of time for you, I was glad that you'd have a break before deciding what to do with your law degree. I warned you though that military life might well drive you off the tracks and cause more problems. You had made up your mind and you went ahead with a commitment."

"I know," David said. "Who could have predicted that the war on terror would have us embroiled in the Middle East, Iraq and Afghanistan—and, after that, North Africa and the Arabian Peninsula would explode. I didn't really bargain for a war, I have to admit."

"On top of it all, against my advice," he said, smiling warmly, "right after graduation from college, you got married. We both knew it wouldn't last and it didn't, of course." Willard said. "Then, after you got back from Iraq and were back in law school, I couldn't believe that you got married again, this time to Lucille. I didn't think you made a good choice. I couldn't imagine it would last. Actually it has lasted, if you can say that, longer than I thought. As far as I could see, she was desperate that she would lose you, and she was probably right about that. That happened anyway, right? It was just a question of time. You were perfectly willing to settle for something less than happiness, less than love."

Willard continued. "I remember that you called when you were back in the States on leave before you went to Yemen and Djibouti. You sounded desperate. You came over that same evening, and we talked well into the night. You weren't through with the military but, by that time, the worst had already happened. I've never seen you so sick with despair, remorse and, I think, maybe even a little unhinged mentally, although you refused to consider that you needed help. You kept saying that your weakness of character had done you in. You hadn't developed a strong moral compass, and it led you to go along with some killings. You said you didn't realize in time what was happening, and you felt frozen in time and space and unable to react. For weeks after, you felt as though you had crossed a boundary from reality into a nightmare. I felt that you were overreacting and that maybe it had to do with something in your childhood. You kept coming back to that over the course of years but never seemed able to talk about it. Maybe I should have pried it out of you. Maybe I still should."

"I know. Maybe so," David agreed. "That same problem is rearing its head now. It never got resolved. I was suffering from what they call moral sickness. I was haunted by what had happened. It possessed me in a way. I was stuck like a bug on a pin, a point of indecision, like Mr. Thompson in Katherine Anne Porter's *Noon Wine*. Do you remember how that story has always fascinated me? I couldn't find a way to get away, how to handle guilt—remorse and fear too. That was the first time in my life when I actually worried that I would lose my soul for good. I have not dealt with it still, and it looks as though I'm about to face it again."

"I'm sorry to hear that," Willard replied. "I felt then that I couldn't offer you any real comfort, certainly not with the shallow theology that organized religion too often spews out. Jargon is jargon and I've never had any use for doctrine of any kind, dogma, religious or otherwise. My faith is not based on what religious institutions say or do. It's in what Jesus Christ said and did, especially the Gospel of John and the letters of Paul. Those books hold the key to solving the world's problems today, if we could just extract and apply them."

Willard went on, "But, I could see that you were deep in despair then, in the dark night of your soul, the abyss. I remember telling you that accepting the depth of despair and suffering was the only route to the depth of knowledge and spiritual understanding that could ultimately lead to atonement and, finally, redemption. That's about where we left off and I thought everything was falling into place for you."

"I thought so too," David said. "I never felt it was completely behind me though. If I listed all the symptoms I've had since getting back from Iraq, and it's been more than a dozen years now, you'd say I have PTSD. I've never pursued that route. If anything, I've avoided it because it would have destroyed my chance for success in public life, frankly. The combat experience usually exacerbates a condition that already exists in a person. The experience can be uplifting once in a while but, by and large, it is brutal and dehumanizing of the self and others. What we see and what we do puts a lot of people over the top, but it isn't as though it's a virus that we catch. I have no intention of trying to get diagnosed. It's the last thing I want."

"I get it," Willard said. "When you're ready, go ahead and bring me up to date and tell me what's troubling you."

"A lot has happened," David said, "some good, some bad. My career is going well but there are serious tensions there. I have opportunities for advancement, but I fear that the memories that I dread the most are about to surface again. My marriage is in shambles and my relationship with my kids is suffering. I'm on a path to achieving my ambition, but I don't know if it will be better or if the cost will be too much. The truth is that I don't know where I'm headed, and I don't feel as though I'm getting to the root of my problems. I'm not sure of the person I am or the person I pretend to be. I'm a little like Jean Valjean. I'm heading somewhere but I'm not sure where. The past, my Javert, is pursuing me and it's gaining on me."

They talked into the afternoon and well into the night, with David holding back only on what were still unreachable areas of his memory and his mind. They parted the next day, after a long walk on Tuckernuck, vowing to meet again in a few weeks and to keep in touch about developments. With all there was to talk about, David forgot to ask Willard about the enchanting woman he'd seen on the ferry. He would carry her image with him and be sure to ask next time they got together. Although no solutions to the still unfolding drama appeared, David felt relieved to have a clearer moral compass to guide him.

PART TWO

"There is a luxury in self-reproach. When we blame ourselves, we feel that no one else has a right to blame us. It is the confession, not the priest, that gives us absolution."

—Oscar Wilde, *The Picture of Dorian Gray*, 1890

32

O n his way to work the next morning, David began formulating his legal strategy. He had already decided to enlist Richard to represent him as a witness in Nick Serrano's trial. Herb Gerson would represent him in the divorce action when the time was ripe. Beyond that, he felt a need to have someone close at hand to speak with confidentially, while staying in control of the flow of information about the Ramadi affair. Willard was too far removed from the political situation to help. Richard and Herb were trustworthy but were equally friendly with virtually everyone in David's support group. When David consulted them in their legal capacity, he wanted to be in a position to manage the information. He would reveal only a carefully crafted version of the events. They were lawyers and would not be judgmental about their client's actions. Legal training had liberated them from passing judgment on a good client with a challenging legal problem.

Lawyers were used to situations in which clients controlled the information. His story needed refining. Despite the necessity that a lawyer should know all the facts, he was plotting to control the legal solution by holding back facts and formulating his own strategy, thereby depriving his lawyers of the complete picture. Now he understood the client's point of view. It was a question of trust, he supposed.

Who did that leave to confide in? Jeffrey Webster? He was a good friend at the Court who cared about David's welfare, but the relationship with Jeff wasn't close enough for him to share the shocking details of his past. At the moment, he needed to talk to someone who was directly involved in the present political venture. He was looking for practical solutions. There would be time for Willard's moral advice.

It came down to Dana. They had been careful about contacting each other. Their only meeting had been in New York, where they had a fast lunch in a nondescript restaurant when David had to be in the city for a day. She told him she was gradually distancing herself from Jake. Her new job kept her in the city all week and traveling on weekends. It gave her the time and space she needed to cool the relationship while she reassessed it.

"Jake is wondering if something is wrong," she said to David. "He keeps saying 'What did I do wrong? Tell me. I'll fix it.' I assured him that he hadn't done anything wrong. But I can tell he isn't satisfied that he's gotten to the bottom of it. Jake is so self-focused that he can miss the obvious. He'll start wondering if there's someone else. He may even get paranoid about that.

What could I tell him, if I wanted to? Would I say, 'Yes, Jake. I had sex with one of your best friends. Just hang in there, darling. It doesn't mean anything right now.' Can you hear me saying that?"

"Of course not," David replied, taken aback that Dana had been so direct, so revealing of her feelings. He decided to take her words seriously. He leaned across the table until his face was six inches from hers. "I care about you. I'm not stuck forever, but I agree that we can't say anything right now or do anything. There's a lot riding on it, but Jake's feelings are important too. It tears me up."

After that conversation, David knew he should put the idea of an intimate relationship with Dana out of his mind. But she was a person he could turn to for an assessment of the whole situation. She knows her way around, he thought. She knows the President because of their mutual affiliation with the Global Crisis Network. He would need assurance. Even if she continued her relationship with Jake, maybe he could talk to her in confidence. He'd have to be sure she hadn't revealed what he'd told her so far. It was not easy to control all the information. There were too many loose ends. What would he tell her? How much should he reveal?

He decided to text her at work. Dana replied quickly. She'd be in New York all week and Thursday would work best. They could meet at the small apartment she shared with the GCN executive director, Sue Chang. Sue was out of town and wouldn't be back until very late on Thursday night. They would have privacy. David made it clear that he planned to return to New Haven the same day, but he made a reservation at the Yale Club in case it got late. This would work well. He could go to Hartford on Wednesday. Nothing urgent was going on at the Court.

The day crept by slowly and Wednesday was uneventful. He had no further contact with Burkhardt. David heard that he would leave soon for the annual July meeting of Chief Justices, this year in Reno. Good. He'd be out of the way for a week or more. Burkhardt always turned his stay at conferences into personal golfing vacations by claiming he had other meetings to attend. David had lunch with Jeff Webster but kept the discussion light. Jeff had heard the gossip that was circulating about Nick's visit and wanted to know more about it.

David downplayed the incident. "That guy was my platoon sergeant when I was in Iraq. He and I didn't get along. He shows up once in a while. I guess he's had a tough time. He's ragged around the edges, shall we say. Mental health problems, I think."

"Guess so," Jeff said, grinning. "I heard he was way out of line. Burkhardt got all pissed about it. What a pain in the ass that guy is. Burkhardt, I mean." Jeff said, laughing out loud, and whispering, "an insufferable, arrogant blowhard. He got lucky with one Governor and jumped to the front of the queue. That's not the first time or the last, of course."

33

David took an early train to New York on Thursday, explaining to the boys at breakfast that he had a full day of meetings with his ABA advisors and other people who were helping him. It was strange, he thought, how casually he could lie to suit the circumstances. There was a time when he prided himself on being truthful even when it was against his own interests. Perhaps all the years working within institutions, the military and the law, had worn down his defenses to the temptations of lying-on-demand.

The boys were still in school and Lucille had volunteer commitments on Thursday and Friday so he felt free. He had no illusions that he had been attentive to Lucille's or the boys' needs for a long time. Nor had he been easy to live with. But he convinced himself that Lucille was primarily responsible for the breakdown. Alcoholism had derailed her years ago and made any positive change impossible.

During the train ride, he caught up on news and then spent two hours in the Yale Club library getting his stories in order. He was amused at the lawyerly way he went about that task. He'd need this workup for Herb and Richard. He had a tentative appointment with Herb on Friday morning if he stayed in the city. If not, they'd talk by phone. He couldn't afford delay in planning strategy in case Lucille took precipitous action.

Dana had given David instructions on getting to her apartment on East 80th Street and retrieving a key from the doorman. He was welcome to get there any time after 2:00 p.m. She'd try to be home before 5:00. They could talk there for the sake of privacy and then go out for a bite before David returned to Grand Central. He decided to walk. It was overcast with a light drizzle, but David ignored the dampness and enjoyed the refreshing coolness of the light rain. He had used the Club gym before lunch, helping him to gain focus. He wondered indifferently what he'd be doing a year or five years from now. By the time he reached the apartment, about 3:30, he felt refreshed and optimistic. Knowing that he could tell most of the story to someone he could trust lightened his load.

David sat down at the ebony Yamaha baby grand piano in the living room and made an attempt to play a few pieces from a book of classical music that he found in the bench. He had once been a fair pianist, for his own pleasure, not for performance. He hadn't played in years but he made a mental note to take up the piano again someday when he had time. The piano had, in earlier years, been a way to regain his equilibrium. He glanced at the *Times Book Review* that was sitting on the coffee table, then dropped off to sleep on the sofa with sunlight bathing him in a soothing stream of warmth.

He awakened later to the sound of a key in the door. He sat up and opened his eyes in time to see Dana looking him over, a smile brightening her dark green eyes. "Hey," she said in a melodious tone, "Catching a few are you? This apartment gets the sun in the afternoon. It's great for naps, although I hardly ever get the chance. I bet you don't either. It's good to see you."

"Hey, yourself. I'm glad to see you," he said. "It's great to be here, to see where you live. I like this area of the city. It's a perfect walk from midtown, interesting, not too crowded. God, I haven't relaxed in days, more like weeks or maybe months. Relaxing could become a habit if I got the chance."

"Do you want a cold drink? Beer? Wine?"

"A beer would be great," he said. "Can I help?"

"No. That's easy. Be right back," she said, disappearing down the hallway. David had a few moments to consider where to start his story. Best to skip the details, he thought, and get right into the present dilemma. He could always backfill the details of what led to the crisis. Dana returned in moments and settled at the opposite end of the sofa.

"Tell me what's up," she said eagerly. "I'm sorry not to have stayed in touch more, but I've had a steep learning curve to deal with. Turns out I'm not only Deputy Counsel at GCN, but director of special projects, which includes everything that isn't crisis intervention. I love the place, though. I think this organization is the future. It's committed to neutral, crisis intervention and diplomatic negotiation with no agenda of its own, just to facilitate peaceful resolutions. We have a very diverse panel of negotiators, mostly foreign nationals. Some are from countries that are not friendly to the U.S. No one could accuse us of being biased. It's like a mini-UN except that it's effective and flexible and far less expensive to maintain. It's what the UN was supposed to be before it became a petrified bureaucracy, a forum for posturing and complaining."

David was about to jump in with a defense of the UN, but Dana added, "I know. Some of the agencies do very good work, but when it comes to acting on international or humanitarian crises, it's too easy for one or two countries to block anything that might work."

"Fascinating," David said. "I'd like to hear more about that and what the President did when she was running GCN. Organizations like this that try to work out conflicts before they ripen into violence are the future, if we can ever get people to take a long range view of problems."

"I'd love to talk about it," Dana said, "but we need to get to what you want to talk about now. This sounded urgent."

"Okay," he said, still conflicted about how much to say. He hadn't resolved the trust issue. "Can I say first that you look fantastic, all business and professional and capable, but exotic too."

"Thank you," she said, "but please, tell me about your problem."

"It's difficult to know where to start so let me lay out what I face right now and you can ask questions. I hope you'll give me feedback to be sure I'm on the right track," David said. Dana nodded.

34

We know the President has a short list of candidates, although it's not necessarily the final list," David informed Dana. "We know that Lehman is determined to uncover any secrets that could embarrass her, especially since the Senate probably won't confirm her nominee without a fight. I have no problem with that; it's a cardinal rule of politics. Lehman knows that something happened with my platoon in Ramadi while I was there that resulted in an investigation. What he doesn't know, and you don't unless Jake told you, is that the entire record of the investigation is either corrupted or missing." David looked directly into Dana's eyes to see whether Jake had told her that information. She shook her head no and said, "Jake didn't say a word about that. I've hardly seen him since getting back from New Hampshire."

"I was going to ask you about Jake," David said, "How he is, how things are. Maybe we can talk about that later. But for now, Jake and I spoke about this and he volunteered, or maybe I should say, insisted, on finding out about the investigation report. He found out that the digital file that was created and put on the SIPRNET has been corrupted, probably deliberately. You know what the SIPRNET is, right?"

"I've heard Jake mention it. I know it's a digital network but I don't know what the acronym stands for."

"It's the Secret Internet Protocol Router Network, the official digital network used by the military. It's accessible worldwide. It's supposed to be supersafe and accurate, but it's accessible to so many people, including a huge number of military personnel from top to bottom, that it has lots of flaws. Anyway, the print version is also gone. It's not in the file at Fort Benning. It was brought there from Iraq when the company returned to base. Jake said he'd try to find out more but I haven't heard from him. That was two weeks ago."

Dana was listening intently. David could see her weighing Jake's role in this and feeling confident that they hadn't discussed this. What did that mean for his relationship with Dana? She wouldn't expect that Jake would reveal anything to anyone. He was absolutely firm about that. Dana was shrewd. She'd actually approve of it.

"Something happened," David went on, "that gave me a clue as to what happened to the report. The person at the center of the investigation, Nick Serrano, my former platoon sergeant, showed up and threatened me. He's been charged with a homicide in Philadelphia. He's been in and out of trouble since the service. He wasn't such a bad guy then, although we were enemies of sorts, but I guess he went off the deep end somewhere along the line. He's full of rage and aggression now and obviously violent. His lawyer wants to mount a PTSD defense to the homicide and that's where I come in."

Dana interjected, "Who'd he kill?"

"He's charged with killing some guy, a friend of his live-in girlfriend, and attempting to kill her," David said. "I don't know the circumstances. Serrano says they were shot in a parking lot near the bar where she worked in Philadelphia. He says he wasn't involved. I get the impression that the defense is not that he didn't do it but that he had a flashback to combat in Iraq and isn't legally responsible. Of course, it's a little more complicated than that."

"Where do you come into this?" Dana asked.

"He wants me to testify that his combat experience in Iraq caused his PTSD. He says he was diagnosed, but I don't know that for a fact. I don't know a lot because we parted, shall we say, abruptly on the day he came to see me. He wants me to testify about the trauma as a basis for his PTSD. Well, God knows, there was plenty of trauma every day we were there and the threat of it every hour. But that's the back story, a long complicated back story."

David went on. "I'm involved in that story. I had a role. I was in command after all. I knew what was going on. There were Iraqi women involved, one that Serrano was involved with. When I learned about it, I tried to persuade him to stop fooling around with the locals. That's practically a capital offense in an AQI area. He didn't stop. I let it go rather than confronting or reporting it. I was hoping it would take care of itself. It didn't. It blew up right in our faces.

"AQI insurgents retaliated," David added, "not against us, but against his woman, just a girl, really. They were all over the place. It was still a hot area at the time. They murdered her; I mean brutally murdered her. A few soldiers from my platoon retaliated against the insurgents. Serrano led the retaliation. There's a dispute about whether he was authorized or not by me. But if I didn't authorize it, which is subject to interpretation, I certainly didn't prevent it."

"What do you mean there's a dispute about authorization? That sounds evasive, like typical military bullshit. Did you or didn't you?" Dana asked.

"What I mean is he claims I gave him an order to retaliate. I deny that. Anyway, some civilians and two of our own soldiers were killed. We're talking more than twenty deaths, closer to thirty. When it came to light, a lot of us, up and down the command line, helped to make it go away, officially that is. It didn't entirely go away but the embedded journalists who were hanging around didn't get the stories they wanted. They were ticked but they knew they couldn't do anything about it. They depended on being embedded to stay there.

"In the end, Serrano was sent home and ultimately discharged but not prosecuted. It was an informal investigation, in-house and private. I think

Serrano's wondering whether he can still be prosecuted for the murders of civilians, and I don't know the answer to that. What is the statute of limitations on murders in federal court? Does it depend on the degree of murder? I don't know. Nobody got serious punishment, just administrative garbage. There was a hearing and most of us testified. It should all be in the investigation report. I guess some people, journalists in particular, would call it a cover-up. It was a very sensitive time in Al Anbar Province then. In 2007 the surge was still going on, although it was nearly over. We were trying to take—or retake—Fallujah and Ramadi, the places that were lost a few years before that to insurgents. The fighting has never stopped there. It won't ever stop any more than the fighting in the Middle East will ever stop."

35

What a story," Dana exclaimed. "No wonder you're upset. So this is the missing report. What a time for this to happen, with the nomination pending and media attention focusing on Al Anbar because of the latest fighting. Conditions are more volatile there now than in a few years."

"I know," David said, clearly subdued. "There was a brief respite when we withdrew, then it exploded. Like my life."

"My main concern is the impact on you," Dana said, "but I can't help but care about President Madison too. She's the smartest and most courageous President we've had in a long time. She thinks long term even if nobody else does, and she rejects the stale jargon and the worn-out ways of viewing international relations. She has the background in history to understand the context of the conflict in the Middle East and North Africa, and Latin America, the Far East too. She's vulnerable politically but willing to take risks even if she sacrifices a second term. How often does that happen?"

"I like her too," David said. "Frankly, I'm in the competition because of a few friends in the right places and a few lucky breaks. I'm the longest of the long shots. I know that presidents see their Supreme Court appointments as legacies, but, once the appointments are made, there's no predicting the long-range performance. Why is she so different from other presidents? Isn't she going to make the nomination for tactical advantage with her agenda, and the likelihood of confirmation?"

"You're wrong in that," Dana said emphatically. "I'm not naïve, but I know she's different. Sure, she's not oblivious to political advantage, but she's interested in having you on the court to support a global outlook rather than the provincial approach that has prevailed for too long. There are lots of cases the Court could take that deal with issues bearing on foreign policy, where a global approach could work. I won't deny that she has vision and she knows that your combat record makes you acceptable to most everybody, even the right-wingers. Since 2001, this country has seen millions of veterans come back from the wars. She's well aware that there never has been anyone with a voice for veterans on the Court. There have been veterans, yes, but not someone like you at a time when veterans are highly visible and outspoken. You're unique, a combat veteran with progressive views."

David listened intently but began nodding his head when Dana talked about his military record. "Well, Dana, I appreciate what you say but my record is problematic, and I don't know if I'm worse off if the record never shows itself or if it does. I'm convinced that Serrano is responsible for the corruption and the disappearance of the print file. He'll hold the written report over my head. If I testify, he expects me to lie about the facts. Sure, there sure was trauma, no mystery about that. He actually fell apart when the woman he was involved with was murdered. That's probably what set him off on a rampage. The trouble is he took down civilians who sheltered the insurgents as well as those bastards, themselves."

"If you want to put yourself down and be defeatist, you'll lose your support, including mine," Dana said. "When is the trial? How's the timing?"

"Serrano says the trial is set for the first week of September. I could probably wage a battle against being compelled to testify, but he has information that would make me look very bad. In fact, I could probably be charged with perjury during the investigation and the hearing. Yes, there was a hearing, although it was perfunctory because the command was determined to suppress this whole incident, keep it out of sight and out of the hands of the media. The two embedded journalists were nosing around all the time. Command was careful not to let them get any information and to conduct the closed hearing without giving any notice."

"Didn't they get access to some information? Couldn't they talk to the witnesses?" Dana asked.

"Yes, of course, but they knew they were vulnerable. One time, the battalion commander even threatened to throw one of them out. The journalist capitulated and never ran a story again without getting permission. Being embedded was their bread and butter. But still I think they were biding their time, hoping for the right opportunity that would be worth the risk of getting tossed. Those journalists had a good life under the circumstances, well protected and safe even though they were on the edge of danger. Not all journalists wanted to be in that spot but, for those who did, it was a good assignment. As long as they followed protocol, they were safe in Iraq and Afghanistan. Those who were in less organized, less controllable places where the American military machine wasn't in control—Syria, Libya, Yemen, Somalia, Ivory Coast, even Pakistan. Those are very different stories. There wasn't as much fighting but it was less safe."

"I never thought about that," Dana acknowledged. "I always thought, wow, those journalists in all war zones, they're the greatest. But I see what you mean. Not all war zones are alike in risks."

"Right," David said. "I admire journalists too and some are very brave and dedicated but others find a way to be safe while seeming to risk their lives."

"Anyway," David continued, "the other issues are my personal life, calm at the moment but it can blow up in my face any minute. And, I've also got a hostile colleague if you can call him that, the Chief on my court. He'd love to embarrass me, to ruin me. He saw Serrano the day he came to the court. The Chief tried to bully me in his arrogant way. He's a threat, not a big one at the moment, but a threat anyway."

"You're right to go easy on that. You don't need another problem," Dana added.

"What about Jake, speaking of threats?" David asked. "If Jake ever got wind of my role in the Ramadi incident, he'd blow his top. He wouldn't tolerate that lack of leadership for a minute. I think Al Qaeda took out the woman as a warning to the other women who were hanging around with Americans. The hardliners had no use for their women mixing with our guys. That was against their rules. It was a death sentence for women and anyone else in the wrong place at the wrong time. One of our missions at that point was to win over Iraqis but most people don't realize that the fundamentalists were dead set against letting that happen. Anyone who cooperated with us was in jeopardy. That's one reason why we had to root out the insurgents. There was another reason too. AQI didn't like the military hiring the sheikhs. The Arab Awakening was threatening to their control over the people. The girl's father was one of them. He was one of the important leaders. He recruited other sheikhs with offers of big money to recruit the Sons of Iraq. They fought the insurgents. But that's another story."

36

I made some mistakes," David said. "If I could do it all over again, would I do anything differently? You bet. I'd put a stop to the relationships with the Iraqi women. The relationships were like accelerants poured on a fire that's already out of hand. If that didn't work, I'd get command involved. Serrano would have been transferred. I messed up in not absolutely preventing him from handling the retaliation. I could have gotten the Sons of Iraq to do the dirty work instead. They would have avoided civilian casualties.

"As far as the investigation whitewash was concerned, that's a harder case. The whole military apparatus depended on protecting ourselves above all else. It's really no different from any institution, just on a different scale. The word was 'Keep this quiet.' The standards are different in the military. What is valued and what is not are entirely different. The day you go in, your world turns upside down. Preserving life is now at the bottom of the list, except your own and your buddies. Killing is what you do. It's another tool in your toolkit, one you turn to damn quickly. If in doubt, shoot."

David was wound up now. "If protecting your buddies requires lying, you do it. Lying is just another tool, a weapon to help accomplish your goal. The lying starts long before war breaks out. You've heard it said that the truth is the first casualty of a democratic society when war is at stake. I learned something similar in law school, and in politics too. They just call lying by different names, like argument or rhetoric. If you're in the military, don't complain. Don't whine. Don't ask for help. Don't ask for an exception. There are no exceptions unless they serve some other military purpose. The order is the commandment. Military orders trump the Ten Commandments.

"The day you get out and get back home, the world tips upside down again. You step onto a different planet. You have different rules. Is it any wonder so many soldiers of all wars are strung out? Go off the deep end? Get mental illnesses like PTSD, depression, addictions? Commit suicide? My God, the wonder is that they all don't, and most of these guys and women are just out of adolescence for God's sake, still forming their brains and they get all screwed up. And once you're discharged, the government says go away and don't come whining to us. Take care of yourself and get on with your life and, oh, thanks for your service. Oh yeah. Sorry we didn't accomplish much, or anything. Maybe it was a big mistake after all. Have a nice day."

"I understand," Dana said softly. "One of the best courses I ever took was about the American experience in twentieth and twenty-first century wars.

106

War is old. It's been around for a long time. It was designed by people who are not in the trenches or the jungle. They're in offices and gated communities, on Wall Street and in defense plants. They're in Congress and in the White House. They shuttle back and forth between the Pentagon and the private sector in high salary jobs. How many generals have to worry about getting blown apart by an IED or a RPG? Not many. As for the people back home, if it doesn't affect their standard of living, they don't see the relevance."

"It's sick, isn't it?" David asked. "That attitude really sucks. I suppose I sound like a sore loser. Maybe I am. Maybe I was a wimp when I wrote that book about what it is to be a soldier. I was trying to ride both horses, not offend the military and not offend civilians. My next book will hit hard. If I don't get this, I'll write that book. What the hell do you think I should do besides hire a lawyer to advise me about this trial and another for the divorce? That's as far as I've thought it out."

Dana had a pained expression on her face. She brushed away the sense of disappointment in him that no doubt he could detect. He understood that she was sympathetic to all he'd been through and that she knew how good people can make bad decisions, or no decisions, when they're under pressure. The situation had become complicated.

37

avid studied Dana's face, wondering how disillusioned she was with him, with all that he'd done and failed to do. He didn't dare move, half anticipating that she would tell him to leave. She surprised him when she moved over until she was nestled against him, wrapping her arms around his chest, stroking his head. "Oh, David, I had no idea you had gone through all that and were carrying all that around. I understand what you did and why.

"My grandfather was never the same after his tour in Vietnam," Dana went on with obvious emotion. "As a child, I knew just the shell of the person he had been, according to everybody in the family. Someday I'll tell you about that. You're such a good, sensitive person, so worthy." She was holding back tears, perhaps for herself and perhaps for David's pain, his guilt, whatever he had done or not done. "If it means anything, and I mean this in the right way," she said, "I forgive you. I forgive you for all you've done or failed to do that causes you to suffer."

"I love you, Dana," David said, surprising himself that he had blurted that out, when he had meant to hold it back. He wasn't at all sure he meant it. "I don't know where that takes us, but we can figure that out later."

"I don't know either. It's complicated. It can mean what we decide it should. It can bring us together as a couple someday, or it can just mean that we care about each other as friends, as loyal, understanding friends. You need to know how I feel about you, and I'd like to do that but I'm afraid to move ahead too quickly. I've been hurt before and I've done some hurting too. You're a good person, a fine person, and I do love you, but I don't know yet what that means. I love Jake too, but that's different."

"That's enough for me now. We can take it where we want, but love shouldn't be held back. It's a healing love and that's the way I take it now," David said. "It's enough if you just hold me for now. That's enough. This is right. It isn't disloyal. Love needs to be expressed. What we do with it is another thing. We'll find a way."

Before they understood what was happening, compassion evolved seamlessly into fierce physical desire. For those moments, David was spared his pain and bathed in a sense of relief and release. It was as though his deep wounds, the lacerations of his soul, were healed. He knew it would not last, that he would have to face the trials, all the trials, and perhaps more because of these moments. But for now, he felt whole. Was this redemption? He felt as though he had not yet atoned for his wrongs, his crimes, but that in some way he had been granted absolution for the moment.

They awoke several hours later. David had not meant for this to happen. He wanted to keep the relationship but not to complicate their lives. Dana spoke gently. He shifted his body and looked at her. She seemed untroubled "How do you feel about this?" he asked stiffly, trying to keep the anxiety out of his voice. She looked at him intently "I'm okay with this. I mean, not just okay, more than okay. You don't have to worry that I'll reveal anything. I won't. My relationship with Jake is close to the end. When the inevitable happens, he'll have to face the fact of our day-to-day tension as the reason. When we moved in together, we agreed that neither of us would make a claim on the other."

"But you know Jake," David said. "He can't stand losing and he doesn't miss a thing."

"I can't say I've been thinking much the last few hours," Dana said with a smile, "but I have some thoughts about what you said and what you should do. Do you want to hear them?"

"Absolutely," he said, sitting up. "That's what I really wanted from you, why I came here today besides just wanting to see you, of course."

"Okay," she said, pulling herself to an upright position, "here goes, even before I have coffee to wake myself up. The trial is in six weeks, right? Anything can happen between now and then. Don't brush Nick off now. Let him think you will do something for him, that you'll have to work out what that is. Talk to his lawyer or have your lawyer do that. Tell him that you won't let him down but that you can't lie. Say that you will help but in a way that you have to plan carefully. After all, the guy did go through tremendous trauma, right? This is not fiction. He probably does have PTSD based on his combat experiences."

David started to interrupt. "Wait, please hear me out," she said. "You can testify about his trauma and avoid getting into problem areas. You need to get him off your back now. Who knows, maybe just the fact that his lawyer can tell the prosecutor he'll have you as a witness will be enough to get him a plea bargain. He's got risks too, lots to lose. Don't make a specific commitment or promise. Give yourself bargaining room and play it cool. Whatever happened, whatever you did or didn't do, was long ago. You have a lot at stake now. That's your priority. In the meantime, give yourself breathing room and wait to see what happens.

"If he ultimately isn't satisfied," she said, "he may be vindictive, but he *will* be that if you do refuse him. Don't do it now. Postpone it. It won't be any worse later if you lead him on now. In the end, you can act in your own best interest. Going out of his way to get you in trouble won't help him. He may well decide not to do that even if you turn him down. But on the other hand, maybe you'll avoid the whole thing. You don't know for sure what information he has. You think he has the print file but he may not. It's worth buying time for yourself and, when the time comes, you can figure a way to keep the lid on him and protect yourself. By then you may be in a secure position with the

President or, of course, it could be all over by then."

David nodded, waiting.

"What lawyers will you use? Do you know who you want to handle your divorce, assuming that goes forward?"

"I'm not sure," David replied, "someone in the firm, but it should be a divorce specialist, probably Herb."

"That should be an easy one, then," Dana said, "You need the best criminal defense lawyer at the firm. That's Richard, right?"

"Definitely," David said. "I'll see Richard tomorrow, hopefully. Herb does some criminal too, white collar stuff, but I'm more comfortable with Richard. We were always on the same wavelength at law school. Herb and I are not as close. Richard just takes things the way they are, no questions asked. They're both loyal."

38

As they sat on the sofa, David lulled into a relaxed state by physical and emotional closeness with Dana plus his own vulnerability, any concern about Jake seemed too remote to cause immediate alarm. The sound of a door bolt snapping in response to a key in the lock startled them both into action, grabbing, struggling to pull their clothes on quickly, clumsily. It seemed futile. "Oh my God," Dana whispered. "It must be Sue. She's way early." The door started to open. Dana called out, "Sue. Give me a minute. Wait please. I'll be ready in a second."

A woman's voice said with alarm, "Okay, sorry I'm early. The meeting broke up much sooner. I should have called from downstairs. I'll go get coffee and be back in a half hour."

"Oh sweetie, you don't have to do that. Just give me, us, five minutes."

"Okay," Sue said. "It doesn't matter. Take your time. I don't mind."

"Thanks, but it's okay. Almost ready," Dana said, as she continued to dress. David was now fully decent, with everything but socks and shoes on. Dana went to the door, with a nod from David. Sue came in, concern on her face, along with an apologetic look in her eyes. "Sorry, Dana, I should have called from downstairs, but I never thought."

"No reason to think that," Dana said. "I had no plans. Sue, this is David. David, Sue. You met at our place, Jake's and mine, in New Haven." Dana was trying hard to bring normalcy to an awkward situation. Both David and Sue nodded. "David and I are going out for a bite. Do you want to come along? We owe you."

"No thanks. I'm beat," Sue said. "I need to relax. Don't rush away on my account. It's fine, really."

Despite Sue's words, David could still see disapproval etched in her face. David wondered whether she had a separate relationship with Jake. The thought of it made him tense, casting a cloud over the glow of intimacy.

A short time later, David and Dana walked the short distance to a neighborhood Italian restaurant, La Strada, and found a quiet corner. They shared a laugh about being caught in delicto.

"I'm concerned about Sue," David said. "Do you trust her to keep what she saw private?"

"It's fine. I'll speak to her when I get back. As far as I know, she doesn't talk to Jake on her own."

39

After they placed their orders, Dana asked, "Would you talk about why you enlisted in the Army?"

"Sure," he said, glancing around. "Glad to tell you why I joined up. The culture in my family was that going into the military made a boy into a man. It was a natural part of growing up, at least for my grandfathers' and my uncles' generations. I had heard them all tell their war stories. They passed along the mystique about going to war. It was heroic. It was about defending your country, defending freedom. It was about good versus evil. It's different now. After the World Wars, you could hardly say that going to war was heroic. But political leaders still try to model their wars after the great wars. That's the big lie.

"It was always in the back of my mind," David said. "The physical part appealed to me too. It was an extension of sports, I guess. Another is that I really needed to get away from law school. I didn't like it at all. I needed to get away from the marriage too. There's one more strange twist. I took pleasure in knowing that joining up would anger my father, given our dysfunctional relationship. He was the exception to the family tradition. He disliked the idea of military service. He refused to speak to me the whole time I was in the service and after I got back. I suppose that joining up worked for me in a perverse sense because it got to him."

"That's incredible," Dana said. "Such a simple decision became so complicated."

"Yes, it's true," David continued. "Yale didn't have ROTC. It was banned for a long time and not reinstated until just ten or eleven years ago. If that had existed, I probably would have chosen ROTC. I would automatically have become an officer. I went to OCS, got my commission and went off for three years. To tell the truth, it felt really good to be out of law school, even though I expected to return. The Dean promised I could return without reapplying."

"I can't picture that," Dana said. "You seem so focused, so determined to go after what you want. I can't imagine you being so weary of law school that you would quit. But it doesn't sound like an impulsive decision."

"It does seem strange doesn't it?" David said. "But it's where I was then. I'd done pretty well the first year and the Dean said I could do anything I wanted if I kept my grades up. He virtually promised that I'd get support for a federal circuit court clerkship if I wanted it. I figured I had very little to lose by cutting out for three years. Of course, I could get killed, but I was depressed and willing to risk just about anything. I had no sense of how long the three years would feel. It did provide the impetus for my first wife to end the marriage. That was a good thing.

"Willard tried to talk me out of it but I felt I had to do it. He was right about it not being a good move but, of course, he acknowledged that he had had to find his own way too. After all, he spent three years in the CIA after Yale. He realized later that he had been part of the one American institution that represented everything he came to believe was dangerous for democracy. I felt free once I was away from New Haven. Of course, there were plenty of demands and restrictions. But I've always felt that freedom was a state of mind. Even when I felt like a prisoner at home with my parents or in the marriage, or whatever, I could be free in my own mind. No one could reach me there."

"I see that," she said. "I don't know you that well, but I can see you retreat into your mind. I've never seen anyone quite like you in that way. It's unusual emotional control. I'm a control person but I don't lock up my emotions that way. They find their way out by themselves."

"I knew it was possible that I could be thrown into fighting a war in the desert," David said, "but I wasn't capable at the time of realistically appraising what that would be like. I thought, oh well, it would be exciting and a career boost. The military had regained some status with the public. There was even excitement at the very beginning. Eventually, everyone got worn out. I always liked physical challenges and thought I was pretty well suited to it. I didn't imagine what a boring grind it would be day by day or how unprepared I was to face the decisions, the split second decisions, and the training to develop reflexes to shoot to kill. That may be one reason why I did it, to make myself face physical danger and big moral decisions. It turned out to be my downfall, my Achilles heel."

"I didn't think you had an Achilles heel," Dana said. "But you must know. It's good that you can analyze this and figure out why you did something that seems so unlikely and so contrary to everything about you. I can't figure it out. You're not the kind of person I would ever imagine as joining the military."

"I understand," David said. "That's the way everybody reacted. I never imagined facing so many bullies like the ones I'd faced, or escaped from, as a kid. I thought that part of my life was behind me. Frankly, I didn't deal with them any better than I did as a kid. I was no match for the ruthlessness of guys I met. I lived with more than one sociopath, although I didn't recognize that until later. We make up reasons for people's behavior, excuses to make them seem normal. Later we realize they were not. We wonder why we couldn't see that at the time. We wonder why we didn't stand up for what was right. I'll tell you the whole story sometime."

Dana said simply, "I understand. I'll be ready when you want to."

As they prepared to leave, David felt more at ease about today. For the moment, he pushed out of his mind that they had plunged into physical territory again and that Sue's early return had put him in jeopardy.

"I'll head back to New Haven tonight. That will avoid questions about where I am and who I'm with. I'll get in touch with Richard and Herb first thing tomorrow much as I'd like just to stay with you."

Dana nodded agreement. "It wouldn't work out with Sue here anyway," she said.

"I should check in with Jake," David said as they headed toward the door, "just to be sure everything is okay between us. I'm going to call him tomorrow."

"I haven't said anything to make him suspicious or doubt me," Dana said, "although he knows I'm pulling back from our relationship. We haven't talked for a while. It sounds right to talk to him. Maybe he's found out more that will help you. You should keep your relationship with him strong. He's loyal to you and you want to keep it that way. Anyway, this may sound abrupt, but we have no idea what the future holds for us. It would be a stretch to imagine that we'll be together a year from now. Your friendship with Jake goes back a long way."

David was startled by the conviction behind her statement and gazed at her, silently. "You're right of course," he said, feeling the sting of her remark. "I know you need space now. I respect that and it's probably best for me too. Everything is such a goddamn mess right now."

They parted with a quick embrace as they passed through the foyer, aware of the need for caution. You never know who is watching, he thought. What if Jake is coming to surprise, or check on, Dana? He would know exactly what happened. I'll talk to him tomorrow and be prepared to cover for this in case we've been seen.

40

David arrived home to darkness, inside and out. It was after midnight. Leaving all the lights off struck him as an assertive action on Lucille's part. What could he expect? He hadn't communicated with her and had been gone for the whole day. As he walked quietly through the downstairs area, he was overcome by fatigue. He had no stomach for a confrontation. The house was still and he heard no sound anywhere. He crept up the stairs and went into the office on the second floor. Without changing, he lay down on the day bed. He would call Jake early. He'd be able to detect any tension in Jake's voice. He wouldn't tell Jake yet about Nick's trial.

Dana wouldn't be likely to talk with Jake this week. With the latest outbreak of violence in Yemen and Syria, the GCN was in high gear and she might even be sent on her first trip to the region. One of the trouble spots in Africa was expected to break out into violence again too. Conflict and violence spread like wildfire through the Middle East-North Africa region. The altered map of the region, altered by a violent cycle of domination and submission, sect by sect, had not brought any noticeable increase in peace and harmony. It was like, as some commentator had said, there were dozens of ISIS and Al Qaeda branch offices, along with dozens of other sectarian franchises operating throughout the area, constantly morphing into new organisms, like a parallel universe composed of viruses. The odd thing was that once these outlier groups gained power, they sometimes pretended to be governments in order to hold onto power. But that was just a device. Behind the lure of providing government stood the threat of violence as the enforcer. It was impossible to predict where the next firestorm would be or what the next accelerant might be. At the heart of it was the perennial tension, with periodic outbreaks of violence, between Israel and its captive, Palestine. Year after year, decade after decade, that hostile relationship seemed to be the cauldron that brought other violent episodes to the point of boiling over.

David would have relished a career in conflict resolution on this level. He envied Dana for being right in the middle of it. Maybe he'd still end up there, especially if he didn't get to the High Court but managed to keep his reputation intact. Perhaps he would not be content with any prize he acquired once the pursuit was over.

He resolved to go easy on the conversation with Jake and then call Richard. He hoped that Richard could see him today. That meant going back to the city or waiting until evening when Richard would be home in Westport. That would be better. The big question now was whether to agree to testify. He'd talk to Herb as well. Should he ask each to keep what he said in confidence, that is, to keep it from the other? That was awkward. Lawyers performed better when they thought they were trusted. They would comply with whatever David wanted but would wonder what he was afraid of. With these thoughts swirling in his head, David drifted into restless sleep, waking three or four times until he got up feeling his usual fatigue at 6:00 a.m.

David had breakfast with the boys. Lucille came in and out of the kitchen several times. She made no direct contact but seemed to relish being as intrusive as possible. He decided to go to his New Haven office where he could have privacy for his phone calls. He felt apprehensive. After the boys went out for the school bus, he got ready quickly and left a note for Lucille that he'd be in New Haven all day and had a meeting at night. That would cover seeing Richard in Westport at his home.

41

David got to the New Haven courthouse and headed up on one of the staff elevators to his tenth floor office. The courthouse was only a dozen years old but already showing signs of poor maintenance. The cycle of state overspending for political advantage, followed inevitably by gloomy announcements of deficits and urgent pleas for austerity, was maddening. David's office overlooked the predominantly Gothic architecture of the university campus. He could identify nearly every building in which he had lived or attended class. The campus view was a welcome change.

As soon as David was settled, he dialed Jake's mobile phone. Jake answered immediately. "David," he said sharply, "Where have you been? What's going on?"

"Hey, I'm sorry not to keep in touch but, actually, very little. Nothing new as far as the status of the file is concerned and nothing new from Bradley or the White House, not that I expected to hear anything. How about you? Anything else turn up?"

"Nada," Jake said. "Any thoughts about what I should do next?" An uncomfortable silence followed, broken finally by David.

"Not really," David said, before blurting out the information about Nick's visit, under pressure to say the words he'd previously decided to withhold. "I heard from a guy in my platoon, and he wants me to testify in a trial he's involved in. I suspect he may be the one who messed with the files."

Even before he had finished divulging the information, David regretted his impulsive disclosure, overriding his better judgment. Jake responded with acute interest. "What's this guy's name? What was his rank? What's the trial about?"

"He was my platoon sergeant, a rough guy, capable sergeant though. He's been arrested for homicide and attempted homicide. Shot his girlfriend and killed her male friend. That's all I know. I have to talk to Richard today about how to handle this, whether to testify or not, how it might impact me. That's all for now but I'll keep you posted. I don't need this. Bad timing."

Jake wasn't through. "So you think he might have taken the file or destroyed it? Why?"

"I don't know. Just a hunch. Nothing to hang that speculation on, but I'll keep in touch."

"Okay," Jake said, "but wouldn't you support the sergeant if he's in trouble?"

David felt on the spot. "I would ordinarily—but he's looking for me to embellish the truth, make things up."

"Oh. Okay, keep in touch, and I'll follow up any leads that we can get."

"Right," David replied quickly. "Will do. Thanks for helping out. How's everything with you?"

"Oh okay," Jake said unenthusiastically with a note in his voice that David interpreted as disappointment. "I'm doing fine. Work is real busy, and that's all I have time for." Then, abruptly, Jake added, "Have you talked to Dana recently? She's in New York all the time and I haven't talked with her in," pausing, "quite a few days. Thought you might be in touch with her. I know you like to talk with her, right?"

David paused to plan his response, stammering, "Yeah, we talked a little while ago, I forget exactly when. A few days ago, just a brief conversation, mostly about her work with GCN, which I'm really interested in, you know. With the President emphasizing peaceful conflict resolution, I wanted to see if Dana had any insights into what she may be thinking, you know, for the nomination process."

There was awkward silence on the other end, after David's disjointed response. Jake paused for what seemed to be minutes. "Oh, yeah? When did you get interested in GCN private dispute resolution stuff? When was that? Why did you talk? I don't get it."

Jake had a habit of piling question on question. It was a good thing that wasn't allowed in court. It was impossible to keep track of all the questions and their implications. "A few days ago, I think." David had to decide whether to say that they had seen each other, as opposed to talking on the phone. He decided against it although his heart was racing."

"Okay," Jake said, letting go for the moment. "We'll catch up real soon. Keep me informed. Give Richard my best. Take care of yourself."

"Sure will, Jake," David said, wondering if Jake's last statement was an expression of concern for his welfare or a threat to it.

"And if you talk to Dana," Jake said, "tell her to fucking give me a call." He paused, probably aware of the bitterness the remark reflected, and added, "Forget that. Forget I said that."

"Okay, Jake. Talk to you soon." Any illusion of comfort evaporated with Jake's biting remark.

After he ended the call, David sat still and let his heart slow down. Take it easy with the Dana thing. It's too risky, he thought, realizing that he was focused only on the implications for himself, not for Jake, and not for Dana. "What a selfish bastard I am," he said aloud. "Always thinking of myself first."

42

After checking in with his law clerks, David was assured that no urgent business required his presence in Hartford. Relieved, he flipped to Richard's number on his cell phone, reaching him on the first ring.

"When can I catch up with you?" David asked. "I need to talk to you about a legal matter in person. Do you have any time today? I could catch a train this morning or drive to Westport this evening."

"Sure," Richard replied without hesitating. "I'm jammed all day but I'm going home early because I have to go to a school play tonight. I should be home by 4:30. I'd have an hour at least. Will that work?"

"Terrific," David said. "I'll be there at 4:30. Shall I pick you up at the train?"

"No thanks," Richard replied. "The car's at the commuter lot."

"Thanks, that's perfect."

David needed to decide how much to tell Richard and to emphasize that this was an attorney-client conversation. He needed Richard's advice and protection. He'd have to disclose details to let him know what was at stake. He'd better touch base with Bradley too. It wasn't easy to motivate himself to deal with these tasks. He'd play it by ear whether to tell Bradley about the trial. He didn't want Bradley to pull back in his efforts.

No answer. Bradley was back in Washington and, no doubt, managing a demanding schedule. He was expert at juggling a dozen things at once. David called back in half an hour.

"Just touching base," David began. "We haven't talked in a week. Anything new on your end?"

"Great timing," Bradley said. "I was going to call you later. There's promising news. Lehman called me late yesterday and said the President wants to move forward on the nomination, starting by interviewing her short list. You're on it. Lehman asked about the missing file. When I said there was nothing new he said that would be part of the FBI background check, if it reaches that stage."

"The President wants to meet you," Bradley added. "I know she's meeting with at least six candidates. It would be the end of the week, Thursday or Friday."

"I can do either," David said, checking his watch, excited at the news. "That's great. What happens next?"

"Let's plan on Thursday. Come down on Wednesday night. I'll try to arrange the meeting for first thing in the morning. You can stay with us in Bethesda."

"Fabulous," David said.

"Check with me tomorrow and I'll confirm the day," Bradley said.

David made a quick decision not to tell him about the trial until he got there. "Who will be with the President?"

"Definitely Lehman, probably the President's Chief of Staff, maybe Lehman's deputy. Probably that's it. Sometimes the President clears everybody out and talks one on one. Is there anything new I should know?"

"Nothing that comes to mind," David said.

43

David drove to Westport in the early afternoon on Wednesday, just missing the brutal rush hour traffic heading south on I-95. When he arrived in Westport, he decided to stop for coffee rather than get to Richard's house early. Because Richard's wife, Constance, worked as counsel for a law firm in the city, only the dogs would be home. David could have arranged with Richard to go into the house, which he had done many times, but neither of them had thought to mention it. He didn't feel comfortable doing it on his own.

He wouldn't have to worry about privacy. Richard and Constance were loyal friends and good lawyers. There was no concern about confidentiality. They made a point of avoiding career talk to avoid conflict of interest problems. David enjoyed sitting in the coffee shop for a half hour. Although the place was crowded and noisy, he found it conducive to organizing his thoughts. Strange how solitude can exist in in the midst of noise and activity. He had a friend once who wrote his mystery novels sitting in a fast food restaurant.

David's extreme caution about protecting his past troubled him on some level. He would prefer to be open and trusting with his close friends. He envied people who could do that, revealing themselves as they are. David attributed his inability to his withdrawal from his world after the incident with his brother. He was responsible, of course, but his parents shared in that even if not directly. Neither he nor they imagined that his resentment would metastasize as it did. It was as though an impenetrable fog concealed the fact that he and his brother stood on the very edge of a precipice—until the moment of truth.

It was time to drive the short distance to Richard's Pennsylvania-style stone farmhouse in one of Westport's finest neighborhoods. The house was situated on a large, lightly wooded, landscaped lot. The house looked as though it had sprouted centuries ago from the earth on that very spot. Considering their successful careers in the city, the Sellers lived well but modestly. David reflected that he also had made a substantial income when he was with the firm. He surrendered that when he accepted the Court appointment. There was never enough money now.

Although it was a sacrifice to leave practice so early in his life, the reality was that he had been bored with the routine. He much preferred to work without being preoccupied with winning or losing. He had no quarrel with his former partners. It was a question of what suited his legal interests. He felt that making policy, rather than judging disputes, was his forte. The judicial option had come along first. He thought of it as merely one move in his career but he realized that his future could blow up in the perilous world of politics.

Before David could ring the bell, Richard opened the front door and greeted him warmly. After getting cold drinks in the kitchen, they sat in Richard's home office, a large, oak-paneled room with bookshelves extending across two walls. He had all the latest technology for work and entertainment, including a communication system that enabled him to join the firm's video conferencing network when he worked from home. He was relaxed and didn't seem pressed for time but David could see that he wanted to hear the reason for the visit.

"It's great to see you," Richard began. "We don't get together often enough. I miss our squash games and the pick-up basketball too. I still play squash at the Yale Club but my better judgment finally sidelined me with basketball. I can't race up and down the court the way I used to in college. It was fun while it lasted and winning the Ivy twice in our four years was a highlight. But tell me what's on your mind? You sounded serious."

"It is serious," David said. "I need advice about how to handle a demand that I got to testify in a criminal trial out of state, in Philadelphia, involving a guy from my old unit in the Army, my platoon sergeant."

"No kidding," Richard said with surprise. "I didn't figure it was anything like that. I thought it had to do with the Supreme Court business."

"This could impact that," David said, revealing his concern.

"Yes, I suppose so," Richard agreed. "Is your testimony a problem? What's the trial about? Can you give me some background? The more detail, the better."

"Yes, of course. I do want you to consider this a formal legal representation, for purposes of confidentiality. This is a very sensitive time for me and I know how meticulous you are."

"Absolutely. Nothing leaves this room unless you authorize me to speak to someone about it," Richard assured.

44

et me frame the issue and give some background," David said, "and then fire away with questions, anything you need to know. The sergeant, Nick Serrano, has been charged in state court with homicide and attempted homicide. There were two victims, one dead, the other barely survived. The information I have is that he's charged with second-degree murder. There's no claim of premeditation. Apparently, it was a relationship breakup that went sour. Serrano's lady friend didn't come home one night so he went out looking for her with his Glock 22, 44-caliber handgun. He found her with a male friend, just a friend I understand, in the parking lot of the bar where she worked. Serrano shot first without asking questions. He killed the guy, and nearly killed her. He has a criminal record. He was a competent sergeant, although we didn't get along much of the time."

"So where do you come in? I don't see why he'd want you to testify."

"His lawyer has come up with a PTSD defense. He's had some fairly serious sentences for violent crimes, mostly arising in domestic disputes or fights that got out of hand. He faces heavy time if he's convicted. His lawyer needs testimony about the traumas he experienced in Iraq. I spent more than a year with him on base in the States and in Iraq. I also was a first-hand observer and directly involved in an event, really a series of events in 2007 and 2008, which got him informally disciplined. He was damn lucky it didn't get to the division level with a CID investigation. His lawyer thinks I can lay the groundwork for a PTSD defense."

"Was he ever diagnosed with PTSD or did he at least report symptoms?" Richard asked. "If he never laid the groundwork, he might have a tough time, especially if he was denied benefits."

"I'm not sure about all that," David said. "He told me he was diagnosed, but I can't rely on what he says. He came to see me unannounced at the Supreme Court one day not long ago. He was aggressive and demanding, threatening actually. He always was a bully and he's worse now."

"Threatening? What did he threaten? Does he have some hold on you? I would say you should avoid getting involved unless there's more to it. He sounds like a problem guy who could be a problem for you. Who's his lawyer, by the way? Maybe I know him."

"The lawyer's name is Myron Stewart, if I got the name right. Familiar?"

"Oh, my God. he sure as hell is. Stewart is a well-known, I almost said notorious, criminal defense lawyer in the New York area. His main office is in the city but he's admitted in New Jersey and Pennsylvania. He's a rough customer but, I have to say, a very effective lawyer in his own way. He's the kind of lawyer who gives lawyers a bad name. He's loud, aggressive, a bully. Ruthless too. He's willing to do just about anything. But he performs very well in a courtroom. He has a reputation for getting what he wants. He's never been suspended, but I don't know why. It sounds like your guy went to the best, or maybe I should say, the worst. You would think this guy would antagonize jurors and judges, but somehow he does well with juries. Lots of DAs are scared shitless by him. He'll use every underhanded trick in the book, personal stuff, you know. He'll go after them and make them look bad. A DA who is running for re-election is a sitting duck for him. Judges give him a lot of slack too. They know he can make them look bad. He has confidence oozing out of every pore, works a lot for organized crime figures and politicians in trouble."

"That's bad news," David said with alarm. "Just what I need. No wonder Nick had the balls to barge into my chambers and demand that I testify for him or . . ." David said, pausing.

"Or what?" Richard broke in.

"Or he'd smear me with accusations," David said reluctantly, "accusations that I participated in covering up his misconduct in Iraq. I was his commanding officer, and I bent over backwards to protect him, to help him avoid serious punishment. I probably didn't tell the brigade commander who conducted the interrogation hearing everything."

"Probably?" Richard asked.

"There was a big question about whether I authorized some missions, three actually, to root out insurgents. Al Qaeda had murdered an Iraqi woman, Nick's woman. We all cooperated not to let the incident explode in the press. A lot of civilians got killed in the process and two of our people, one male, one female, got killed too."

45

t did not go to the CID, I take it," Richard said. "So there was no court martial. Only informal discipline?"

"Right. The report was conveyed back to the States pursuant to protocol, presumably to Fort Benning. From there it would have been uploaded to the SIPRNET. The report contains a sanitized version of the events that happened. It didn't mean a damn to anyone then but if it all comes out now, it won't look good for anybody, all the way up the command chain."

"You were interviewed under oath, I assume," Richard asked. David nodded affirmatively.

"Did you tell the truth in the investigation report?" Richard asked, "and in your testimony to the commander?"

David paused. "I suppose not the whole story," he said cautiously, searching Richard's eyes for a reaction. "I went along with what Command wanted. Protect our own. Don't let the media get hold of it. We had a couple of embedded journalists in our company that were always snooping. At the time, they didn't even know the informal hearing was taking place. One of the journalists eventually got on this story and he's still around. Serrano had been involved with an Iraqi woman and disregarded my order to end it. There was more to it, other soldiers and other women. Eventually, AQI retaliated. You know they hated any interaction with Americans. There's more. Her father was a sheikh. He was an important Al Anbar Awakening leader. It's a mess but you can see there is a good deal to lose by refusing to testify at the trial, if Nick retaliates. Of course, there's a lot to lose by testifying too. Stewart could really put me in a spot by trying to bully me to lie—to lay the foundation for a PTSD defense. There's more to the whole thing but that's enough to give you the picture."

"Does he have a psychiatrist lined up to testify about PTSD if there's enough evidence to establish the underlying trauma?"

"I don't know," David replied. "I imagine so. It isn't difficult to get a psychiatrist to support PTSD. Anybody can get an expert to say whatever they want."

"When's the trial? Is there a chance that you can defer it until after you get the nomination, which I hope you do, and get confirmed? Then we can tell him to go to hell."

"I doubt it. The trial is scheduled for the first week in September. There's no telling when the nomination will be made. This is really confidential but Bradley just told me that the President is doing a first round of interviews. It

125

looks as though I'm on the short list for that anyway. I'm going down to D.C. next week."

"Great. What about the record? You mentioned a written record, which is standard. It's just about as standard for it to be lost or *misplaced*," Richard said, laughing. "Do you have a copy? Did you ever see it?"

"That's another problem." David admitted. "We can assume the print record got back to Fort Benning when the company, the brigade actually, was sent back. And we know, or at least surmise, that it got uploaded to the SIPR-NET sometime after 2009 when the Army went electronic. But it appears that the written report has gone missing and the digital record has been corrupted. Jake checked into it and so far hasn't gotten any leads to solve the problem. Of course, I'm not so sure I want it accessible. But Serrano may have stolen the print record as his trump card."

"This gets more involved, intriguing actually. It would be an interesting challenge to unravel it if there weren't so much at stake for you," Richard said.

"Exactly," David said, smiling. "I figure it had to be Serrano or someone who did it for him. That's easy, as you know. So many people have access. Serrano had protection from Command in Iraq. He was the guy who could get anything for anybody. He probably did the same at Benning. Anybody could have corrupted the record and stolen the print copy. Serrano went back there after the deployment. He never went back to combat again. He went off the deep end after his woman was slaughtered. We haven't had any contact for a long time, since we left Benning in 2009.

"I did hear from another guy in the platoon," David continued, "who also has been approached by Nick. Nick did have a rough time, mainly of his own doing. He got attached to this Iraqi girl probably in her late teens. He was already married, but I think his wife was cheating. He also ran a dating service for other guys, officers too, and that probably was the pretext for the AQI attack on the sheikh's family. The girl was the logical target because of what she did. Nick went nuts after this happened. He wanted revenge. He begged me to order him to root out the AQI thugs who did it. I'm sure Stewart would want me to lie and say I did. It could be a brutal cross-examination too. I'm not sure I could survive all that and still be a viable candidate. What do you think I should do?"

46

This is tough," Richard said with a troubled look on his face. "I want to see if there's a way to avoid a head-on collision between the trial and the nomination. I'm thinking we could get the trial postponed or substitute a deposition or a statement that the prosecutor could see. That could lead to a plea bargain that both sides could live with. It would extricate you without taking the witness stand. You're right that either or both sides could make you look bad. I worry that the President would be gun-shy and discount you as a candidate based on this baggage alone. Who else knows about this? Bradley? Lehman?"

"Jake and Bradley know something about it," David replied hesitatingly, "Dana too."

"Dana? Why Dana?" Richard asked, glancing at David.

"We've talked a few times. You know we rode back from New Hampshire that day and I told her some of this," David admitted. "She's a good listener and smart too."

Richard's skepticism was revealed on his face. "You knew way back then?" he asked, his voice conveying mild disapproval.

"Yes, I did and, yes, I said nothing," David replied defensively. "I didn't think it was going to be a big problem. Larry, another guy in my unit, told me he talked to Nick. After that, Nick came to see me, and I could see it was going to be trouble."

Richard was silent for a moment, looking away. "Are you going to tell Bradley the whole story before the White House meeting? And Lehman? What about the President, in fact?" Richard's challenging tone surprised David.

"Bradley knows that I've been asked to testify in a trial. As for the others, I'd prefer not to, especially if we may be able to avoid the problem. It could be fatal to my candidacy just to reveal it."

"Right, I know," Richard said without eye contact. "Is there anything else I should know about this?" He paused. "Then we have to talk about what you want me to do."

Despite David's reluctance to discuss further vulnerability, he added, "First, I'll mention two things. Before I went on the bench, when I was working for the Senator, I went with him on a legislative fact-finding mission to Baghdad. We stayed in the Green Zone, of course. As you might expect, it was mostly a window-dressing tour and didn't accomplish much.

"During those months when I was still in Washington, I thought a lot about the Iraqi woman's family, the ones who survived I mean. I wanted to apologize for what happened, to make up for it, get it off my back. I felt I didn't do everything I could have to protect the woman. If I'd put a stop to the relationship, she wouldn't have been killed and the others too. It was dangerous in Ramadi."

David went on. "The Senator put pressure on the Colonel to send me in a small convoy of Humvees. We went to the house where the woman's family had lived. I had picked up enough Arabic to say what I wanted to.

"I was able to speak to a few people. It didn't go too well. The aunt started accusing me and all the women were crying. The men got angry. They were all hostile. They felt the Americans had caused all this. They blamed me. I imagine they may have been harassed by Al Qaeda since then and their lives became miserable, even more miserable than before. The soldiers who accompanied me finally insisted that we get out of there. So it went quite badly, and I suppose got into some report somewhere. I was in Iraq one other time with a State Department delegation. I thought about giving it another try, but there was no cooperation when I sounded them out. Probably just as well."

"That sounds right to me," Richard interjected. "I would have advised against taking that risk. It never works, just stirs things up and increases animosity. You're damn lucky it didn't blow up."

"The other thing just for your information," David continued, "is that our company had journalists embedded. One journalist, with the *Washington Post*, was also planning a book. He spent time with various platoons, including mine. Name was Caruso, Frank Caruso. I think he published a book and got a documentary produced too. He was always nosing around, particularly to find out what was going on after the incident at Ramadi. The brass didn't want him to find out about the investigation for obvious reasons. There was definitely pressure to bury the incident, which resulted in Nick getting a better deal than he should have. But, since the local sheikh—the girl's father—kept coming to the base to complain about what had happened, it was hard to keep it quiet."

"I understand," Richard said. "That happens all the time. The military is afraid of that kind of publicity. It can blow sky high, ruin careers, even reach into the Pentagon. It could also ignite an ICC investigation and you know what that means."

"There's more to it," David interrupted. "Caruso wrote a story later about what happened there, mentioning that a lot of civilians were killed. In fact, it was that article that gave me the idea to visit the survivors. I've seen Caruso's byline in the media. If he gets wind of the trial and my testimony, he could show up and turn it into a circus."

47

He's bound to figure out everything that happened," David said, "a cover-up and a whitewash. That kind of publicity would be disastrous for me not to mention the military in general. If Nick and his guys didn't intend to kill everybody in sight, they didn't avoid it either. This is an IED waiting to be detonated. Caruso works out of Washington so he will hear about the trial."

"Whew," Richard said, letting a sigh escape, "this is more complicated than I thought. We need to simplify the situation, minimize the risk of damage. First off, I think you're okay not mentioning this to Lehman or the President for now. We don't have to speculate about the trial. We don't want to ruin your chances when it may not materialize. I'll get in touch with Serrano's lawyer, much as I dislike the guy's tactics. If I can placate him while we stall, it may take the heat off and you can concentrate on strengthening your position with the White House.

"As far as the incident goes," Richard said, "it happened in heavy combat during the final phase of the 2007-08 surge, right?"

"You could say that, although technically, the surge was over," David said.

"I'm a little fuzzy about that. I've done a fair amount of military law practice. I've represented quite a few veterans on criminal matters. I fell into that groove because not too many lawyers were interested in it. My law school professor became a good friend. He's still the leading expert, but I know my way around. It seems to me that your situation can give rise to persuasive arguments justifying what you did, without sounding like a Nuremberg-type excuse. If it seems best for you to testify to avoid a blow up, we'll try to come up with a strategy. But my first choice is to avoid it entirely if we can."

"That would be great," David said. "It's by far the best outcome."

"It's crucial to keep the focus on Nick's trial," Richard said, "his problems, not yours. We want to avoid a story breaking about a war atrocity. This is a closed matter that goes back more than fifteen years. As you well know, there's never been a thorough study on Iraq like the Vietnam Veterans Readjustment Study and we don't want to get anyone in Washington excited about doing one now. There *should* have been a study like that for the sake of the country. But as with all wars and the aftermath, war fatigue set in. Then the so-called post-war period mutated into an extension of the war or maybe a new war, in either case, a forever war. Our goal is to keep the lid on that affair in Ramadi."

A concerned look clouded Richard's face. "I have to say something else. I don't want to load it on or get you worried. First tell me, did you resign from the service when you completed your reserve commitment or were you discharged?"

"I resigned my commission. I knew I'd finished that part of my life. I knew I wouldn't want to go back in, get reactivated or rejoin. So I finished my eight year obligation and resigned."

"That's what I recalled, but just wanted to be sure. You're not subject any longer to military discipline, court martial that is?"

"Right," David answered, wondering what Richard was getting at.

"You know about MEJA, right, the Military Extraterritorial Jurisdiction Act? Do you remember that? A lot of people are not aware of it."

"I am, but I didn't think of it," David replied.

"Technically," Richard said, "you could be prosecuted for a felony that you committed while you were in the service. You're subject to prosecution in a civilian federal court. Of course it would have to be a federal felony on which the statute of limitations has not run. I'd say that, after the time that has passed, it would have to be murder or conspiracy to commit murder."

"My God, you're right," David said slowly. "There's no limitation on a murder prosecution. But is that true for conspiracy to commit murder?"

"Yes," Richard said without hesitation. "I believe so. This has hardly ever happened. But we need to avoid a situation where some ambitious federal prosecutor who wants to run for governor or campaign for the federal bench gets the bright idea to bring a murder conspiracy prosecution against you. It would be a stretch I suppose. The theory would be that you conspired to murder the Iraqi civilians in retaliation for what AQI did. MEJA isn't used very often and it would be a fairly long shot but it's not impossible. It's been used mainly for civilian contractors and in a few notorious cases, like the case of Steven Green, which you remember I'm sure."

"I sure do. I knew about that incident. It happened not long before I got to Iraq. I was in officer training school when it happened. It took place in a different area, south of Baghdad, but when Serrano's rampage happened, it crossed my mind. I was afraid the press might call it a war crime. I never imagined that, as the commanding officer, I could be charged with conspiracy to commit murder. Serrano claims I authorized the retaliation. That sends chills up my spine, but I'm glad you thought of it. It's a shock to contemplate. That would change everything, from being in jeopardy politically to being in jeopardy for my life."

48

We have to keep MEJA in mind. And we need to keep the focus off Iraq and solely on Serrano's problems."

"How do we do that?" David asked. "The problem is he wants me to testify that he experienced traumas in Iraq, this one in particular."

"But if his lawyer directs you to, let's say, ordinary traumas, you shouldn't volunteer anything about this incident," Richard said. "You were together for over a year in combat, right? There must have been traumas on a daily basis. Stewart might prefer to stay with safe traumas and leave the Ramadi incident alone. The prosecutor certainly isn't going to ask you to expand on the traumas that Serrano experienced. The prosecutor may not know anything about this whole business unless somebody tells him, which is why we need to keep this out of sight."

"That makes sense," David said. "What happens next? Should I tell Bradley the whole story before I go to the White House next week? He wouldn't want to withhold information from the President. It's amazing how he survives in the political arena. He's the one who made this possible for me with his contacts and his personal credibility. Do I owe it to Bradley to tell him everything, let him know all the risks?"

"As a friend to you and Bradley, I'd have to say that's a personal decision for you to make. As your lawyer, I'd say what will happen with the trial is speculative. It may never happen. If it does, you may be able to get through it unscathed. As a lawyer, my advice is not to tell him now. Go ahead with the meeting. It's very much preliminary, I'd imagine. That's my advice as your lawyer. But you have to decide what you owe Bradley as a friend."

"I'm comfortable with your legal advice for now," David said, relieved. "But what if the President asks me whether there's anything I know of that could embarrass the White House or impede my chances of getting confirmed if it became known? I've faced that question I can't tell you how many times in the past ten years, for my Senate job, my clerkships, and the Connecticut Supreme Court appointment."

"I'd say," Richard replied without hesitating, "you should answer in a way that will appear truthful in retrospect if the Serrano mess comes out, but is so general that it won't alarm the President or Lehman and won't lead to additional questions now."

David was quiet for a moment. "How's this? 'Madam President, as you know, I've had a great many experiences during my life, including a long deployment in Iraq during the surge. Then there's my political work, legal work, and judicial work. I suppose there have been any number of things I've said or done that someone might take issue with or criticize, but I would answer your question in the negative.' Is that too long? Is it evasive? Would it lead to more questions?"

"It's basically what I had in mind. Work on the language. It sounds stiff and contrived. And cut it in half. Your delivery will be important. I just thought about your domestic situation. What about that? Where does it stand? Can you hold off a divorce, if that's what is going to happen, until later in the fall?"

"I hope so," David said with doubt crossing his face. "It'll end in a divorce. I'm sure of that. I think I can hold it off for a while. Lucille is unpredictable. With her alcohol and prescription drug problems, I never know what to expect except that she can be vindictive. Did I tell you? She talked to John Morehead and he called to assure me that he wouldn't do anything without letting me know. He said if it goes to a divorce, he's willing to help us to work things out amicably. I've always gotten along with him but, of course, there's no assurance. Then when I was reluctant to waive a conflict right away, he got hostile. Our conversation ended badly. I don't trust him. I could force him to recuse himself since we've both been close socially with him and his wife for years and he's done legal work for both of us. But she could go to someone a lot worse. I'd like Herb to represent me, if he agrees. I haven't asked him about it. Do you think he'd represent me, or would he feel there is a conflict?"

"I feel confident that he'd represent you. He's never represented Lucille, right?" David nodded in agreement. "He wouldn't let you down but, of course, she might try to get him recused. She could end up a lot worse too if you were to get another lawyer from the shark school."

"I know you have a school performance to get to. Is there anything else we need to talk about?"

"We've covered it. I'll make some notes about our conversation, just reminders, but I'll keep this information on my home computer. Constance and I keep our law practices completely separate and private. I'll get in touch with Serrano's lawyer within the next few days. I'll let you know what comes of it."

"You can go to Washington with a clear mind. It's in your lawyer's hands. That gives you a layer of insulation. We can talk when you get back. I won't share this with Herb—but later, after you consult him, you can decide if you want us to exchange information back and forth. No one else in the firm will know the details. My purpose in talking with Stewart is to quiet things down, not to give assurances, but to let him know it's not being ignored."

"Great, thanks. I feel relieved to know that you're on top of this. The MEJA business is scary. I'll put that out of my mind, but it's something I'll have to consider."

"Take care. Focus on what you need to do and feel free to call or text any time day or night. No kidding. Any time at all."

They walked to the door and shook hands warmly. David proceeded to his car for the drive home. He decided to give Dana a call. Before he got on the highway, he'd text her and then stop for a call if she was free to talk. Tomorrow he would call Bradley to finalize the White House meeting.

49

Before David reached the highway, he received a text from Dana. He pulled into a Dunkin' Donuts parking lot, and sat with coffee at a corner table in the nearly empty shop. She answered on the first ring.

"Hey, haven't talked to you in a few days. I've been missing you," he said easily, although he had barely thought of her since returning from New York. "Is everything good? Are you at work?"

"I'm at work. We're in the middle of another crisis in Africa, Sudan again. I may go there with a negotiating team any day now. I'm just waiting for the word. What's happening? Is there anything further about the trial?"

"Nothing new but I just left Richard's house. He's going to represent me. He'll call Nick's lawyer. I won't have to deal with Nick from now on. Richard will try to come up with a plan to avoid or at least minimize my role."

"Great," she said, sounding relieved.

"Bradley got a call from Lehman. The President wants to do a first round of interviews with candidates. I'm in the group. I'm waiting for confirmation of when I'll go to the White House this coming week. Of course, it's just preliminary, a first cut."

"Wonderful," Dana exclaimed enthusiastically. "Are you going to tell Lehman and the President about the trial?"

"Not at this point. Richard thinks it would create complications over something that may never happen. He's hoping that I might not have to testify at all. I'm not as optimistic as he is but he advised me to keep the trial business to myself for now."

"What about Bradley? Shouldn't he be told?"

"He said it wasn't necessary to tell Bradley yet."

"Are you sure that's Richard's advice?" Dana asked.

"Of course. What do you mean?" David asked.

"I'm just wondering if that came from Richard or if that's what you want to do. I feel badly for Bradley. He depends on his reputation for being a straight shooter. Don't you trust Bradley to handle the information?"

"It's not that I don't trust him. It would burden him with information he doesn't need to know right now."

"That's bullshit and you know it," she said angrily. "You sound like a political hack, using language like that."

"Those were Richard's words and he might—"

"Excuse me," Dana said, cutting him off. "Nice lawyerly language is what I should have said, legal-political bullshit language."

"Richard is worried that Bradley might feel he has to disclose it to the White House right away."

"That's precisely it, isn't it? It's all about you. Isn't that selfish, to jeopardize not only Bradley's reputation for the sake of getting something you want but to mislead the President too? Don't they deserve better?"

David could feel his temper rising in the face of her unexpected attack. "Richard says just cool it for now. It may not amount to anything. It would be the kiss of death to my candidacy. Why the hell should I do that?"

"It's your life and your reputation," Dana said. "Of course, you've got your lawyer's advice as an excuse for not making a moral decision. Sounds like you'll just perpetuate the cover-up."

Stunned, David replied, "That's a low blow I didn't expect from you, with all that's happened between us."

"With all what's happened? Not much. And not much more in the future if that's the way you handle moral decisions. Look, I have to go."

Anxious to change the subject and keep her on the phone, David asked, "What's going on with Jake? I touched base with him very briefly earlier today. He was a little jumpy, I thought."

"You called him? We talked for a while the other day, and he got pretty aggressive, wanting to know what was going on. He thinks I'm cheating on him. I told him I was busy with work, and I needed to concentrate on my career. He said, 'That's bullshit. You're messing with somebody else. I know it, and I don't like it.' Frankly, I felt alarmed. I have no intention of going back there. You should also leave him alone. He might start asking you questions, and I don't think that would lead anywhere positive. It would certainly not serve your interest, since that seems to be the only consideration here."

"This is not good news," David said, ignoring her jab. "I'm sorry you have to put up with that."

"Yes," she replied. "I have to go, have a meeting in a few minutes. Let me know when you're going to Washington."

"I will. Take care of yourself, Dana. I'm sorry that you don't approve the way I'm handling this."

"I don't. It's nothing but the usual self-serving bullshit."

The call ended with simple goodbyes, leaving David agitated about what he was doing and dubious about the future of the relationship.

50

David finished his coffee while deciding what to do next. It was unsettling to hear about her encounter with Jake. It had been a mistake to get involved with Dana. Jake was not a person to mess with. When there were too many secrets to keep in mind, too many deceptions and lies, life became complicated. Dana's sharpness was especially unnerving.

David called Bradley, determined to keep the conversation to basics. The White House meeting would be Thursday afternoon, with Friday as a backup in case the President was engaged in dealing with the African crisis. She had meetings all morning on Thursday. David should arrive in Bethesda on Wednesday after five o'clock, and they'd have a light supper before discussing what to expect in the interview.

David arrived home just after eight. He saw the cryptic note on the kitchen table as soon as he flipped on the light switch. "Gone to my mother's lake house. The boys and I need a break from the tension."

He was relieved in one sense but also felt, strangely, dismissed and ignored. The chasm between them was growing. No doubt, Lucille did what she could to widen the breach. At their ages, the boys probably took it in stride, but as time went on, it could become difficult to reverse. Throughout the day, his mind kept returning to his deep sadness about the boys. The distance between them tore a hole in the fabric of his life and he wondered if they felt it too. It disturbed him that Lucille and the boys would be with her mother at this critical time. She had always sided with her daughter, brushing aside the drinking problem, which they shared.

Later on, he ate a few bites from leftovers in the refrigerator, his unceremonious style of eating just enough to take off the edge. Despite his fatigue, he spent a restless night, accompanied by elusive nightmares. In one, he was about to set out, totally unprepared, on foot in the desert. He was driven by urgency without knowing what his mission consisted of. He had frequent desert dreams with heat, dust in the lungs, fatigue.

In the pre-dawn hours, he had another dream. He was walking first through a marsh, and then on a beach with four men, trying to sidestep flooded areas. The mission seemed desperate, something about saving a small child who was sick or injured. She was present but not within sight. It was nighttime but the marsh was filled with people who paid them no attention. What on earth was that about? He would add these to his store of dreams of doubt and indecision, obstructed missions and nightmares, scenes of war and dying people sprawled about in pools of water and spilled blood.

He had come to understand the structure of his dreams. There was usually a story line drawn from his experience, recent or long past, that he could practically always identify. The subject seemed to be whatever was troubling him at the moment. It was fascinating how the sleeping brain operated, like a film crew, with a director and actors dramatizing his life.

He called his secretary and his clerks to tell them he would not be in before Friday at the earliest, maybe not until Monday, but that they could reach him anytime. He didn't tell them where he was going. The law clerk network was greedy for information and even casual remarks would not stay private for long. Burkhardt always had his ear tuned into the network.

51

David arrived at 6:00 p.m. at Bradley and Ayako's house in a neighborhood of contemporary homes in the area of Bethesda bordering a branch of the Potomac River. He always looked forward to a visit to the authentic Japanese-style home, with furniture and works of art acquired on their many trips to Japan, most of them in Kyoto where Ayako had lived until coming to the United States for college.

After a quiet dinner with the two friends, David retired with Bradley to his office on the third floor. It was easy to slip into a relaxed mood while viewing the dramatic rocky banks and surging rapids. Bradley relayed the news that the meeting was set for Thursday afternoon at four o'clock when the President expected to be through with a day of intense meetings concerning the explosive conflict in the Middle East, resulting in more critical than usual refugee problems in the region. The world's refugee population had risen to a new height. The world community had yet to find solutions for this grave problem since so many countries had posted no trespassing signs at their sea and land borders.

"What do you know about the meeting? Who do you think will be there?" David asked, revealing his anxiety.

"I asked Lehman about that. He'll meet with you first. His deputy, Julie Crimmins, will probably sit in. I'll be at the White House for a meeting earlier in the afternoon. If the timing works out, I might still be there to greet you after you pass through security. Drive directly to the main gate of the White House and identify yourself to the guards. They'll expect you. A staff member will meet you, whether I'm there or not, and take you to Lehman's office. You should plan to arrive at 3:30 p.m. Earlier is okay but they operate on a tight schedule so you'll just spend extra time waiting downstairs. It's best to be right on schedule.

"Lehman and Crimmins will spend twenty to thirty minutes with you. Feel free to ask questions. I'm not sure where the interviews will take place. Sometimes they're in the Map Room, which is on the ground floor of the residence. That area connects with the first floor of the West Wing and the East Wing. It's a fascinating room, with a rich historical background. Lehman is fairly candid with me. He thinks this series of interviews is premature. He'd rather wait until late in the fall because the Senate isn't likely to get moving on anything until then anyway. I get the impression that Lehman is not enthusiastic about your candidacy but not opposed either. I'm not sure of all the reasons.

"The President cares deeply about this vacancy," Bradley continued. "As a lawyer, she knows that Supreme Court appointments are crucial to a President's legacy. She envisions a Court that will operate in the modern world, one that will consider international precedent and human rights declarations, and be tough when it comes to *war on terror* issues that threaten Constitutional rights."

"I can't imagine Congress loosening up on those issues," David said. "What's in it for any legislator to take the risk of supporting less surveillance?"

"She's realistic about that. She has strict standards for military as well as civilian drones. She has a global vision of the world in which the U.S. asserts moral authority but is not cast in the role of the world's policeman. She sees a world that is in balance, but with shifting patterns and rhythms that have to be tolerated in the short term. She wants a Supreme Court that respects precedent but that isn't afraid to apply it in ways that recognize the world we live in today. We should respect but not be held hostage by the past."

"I admire her efforts to protect civil liberties," David said, "and to control the use of Special Forces to do targeted killings, now that the CIA has been reined in. But Congress has other things in mind."

"True," Bradley added. "The President is not anti-military, but she has controlled the CIA and is fighting for civilian control of Special Forces. They're a good alternative to deploying troops every time there's a brushfire to be put out, but they can't have autonomy. It's hard to contain clandestine activity once it gets a foothold. It builds a fortress inside the government."

"I'm not sure I see how this affects her Supreme Court appointments though," David said. "Should I be prepared to talk about foreign policy?"

"No, not necessarily," Bradley said. "But you need to know the way she sees the world. We can't segregate domestic and foreign policy any more. It's all related. It's a different world. She's looking for people who are not afraid to reshape the way we govern. That includes the Court. That doesn't mean precedent gets tossed out the window but she wants justices who are in step with the world we live in now, in the twenty-first century. She's not looking for a radical approach to the law but wants people who are open to fresh approaches to difficult issues."

"What do you think she'll want to talk about?" David asked. "Is she likely to carry the conversation and then gauge my reaction? Will she ask a lot of questions?"

"I'm not sure." Bradley replied. "She can do both well. She was a damn good trial lawyer before she got into politics. She knows how to ask penetrating questions but she knows how to listen too."

"If she's looking for someone with a clear, consistent philosophy and a game plan, like Roberts had when he was being groomed, I'm not the person."

"I don't think she's looking for that as much as flexibility—pragmatism *and* principle. By the way, what's going on with you these days? Is there anything I should know? I like to level with Lehman. He trusts me. The President trusts me too. That's vital to me."

"I can't think of anything," David said, fully aware that he was omitting mention of the trial. "One thing. The marriage situation is getting worse. There's a lot of confrontation. I feel the tension even when I'm not there. Lucille is working to distance the boys from me. I don't have the energy to fight that battle. I'm just hoping for a ceasefire until the nomination is resolved. Herb will represent me."

"Sounds good," Bradley said. "Let's get some sleep. You need to be rested for tomorrow. How are you going to spend your day? I won't be able to spend time with you."

"I'm not sure," David said. "I'll hang out here for a while if that's okay and then head into the District."

"Sure, Bradley said. "We'll both be at work early. Make yourself at home. Use my home gym in the first level or take a swim in the pool."

David felt relieved by Bradley's inherent optimism. But, of course, he realized that he had provided him with a filtered version of his circumstances, one that stripped it of uncertainty and risk.

52

Alone in the guest room, David's mind drifted to his situation and to the close scrutiny to which his war service was bound to be subjected sooner or later. Although the war was never far from his thoughts, his unpleasant memories had generally remained safely secured in his subconscious. Now that the seal had been broken by Nick's arrival, scenes from the past flashed through his conscious mind when he was alone. He was amazed at how many toxic memories seeped out of the dark places in his mind, as dark as Grendel's lair in the Beowulf legend.

What a difference there was in observing war from a safe place. It reminded him of a movie in which a nun who had taken a vow of poverty refused to be interviewed about her work with the poor. 'I have to *live* poverty, not *talk* about it,' she explained. David was aware that he too had written about war experiences from which he had been protected. He had never felt the pain and loss of the devastating injuries that some of his soldiers had. He was troubled by the concept of *moral injury*, which seemed too facile in some respects when it was employed to benefit people who did wrong.

David had criticized veterans who refused to talk to friends, even spouses, about the horrors of war. He said they should make others understand. Without that, war would be perpetuated ad infinitum because it would be a dark secret protected by those who waged it. It would remain that way, playing into the hands of the politicians and profiteers who thrived on war. For them, war was the wild card in the game of foreign policy that enriched them with power or wealth. If we lack the capacity to understand the pain and loss of others, we are destined to be the prisoners of our worst natures. Our species depends on communication and empathy to survive.

And yet the mythology of war is passed from generation to generation by some ancient edict. In recent history, it began to lack the palpable feel of killing except, of course, on the part of terrorist groups outside the margins of the *civilized* world. Still each generation of warfare marches side by side with each war a prelude to the next. With these thoughts swirling through his head, he dropped into fitful sleep.

53

David arrived at the White House earlier than the appointed time. After clearing the first security checkpoint at the front gate, he proceeded to the next and, after being cleared, parked his car and walked to the entrance. He identified himself and was directed to a seat. Ten minutes later, Bradley appeared. "I knew you'd be early," Bradley said, laughing. They chatted for a few minutes until a youthful staff member came for David. "We'll be going directly to Mr. Lehman's office," she said pleasantly. "Have you been here before?"

"Just once," David said, "for a brief ceremony. This is a special occasion." David didn't try to keep track of the circuitous route to Lehman's office. After twenty minutes, he was told Lehman would see him. As they entered his inner office, two other people were seated in the room. After a lukewarm greeting without a handshake, Lehman introduced his assistant, Julie Crimmins, and a deputy chief of staff, Abby, whose last name escaped David. "Glad you could make it, Judge," Lehman said brusquely.

"Feel free to use my first name if you like."

"That's okay," he said leaving the invitation hanging in midair, and went on. "I know it was short notice but the President decided she'd like to start having conversations. It's preliminary, you understand, and I have two warnings. One is that the President expects absolute confidentiality. Keep this conversation to yourself. Don't mention it to anyone, including the fact that it ever took place. If it ever appears in a newspaper story, you're finished."

"Does that include Bradley?" David asked.

"I don't recall stating any exceptions," Lehman said abruptly, with a disapproving look. "Second, the fact that you have been invited here indicates nothing about the final selection process or who the nominee will be. Do you understand this?"

"I do, absolutely," David said, recovering quickly. "I'm grateful to be here."

"There's no reason to be grateful. That's the point," Lehman said dismissively. He went on, "Just to let you know the way President Madison operates: you can anticipate that the conversation will likely be fifteen minutes to a half hour. I'll be present but, occasionally, she decides to talk alone with a candidate. She likes to get a sense of who a person is. As a lawyer, the President has great respect for the Court as an institution, a living institution, and she wants to be sure her choices will contribute in a lasting way to the Court. Unlike some presidents, she makes up her own mind."

As David was about to respond, Lehman asked abruptly, "What's the status of the investigation report? Do you have a copy for me?"

"No," David said. "I'm sorry. Nothing yet. The print copy is missing. The digital record is corrupted. Records like this are kept by the company, battalion, or brigade that made them and then brought back at the end of the deployment, so they frequently go missing at some point. There are too many people who have access to SIPRNET and it's a confusing, disorganized filing system, if you can call it a system at all. I can answer any questions about my service time. I had to refresh my memory when I wrote the books a few years back. I did a lot of research to get things straight."

"That's not good enough. You should know that." Lehman responded. "Not acceptable. We will not let the President walk into an ambush, with all due respect to your memory."

In an effort to shift the conversation to neutral ground on the heels of Lehman's stinging remarks, David ventured, "Is the President considering a study of the wars similar to the NVVRS following Vietnam? Some years ago, a small group of people tried to get Congressional support for a commission. We compiled a list of a hundred names of prominent people, in the arts, writing, public service, non-profits, and some political people. It never got off the ground. That's the trouble with wars. There's never closure because there's no interest in reopening wounds."

Lehman answered dismissively. "What the President is considering or not is inappropriate for me to discuss with you. Your views about that are interesting but irrelevant. But I can say that the President is very concerned about the endless controversy about the government's failure to help veterans. It's been ten years since the VA was criticized for its delays and deceptive record keeping. She is aware that the problem still exists."

Just as David was preparing another attempt to recover civility, a security guard knocked and reported that the President was ready to see them in the Map Room. They followed the guard to the spacious parlor on the first floor. A few minutes after their entry, the President's arrival was announced by her deputy chief of staff, who introduced David to the President.

54

"G ood afternoon, Justice Lawson. Thank you for coming to visit with us on such short notice," the President said with a warm, engaging smile. She appeared relaxed after what must have been a stressful day, immaculately dressed in a burgundy suit that was dramatic and dignified. She had a graceful bearing. David observed that she didn't look any more like a college professor, her original profession, than he did. The year in office had transformed her image into that of a global leader.

"Good afternoon, Madame President, Please just call me David. I'm used to being informal."

"Thank you, David, I'll accept that invitation. I'd make a similar offer but I'm afraid it would shock my staff and everyone else who heard about it. I've heard a great deal about you, and I admire what you've written as well as what you've accomplished in your life so far."

"Thank you. I've tried to keep busy," David acknowledged.

The President went on, unhurried. "Andrew, or perhaps Bradley Thompson, who I understand is a friend of yours, may have explained that I've decided not to wait until fall to have a few conversations regarding the Supreme Court. It's early in the process, and I may add names to the list as we go along. You wouldn't be here, though, unless I felt that you appear qualified for the position. As you can imagine, we have identified other qualified people." David nodded.

"In any event, we have only a half hour," the President added, "and I have a few questions."

"I understand, Madame President, I'm happy to answer anything."

President Madison continued, "First, I'd be interested to know why you chose to go to law school and then made a decision to interrupt your legal study to enlist in the Army. What was so compelling about the service or so unsatisfying about law school that led you to follow that path?"

David smiled at the reference to law school. "It was a little of both. As for why I chose to go to law school, I was following a plan that I had in my mind since junior year of college. As a political science, economics, and philosophy major, I was fascinated by the role of law in society, the public aspects of law. I thought I might practice for a few years and then get into politics. A legal education seemed to be the right foundation for a career in public service."

"I see," the President said. "Then you didn't intend to have a career as a practicing lawyer?"

"That's right. I also thought about going on for a graduate degree in political science, but I wanted to work in the real world, so to speak. I left after one year of law school because I had serious doubts about whether I'd made the right decision. I wasn't interested in the subjects. I couldn't see the big picture. It seemed like a lot of detail that was irrelevant to what I wanted to do. There was another factor. I got married during the summer before law school and it wasn't working out well. It was impulsive. We didn't know each other that well and neither of us was ready. The year was stressful and I felt I was wasting my time. I needed to get away.

"As I talked about leaving school," David continued, "my wife made it clear that she wasn't following me into the Army if I chose to do that. She was going to stay at home with her family and would seek an annulment. That was fine with me. So the plan also enabled me to get away from the marriage. The Dean assured me I could return without a problem. There was no downside to leaving. Besides, I'd believed since childhood that the military was where men were supposed to prove themselves, the traditional rite of passage. I'd never gotten that out of my head. It was a family tradition. Once I'd made the decision, it was a great relief, and I completed my first year better than I'd started it. When I returned, the marriage was over, and I finished without a problem."

"Thank you for being candid about that," the President said. "Now I'd like to ask your overall impression of the military and how combat affected you. I read your book about your combat experience, and my staff provided me with copies of a few articles you've written plus a few talks that you've given. You've been forthright in confronting the military and political leaders about their hypocrisy. You pointed out the dishonesty in failing to level with the public about the reasons for war plus failing to deal with the suicide rate and military sexual assault. My staff tells me that you still speak out on those subjects but have toned it down a great deal since becoming a judge. I'd like to hear in your own words what you think about the present policy on governing the military and on military interventions."

"Of course," David said, without hesitating, grateful for the softball question. The hardballs were probably coming later. "I've been more cautious about what I say now that I'm on the bench. I have to think about the impact of whatever I say on how the public will perceive me, and the court. The Code of Judicial Ethics is front and center, of course. As far as suicide and sexual assault go, I don't believe that the military or our political leaders have tried to get to the root of the problem. The attention to those subjects varies according to how much media pressure is put on. When the media publishes something alarming about an issue, Washington reacts with talk but no solutions. When Washington turns to something else, the media abandons the original issue.

"The policy of your administration," David said, "in curtailing military interventions with troops on the ground has helped a great deal, as a practical matter. In other words, we haven't been in any ground wars since we finally pulled out of Afghanistan and Iraq three or four years ago. Of course, Special Forces are still directly engaged—subject to civilian control—but, apparently, they are better able to stand the psychological stress of danger and killing. I believe that the Army just ends up blaming pre-existing conditions as the key factor in suicides and still doesn't acknowledge its responsibility."

"Are you saying that the only solution is never to use troops on the ground again?" the President asked. "Much as I'd like to avoid that, we can't rule it out totally, and there are always compelling humanitarian situations. Don't you think that pre-existing conditions are part of the suicide problem?"

"The problem with all the studies is that they don't answer the question about why soldiers and veterans feel suicidal despair. All the studies show is that people with pre-existing mental disorders are more likely to act on their impulses. They ignore the question of what we should do about the factors in military life, or after military life, that lead people to have suicidal impulses and desires. That's a no-brainer. The reasons are obvious. The problem is no one wants to face them. Besides, in my view, history has shown that wars create more problems than they solve. It's an age-old lesson that we as a society, along with most others in the world, turn our backs on. Your admin-istration has provided a temporary fix, but this country has never been known for our consistency from one administration to another or from our long- or even mid-term planning. We read that the U.S. used to be called the *one move chess player* when it comes to foreign policy situations—military force alone."

David continued. "I don't mean to diminish in the least what you've done, but the changes may not be permanent. If anything, our political history shows that each administration designs a reaction to the previous one. As long as we keep doing this and not coming to grips with war and what it fails to accomplish, we're destined to repeat our mistakes. That's why some of us called for a national study of the original decade of war in the Middle East. You know what happened. In the end, all the financial and human cost of Iraq and Afghanistan went unexamined and no one took responsibility. No lessons were learned and now those wars have been superseded by a seamless series of successor wars. Unfortunately, the stage is set for the next disaster after you leave office."

55

appreciate your comments," President Madison said. "I haven't ruled out a commission like the NVVRS. I don't foresee Congressional support for a bipartisan enterprise, but it could be a Presidential program. It would be difficult to control its scope so it couldn't be co-opted for personal political gain. Does it interest you on a personal level?"

"It does. But I understand the complications," David said.

"Let's get to the purpose of our visit," the President said. "Did you suffer any ill effects from your time in the service? Were you ever diagnosed or treated for any physical or mental injuries or illnesses?"

"I didn't have any major physical injuries. I have experienced symptoms that may or may not add up to PTSD. I didn't pursue treatment or diagnosis. I felt that I could manage and get on with my life without seeking treatment. I had no interest in trying to qualify for VA disability compensation. I saw more risk than benefit to that. Because I wanted a career in public service, I couldn't afford to have a history of mental health complaints. Although PTSD is a legitimate illness or injury, the stigma related to mental illness still exists in military and civilian life. It shouldn't be so but it is."

At this, the President turned to Lehman and the deputies and said, "Arthur, I have a couple of questions that I want to ask Justice Lawson privately." Turning to David, she said, "I may find it necessary to discuss what you say with my staff, but I'll ask my questions in private." Lehman and the two staffers got up quickly, nodding their assent, and left the room.

The President continued: "I want to assure you that I will protect your privacy as much as I can, but I would like your absolutely candid answers. Would you tell me what symptoms you have had and whether they are current? You know, this could all come out in Judiciary Committee hearings if it were to reach that point."

David felt obligated to reveal his symptoms. "I'm referring to several things, sleep disturbances for one. I've had nightmares and what I call flashbacks, although I'm not sure they meet the psychiatric definition. I witnessed people on both sides suffering horrible deaths and injuries. I am bothered by heightened anxiety sometimes. For a while, I couldn't turn off the adrenalin, but that's mostly diminished over the years. It's been stressful on my marriage. Those experiences take a toll on everyone, but some handle it better than others."

David went on. "It's hard to know precisely how much the war is responsible for these problems because my theory is that a lifetime of experiences contributes to PTSD. My childhood was not easy. I had a difficult, distant, relationship with my parents, and a divorce after a very short ill-advised marriage, plus my current marriage, which, I have to say, is not as happy as I would wish. I suppose all this sounds discouraging and maybe even alarming. I hope not," David added.

"Thank you for telling me. I assume that you have not gotten treatment for any psychiatric conditions?"

"Correct," David said.

"Even though untreated, are there any psychiatric symptoms that interfere with your work or daily life?"

"No," David replied quickly.

"Do you anticipate that the status of your marriage will change for the worse in the near future? In other words, is the possibility of separation or divorce imminent?"

"The marriage is holding at this time, and I don't anticipate that will change in the near future," David said.

"My next question is whether there is anything I should know that might affect your confirmation process or reflect badly on the White House if you were to be nominated?"

David had anticipated this question with apprehension. How could he be honest with the President and, at the same time, not put an end to his chances of being nominated? He had thought about it at length after Bradley had warned that the question was inevitable. Bradley emphasized his strong opinion that a potential nominee to a high position has a moral obligation not to mislead a president. He conceded that self-interest leads most candidates to rationalize the obligation away.

David also had in mind Richard's advice to keep details about the trial to himself for now. These conflicting thoughts flashed through his mind as he concentrated on remaining in the moment, avoiding an awkward pause.

"Madame President," he began, trying to look natural in repeating his con-trived answer. "I've thought long and hard about this. I realize that I've had a public life. I've been outspoken about my thoughts on a lot of controversial subjects. My private life, public life, and my military life are open books. I've probably made enemies along the way. My performance in Iraq is fair game for scrutiny. As your counsel knows, there was an investigation of an incident in which civilians were killed. There was an informal investigation, but it did not focus on anything I did or did not do. Very little came as a result of the investigation. It never became a Headquarters matter, a CID matter. We've tried to get the investigation report but the print copy is gone, which is not so unusual, and the digital copy can't be accessed because it was corrupted."

"I'm aware of all that," the President said, with slight impatience at his ob-viously rehearsed statement.

"From time to time," David continued, "I hear or read about events that happened during my deployment in Iraq or about people with whom I served.

In fact, I heard recently some damaging information about the person who was the subject of the investigation. I don't foresee any problems in the near future. As far as the symptoms caused by my combat experience, if we can call them that, I don't believe there's anything that would affect my capacity to carry out any position."

The President paused briefly, as she gazed straight at David. "To be candid, that answer leaves many unanswered questions, but I appreciate what you said. I would ask that you let me, through my counsel, know of any major change in the circumstances you've mentioned. I don't intend to make a commitment to anyone during this preliminary process. My ultimate choice will be to benefit the Court and the country.

"I have one final question," she continued. "What do you believe would be the most important contribution you could make to the Court? Let me put that in a slightly different way. You know how it's common to say that an important part of a president's legacy is her Supreme Court appointments. If I should decide to appoint you and you serve, how would that affect my legacy?"

"That's the hardest question of all," David said as convincingly as he could. "I don't like to judge myself except in the most demanding and critical terms." He knew he was being disingenuous because he was about to present the most blatant self-promotion he could manage. He hadn't expected this question. Realizing that he had not been forthcoming about his personal situation, he chose his words as carefully as choosing steps across a high wire.

He began with all the confidence he could muster, "I believe I have the ability to do the job, but I'm certainly not the best legal scholar you could pick. I'm a white male, which means you get no credit for a groundbreaking nomination that brings diversity to the Court. What I can offer is my life experience, which involves some very human failings, some bad choices, switching gears and changing my mind—like leaving law school—mistakes, decisions in commanding my units that I now second-guess, lack of the level of courage that I had hoped for.

"My experiences and accomplishments have been flawed, as much if not more than other people. I believe I'm more introspective than most people. I rate myself high on the empathy scale, so I can put myself in the shoes of other people who are different from me. I have grappled with tough moral issues, the hardest of all involving life and death, and have examined and reexamined my choices. I approach my work without an agenda that dominates judicial decisions. I see life and the world through a wide lens and an open mind. Those qualities are what I can bring to the Court. How my opinions would be perceived, I can't say. But I hope that choosing someone with my makeup would be respected regardless of the particular opinions."

The President gave no clues to her reaction. David was silent, searching her face, waiting for a visual cue. She smiled warmly but formally.

"Thank you. I enjoyed hearing your answer." She rose quickly. David jumped to his feet in response.

"It was a pleasure to meet you, and I hope that, no matter what happens, we'll have occasion to talk again." She walked toward to door, opening it and turning to David with an outstretched hand and a warm smile.

"Good luck with the challenges you're facing and keep in touch. You can get updated information to me through Andrew Lehman, and you don't have to reveal all the details when you let him know. If I need to know more, I'll let you know. I can't commit to a schedule because there are too many uncertainties daily. But my hope is to bring the Court to its full strength as soon as possible.

"Goodbye Justice Lawson," she said formally. She was gone as quickly as she had entered the room. Andrew Lehman entered the room within moments after the President left. David realized that he knew nothing of her reactions, but he couldn't help feeling deflated about his handling of the probing questions.

"I hope you had a good talk. The President is remarkable, isn't she?"

"She is indeed," David managed, swallowing his surge of emotions after the final exchange, relieved that he had finished his precarious high wire walk. He felt a cloud of anxiety descend on him as soon as the moment dissolved.

"I'll walk you out," Lehman said. "Keep in touch with me about the investigation."

56

As soon as David left the White House compound, he called Bradley. He realized that he had misled the President on the threat from Nick Serrano and on his marriage situation. No President in her right mind would nominate a person who was going through a bitter divorce or one whose credibility was challenged. If he cooperated with Serrano, he might appear to be helping a murderer escape punishment by faking PTSD. If he didn't cooperate, he would appear to be an incompetent military officer who had failed to prevent civilian deaths or bring to justice a subordinate who committed war atrocities. Testifying was a no-win proposition.

When Bradley answered, he asked, "How'd it go? Did she ask tough questions? Did you get time alone with her?"

"I thought it went fairly well," David said. "Lehman and two deputy staffers sat in but the President excused them for the last twenty minutes. She asked some hard questions. She didn't reveal her reaction. I was as candid as I could be," he said, relieved that Bradley could not see his face. "But I have no clue as to where I am in the running against the other candidates."

"I could guess who the others are," Bradley replied, "but that's irrelevant. It's not a horse race. How was Lehman?"

"He was fine, abrupt and rude when we met in advance. I don't expect help from him based on his attitude. It's late to drive back tonight. Is it okay if I stay over?"

"Absolutely," Bradley said. "We won't be home until seven. Make yourself at home. The housekeeper is there today, all day, so the house will be open."

"Great. See you tonight."

David decided to stop by the Army and Navy Club where he had guest privileges as a veteran and as a former Supreme Court law clerk. He hardly ever used the club while he was in Washington. The clerks liked to gather there or at the Cosmos Club and he joined them once in a while. He had always disliked private clubs. Something about their exclusivity made him uneasy. They were good places to network. The Army and Navy Club was less pretentious, more comfortable.

It would be a place to make his phone calls. The club retained its prohibition against cell phone use in public areas, but he had use of a hospitality suite. He'd call Dana and check in at home as well. Dana was at her desk when she answered. Her voice was reserved.

"Hey, how's it going?" he said.

"Where are you?"

"I'm in Washington, just left the White House."

"Oh, of course, I forgot this was the week for your meeting. It's been hectic here. I have to make a quick trip tonight to Washington. We have a meeting at our D.C. headquarters. A couple of new crises are about to break. They're not even in the news cycle yet."

"Can I catch up with you?" David asked.

"I won't be free until late, probably eleven o'clock, and they're putting us up at the University Club since all the hotels are booked. It's tourist season you know. Morning is possible."

"I'm staying with Bradley in Bethesda, and I have to get out to his house. I'm under no pressure to get back at any particular time tomorrow. What time can I see you in the morning? How long are you staying?"

"Not sure. I have a ten o'clock meeting so come in as early as you can. If you get in by nine, we could have breakfast here; if not, we might be able to meet for lunch around one."

"Okay," David said. "Morning sounds best. I'll text you. Is everything cool with Jake?"

"I'll tell you about it. Not really. He seems to be going off the deep end. He got very abusive, verbally I mean, accusing me of all sorts of things. He said he knows about us, whatever he means by that. I said that was ridiculous. He said he's not through with that and that he never loses. I'm afraid, to tell the truth, not for myself, but for you."

"Do you think I should talk with him?"

"Are you kidding? No! Not a good idea," Dana said quickly. "You amaze me sometimes. What good would it do? Would you lie? I mean there's nothing between us really. What we've done doesn't amount to anything given the nature of Jake's and my relationship. But you wouldn't want to reveal our getting together would you?"

"No, I suppose not. That would be hard to explain. And lying, I've done too much of that, and I may be stuck with doing more before this whole nomination business is over. That's a hell of a thing to say, isn't it?"

"You have? You will? I don't know what you mean," Dana said.

"We can talk about this tomorrow."

My God, David thought, this is getting worse and worse. He didn't feel like calling Lucille but maybe he'd be lucky and get voicemail. He rang her cell phone and, oh shit, he thought, she answered.

"Where are you? Didn't you get my email?" Lucille's voice was slurred. "Marcus had an accident fooling around playing soccer at the lake. It's been crazy the last two days. He fractured his femur and was rushed to the ER in an ambulance. They operated on it. I didn't even know where you were."

David reacted defensively. "So why didn't you pick up the phone and call me? You took the boys out of state without asking me, for God's sake. You took responsibility for them. How is he? What's his condition?"

"Why didn't I call you? I've had enough to do without trying to track you down. You didn't care enough to let me know what was going on."

"Thanks. That was thoughtful," he muttered. "But for goodness sake, tell me how he is. Was the operation successful? Where is he now? How long will he be hospitalized?"

"What?" she asked. "I'm not answering questions now."

"When are you coming back? I can come right out there."

"No, I don't want you to come out here. I'll email you his contact information. He's getting out of the hospital tomorrow morning and then we're going home. Where are you anyway?"

"I'm staying with Bradley in Maryland. I had meetings."

"Let me put you on notice," she said belligerently. "Obviously I'm on my own and I intend to make that official."

"Wait. Hold on. This is a critical time."

"Your life is a series of critical times. Find yourself a place to live."

"You've been drinking," David charged, out of patience. "Don't make decisions when you're drunk. Don't think you're home free. If you didn't have a glass in your hand, you could get your act together and stop blaming me for everything."

She slammed the phone down. David's heart was racing. What else could go wrong? He'd call Marcus as soon as he got the contact information. Now he hesitated to call Richard, for fear of another problem, but decided that he should. He didn't like to duck bad news. He dialed Richard's number.

57

David's call to Richard went to voicemail. In the meantime, three new voicemails had appeared on his phone while he was at the White House. There were calls from Larry Cutter, Jake, and John Morehead. David winced at the expected bad news that each represented. He'd return the calls without delay so he would know the full picture before talking with Richard.

Larry was first. "Hey, Larry, it's David. What's happening?"

"Good to hear your voice, Captain. I called just to touch base. I wondered whether you decided to testify or not. Nick told me that he went to see you."

"Really. He told you that? I haven't decided yet. What about you?"

"Yeah, I am. I said I would. I met with his lawyer and got the whole picture. He put a lot of pressure on, but it's not a big problem for me. I have nothing to lose, except my time. There was plenty of shit that went down that I can talk about. We all went through hell. His lawyer wants me to kind of downplay Nick's role in the whole mess with the female. I should just say that he tried to clean up the insurgents for what they did, what happened, you know, and that there was no other way. I know that's not exactly the way things were but what the hell, it doesn't matter to me."

"What did you think of his lawyer?"

"Man, he's a piece of work. He and Nick are two of a kind. He's one tough bastard, a big mouth, a bully. I mean he didn't bully me because I agreed to say what he wants. It's nothing to me. I know it's different for you."

"That's for sure and, if we don't tell the same story, it causes a problem for me. That would give the prosecutor a chance to zero in and raise questions about both of us."

"You mean you are going to testify?"

"I don't know for sure. I haven't made a final decision but, if I do, it has to be the truth. Nothing but. I can't do anything else, and our stories have to mesh. I'll let you know what I decide and then we can talk."

"Geez, David, I don't want to make this hard on you, but I can't fight these guys. They'll beat the shit out of me."

"But you have to tell a story that's consistent with the facts to both lawyers. The prosecutor can tear you apart otherwise. Just take each question one by one and answer with the truth and you won't get in trouble. You could get arrested if you lie, you know. The main thing is that we have to be sure we don't contradict each other. I don't think Nick is going to go gunning for you.

Have you talked to Nick?"

"Yeah. Just the once since I talked to you. He was okay, thanked me. It was after I talked to his lawyer."

"Did the lawyer go over the whole story with you?"

"Well, yeah, I guess so, mainly that these Al Qaeda bastards killed the female, among others, and Nick was in charge of the cleanup. Went out three times with a squad and took care of all the bastards."

"What about the civilians who were killed? What did the lawyer say about the civilians who were killed and the two of our guys who were killed?"

"The lawyer said not to raise it. But if the prosecutor asks about civilians, just say you don't know the details. I wasn't on his squad but, if they were killed, it's just that you can't avoid it sometimes. It's fucking war. You don't know who's who and you have to protect yourself and your guys."

"What did he say about the investigation? What about the fact that Nick got a walk?"

"He didn't say nothing about that."

"Did he say anything about having a copy of the investigation report?"

"Nope. I don't recall that."

"Well, let's stick together. We'll talk before the trial when I know what I'm going to do. Keep this conversation between us okay? Don't repeat it to Nick if he calls you."

"Okay man, I got it. Hey let me know if you decide to come down. We can get together."

"Yeah, thanks for letting me know what's going on. I'll be in touch."

58

David listened to Jake's message. It was terse, as though Jake was speaking through clenched teeth. "I need to talk to you now. I know what's going on but I want to hear it from you. Lucille says that you're away and she doesn't know where you are. Get in touch with me right now."

Oh great, David thought. This was bad. Jake was on the right track, of course, but it was hard to say how much he knew. He was incredibly resourceful. As a well-trained SEAL and later a CIA operative, Jake knew the importance of withholding judgment until he had the facts. On the other hand, once he got the minimum of facts, he decided on a course of action and could not be diverted.

The worst of it was that Jake was one of his oldest friends. They had been close since before college despite their polar opposite personalities and outlooks. David regretted risking Jake's trust in him. If Jake were convinced that he had been disloyal, there was no telling what he would do. He would take matters into his own hands. He had a strong sense of duty and morality, but it was a different morality from David's. Jake's was based on honor, his own and the military's.

David figured it might be wise to talk to Jake and try to avert a bigger confrontation. Why was everything blowing up at once? On second thought, maybe it was best not to talk to Jake right now. He needed to make some decisions first. He'd be seeing Dana tomorrow morning. She might know how to handle Jake. She sounded upset though and obviously this had her rattled.

While David was stretched out on the sofa in the hospitality suite, his phone rang. He checked it to be sure it wasn't Jake again. He'd have to duck those calls until he got back. Damn Lucille. She probably gave Jake an earful. When she was drinking she had no restraint. He wondered whether she'd gotten in touch with John Morehead again and whether that was the reason for John's call. There were bigger problems.

The call was from Richard. He was relieved. Richard was looking for an update.

"It went well with the President," David said. "I couldn't hope for anything better. I was wondering whether you reached Nick's lawyer."

"I did. Stewart called back this afternoon. He's a tough son of a bitch. He said he's got to have you as a witness, period. You're crucial to the defense. I tried to convince him that it's unheard of to insist on a judge testifying. It's unfair and unreasonable. There are lots of others who could testify. I didn't want to emphasize the bad timing too much. He already knows about the nomination and senses that he has you in a corner."

Richard continued. "He wouldn't back off and I don't think he will. He's ruthless. He doesn't give a damn about your position or your wish list, as he put it. He's got a client to represent and, one way or the other, you will testify. I said he needs your cooperation and, while I'm advising you not to testify, we would listen to a proposal about some very limited testimony. He said, bullshit, if you don't agree to come down and answer whatever he asks, he'll notice your deposition in Connecticut. It'll be the most goddamn wide-ranging interrogation you ever imagined. He said he'd nail you to the wall and would release the deposition to the media. He said he'd get it before the jury too. He did concede that he's still interested in getting a plea deal for his client and having you on the witness list might help. He said something about loyalty and asked whether saving your own skin was all that's important to you. I'm just telling you what he said."

"Damn," David muttered. "He can do that, can't he? I mean get a local lawyer to notice the deposition and feed him the questions, and make it as broad as he wants? You can advise me not to answer questions but, if I refuse, it would look like I'm covering things up."

"Right, he can do this under the statutes. It won't be pretty but we could control it to some extent."

"What do you think I should do? Agree to go down there? Try to make a deal as to what he can ask so the prosecutor doesn't have a field day? Some Philadelphia DA might want to make a name for himself."

"I think the best strategy is to agree to testify at this point. That way we preclude a deposition. At the last minute, we can try to hold him up with some excuse and get him to agree to limited testimony. You have to tell the truth but you don't have to volunteer and, if you forget some stuff, so be it. It's been years since this whole business happened. If he knows you may say things that will damage his client, he may have second thoughts. He cares mostly about his own reputation. This guy hates to lose and he's greedy. I doubt that he gives a damn about Nick. It's really about himself. He doesn't want to be embarrassed, and he wants to win. So we should go along for now. It's only a few weeks away. I may be able to get him to give me a list of questions that he wants to ask. We can argue about ones that you don't want to answer and then leave it up in the air. Let him hang out there for a while but with enough assurance so that he won't try to depose you. Time is short."

"That doesn't sound as bad as it did when we started talking," David said. "I wish the damned thing would go away. Maybe it will, if the prosecutor is uncertain whether he'll get a conviction. Will you be able to get someone down there to monitor the trial and see how it's going? Maybe before the defense has to start, they'll make a deal."

"Yes, I'll have someone in the courtroom all the time, my associate, Barbara Stearns. We'll watch it closely. He said he'd call his other witnesses first.

I know why. He can control them and he hopes to box you in, to make you go along with the story he gets them to tell. He thinks you won't want to contradict the other witnesses and set yourself up for a harsh cross. It can actually work to your advantage because you'll have the last shot at reconciling everything the way you want to. Of course, his client will testify at the very end, if he does at all."

"Sounds like a logical strategy," said David. "I like your approach."

"Who else besides Larry does he have?" Richard asked. "He didn't tell me all the names but he mentioned there would be a couple of guys who were in Nick's squad on that mission. Doug? Al? Do those names ring a bell? Also two widows of guys who committed suicide."

"I know of one. What would he gain by doing that? That sounds cruel."

"Apparently, they're all glad to back up Nick. They'll testify about the PTSD that their husbands suffered, how messed up they were, and how it led to their suicides. Apparently, he stayed in touch with the guys and families and helped them out financially over the years."

"I didn't expect that. I was on pretty good terms with the whole platoon, and I figured that no one would go out of their way to screw me up."

"I can ask Barbara to look into that when she's down there."

"Thanks, Richard. I don't know what I'd do without you. By the way, I may need to contact Herb. I have a feeling that Lucille is going to escalate the situation. You might mention to Herb that I'll call him this week."

"Sure, keep your chin up. We'll beat this. My goal is to make it go away with as little fuss as possible and to keep it under the radar."

59

David was exhausted after the long day, not to mention the phone conversations. It was not easy to assimilate all the information he'd received. It was time to drive back to Bradley's. He thanked the club manager, whom he had gotten to know during his Washington days. A walk through the library and the fabled Daiquiri Lounge enabled him to take a quick look at the photographs on the walls, the memorabilia, and the stacks of books on military history. It occurred to him that his photograph might be hung there if he made it to the Supreme Court. At the rate he was going, he thought, he'd be more likely to see his picture splashed across every major news source if he was accused of perjury or prosecuted for conspiracy under MEJA.

He maneuvered the daily snarl of District traffic to Bethesda. He pulled into Bradley's driveway in just under an hour. Bradley and Ayako had arrived home and were sitting on the porch. Bradley asked about his day. Having in mind Lehman's admonition about confidentiality but recognizing that Bradley had to be an exception, David recounted the visit.

"I like the way the President handled the meeting," Bradley offered. "I think she trusts you and feels that you're on the same wave length. That's a crucial factor. But she knows something is brewing about the investigation, so she's bound to be guarded. I see Lehman once a week and I'll keep my ears open. I'm on a foreign policy advisory committee that he chairs. I'm pretty much in accord with the White House position but others are not. She's the first president in a long time who isn't afraid to put people with different views on advisory committees. That's a smart move.

"She takes the committee very seriously," Bradley added, "even drops in once in a while. We're focusing on North Africa now. The problems never go away and never get any better, and we still have only a small toehold in Djibouti. It's been more than ten years since the Al Qaeda network disintegrated to some extent and the Islamic State network became the major threat. It's a franchise system, somewhat like Al Qaeda but far more extreme and obviously more violent. It's like a network of franchise operations, with different names, through Africa and the Middle East. But it's branching beyond that region too. It's really a threat wherever there's a Muslim population to draw on. We're even worried about South America and Southeast Asia. Of course, if we make headway in stamping it out, it'll be replaced by another extremist group. There's no end. Extremists will always exist."

After a quiet dinner, David excused himself. He knew they got off to an early start in the morning and he needed to also. He was not about to reveal that he was meeting Dana. Before leaving in the morning, Bradley told him that Jake had called him a few days ago.

"He wanted to know if I'd been in touch with you. I said that you were staying with me for a couple of days. Jake was surprised and said he'd been trying to reach you. He sounded tense but didn't say what it was about. I told him I'd pass word along to you, and he said he'd appreciate that. He said you and he had urgent business to deal with the moment you got back. Do you think it concerns the report?"

David felt alarm circulate through his body, and his stomach clench with discomfort. Oh great, he thought. Jake was honing in for the kill. At least he didn't badmouth me to Bradley. David knew that Jake and Bradley had a good relationship but they were not as close as David was with each of them. They hadn't lived together during college or law school, as David had with each. David said, "I don't know what it's about, but I plan to call him as soon as I get back. I know Jake is intent on getting hold of the report. I'm hoping it may not be such a big issue with the President."

"We can hope," Bradley nodded.

David decided to drive into the District and park at the Club. He sent Dana a text that he'd be in the lobby by 8:00 and would call from the desk. He felt some apprehension, not knowing exactly where her relationship with Jake stood. He was nervous about the possibility of being seen with Dana. But it was too late to change what he had put in motion. He felt tension about meeting Jake. Jake would be difficult in a confrontation. David's choices were limited to candor or denial. Both were risky. Jake would not forgive anyone violating his territory or his prerogatives. He was possessive to the death, so to speak. Maybe Dana could shed light on the situation.

60

David called Dana from the lobby a few minutes before 8:00. He was relieved that she had ordered breakfast from room service as an alternative to going out, for the sake of privacy, she said. She admitted to feeling slightly paranoid about being spotted by someone who knew Jake. David was at her door in five minutes.

She greeted him without any word or sign of affection. She directed him to a small table with a breakfast tray. No need to force the issue. It was wise to cool the relationship for the time being. That did not prevent him from feeling mildly disappointed that she was pulling back. After a few minutes of light conversation, he felt his resolve to maintain distance slip away, but she showed no sign of warmth or even pleasure at his being there.

They ate in silence aside from casual remarks. Dana asked about the White House visit. David offered only a few basic comments, feeling reluctant to share information with her. He asked about her trip to Washington, and she explained that it involved upcoming negotiations in Africa. David sensed that they both were poised to bring up the troubling subject of Jake's hostile reaction and what seemed to be a final breakdown of Dana's relationship with Jake, and probably with him too. He hesitated to describe Jake as paranoid because in this case his suspicions were grounded in reality.

Dana broke the silence. "I'm really alarmed at Jake's response. He'll hold onto this until he finds out the truth. If he finds out anything to support his suspicion, he won't stop until he has retaliated. I don't feel I did anything morally wrong because we had not reached the marriage stage, but, of course, I wasn't open and honest with him either. But you and he have a special relationship, and he will feel that you betrayed him. I think he's justified in feeling that way. I don't mean to criticize because I'm as much at fault as you. We let our emotions run away with us. I can't imagine what we were thinking about at the time. We have to end this relationship, whatever it is, at this point. Since you're thinking of contacting him, what are you going to say? I've already denied that there is anyone else, so I'll stand on that."

"I don't know," David said. "If I tell him what happened, he and I are finished and he'll want revenge. If I lie, I'll buy time but not for long. Eventually, he'll make me pay a price. My relationship with him is doomed either way. He'll never trust me again. He won't deny his instincts, once he's identified a threat or a wrong. I should probably avoid him as long as possible, maybe until the nomination is settled. If he seeks me out, I'm not sure how to handle it.

"On another subject," David continued, "I did reveal to the President that I had some stress symptoms following the service. I tried to downplay it. Isn't it a shame that the stigma prevents getting help when it's most needed? It seems like a classic Catch-22. If you are mentally ill, it's your duty to get help. But if you do, they penalize you. Even with all the mental illness in this society and all the people who are on prescription drugs, the stigma continues. It's fatal if you're in the public eye, or just looking for a job."

Dana rose from her chair. "I have to get ready for my meeting. We'd better not communicate or see each other unless there's some critical warning we need to convey. Is texting to your private number the best way? "

"Yes, and how about you?"

"Send a text to my cell. No one else has access."

David felt his heart sink. He wasn't sure whether he still cared about her. They barely got started on a relationship. It seemed unlikely to be revived now. Not only that, he had elevated her to be the only person to whom he could confide and turn to for advice, besides Willard. That was a lost cause at this point. He wondered whether pursuing the nomination was worth all the incipient damage to relationships. He contemplated his deteriorating marriage, fractured friendships, betrayal of trust, loss of love, and the loss of self-respect. He consoled himself that he would find new relationships if he got to the Supreme Court.

They parted, David with unspoken regret, unable to read Dana's body language. She gave no signals about how she was feeling except her impatience to have him leave. Did she not care at all?

"Dana," he said in a subdued tone, "I hope there is still a chance for us when this is over. Don't write it off."

"We have to let go of that now. We should communicate only to protect each other. But let me know what's happening with the nomination."

"I'll let you know," he said and left quickly without prolonging the awkwardness of the separation. He heard the door close firmly as he headed down the hall for the elevator, hoping that Jake would not appear around the corner or step off the elevator. He reached his car without incident.

61

Before getting on the Beltway out of the city, David stopped at a gas station. He was surprised to find a new voicemail from John Morehead. He pushed "listen" with a sense of foreboding. Another crisis, he wondered?

"David, John Morehead here. Give me a call would you? I understand you're out of town. Lucille came in to see me yesterday. She instructed me to go ahead with a divorce without delay. I tried to talk her out of it but she's adamant. I don't know why the urgency. She says the timing is right. Look, I'm not eager to do this, you know that, but I don't have much choice. You should ask yourself whether you have a real choice about waiving the conflict. If I'm not her lawyer, she says she'll hire somebody tough and ruthless. Those are her words. So there it is, David. Let's talk about this. I want to do what's best for her and you, both of you. I hope you know that."

So I need to deal with a divorce on top of all the other pressure. Maybe Jake has been in touch with Lucille about his suspicions and she's fired up.

The next message was a surprise, Burkhardt. What the hell does he want?

"Lawson," he bellowed in his street voice, at a volume twice what was necessary. David wondered what audience was sitting in his office. "Where the hell are you anyway? We've been looking for you for two days. No one knows. Not even your clerks. Are you still a member of this court? I called a court conference for Friday morning, and we've got everyone coming in at 10:00 except you, of course. Even your wife doesn't know where you are. For Crisssake, you'd better show up in the morning unless you're being held hostage. It's now Thursday afternoon, 4:00 p.m. If you're not here, I'll have no choice but to report your absence to the Judicial Complaint Committee. By the way, I'll suspend you from sitting."

Burkhardt slammed the phone down heavily, violently enough to puncture an eardrum. David was aghast at the crises brewing in every sector of his life. They were all blowing up at once.

Another message was brief and abrupt. Jake's voice was unmistakable and tense with bottled-up rage. "I said to call me. I've heard nothing. No one knows where you are. We need to talk now. I expect a call back. It's Friday morning at 7:00 a.m."

There were other calls. His law clerks had tried to reach him on Thursday afternoon. There were texts from them about the Friday conference and a late August conference. Burkhardt always liked to gear things up in the last week of August since the first round of arguments was scheduled right after Labor Day. Before that change, the court never got into gear before the third or fourth week of September. Burkhardt would hit the ceiling when David told him he likely couldn't sit during the first or second weeks of September. He had no intention of providing a reason.

There was no way he could be in Hartford today. It was already after 10:00. He texted his permanent clerk. "Got messages. Detained out of state. Back in state late this afternoon. Let CJ know cannot make conference but will call this afternoon."

He was not going to Hartford today even if he got back to Connecticut before the day was out. The thought of a confrontation with Burkhardt was distasteful. It would be brutal and Burkhardt would ensure that it was not private. He would seek to embarrass him in front of the entire court and the staff if he could by shouting in the hallway to get attention. Burkhardt was the least of his problems. He'd call him from his New Haven office. He'd have to figure how to take care of the bullying SOB when he had more time. It was intolerable, but he was too vulnerable to get embroiled in street fighting with Burkhardt.

He jotted down notes of the calls he had to make: Herb, Richard, Morehead, Burkhardt, Jake. It occurred to him that letting Morehead go ahead and represent Lucille couldn't do any harm, but he'd have to get Herb involved to protect himself. Herb was good at that, tough and effective but always professional, never confrontational. He'd have to make financial concessions to Lucille. She wanted that even more than humiliating him. He'd give up custody, which wasn't necessarily great for the boys. But he wasn't in any position to secure custody, much less to carry it out. He could see the boys regularly, and they were used to managing on their own. He was thinking of himself first, of course. Wasn't that always the way. Well, if he didn't, who would? It had always been that way since he was their ages or younger. He'd have to talk with them about that when he got a chance.

David sat immobilized for a few moments. I need a strategy, he thought. I feel as though I'm juggling half a dozen torches in the air. I need to talk to someone. Maybe Willard is back in Boston. Near the end of the summer, he sometimes goes back and forth to the island. He dialed Willard's Boston number.

David was relieved when he answered the phone. "I was hoping I could see you this weekend. I didn't know whether you'd still be on the island or back in town."

"Good to hear from you. You've been on my mind since your visit. I've been wondering what's happening. I haven't read anything and I don't know if that's good or bad. I came back for a few meetings in town this week. Love to see you. When can you come up? Tomorrow?"

"Yes. I'm on my way from Washington back to New Haven, and I could drive up first thing in the morning."

"Great, about what time? I usually go for a long walk in the morning."

"How about 10:30?"

"Sounds good," Willard said. "You sound concerned. Is everything okay?"

"Not really. I'll explain when I see you."

David hung up and pulled out of the lot heading for the Beltway. Friday morning meant dense traffic everywhere. He could count on seven hours driving time to New Haven. He'd have to stop along the way and make some of these calls. He'd do that when he got to Maryland or Delaware.

62

David pulled into the first New Jersey Turnpike stop. He reached Dana by text, and she texted back that she was in a meeting. She called in ten minutes, sounding annoyed that he had called. "What's up?" she asked abruptly. "Better be important. I left a meeting." In answer to his hurried response that it concerned Jake, she replied impatiently.

"Jake called me, looking for you," she said. "No, I did not tell him that we met this morning. I said I hadn't seen you since I couldn't remember when. He seemed satisfied."

"You never let him know that we've been, well, together, right? I mean, you know what I mean."

"Oh for God's sake, David, I can't believe you interrupted me for that. I said I've never told him. How many times do you want to hear that? Don't let fear tear you apart. There's no purpose in telling him anything. That will set him off. As long as he's in doubt, he won't retaliate. If he finds out, he will. Period. It doesn't matter how he finds out. There's no gold star for letting him know honestly. Have you got that?"

"Yes," he said, stunned by her harshness. "Fine. Sorry to bother you. Won't happen again." He hung up.

He knew instinctively that she was right. He called Jake's number hurriedly before he got cold feet. Jake answered. David felt chills at the icy rage in his voice. "Where the hell are you? I've been calling all over. Even talked to Lucille." That's it, David thought. That's why she's steamed up.

"Jake, sorry, meant to get back to you sooner. I'm travelling back from a meeting in D.C. about the nomination. It's going to be late and I'm away tomorrow. Meeting in Boston. Can we talk on Sunday? Or Monday?" Pause.

"No. I'm free right now. Come to my house. We need to talk now, not two days from now. I have two important things to tell you. One of them will surprise you."

"Look, Jake. All right, I'll come right to Olive Street. You don't care what time it is?"

"Right," Jake muttered. "I'm waiting."

He left Herb a long message. "Richard may have told you that I'd be in touch. The bottom line is that Lucille says she wants to go ahead with a divorce. This is horrible timing for me, as you know. She talked with John Morehead a couple of times, asking him to represent her. He told me a while back that he was willing but only if I'd agree to it. His tone has changed. He's pressing me to agree, saying that Lucille is threatening that she will get some shark if I don't. I hope you will represent me. Should I agree to let Morehead represent her? The downside is that he knows a lot about me from our social friendship. The upside is that I think he would not be as bad as her next choice, somebody who'd love to sink his teeth in me. Give me a call please."

That was it. He'd have to wait to hear back from Herb. He made a quick stop for coffee and drove on. Dana's stern warning made it easy to deal with Jake for now. Deny everything. If nothing else, Jake was predictable. He would not act until he knew enough facts. He clearly had betrayed Jake. But nothing was to be gained by giving Jake the opportunity to destroy his career, maybe even his life. He felt pain at the damage to the relationship but this was no time for weakness. This was survival, something he became skilled at in childhood. Damn, he thought, he could be as tough as Jake, almost. He knew how to go for the kill too, if he was forced to. He'd been prepared to do that as a routine matter every day in Iraq and he'd proven himself capable of carrying it out when he had to.

As he worried about what Jake's surprise might be, he recalled the President's question about whether he knew of anything that would cause confirmation problems and embarrass the White House. David recalled his contrived answer, designed to be evasive. Contemplating that conversation, he moved onward through the heavy Friday night commuter traffic of New York City and headed for Connecticut. Usually he felt a sense of relief when he crossed into Connecticut. Tonight he felt dread as he moved closer to New Haven and a confrontation with Jake.

63

I t was after 9:00 when David pulled up in front of Jake's townhouse. At an earlier time, Jake had talked openly with David about Dana. He was attracted particularly by her candor and her fierce independence, both of which had worn thin for him over the course of months. She had been attracted to him for different reasons, mainly his confidence and single-minded determination that anything was possible. He had unusual physical strength and an iron will to conquer every challenge. In some ways, each admired in the other the attributes that each wanted to possess. As so often happens, the very qualities that attract so strongly in the first place turn to be the ones that drive people apart in the end.

Both lacked the capacity to share power and to compromise their interests Eventually, Jake went for days at a time not speaking with Dana. Long before that, he had stopped talking to David about the relationship. David attributed the silence to Jake's work, always urgent and clandestine. David never knew whether Jake was working solely in private operations or whether he undertook special missions for the CIA. David surmised that Jake's connection with the CIA had never been severed completely. He wouldn't have been surprised in the least to learn that Jake was taking on secret, dangerous missions or that his activities might resemble those of the fictional Jason Bourne. It was not uncommon for Jake to fail to show up for meetings.

Jake opened the door forcefully and waved David in without a hint of warmth or civility. David did not look forward to this session. He was up against one of the toughest operators in life and death crises. How could he keep the truth from surfacing in an encounter with Jake? He'd gotten through tough situations before, he thought.

David followed Jake to the kitchen. They sat at the dining table in the renovated kitchen. Jake had remodeled the house after he moved in. Although it had been allowed to deteriorate for years, he hired and worked alongside a builder to restore it in a style consistent with the early 1800s. Jake put two cups of coffee on the table.

He started in on David. "I'm disappointed in you. We've had a long friendship. How many years? Since high school, right?" Jake always got right to the point. No messing around. No small talk. "I'd like to hear it from you."

"What are you disappointed about? I can't think of anything I've done to disappoint you."

"Don't play fuckin' games with me. You know what I'm talking about. Dana, that's what. Tell me about your relationship. Suddenly, she's ending mine and starting yours."

"We're friends, same as before," David said. "I've always liked Dana, respected her. She's smart, has good judgment, and she's a good resource. I've got a lot of decisions to make and I've talked to her a few times. The first was on the ride back and forth to New Hampshire. You didn't show up, if you recall."

"Yeah, well I have information that you two stayed on by yourselves and that you've seen her since," Jake said, visibly angered.

David knew he had to cover himself but didn't know whether Dana had told Jake they'd talked in person since the New Hampshire weekend. He should have asked her. Too late. He plunged ahead. "We took a walk before heading back, then got our stuff and drove home. You were here. I stopped for gas and for coffee on the way back. I did see her one time in New York. I wanted to hear her thoughts about the President since she had worked with her at the Global Crisis Network. That's it. I didn't know I needed permission from you to talk to her." David could feel his irritation mounting.

"What about Washington this week?"

David knew he had to wing it on this one, as on the New York meeting, not knowing what Dana had said. He assumed that she'd denied everything, as she said, and hoped to hell he was right. "No," he said firmly. "I did call her to let her know how the White House visit went."

"You're not telling me everything. That much I know. You're a liar. I'll find out the truth sooner or later. Making it more difficult will not help in the long run. I know I can't trust you now. What your relationship is with her is not the only issue. It's your goddamned disloyalty. I don't trust you worth shit, just so you know."

"I'm sorry to hear that Jake. You're making a mistake."

"Lucille said she believed you were in Washington to visit Dana. She is convinced of it."

"When did you talk to Lucille and why?" David asked, counterattacking, irritation shifting gears to anger.

Jake glared. "I was trying to locate you, which you seem to have made as difficult as possible."

"What gives you the right to tell me what I should do? Prying information out of Lucille is a violation of my privacy and loyalty, if you're so concerned about privacy and loyalty. Who are you to make accusations about loyalty?"

"You have no reason to be proprietary about your relationship with Lucille. I didn't exactly have to pry it out of her. She was more than willing to talk. She invited me to talk with her anytime."

"Did you visit her or use the phone?"

"What?" Jake said, laughing bitterly without humor. "Do you think I'm interested in Lucille? You know how I feel about alcoholics. They're not worth shit, except to get information," he said with a sardonic grin. "In fact, I think she's a worn-out piece of shit. I hope you have a good lawyer. And I think you can kiss your appointment adios."

"Oh really. What do you know about that?"

"That's the surprise I mentioned," Jake said with evident pleasure. "You know the record of the investigation that I tried to get to do you a favor? It seems to have surfaced, my friend. I had a chance to look at it, in fact, and I understand why you were glad to have it missing in action."

"Oh really, how's that?" David asked calmly, trying to conceal the alarm that he felt.

"I'm glad to let you know because you'll hear about it soon enough from the source. Let's just say that I paid a personal visit to the source. I had an interesting conversation with your old Army buddy and his lawyer. I would say you're boxed, my friend, my former friend, completely boxed. You've planted the seeds of your own destruction."

"Oh," David snorted. "You sound like an Old Testament prophet. Are you on the criminal defense team for Nick Serrano?"

Jake laughed bitterly. "Your old buddy was glad to talk with me, and I was glad to take a look at the record. He's got your number."

"And did you learn how he happened to have it in his possession, or don't you care?"

"I have nothing more to say," Jake said. "He was an NCO, but you were a commissioned officer and his superior. By the way, your present superior does not hold you in high esteem. I'm sure I don't have to remind you about that. You've burned a lot of bridges with your ambitions, judging by your lack of supporters."

"You son of a bitch," David said. "You've been snooping around Hartford too? Incredible. Is this one of your personal CIA missions? You think you can get away with anything you want. We have new rules to play by, don't we? I've never known you to operate on bare assumptions. You're way off base."

In the course of the thirty-minute conversation, Jake had gone from controlled anger to open disbelief, to controlled rage, to threatening, and finally back to rising anger at David's last accusation. Jake prized nothing more than his adherence to military discipline. He was, once and always, a highly disciplined warrior, whereas David had left all that behind when he resigned his commission. David prided himself in owing allegiance to no person and no group. He had separated himself psychologically from his parents at an early age and had never again fully surrendered himself to any outside authority.

"When somebody kicks me in the teeth, it's no holds barred," Jake said, his eyes darkening with hatred.

"I see," David said. "I'm glad to know where you stand. Thanks for warning me. I guess our years of friendship that you remember so fondly don't create any tolerance for friends under pressure."

"We're through. I'll find out about everything. In the meantime, I guess you have immediate problems to deal with. I don't need to do anything. You're doing plenty to yourself. You think you're under pressure now. Wait a while."

"I'll find my way out." David walked straight to the front door without turning around or speaking. He had nowhere to go but home, if he could call it that. Jake wasn't off the mark when he said he was boxed. Good word for it. But he'd survive. He was surprised Jake had not pressed harder about seeing Dana. He was surprised, although he shouldn't be, that Jake had tracked down Nick and his lawyer and actually met with them, and Burkhardt. He stops at nothing. At least he knew what to expect.

64

The house was dark when he pulled in the driveway. He knew Lucille would be back. He was careful not to wake anyone. He lay down on the sofa in his office and drifted off to restless sleep littered with all the problems he faced. He took deep breaths and concentrated on pushing them away. He had learned that technique years ago when he was experimenting with meditation. Later, after getting back from Iraq, when he was tortured by hyper-vigilance, it was one of the mindfulness techniques he learned at the VA in a mental health class. At least he got something out of it.

David developed a theory, mostly kept to himself, that soldiers who went into combat in a stable, healthy condition, and who weren't enlisting out of desperation, returned to civilian life in about the same shape as when they went in. Most of the people who came out with serious mental health problems were those who had some problems—alcohol, drugs, mental illness—when they went in. Many of them were hoping they'd come out in better condition than when they went in. It rarely happened.

Of course, some soldiers had unusually horrible experiences or suffered devastating injuries. Everyone, no matter how healthy and strong, had a breaking point. He had observed that suicides tended to be those who were in a desperate situation before they went in or those who saw the military as their last best hope. Others had a promising future only to get home and run into some insurmountable problem that drove them to despair. The perception that there was no escape is hardly ever accurate. But people can't think clearly when they're drowning in despair.

Perhaps anyone could reach a breaking point for suicide as well as mental illness. David couldn't imagine committing suicide but then he'd never been that close to despair. He felt that he had retained his ability to perceive and think in a healthy way, despite occasional discouragement, anxiety, and fear, and had never entered the dark realm. But no one could rule that out. Public humiliation and devastating losses could trigger an episode. Once mental illness took over at the psychosis level, anything could happen.

He wondered how he would react if all the losses he contemplated actually happened. If he were publicly humiliated at trial and lost everything, might he contemplate suicide? Who could tell? If only those who contemplate suicide could know that they are at risk of destroying the only chance of relief and release. He fell asleep with these morbid thoughts, wondering if this was to become his dark night of the soul.

When he awoke, he was aware of silence downstairs. He dressed in casual clothes that he had in the outerwear closet, jeans, long sleeve UA shirt, and running shoes. He had to get underway by 7:30 but hoped to touch base with the boys. Despite their reserve, the boys were glad to see him and seemed eager to talk, the first occasion since the sudden departure for the lake house. He was relieved that Marcus would make a complete recovery—well, except that he was wearing a cast on his leg like a badge of honor. They spent an hour over breakfast before Lucille emerged, at which point the boys immediately became quiet, guarded, and preoccupied with nothing in particular. She evidently had not expected to see him in the kitchen and looked even worse than usual. She appeared hung over. He had mixed feelings. Now that she was going to start litigation and end up going for his carotid artery, he hoped that she'd come apart at the seams. Let her ruin herself, he thought. He had tried for years to rescue her from alcoholism. Nothing had worked.

She barely concealed her contempt for him. The boys' evident pleasure at being with him compounded her displeasure. It seemed unfair to her in view of her dedication to their needs. He told her quickly that he was driving to Boston to see Willard. He put it in terms of Willard needing to see him. She didn't react to that subtle device. The boys asked whether they could come along, and he had to refuse. There was no place for them in the serious conversation that he needed to have with Willard. He promised to return as soon as possible and spend time with them. They were placated for the moment. He'd have to follow through with that. He preferred not to mention, at least not in front of the boys, the call from Morehead.

65

David arrived at Willard's apartment on Beacon Street in two and a half hours flat, despite stopping to text Dana about his conversation with Jake and to place a call to Richard to set up a time to talk. He would reveal that the report had surfaced. How could Richard help shape his testimony if he didn't know about it?

The existence of the report brought David's statements into question. He had not told the whole truth at the investigation hearing. At the time, he had wilted under pressure from his superior officers to play along in minimizing the incident because the two embedded journalists would have been certain to write about it, and their stories highlighting civilian deaths would have been carried by every wire service.

The enemies of the United States were hungry for any allegations of misconduct by Americans. The slaughter of innocent civilians, especially because of an American NCO's improper conduct and failure to follow orders, coupled with a failure of leadership on David's part, would have been big news. The problem with the report was that it might contain conflicting versions of what had happened. David did not recall whether he had seen the report years ago. The entire transcript was no doubt appended as well with the commander's final remarks, justifying what was, in essence, a whitewash. The non-judicial handling of a matter that clearly should have gone to a court martial was patently inadequate.

If the facts got out, it could be another Abu Ghraib that, coincidentally, was located not far away from Ramadi. Maybe it didn't rise to the level of a My Lai atrocity because of the difference in sheer numbers of deaths, but it was bad enough. The military response was to justify Nick's retaliation, the good soldier acting to defend his turf. When the facts emerged in the press, Nick might possibly be given a pass by public opinion. But misconduct or failure to lead by an officer would be judged more harshly, and cover-ups were universally condemned.

David's train of thought ended abruptly, thankfully, when Willard opened the front door. They went out to the small stone terrace in back of the apartment. Willard had decorated the terrace with plants. He assured David that their conversation could not be overheard. David brought Willard up to date on all the events that had brought him to the brink of testifying, while he was defending himself against attacks by Lucille and Jake. He disclosed that he

174

was worrying about the possibility of prosecution for a war crime years after the war.

Willard listened attentively, and David knew he was assessing the situation with his unique moral framework. It was a wonder to David how Willard could be entirely supportive while at the same time candidly analyze critically the moral choices to be made.

Willard had nearly always held his own feet to the fire when it came to moral decisions. He had a remarkable capacity to suffer the consequences without complaint. But he acknowledged that he had failed to do that at times because he had not perceived or understood the choice and sometimes because he had failed to muster the strength to do what was right. He was always, in David's experience, honest in evaluating himself or others.

66

When David had finished, he said, "What are your thoughts?"

Willard began. "You know I'm glad to give feedback. But have you made a decision?"

"No, not entirely. I look at the situation piece by piece. I can't stop Lucille from starting a divorce action. I tried to get her to hold off for a few months. As far as Jake is concerned, I've lost control of that situation. What I did was wrong. I can't change what happened, and Jake is unforgiving. If I admit what happened, it would not change anything. I can't argue that it's morally right to deny everything, but, if I don't, Dana will be in trouble too, and I'll pay the consequences anyway.

"The trial is the big thing," David said. "It may be that I won't have to testify or, if I do, that it won't result in serious damage. The decisions in this matter were made a long time ago in Iraq in the middle of a war. To protect our own men and women was a legitimate choice. I could have refused to go along with the cover-up but what good would it have done? It would have brought disastrous publicity and criticism down on our company, not to mention the whole battalion and the brigade, even the government itself. Nick did eliminate the insurgents who had been besieging us continuously. Yes, he killed a bunch of innocent people but that could have happened even if someone else had conducted the retaliatory strike."

"I'm with you so far," Willard said.

"I didn't act firmly to stop Nick before his relationship with the Iraqi girl became a problem, and I didn't intervene as I should have. But exposing him and our whole military to condemnation by forcing a court martial would not have solved anything. I admit that I fell short, but those were judgment calls. I know that sounds like rationalizing the result, but there it is. As far as the President goes, it may be unnecessary to tell her the whole story. She isn't publicly committed to me at this point. If she nominates me without knowing this, that would not be right, but I have no reason to think that will happen before the trial. Jury selection is starting in a couple of weeks."

"Fair enough," Willard interjected. "You're facing it head on. While I might not agree completely with your plan, I'm glad to see that you're not ducking the issues. There's some rationalization, of course, and you are clearly subordinating morality to practical consequences for yourself. No question about that. You've asked what I think. You know that I never tell anyone what to do. No one can make your moral choices for you and, as far as setting priorities, only you can do that. The weight you assign to the moral choices varies according to your priorities. In other words, you weigh the moral choices against your main priority, securing the Supreme Court nomination. Only you can decide whether that is justified."

"It's disappointing to hear you put it that way, but I can't argue with it," David said.

"By the other choices, I mean your marriage and parenthood, your friendship with Jake, and with Bradley and the others who are supporting you. Your potential future relationship with Dana is another. She's the only one whom I don't know, but I can understand why you value her so highly. She sounds like someone I'd like, but, from what you tell me, that relationship may not work out. Is securing the nomination important for anyone but yourself? In other words, do you believe that it's essential for the good of the people that you have the Court seat? Or is it just the culmination of your career that you long for? I can't answer those questions. I have a hunch that if you get it, it won't be the culmination of your career. There'll be something else beyond it that compels you, and you may wonder why it seemed so important.

"You have within your reach," Willard said, "the capacity to do a lot of good, to serve as a sterling example of integrity and moral worth. I'm not at all sure the best way for you to do that is by being a Supreme Court justice. It certainly is not if you acquire that appointment by violating or compromising your highest standards, which should be the highest standards that you can imagine. You know that I don't think much of success as a valuable human pursuit. It usually brings no satisfaction and accomplishes nothing. It evaporates in the course of a human life. I have a different framework, more of a transcendent standard. I'm not saying that I always apply it the way I should, but I believe in it."

"I think serving on the Court would be my path to contributing to the good of the country," David said, "but I understand that you are looking at it, at everything really, from a different perspective. I can't put myself in that place. At least I don't think I can. Maybe it's just that I don't want to."

Willard went on, "I realize that you see certain actions as absolutely being the death knell to getting the nomination. You're probably right. After all, a bunch of flawed human beings is going to react to what you do, and they're going to be governed by self-interest. The President may react differently. From what I see, she is a rare bird, the likes of whom we haven't seen in a long time. It's a miracle that she got the nomination and won. No one thought she would. She is worth treating with the utmost respect. She might not ditch you the way others would if you tell her the truth. Maybe she deserves that much from you. You have to decide.

"I have one more comment." Willard said, pausing briefly. "If you join the conspiracy of people who talk about war in the usual antiseptic way, you'll be doing a great disservice to the human race. War was created by people with near absolute power, kings and rulers, as a means to get something they wanted. Ordinary people bear the burden. We need to call it what it is.

"In order to get ordinary people to do what they want, those in power promote myths about war, glorify it, produce sanitized versions, even elevate it to a place of honor in human society. Ordinary people have little choice in the matter to begin with, and they buy, on some level anyway, the myths about war becoming the path to manhood and honor. They even accept the notion that war has spiritual value. People hardly question the myths any more, until they come face to face with the reality of war."

Willard was getting worked up. "War has been portrayed as, not only glorious and heroic, but inevitable and inescapable. Rubbish. If you publicly sugarcoat the ugliness and horror of war, as you did when you went along with the cover-up, you perpetuate the fraud on humankind. Decent people have had to do despicable things in the name of war. For God's sake, and I mean that, do your part in dispelling the smokescreen that protects war and its consequences. Okay, that's my sermon for the day."

They talked on for two hours before strolling to lunch at one of Willard's favorite restaurants, Cheers Beacon Hill, and lingering afterward on a park bench in the Commons. As David prepared to leave, he felt the sense of being grounded that he always got after being with Willard. He felt a pang of anxiety at the thought of returning to his problems from this safe haven. Willard's moral confidence, he would call it his faith, bolstered David's confidence. At the same time, it forced him to contemplate shouldering a burden of moral responsibility for his actions. He felt weighed down by a sadness that he didn't understand. Perhaps it was a realization of how dependent he was on Willard for guidance and that Willard was not immortal. He did not want to think about a time when he could no longer turn to him.

David might not be prepared to act with the moral strength that Willard would like to see, but at least he now had a touchstone. One point that Willard made he took to heart, that was letting the President know all the facts before she committed herself publicly. She did deserve this, but did he have the courage to disclose the facts? Once again, he began thinking of ways around outright disclosure. What if he minimized the importance of the trial and simply told Lehman that he had to support a wartime buddy, hoping that he would not inquire further?

Before leaving for the drive back, David asked Willard a final question. "I forgot to ask you about a woman I saw on the ferry when I came to see you the last time on the island. She appeared to be a little older than I, maybe late forties or early fifties. She was sitting out on the back deck in the rain when I went outside, wearing a blue parka with a hood. She was striking, and I don't mean beautiful like a film star, but she had an aura about her that made me keep glancing over at her. I'd say she was on the tall side, slender, with green eyes, and a good Nantucket tan. She looked like a native, not a visitor. Do you recognize her from the description?"

Willard erupted with laughter. "I do, indeed," he said. "You didn't miss much. I know just who you mean. She's a minister, the rector of the Congregational Church. She's from an old Nantucket family, as I am. She spent most of her life in Boston and Cambridge. Her background is psychology as well as theology, and she taught at Boston University Theology School. About five years ago, she came back here to live and eventually took over the church. She's a very good friend of mine. She's an avid sailor, swimmer, runner, quite an athlete."

"What's her name? Tell me, for God's sake, literally," David said.

"I can tell you're impatient, aren't you," Willard said, laughing again. "I don't blame you. She's an absolute gem, and you have her age about right. Her name is Ruth Lambert. Her maiden name was Bernard. The Bernard family is connected to the old Nantucket families back to the early seventeenth century. She's spectacular. I see her several times a week and next time you're here, I'll get you two together. She'd be a good match for you. I'm too old for her. I'm feeling my age these days. I have to go for a checkup and probably some medical work later in the fall. I was supposed to go in last spring but I slipped out here before they came to get me." He laughed again with amusement at his own deception and at David's keen interest in Ruth. He was not surprised. The idea of destiny popped into David's head.

67

David headed straight home from Boston. The weekend was reasonably peaceful, and he spent time with the boys as he'd promised. Richard called to let him know the trial was beginning at the end of the first week of September, assuming that jury selection was completed. The judge would be hearing preliminary motions during August. Trial courts did not shut down for a month as appellate courts did.

Richard predicted that David would not be called until the third week of September because the prosecution case was expected to last an entire week. That was fine with David. It gave him time to prepare and, of course, it allowed time for a possible plea bargain.

He might be free after all to hear cases at the Supreme Court during most of the two-week term in early September. He talked to Burkhardt on Monday and kept his temper, enduring the tongue lashing for not showing up on Friday. Herb called him at court and approved the idea of consenting to Morehead as Lucille's counsel. Herb would call Morehead to lay the foundation for deferring the action. He reported later that Morehead didn't oppose slowing the process down a bit.

Richard sent his young associate, Barbara Stearns, to Philadelphia to sit in on the motions and to get to know the cast of players in the trial. She would keep David current through the preliminary stages.

PART THREE

"The truth shall make you free."
    —John 8:32

"[H]e was still in good health when the quarantine period was over, and they told him again that he had to get out and go to war. Yossarian sat up in bed when he heard the bad news and shouted 'I see everything twice.'"
    —Joseph Heller, *Catch-22*, 1955

"Truth is the most valuable thing we have. Let us economize it."
    —Mark Twain, *Pudd'nhead Wilson's New Calendar, Following the Equator*, 1897

68

Early in August, Lucille took the boys to the Michigan lake house for three weeks. One of her cousins had canceled her allotment at the family compound. With few other takers, Lucille got extra time, giving David much-needed breathing room. In addition to reading briefs for the September term, he would write an outline of his experiences during the Iraq tour. This would prepare him with all the details he'd need for the trial. According to assessments by Richard and Barbara, he would probably be called to testify.

After getting a start on the outline, David called Willard to ask whether he could visit him on Nantucket during the following week. Willard agreed enthusiastically and confirmed that a room would be available. He planned to stay on well into September, his favorite time of the year on the island. They agreed on a date for David's arrival. Two days before the day of departure, David called first thing in the morning to confirm the plan. He left a message and, when he didn't hear back by early afternoon, he called again. An unfamiliar female voice answered. When David revealed the purpose of his call, she said, "I'll get someone." David waited, feeling slightly apprehensive. In a moment, another woman's voice greeted him by name.

"Justice Lawson, David, this is Ruth Lambert, a friend of Willard's. I know your name well. Willard has spoken of you often. I'm afraid I have bad news. Willard had a stroke, a major one, last night. I planned to call you later."

"Oh no," David said, feeling alarmed. "How is he? Was there a lot of damage?"

"I'm afraid so. He's in the ICU at the hospital on the island. He hasn't responded since the EMTs brought him there. Depending on his response within the next few hours, they are weighing whether to fly him to Massachusetts General in Boston. They thought it best not to put him through that trauma unless it's necessary."

"Oh, my God, this is awful," David said, barely able to contain his emotions. "I was coming to stay with him in two days."

"He mentioned that. He was looking forward to seeing you. I'm so sorry to give you this news."

"This doesn't sound good," David said. "What's his condition? I don't want to overreact, but what are his chances of surviving? I know he didn't want to prolong his life if it wouldn't be high quality."

"You're right, exactly. I think he had a premonition during the past month

183

or two about his health failing. There's no reason to bring him to Boston unless he needs extraordinary care. I don't think he'd want that under the circumstances. The doctors doubt that he'll be able to go on without some form of life support. I've been trying to get in touch with his children, to let them know the situation. Nothing will happen until we reach them. His son and daughter both live out of the country, as you know, so it's doubtful that they could get here very soon. So far we haven't even made contact."

"I want to come up, Ruth. I'm going to head for the Hyannis ferry right away. I'll just throw a bag in the car and be on my way. Would that be okay?"

"That's wonderful. He would want that, and it would be a great help. Just come directly to the hospital."

Twenty minutes later, he reached Hyannis in time for the three o'clock ferry. The circumstances were so different from the last trip, made with happy anticipation. He sat alone on the back deck, recalling the last trip. He felt bereft already, as if he were losing a best friend, an older brother, and a parent, all at the same time. He felt lost without Willard's steady hand to guide him, especially at this time when he was facing one of the biggest challenges of his life. He sensed that his reliance on Willard might be nearing the end.

When the boat docked, he hurried off and walked up to the hospital. The short walk and the exercise and air had a calming effect. Arriving at the hospital, he went directly to the ICU and asked for Willard's room. As he approached, he felt himself about to drown in deep sadness but, incongruously, experienced a sense of nervous anticipation about meeting Ruth. He knew Willard would be amused to know his conflicting feelings. His eyes would sparkle at the thought of David's interest in her. He might joke about stopping at nothing to bring them together. David took a deep breath and entered the room. Willard, with his normally robust appearance, looked shockingly small and frail, lying there in a cocoon of medical equipment. Ruth, who was seated by the window, gazing absently at a magazine, looked up and walked toward David, arms outstretched.

They greeted and hugged briefly, as she expressed her sorrow. "I'm so very sorry. I know what Willard meant to you. You meant the world to him."

David went to the bedside and gently grasped Willard's hand, glad for the palpable life force still warming his body. David could imagine his soul, present and vital, now about to be liberated, welcoming the journey ahead. When David spoke to Willard, he observed his eyelids flicker and his head move in a gentle nod, as if he knew David was there. David sat for a while with him, speaking in a low voice, struggling to hold back tears, telling him what he had meant, what he still meant, and the unimaginable difficulty of going on without him. "What on earth would I do without you? I am a lost sheep. You've been my moral guide for so many decades."

After a while, David and Ruth quietly left the room to sit in the nearby waiting area. They sat without speaking. Even without words, David was keenly aware of the depth of Ruth's compassion and the strength of her faith.

His heart, aching with pain for Willard's impending death, raced in her presence, in defiance of his conviction that all his attention should be directed to Willard.

The doctor, who had known Willard since she was a child, and later married his nephew, sat with them. She explained that the stroke had been severe and that the testing indicated that he had some brain function, both stem and higher brain. She offered her prognosis. "Although the equipment will keep him breathing and his blood circulating, I don't believe he will regain consciousness in any meaningful sense. We've done quite a bit of testing. Even if he were to regain full consciousness, he wouldn't regain control of his limbs. He'd be confined to a wheelchair. He wouldn't be able to speak or care for himself."

"Wouldn't it be best to wait for a couple of days?" David asked.

"You can wait if that's most comfortable. I think we'll know as much as we can by tomorrow morning."

"How do you feel about it?" David asked Ruth.

"I don't feel comfortable terminating support until we hear from the children. We definitely need to wait for them to respond. It wouldn't be right to act without their approval or without giving them a chance for them to get here."

Ruth and David agreed that it did not make sense to move Willard to Boston. They would await contact with the children, however, before making a decision. They maintained their vigil while they shared stories about their experiences with Willard.

69

Later that evening, back at Willard's apartment, Ruth got calls from both children. They agreed with the decision to terminate life support. Neither would be able to get back to the States for several weeks. They would return for a memorial service later in the fall, probably October. Neither child had seen Willard in several years. They had their own families, one in Brazil, one in Japan. Although they stayed in touch with him occasionally, they had not been back to the States within the past five years. Two of their children had never even met their grandfather. Willard rarely mentioned his children, who had been raised by their mother after the divorce. Strange, David thought, he gave so much to so many people but not to his own children. That is probably my fate with my own children, he thought. Ruth would carry out Willard's wishes to organize a service on Nantucket, with his ashes to be deposited at his favorite places on Nantucket and Tuckernuck. A small portion of the ashes would also be placed in the Coleman plot. The service would no doubt draw many people from his immense international following.

Both Ruth and David were exhausted at the late hour when they finally left the hospital. They agreed to return in the morning to carry out withdrawal of life support assuming there was no positive change in his condition. They parted in front of the rectory, with David crossing the street to Willard's apartment in the Inn. Their plan was to meet at the rectory for coffee before heading to the hospital.

David did not anticipate the intense emotional experience of being alone in the apartment. Willard's presence was palpable, so much so that he had an impulse to talk out loud to him. And yet, he felt alone, with Willard's physical presence about to depart. He thought about Willard's soul leaving his body. The idea startled him. It implied a level of Christian faith that he was usually skeptical about. But then he had not experienced before the death or near death of anyone whom he loved as much as Willard. He had never before wished for the continued life of his soul or had such trust that it was true. Abstract philosophical theories faded into obscurity in the face of concrete human emotional and spiritual experiences.

Open books in various stages of study by Willard rested in dozens of locations. David recalled that Willard grazed literary, theological, and philosophical texts endlessly. Well-worn notebooks were strategically placed in every room, positioned for Willard to jot down his observations and thoughts. David flipped through several notebooks and discovered Willard's newly discovered talent for poetry. "These have to be published," David said aloud.

The entire apartment bore Willard's unique imprint. Strange, David thought, how these material possessions, so treasured in life, amount to so little upon death. Willard was confident about his destination after this life and equally confident that souls, once disembodied, retain in some mysterious way, the knowledge and insight acquired during earthly life. That became assimilated into the collective knowledge of humankind.

David found William Sloane Coffin's book, *Credo*, lying on Willard's dining table open to the section on the end of life. A highlighted section read: "If we are essentially spirit, not flesh; if what is substantial is intangible; if we are spirits that have bodies and not the other way around, then it makes sense that just as musicians can abandon their instruments to find others elsewhere, so at death our spirits can leave our bodies and find other forms in which to make new music." That captured Willard's philosophy perfectly.

David sat, scanning other passages that Willard must have highlighted as he read or reread the book. He knew that Willard rejected most religious dogma but that he was intensely spiritual. He would say plainly that he was ready for whatever God had in store for him. He never defined precisely who or what he thought God was. He'd find out soon enough what was to be discovered.

He chose the sofa to sleep on and drifted off letting his mind wander to thoughts of both Willard and Ruth. His first impression of Ruth during the ferry ride had been prescient. She was attractive enough but her main attribute was an undefined feminine strength and goodness. Her features were pleasing and her presence radiated warmth and optimism. She had a sixth sense about feelings. He suspected that she and Willard were conceived from the same mold. Both had a sense of inner peace, confidence, and empathy. His final waking thought was to look forward to seeing her in the morning. He was in no hurry to get back to Connecticut.

70

They met at eight. They talked over coffee and left untouched the bagels that Ruth had gone out early to get. The morning mission was too solemn to allow for eating at this hour. They decided that there was no one else who needed to be informed before authorizing the removal of life support. They went to the hospital, refreshed by the brisk walk from the rectory. The doctor was already in the room, checking Willard's vital signs. She led them to a small conference room for an update on his medical condition.

David began, "Doctor, what's his condition this morning? Any change?"

"No change," she replied. "He's resting peacefully and I think he understands on some level what I was saying. I minimized the medication so he'd be able to comprehend and maybe even respond. I told him the prognosis, that the stroke was severe, leaving lasting damage. He nodded. I believe he understood. I asked if he wants me to keep the life support going for a while longer. I saw a slight negative movement of his head. I've known him a long time, as you both have, and I feel tuned in to his thoughts and feelings. I'm sure you do too."

"I'm amazed at his responses given the severity of the stroke," David said. "Do you think we could talk to him for a while?"

"Of course," she said. "Take your time. No reason to rush."

They sat with Willard for more than two hours, holding his hands, which radiated warmth, speaking quietly to him and listening for messages. If there were a chance he could hear and be comforted by their presence, they would take all day. Ruth prayed quietly. David was not comfortable in displaying religious faith openly.

"Willard," David said, "We spoke to Josh and Susan last night. They're making plans to come here but it won't be right away. You remember Josh is in Brazil and Susan, in Japan. They wish they could come now. But they said that Ruth and I should make the medical decisions and whatever we decide is okay with them."

Willard appeared to nod affirmatively. David felt that he understood. He went on. "The doctor told you that it's unlikely you can resume living alone and do all that you're used to doing. We're prepared to make arrangements for a bed at Island View Manor, if you would like. You could get therapy and get some of your strength back." Willard shifted perceptibly in the bed and seemed to be agitated as if resisting the idea. He murmured slightly in a way that sounded like "uh-uh."

Ruth joined in, "You don't want that, Willard. Is that right? You don't want to go to a nursing home? You don't want life support to continue?" David felt uncomfortable at the directness of her questions. She was certainly more familiar with these situations, although David had been present at the deaths of too many soldiers to count, plus his grandmother, who died at the age of one hundred when David was in his twenties.

"I'm satisfied that he doesn't want life support," Ruth said. "That's consistent with everything he's always said."

"I agree," David said, "although it makes me uncomfortable to put words in his mouth. That's the lawyer in me. But I feel confident it's what he wants."

They both were feeling exhausted. David wanted to speak with the doctor one more time before giving the signal.

"Doctor, are you still convinced there's no hope of recovery? Did you do any more cognition tests?"

"I did neurological testing this morning with our portable scanner. Judging by all the signs of the stroke and post-stroke activity, he won't regain much more than he has right now."

"Okay," David said. "I'm convinced. Are you, Ruth?"

"As certain as I can be," she said. "I'm in favor of carrying out his wishes." She looked ever so slightly impatient with David. She had reached the point of decision more quickly.

"Doctor, let's go ahead with removal." David said.

"Do you want to wait outside while we disconnect?"

They glanced at each other. "We'll stay," David said firmly. Willard's breathing was labored and he looked uncomfortable with all the equipment enveloping him. He was still but not yet in peace. They continued to hold his hands. The doctor warned that he might continue breathing, alive on his own for an indeterminate time, as long as a few hours but possibly as short a time as a few minutes. There was no certain timing of death in response to the disconnecting of life support.

The doctor left the room. Minutes later the ventilator motor shut down. No change happened in the first half hour. Willard's hands continued to be warm. Gradually, the warmth receded and, within forty-five minutes, his hands were cold. Life was gone. Death had come. David strained for several minutes to see whether he could encounter Willard's soul as it departed the body. He had heard people say that they had actually seen a vaporous presence rise from a body at the moment of death.

He would like to see that as reassurance that the soul was embarking on a journey of its own. He could not be sure that any such wispy visage ascended. He asked Ruth whether she had ever seen the phenomenon. She believed it was possible but remained skeptical about the accuracy of human perceptions.

"Our perpetual search," Ruth said, "for physical evidence of something as mysterious as death or afterlife or God, is understandable. We desperately want to know the other worldly in human terms. We want assurance, evidence. When we hear the voice of God, it isn't likely to be some Old Testament-type voice roaring or doing magical things. It's more likely to be a small voice—or some kind of ambiguous sign—emanating from inside, not outside."

71

They sat a few minutes longer before heading out into the breezy Nantucket sunshine. They walked for a while, stopped for coffee on the pier, and sat lazily in the sunshine.

"What's your connection with Nantucket?" David asked.

"I grew up here. We lived here year round. My mother and father were from old Nantucket families. My father was pastor of the Congregational Church."

"Where did you go to college?"

"I left for college and graduate school, of course, BU for both. Then I taught psychology there for a long time. I finally decided to go to theology school, which had been a long-term goal for me. I planned to teach rather than minister in a parish."

"And you married, right?"

"I did, just about twenty-eight years ago. That ended abruptly five years ago when my husband decided he had enough of commitments. He was tired of marriage and wanted freedom. I puttered around feeling restless and a little depressed for a while. Eventually, I learned that the minister at the Church was retiring at the end of one summer. I was lucky enough to get the job. Since then, I've stayed on the island about eleven months out of the year. I take two vacations, one after Christmas and one after Easter."

"Do you have children?" David asked.

"No. We had no children. The divorce was simple, painful but simple. At this point, I have no regrets and I'm content to be alone. The social environment here is limited and, anyway, my life is full, with ministering, teaching, athletics, writing, and art. . . . Tell me about yourself."

David told her about his life, his poor decisions, and his present opportunities for success or failure. He said he felt that he had never dug down deeply enough to get to the bottom of his morality crisis. He believed it stemmed from his childhood and an experience that he could not face and, therefore, could never put to rest.

"Will you tell me about that experience?" she asked, turning toward him on the bench.

David looked at her without speaking, wrestling momentarily with a decision to reveal the truth. The grief over Willard's death had overwhelmed him. He was ready to give up the long-held secret.

"I will," he said. "It's the first time I have ever spoken about it." She put a hand on his, meeting his eyes with acceptance.

"I caused my brother's death. I killed him actually. He was six, and I was twelve. I hated him. I hated him from the time my parents adopted him. So I ruined his life, my parents' lives, and my own."

"There must be more to it," she said, probing gently. "That's a sweeping conclusion. It sounds like a child's oversimplification of something much more subtle, much more complicated. Would you give me the details?"

"I guess it is sweeping," he said, "but I've always felt that, at some point, I would have to acknowledge the truth, as raw as it is, not as I wish it had been. I directly caused his death. I can't believe I'm talking about this. It's been stuck in some deep place inside me. I never even told the whole story to Willard. It haunts me day and night."

"Are you comfortable here? Is this place private enough?"

"We seem to be alone. Willard guessed what it was, I think, but he never pressed me. It makes me sad that I lost the chance to tell him anything else. It will take a while to accept that. If you're willing, here goes," he said, looking straight at her. "I think you'll be shocked."

"I doubt that," she said.

72

I t happened when I had just turned twelve," David said. "My brother was six, a few weeks away from his seventh birthday. I was born when my parents were older than most, mid-thirties. They had been married for more than ten years. They wanted desperately to have children but it just didn't happen. That's what they told me. They didn't go into detail, of course. Finally, I happened. They adored me, I think. That's what they told me anyway. It was like a miracle for them. I often wondered if theirs was an immaculate conception. I never could picture them having sex. I suppose that's common. But they never seemed to be in love. There was no sign of physical affection between them, not a hint of romantic love. They were good people, good parents I suppose, overprotective, but that was to be expected. They had waited so long.

"After a while," David continued, "they worried about having only one child. What if something happened? Some family members convinced them it wasn't good to have an only child. They said I'd be spoiled and lonely and all that. So they started talking about adopting. They figured they were too old to have another of their own. I was very much aware of their conversations. They even asked me whether I would like a brother or a sister as a companion. They explained the whole thing in simple language, of course. I remember my reaction vividly. 'No, a thousand times no,' I screamed and ran out of the room. Even though I sometimes wished I had a brother or sister, when I was faced with the reality, I wanted no part of it. Finally, they went ahead despite my protests. They did find a child, a boy, to adopt. He was from a neighboring town, an orphan I was told, maybe just to get my sympathy. I don't know the truth. The long and short of it was that it was the perfect arrangement for everybody, except me."

Ruth was spellbound but interrupted for the first time. "How old was he? And you, how old were you then?"

"Ronnie was around two years old and I was about eight. It was never the same for me. I suppose I got over it in one sense or, at least, everyone thought I did. But I did not let go of the resentment, the sense of betrayal. I carried it until their deaths, all of their deaths. Oh, he and I got along in a way, and it wouldn't be fair to say that I suffered or was neglected. Remember the ads for a COPD drug that used to be on TV? People had elephants sitting on their chests. That's the way I felt, suffocated by his existence. My parents focused most of their attention on him. I suppose they did the same for me when I was that little, but, of course, I can't remember that. So it seemed unnatural and I felt abandoned and cast aside."

"Of course," she said. "That's a natural experience for first children, but this does sound extreme."

"Anyway, in the summer when I was twelve and he was nearly seven, my parents rented a cottage at a nearby lake, which they usually did, for two weeks. Those were the only vacations we ever took. For some reason, which still mystifies me, they decided it would be good for us to stay there for a night or two while they went back to the house, which was less than an hour away. My father had to go to work every day and this would spare him going back and forth. Why my mother didn't stay, I can't imagine."

"I'm afraid to hear what happened," Ruth exclaimed.

"They were usually so overprotective. I was amazed. I had mixed feelings. I'd rather have been alone. He'd ruin my time there. My reaction was that it was a horrible burden to place on me. But I felt a little thrill too. I would be in control. What an opportunity to bully him, torture him. Something inside me felt that thrill. It was a strange feeling. It even frightened me.

"I was mean to him the rest of the first day. I was mean a lot of the time, of course, but the point is that on the second day, when they were due back at supper time, we had a big storm, lots of rain with wind and choppy water. The lake looked like an ocean. We had a large Navy Surplus yellow rubber raft. It was the kind you could row or put a small motor on. I loved taking it out and jumping from it. Anyway, I told Ronnie I was going out in the raft. He was afraid to be left alone and afraid of the lake. He could barely stay afloat for a few feet with the dog paddle. He begged me not to go, and I didn't relent, of course. I enjoyed tormenting him. Then he said he was going to go with me. He was afraid to be alone in the storm. I refused but, actually, I was provoking him into coming out with me. That's just what I wanted, to really scare him.

"To tell the truth, I was scared too. For one thing, it was pretty deserted. There were a lot of cottages, some very close, but it was a weekday and no one was in sight. The lake was really rough. I had a hard time launching the raft, but my need to terrorize him drove me on. I sat on the edge of the raft, which actually made me nervous. Ronnie sat on the bottom. He was terrified, but I teased him and called him all kinds of names—sissy, wimp, fairy—the worst I could come him up with at the time. I said he was just a baby. So he moved and sat on the rim opposite me. I could see he was trembling. If I hadn't forced him to do that, he wouldn't have gone overboard."

"What happened?"

"I rocked the raft, pretending that we would capsize. He started crying, wailing, screaming, and this just fueled my appetite for cruelty. I did it all the more. Then, and it makes me shudder to think of this, which I relive every day of my life: a big wave caught us. It actually hit him at just the wrong moment, and he went overboard. At first, I laughed. I just stayed in the raft, watching him flounder. He screamed, which made him start choking on the waves washing over him. He begged for help, and I just laughed and did nothing. I loved it. But then it all changed in a second when I realized what was happening. He was choking, getting mouthfuls, disappearing from view behind the waves. The storm churned up the waves. He started to get carried away from the raft.

"I started to panic when I realized this was out of my control. I tried to row toward him but the oars were useless. I finally jumped in and tried to swim toward him, holding onto the tie line, but I couldn't make any headway. He was fifteen feet away and disappearing in the waves, going under for a long time and then popping up. Through it all, he was gasping and choking and struggling. Then I lost sight of him for good. I was getting tossed around in the water and had a tough time getting back to the raft. I had no idea what to do. Finally I started rowing for shore. What else should I do? I was sick, panicky. I threw up. I was frantic. I was wailing, 'No! Oh no!' over and over and over. But I knew he was lost, and that I was lost forever. I had killed him. I hadn't meant to kill him, just terrorize him. I was in agony. All I could think of was the consequences I would have to endure. As I rowed toward shore, I started repeating 'Oh God! Why did I do it? Why did I do it?' I had no doubt that God's wrath would strike me down."

"Oh, I'm so sorry," she said putting her arm on his. "How terrible, and you were just a child."

73

There's more," David said. "When I got close to shore, I jumped out and ran to the cottage next to ours. The old woman who lived there was on the porch. She said she had seen what happened and had called the police. She asked, more like *said*, in an accusing tone, 'How could you take your little brother out in that storm, much less go out yourself? It was a terrible thing to do. It was a crime to do that.'

"I knew she was right, but I hated her for saying it. It made me sick. Right away my mind went to wondering how much she had seen. What would she tell the police when they arrived?

"My mind turned from grief to worry about myself. I knew I had led Ronnie to his death, virtually murdered him. I thought I would be arrested and spend my life in prison. But when the police got there, she didn't accuse me, at least not that I heard. Maybe no one saw what really happened. I heard her say something about 'fooling around' but that was it. Maybe I'd gotten away with it. Those thoughts were terrorizing my mind. So I went from guilt and remorse and fear for my lost soul, to desperate self-preservation. Then I felt a glimmer of relief, almost joy, that I had escaped the consequences. All that took place in a flash. All I could think of was whether I could get myself out of the mess. I told myself that I would deal with my guilt and remorse later. I think that's when I learned to postpone my feelings, to stop them in their tracks and defer them."

"Oh, David, that's just awful," Ruth said in a distressed voice. "You were just a boy."

"An evil boy, I think," David said.

"No. You were just a foolish child at the mercy of your feelings. You were right on the cusp of childhood and adolescence. Children can't see as far ahead as adults when they're connecting feelings, actions, and consequences. You were overpowered by feelings of resentment, even hatred. Children have those feelings, adults too, but they hardly ever result in bad things. It was a horrible incident, but your feelings were understandable, normal in a way and in part caused by your parents. You did what so many kids do, tease, even torment, and put other kids at risk. And they, your parents, didn't foresee what could happen. And then, later, you had to face a war on top of that. What ever happened? Did they find your brother?"

"The police got hold of power boats and got nets to drag that side of the lake, but they found nothing all afternoon. Of course, the storm went on for a while, and it was hard for them to operate under those conditions. When darkness came, the search came to a stop. We remained at the cottage. There was hardly a word spoken among the three of us. The next day was more of the same. It was agonizing. A day later, his body washed up in the next cove, about a quarter mile down the shore. My parents. . . ." David paused, unable to finish his sentence. "They were absolutely beside themselves. Devastated would be too mild a word. I don't think they ever recovered. They never confronted me or accused me. They heard the story that I gave the police of course, which conveniently omitted any blame except for admitting that I had misjudged the situation. They heard the neighbor's story. They had to know that I tormented him whenever I got the chance and that I held onto a deep resentment. I don't know if they ever felt guilty about their role in the whole business."

"Do you think they ever suspected that you did it deliberately? What did you tell the police and your parents?" Ruth asked.

"I never told my parents anything directly, and they never asked. In all the years after, we never talked about it. Before I told the police my version, I thought about it carefully in the little time I had. They took a statement. I still have a copy of it, believe it or not. It's a reminder of how I could do something very bad, evil, and survive. It's helped me understand how other people, almost anyone, I'm convinced, can commit an evil act."

"I've seen evil," Ruth said, "but that's different. You were a child with a child's inability to anticipate consequences and control behavior. You're holding onto this incident as though the adult in you is responsible for the child's actions."

"When I talked to the police," David said, "I actually put the blame on Ronnie for urging me to take him out. I was clever in the way I did it. I was possessed with enough ingenuity and self-control, under those circumstances, to extricate myself. I couldn't admit that to myself for a long time. I worried for a long time that some other neighbor had seen more and sized up what happened but no one came forward and the police went to every house. Maybe they suspected something, maybe thought I was a monster. I guess no one who saw the scene from a distance was able to interpret it. They couldn't see what was in my mind. If someone had seen me rocking the raft and laughing, they would have known though, but I guess no one did. For a long time, I had nightmares in which I had committed murders and got away with them. But I never knew when they would catch up with me.

"For years, I was concerned about not getting caught for what I did, that I had really murdered him. I don't know which is worse, fearing discovery at any moment or living with the truth about what I did. It was revenge in a way, and that's not the only time I've wanted revenge. I know that I didn't want to stop until I caused him to suffer. Something relentless, a fury, had hold of me. Someone or something knows all about it. God? The Devil? I've always felt that my soul is in jeopardy."

"I have to think about that one," Ruth offered. "I don't think I believe in divine retribution or justice as such. But was your relationship with your parents ever restored in later years?"

"Not really. They buried it, never talked about it. I buried it once I felt sure I had gotten away with it. It ate away at all of us though. Eventually, we all carried on with the routine as before but any chance at happiness was gone. They did their jobs, but I could see they never again took pride in anything I did. I give them credit for doing the best they could, but they were wounded forever to the core. I've carried that memory, that scene, the weight of that guilt with me all my life, the last thirty years. I've had hundreds—thousands—of nightmares and flashbacks to that scene. I still do. That is my curse, at least part of it. I've always felt that there is no expiation or absolution for what I did."

74

That's an incredible story," Ruth said. "I'm sure it's not unique though. Children can't control impulses the way adults can, or are supposed to anyway. And children often grow up burdened by guilt for actions or thoughts out of proportion."

"Can you stand to hear a little more of what happened?" David asked. "I didn't expect to go into the whole thing, but I'd like to finish the story. There's not much more."

"Of course," Ruth said quickly.

"After the first day," David said, "when the search was abandoned because of the storm, my parents were huddled together in their room, talking sometimes, but mostly absorbed in their individual grief. On the second day, my mother kept trying to go outside to see if Ronnie had come home. She'd even ask where he was and when he was coming home. Her mind seemed to slip away, and she couldn't accept that he was dead. My father would bring her back when she went out on the porch in the rain. It stormed a long time on the first day and well into the second. My parents spoke quietly, when they spoke at all, and argued some of the time. I don't know what they said about me although the cottage had no insulation and sounds were hard to keep private. I was alone in my own fear and grief, too, mostly fear that it had turned out this way. I was stunned when I had to grasp that the past can't be changed. I kept going over it, willing it to have a different outcome. But this was the world of reality, not imagination. I think one of the big differences between childhood and adulthood is grasping the difference."

Ruth interjected, "The more I think about this, the more I'm convinced that you have been bearing a burden of guilt far beyond what you should. You didn't intend that he would die as a result of your teasing, even if we call it tormenting. Perhaps you should have known better. You were older than he was. We could even say that you knew there was risk involved. You probably even wished sometimes that he would die. But, as a child yourself, you don't need to assume adult responsibility. I've spent some of my psychology career studying developmental theories of responsibility for crime. I feel confident about this. Childhood, adolescence, and adulthood are clear and distinct stages."

"I get that," David said. "I've wrestled with these questions all my life. I even took philosophy courses and psychology courses looking for answers. When I got to law school and learned about the arguments that lawyers make in criminal cases, this incident was all I could think about. How fine is the line between intention to kill and intention to put someone under your care in such peril that you bear responsibility for what happens?

"Lawyers can make all the arguments they want to avoid convictions for their clients. That's their job, their duty actually, but that's a duty created by law, not one based on morality or religion. Actually, I think I showed my law skills on that terrible day when I began formulating my story and my strategy. Sad commentary, isn't it? This was a question of morality. It seems to me that people, maybe most people, have a lawyer lurking inside their brains to make arguments for them. We call it rationalization, twisting and turning and manipulating the facts to make ourselves feel better or to help us get out of trouble. But that doesn't involve the truth, the Truth with a capital T. There's a little more to the story that reveals more of me. I don't know why I'm doing this except that it is a backdrop to what happened in Iraq."

"I hope you'll tell me about that sometime," Ruth said.

75

Back to that day they found his body. I don't think any of us had slept that first night or the next," David said. "I was in turmoil with waves of terror and grief, not so much for Ronnie, as for the fact that my life was in jeopardy. I knew I had put in motion a force that couldn't be changed. Very early in the morning of the second day after it happened, there was a knock on the porch door. My mother called out, 'Oh, Ronnie's here.' I stayed in my room and listened. It was one of the policemen. He told my father that Ronnie's body had washed ashore. It was in an ambulance outside and could one of them please identify the body. My mother started wailing again and my father kept telling her to be quiet. She had not accepted the fact that he was dead. She was never the same again. She separated herself from her conscious mind, if that's possible, when she couldn't accept his death."

"I know what you mean. I think that's possible although neurologically it's something different," Ruth said.

"My father went outside. I was watching from the window. They opened the rear door of the ambulance, slid out a stretcher, and pulled down the sheet covering him to his waist. I could see this white, water-soaked body. He looked so tiny, so pathetic, and frail, and so awfully dead. It was the deadness that got to me. I was fascinated, despite myself. Finally, I ran to the bathroom and got sick, with violent heaving that I thought would never stop. And then I wept and wept until I had nothing left and lay on the bed.

"While I was still watching, my father nodded that it was Ronnie. The men were all grim-faced. A few neighbor men on the edge of the parking area spoke in low voices to my father. I felt invisible.

"I never missed Ronnie, hardly ever thought of him. I felt that, because he was adopted, that made him less worthwhile. That's just a sense, not rational, but later on it made me realize how in war, American soldiers could kill people from other racial or ethnic groups so easily, so without remorse, deliberately, even unnecessarily, because they were worth less. Our troops were encouraged to devalue their lives. They repeated the dehumanizing racial and ethnic nicknames until they were ingrained. Of course, we're not the only ones who do that. All genocide is based on devaluing other human beings."

"I think you're right about some of this," Ruth interjected. "But I still think that you, the adult, is overanalyzing you, the child, and not giving any benefit of the doubt. I agree that racism and sexism too plays a huge role in making war and killing easier. Think of how the Nazis treated the Jews in the ghetto like so much garbage. They murdered them without any reservation, without hesitation. Look at all the genocide that has happened in this century already, even after the universal condemnation of the Germans. But I think your sensitivity to this because of your experience, not despite it, makes you a finer human being. You are worthy of what you have achieved and of what you can contribute. You've suffered but suffering can have positive results."

"I don't know. That would be nice to think but I can't let myself be seduced by that kind of thinking. It's too self-serving, too easy to let myself off the hook. I've never really gone into this with anyone except Willard to some extent, a long time ago. I've never confessed it openly. I've never forgiven myself, and I won't in the future. I believe that an evil act like that lives on forever in time and space. It can't be erased and it can't be changed. I made a moral judgment. It was wrong, evil. I gave in to the dark impulse in me. How it got control, I don't know but the truth is that what I did was morally abominable."

David went on. "It wasn't accidental or negligent or even reckless. It was deliberate. I should have known what could happen, even at twelve. The fact that I can make this moral judgment actually gives me confidence that there is a God. Where else would this judgment come from? It also fills my heart with fear because I don't believe in forgiveness just because you say you're sorry. Maybe there is some process of redemption following remorse and atonement, but I don't have the courage to do it. That would have to involve a public confession. I'm too weak a person to do that. Maybe I will, someday. But I don't think redemption happens in this lifetime. If I were to reveal this, I would be condemned. I don't think I'd get sympathy, just disgust."

"I have more faith in people," she said. "And more trust in God."

"People will react the way it best serves their own interests. There wouldn't be anything in it for anyone to rush to my defense. Sometimes," David said, "when I've been thinking of what happened, what I did and didn't do, in the war, I have a particular nightmare. I see soldiers parading proudly on a runway. They're wearing dress uniforms decorated with medals, shiny ones with ribbons, representing their courage and honor. Then the picture gradually changes, morphs into a different one. The soldiers have the faces and bodies of skeletons. Their uniforms are tattered and bloody. Their medals have changed. They show acts of murder and mayhem. They are *medals of dishonor*, representing all they have done that is evil. And the ghoul-faced soldiers with their medals of dishonor are so weighed down by their evil and cowardly acts that they can barely stumble along. They are all bent over. They appear to be in great pain. I wake up terror-stricken from the nightmare. It's so real that I lie there struggling to reassure myself. I wonder if this is what hell is like. Whether any of us acknowledge that we bear those medals of moral dishonor or not, they exist. And that goes for the Generals and the Presidents who send people off to kill and be killed. In morality, there are no justifications, no excuses, no lawyering—just the truth."

"I need time to absorb all this," Ruth said. "But I'm glad you told me. This is a heavy burden that you are carrying around. I hope we can talk about it again. I'm getting a little concerned about the time."

"I had no idea I would get into all this. My God, we just met. I'm sorry to burden you. I guess you can call this my *death of innocence* story. I call it my *death of the innocent* story too because Ronnie did nothing to deserve to die."

"What was the funeral like? Really bad?"

"Yes, as you can imagine, it was sad. I went with my parents but I felt invisible again except that, paradoxically, I also felt that everyone's eyes were accusing me. It was terrible. I had to use my skill at shutting myself down and walling out everyone and everything. I actually felt nothing during the funeral or after but I was aware of what was going on around me. It was like I was outside my body and I could see everything from a distance. Some of them were even consoling me afterward. I went along with it. That was my survival plan, in fact, to be a victim so I couldn't be the accused.

"I learned to construct my arguments with great skill. I became an actor, playing the role of the great advocate. It's funny, you know, some people actually said that it was an Act of God that was responsible for Ronnie's death. I played along, of course, not knowing exactly what that meant. Years later, in law school, I came across that concept in the law. I got it. Isn't that ironic? Blaming God for the death? I was afraid my agreeing with that would make God furious. You see I do believe in God. I think that's where our moral judgment comes from. But I'm not convinced at all that it is the Christian-marketed-all-forgiving, easy-going version of God that we've created to make ourselves feel better. We create childish stories to make ourselves feel safe or to convince ourselves that we are exceptional, justified, morally right."

"You've created a version of yourself and a version of God to line up with your feelings as a child after that horrible incident. Yes, you bear some responsibility, whatever is appropriate for a child, but you have built that into a theology to punish yourself. You need to forgive yourself. At the same time, you need to stop feeling your human pride at being so clever as to fool everyone, even God, about what happened, the truth of what happened. And this has very little bearing, I suspect, on your guilt for whatever you think it is you did or didn't do in Iraq."

"I know you're getting at some truths that I've obscured, but I'm feeling wiped out right now. It has been such a relief to tell someone, to tell you. I'm sorry to burden you, though. I would like to understand all that you're saying. Can we talk about it again?"

"Of course," Ruth said. "Good idea. It's been a long day for both of us. Shall we get coffee before we walk back? We'll face this together as we faced Willard's death. We should think about Willard now."

76

David stayed on the island another two days before parting, reluctant-ly, with Ruth and taking the ferry back to the mainland. They made plans for Willard's memorial service and talked several times by phone with his children about the arrangements. His ashes would be held for the memorial service in October. He wasn't fond of burials, even though he joked that all his ancestors would be disappointed if he didn't join them in the Old North Cemetery. The ashes that would be buried there would "keep the old ones happy," in Willard's words.

During their two days together, they had time to talk again about David's childhood story. Ruth urged him to reexamine his early childhood from a new adult perspective. He began to realize that childhood memories come pack-aged the way they were perceived and stored in childhood. That process results in inaccurate memories. They are limited by what children felt and understood at the time.

"It's as though," Ruth said, "we were to accept our ancestors' understand-ing of the universe and treat it as the whole truth. The childhood memories need reexamining and editing to take into account what an adult would have understood at the time. If that doesn't happen, people get stuck in childhood, unable to advance, and bonded to the image they created in that early devel-opmental stage of themselves. Childhood memories need to be dug up. If they are allowed to remain buried, they can't be developed into adult, accurate versions. You've lived in fear all these years, in fear of yourself, actually. In a sense, you haven't grown beyond what you were as a child. You don't need to fear yourself. You're in control of the kind of person you want to be, the kind of person you are. It's true that we can't undo the past. We're bound in some way by what happened in the past, but we are free to make choices that aren't dictated by the past. You need to free yourself and stop being afraid that you will act badly when faced with choices of good or evil, moral or immoral."

David began to appreciate that his buried memories, which he dismissed as too painful to re-experience, imprisoned him by limiting his view of himself and what he was capable of. He realized that his handling of the Ramadi incident, which he was soon to testify about, did not represent a response directed by his childhood mistakes or misdeeds. Ramadi was a complex, nuanced situation in which he was balancing myriad conflicting goals, all constrained by his military office. He needed to seek the truth. In the absence of truth, there is no understanding. Without understanding, there can be no moral choice and action. Truth was the first step toward justice. As Willard said, there can be no justice without truth.

"I know this will help me decide how to testify," David said, "but I'm not sure what that will be. I know that I'll never be free if I evade the truth. I need to rethink what happened with Ronnie and what happened in Ramadi."

"You'll find your way," Ruth said on their last day, laughing. "Diogenes will be with you. He'll be carrying his lantern and looking for you as you go through the streets of Philadelphia. You won't be alone."

They parted, with David promising to return immediately after the trial. He knew that deciding was one thing; carrying it out was another. That would take courage. He would return to see Ruth. He could not have imagined that the woman on the ferry was turning out to be a vital person in his life. That much he knew was true.

77

September came on suddenly, disturbing the complacency that David had gotten accustomed to for three weeks. His daily routine, which gave him time and space to get in touch with himself, was shattered with the return of Lucille and the boys. He was happy to see the boys despite their reserved attitude toward him. Lucille seemed confident although her flushed skin under the summer tan showed signs of heavy drinking, no doubt a key part of her family's daily routine.

The first week of September passed uneventfully, with David reading motions and briefs, as well as completing a draft of his outline. On Tuesday of the first week, he got a call from Richard, who said that the trial would likely get underway at the beginning of the following week. Jury selection had been completed during August and the panel would be sworn in on the first day of trial. The prosecutor predicted it would take about four or five days to present his case. That meant the Commonwealth probably would rest by the end of the second week. The defense case would begin immediately after, taking probably five or six days, which would consume the third week of September. David wouldn't be needed until the latter part of the third week.

Richard was virtually certain that the trial was not going to be averted. David should plan on coming to Philadelphia on Tuesday or Wednesday of the third week. Barbara, who was keeping a detailed notebook on the case, had ordered daily transcripts of the testimony. She would brief David when he arrived. Richard offered to go down on short notice but probably not until the defense case began. The District Attorney had moved for a preliminary hearing on the PTSD defense. Although the judge had not yet ordered a preliminary evidentiary hearing requested by the defense, Myron was hopeful that the testimony might persuade the prosecution to offer a favorable plea bargain. That was a long shot, Richard said. The prosecutor knew that David was on the witness list but nothing beyond that.

The trial judge, Joseph Lacey, a cut above the usual denizen of the Philadelphia trial bench, was becoming impatient with the squabbling lawyers who had consumed nearly two weeks of his summer break—that is, the break he had expected to have by finishing all court business by noon. He disliked trials, which were unusual in a system where nearly every case was settled before or during jury selection. He was known to be competent and experienced in criminal cases, but given his secure position in getting re-elected as long as he wanted, somewhat lacking in ambition and energy. This trial looked as though it would take too long for his taste and demand too many rulings. It was hard to tell how that would play out.

He seemed to get along well enough with the DA, Gerald Peale, a combative and highly ambitious elected official who longed to become a federal prosecutor. But Judge Lacey did not seem to appreciate Myron Stewart's brash, noisy, and disrespectful style. He was familiar with Stewart, having had him on several criminal trials of organized crime figures. The judge was irritated but undaunted by Stewart's bullying tactics. Lacey was basically laid-back in his courtroom style. He had an aversion to getting reversed. Unlike other city judges, he was cautious about rulings, always bending over backwards to rule in favor of the defense, if at all possible keeping appeals to a minimum.

It was unpredictable whether he'd grant the prosecution a preliminary hearing on the proposed PTSD defense. The DA wanted an advance look at the defense case under the rationale of challenging the scientific basis for a PTSD defense in this case. The defense was not claiming insanity as a basis for acquittal but, rather, PTSD as an avoidance-type defense to challenge the prosecution's evidence as to intent or other mental states.

David asked whether Richard or Barbara could get Myron to disclose the questions he'd be likely to ask. That would enable them to shape his testimony. David also suggested a mooting session on cross-examination based on what Barbara thought would be asked. Richard agreed. Barbara would work on that as well as wheedling potential questions out of Myron's associate, Lenny, with whom she'd established a social relationship during the summer session. The stage was set. David spent every day sketching out what he might say. He wished he had a copy of the investigation record so he could be sure what it said.

David's goal was to contribute to convicting Serrano by telling the truth without bringing consequences down on himself. He hated the thought of letting Serrano get away with murder. He knew that to tell the whole truth would expose him to a vicious cross-examination about his earlier story at the investigation. He took seriously the possible public revelation of the record or, in a worst-case scenario, an MEJA prosecution for conspiracy.

Every time David thought of staying with the original testimony, he felt a pang of guilt. It felt like a betrayal of Willard and everything he stood for. But when he considered telling the whole, damned, messy truth, he shuddered at the consequences. He would avoid thinking about the problem until he had to make a final decision. He was feeling strengthened by his conversation with Ruth and by starting to free himself of the grip that the buried childhood incident had bound him with for so long. Still, the truth carried huge consequences for him. He would need more courage than he believed himself capable of to withstand the condemnation that he felt was sure to follow.

78

David was glad to be traveling to Philadelphia on Amtrak on Tuesday of the third week of September. The two weeks since Richard's call had passed quickly. Fortunately, the Court's short first term consisted of arguments during the second week alone so David was spared the uncomfortable task of begging off from sitting. Burkhardt would have extracted a heavy price. With the term behind him, he could concentrate his energy on the trial.

His travel time door to door wasn't much different from taking a flight, considering waiting time and routine delays. He liked rail travel on the quiet car because it gave him time and space to collect his thoughts. It was close to 6:00 p.m. when he arrived at the Omni at Independence Park, the hotel used by Richard's law firm for lawyers and clients in Philadelphia. As soon as he checked in and got to his room, he called Barbara by pre-arrangement. They met in the lobby an hour later, recognizing each other from a brief meeting in Richard's office a few weeks earlier. As he recalled, she was a bright and energetic thirty-year old, with a habit of talking at a rapid pace. She was a bit aggressive for his taste but, at least, she said exactly what was on her mind without any evident filtering. A corner table in the main dining area provided ample privacy to begin discussing the case.

He was impressed with Barbara's attention to detail. Without consulting notes, she had the expected testimony of every potential witness down cold. Richard chose his associates solely for their ability and willingness to work long hours. Barbara was one of a half dozen associates who spent most of their time working Richard's litigation files.

David first directed Barbara to explain the charges and the evidence against Nick. He needed a feel for the case in order to understand why Nick's lawyer was relying so heavily on a defense rather than on attacking the prosecution's case. She summarized the prosecution's case, which included insights she had gotten from the Assistant District Attorney, sitting second chair, whom she had developed as a source.

Barbara rattled off the details of the case. "Nick, who was divorced from his wife, a long story by itself, had burned through numerous relationships over the years. He was plagued by long-standing alcohol and drug problems, since well before Iraq. He had bottomed out a few times, landing in jail or rehab, depending on his luck. Nearly every relationship had involved domestic violence. Beyond that, he had many arrests, and some convictions, including two felony assaults. His current relationship, with Dolores 'Dee' Hamilton, had lasted two years. That tortured relationship had generated several complaints of domestic violence by Dee, who was an Iraq veteran herself. Their relationship had been volatile and violent from the start but had deteriorated in the last two months. From Dee's point of view, it was approaching the final breaking point."

Barbara continued, "She worked as a bartender at a local sports bar. She had an alcohol problem too. In the past two months, she had become friendly, but not romantically involved, with a patron named Harold Wickes, the homicide victim, a Vietnam combat veteran. Nick was insanely jealous of Dee's male acquaintances at the bar. The DA has two witnesses set to testify to this.

"On the night in question, Nick went to look for her after she failed to return to the apartment after closing time. Nick had been drinking heavily and had fortified himself with two handguns. After checking the bar, which had just closed at 2:00 a.m., he went outside and became enraged when he found them sitting in the front seat of a Jeep in the parking lot. Apparently they were just talking. He approached the car with his Glock 21 handgun, his weapon of choice, drawn, pounded on the hood of the car, and smashed the passenger window. Wickes, a large out-of-shape man who was usually able to handle anyone who threatened him, got out of the car and started for Nick. Nick shot him five or six times in the face and chest. He died on the spot. Three witnesses are lined up to testify to this.

"Dee began screaming and tried to slide to the driver's seat and pull out of the lot. Nick fired four or five more rounds at her through the windshield. Then he walked to his pickup, probably assuming she was dead. Witnesses observed this too. Apparently, he was unaware that anyone was in sight. He stopped at his apartment just long enough to grab a few items, hoping it would appear that he had been away. He thought no one saw him leave, re-enter, and leave again from the apartment. Again, there were witnesses who pieced this together.

"There's more," she continued. "He drove out of town, toward New York City, and conjured up a story in case, as seemed likely, he'd be caught eventually. The story was that he came looking for Dee and became angry to find her with Wickes. He claimed they'd been planning to work out their problems. He panicked when Wickes approached him with what he believed was a handgun, and experienced a flashback to his combat days in Iraq, specifically to Ramadi during the surge. He believed that he was being challenged by insurgents during a patrol. So, of course, he reacted quickly and shot the attackers."

"That's quite a story," David said.

Nick was picked up by two alert New York City police officers before two days went by," Barbara said. "He was probably shocked to learn that Dee had survived. He'd been in enough trouble over the years to know to keep his mouth shut. He asked for his lawyer, Myron Stewart. He had used Myron before and over time had sent him quite a few clients. Myron likes representing veterans. It enhances his standing in the legal community, which needs all the enhancing it can get. He's disliked by most lawyers and judges. Who can fault him for doing everything he can, ethical or not, for combat veterans who have served the country?"

"It sounds as though this trial is as much about Myron as about Nick. Do you see it that way?" David asked.

"In a way, yes," Barbara said. "Every case becomes about Myron as well as the defendant, maybe even more. He puts himself on the line in a personal way with jurors. Myron's main office is in New York City, but he's admitted to practice in Pennsylvania. As soon as he got the call, he left for Philadelphia and met Nick at the police station with his favorite bail bondsman in tow. He got Nick released after he waived extradition. The judge on duty for serious bail matters apparently had a soft spot for veterans too. He set bail low enough to get Nick released despite the fact that he fled from the crime.

"Back in Philadelphia at his first court appearance," Barbara continued. "Myron managed to plant the seeds of a PTSD flashback defense with a few choice comments that got passed along to the judge. The low bail stood. It turned out that the victim, Harold Wickes, was not well liked by some of the local police. He was relatively clean, himself, but two of his brothers are connected to the mob. Harold had little respect for police in general but, of course, he had a few fans among, let's say, the less honorable members of the department. He did favors for a lot of people and handed out money in the right places."

"What was the evidence so far?" David asked.

"The police were dispatched in response to a 911 call from a couple of patrons at a club that backed onto the parking lot. They were getting into their car when they heard shots. They saw Nick start up his dark pickup truck which then quickly exited the lot on the far side. They heard moaning from the SUV when they approached it. They saw a body lying in front of the Jeep and saw Dee sprawled across the front seat. By the amount of blood, they thought she would die on the spot.

"The police were there in five minutes, the EMTs right after. At that point, the police thought it might be a robbery gone sour. Dee went right into surgery so they didn't get to talk with her until the next day. She managed to identify Nick as the shooter; she called him her former boyfriend. The police knew who he was from prior incidents. They weren't sure about the motive at that point but they went right to his apartment. No one answered and they got a search warrant. They didn't find much although it looked like he had left in a hurry. They put out an APB.

"Dee was lucky. She had some life-threatening injuries and was in critical condition. But she pulled through. The police talked to her later in the day and got a little more information. She said she hadn't been home, at Nick's place, in three days and had told him the relationship was over and she was moving out. He refused to let her end the relationship, and she was pretty frightened. She went to stay at her sister's and Harold drove her back and forth to work. They had become friends, she said. He knew her sister. When Dee learned for the first time that he was dead, she went to pieces. They stopped the conversation. Maybe there was more to the relationship, but that's neither here nor there.

"In the meantime, they picked up Nick and got nothing out of him, of course. It's a credibility issue as to what happened but Dee came across very well on the witness stand after the police set it up with their testimony. They found the guns. Nick had them both with him. Either he forgot to get rid of them or maybe thought he might need them. He might have known about Harold's underworld connections. In fact, he may actually have thought Harold was armed. We don't know how much Nick knew about Dee's relationship with him. Maybe he actually figured out on the spot that he'd have to rely on a PTSD defense. Nick has been around the streets and the veterans' clubs. He probably knew all about PTSD and what it could do to you and for you. Myron filed notice of an insanity defense, but it's anyone's guess what he'll do, whether he'll go all the way with that. My guess is probably not, from what his associate tells me.

"Myron has been very successful with PTSD mental state defenses for veterans. He hasn't been successful yet with an insanity defense relying on PTSD but has managed to get some good plea bargains. Of course, it's been over ten years since the war now, but there's still sympathy for veterans and PTSD has become more and more credible in court. The defense started yesterday following denial of a routine motion for judgment of acquittal."

Barbara continued. "I figure you won't be needed for a couple of days. You're fairly far down the defense witness list. I think Myron will call other witnesses to lay a foundation in an effort to box you in. He wants to reduce the chance that you'll contradict the other defense testimony. You're the star defense witness, I think. He'll hold Nick until last, of course, assuming that he testifies at all. I think he has to in this case to tell his story about the flashback. He'll adjust his testimony to the witnesses who preceded him. Someone has to testify what was in his mind, his perceptions, what he believed was happening and all that. Unlike some other PTSD flashback cases, there are no witnesses here to support him with his flashback theory.

"They'll create a tight little box for your testimony, just to corroborate the others about the war, firefights, maybe even the killing of the insurgents, and what it was like in general. There's a risk because Myron doesn't know for sure what you'll say. The DA knows about the report that has been 'found,' as you know. Myron is holding tightly onto it. I suppose he's still hoping for a sweet plea deal before or after you testify. The prosecutor might want to voir dire you. The judge is letting the lawyers do just about anything they want. He's trying not to piss off the prosecutors or the defense. He's a cut above the typical political machine judge. He's clever, has a lot of experience, and good instincts."

"I guess that's good news," David said.

"You could come to court tomorrow, but I'm afraid you'd get a lot of unwanted attention. It's better to lie low and I'll brief you twice a day. It's up to you though. Richard prefers that you stay out of sight. You're likely to draw publicity, maybe even a feature story in the media. Reporters will start digging about you. And who knows? You might not even have to testify. Maybe Nick will get his plea deal."

"That sounds like good advice," David agreed. "I'll stay out of sight. There are reporters covering the trial, right?"

"Yes. Two or three."

"Did you catch their names?" David asked. "Was one Frank Caruso by any chance?"

"That's it, yeah, Caruso. He tries to talk to me every time there's a break, and I've seen him talking to both lawyers. He's been there the whole time."

"Damn," David said. "That's the reporter who was embedded in my company when I was in Iraq. He wrote a book about his experience. About ten years ago, maybe more, he did a feature on the survivors of a raid that killed a lot of civilians, wiped out a whole family. I don't know if Richard told you about this. It may come up during the trial."

"Yes, I know about that raid, the Ramadi raid, right? That's what the report is about, as I understand it," Barbara said. "You definitely want to steer clear of this guy."

"I wonder how Caruso found out about the trial," David said. "I wonder if it's me he's after or whether he just recognized Nick's name. I suppose he knows by now that I'm on the witness list."

"I'm sure he does. I've heard him mention your name. He even mentioned it to me but I didn't pick up on the significance at the time."

"Have there been any stories about the trial yet?" David asked.

"I don't know," Barbara said. "But I'll find out. I'll check into that later tonight."

They continued the conversation in David's suite for an hour until he had reached his limit. He was exhausted. He was glad to have a day or two to get acclimated. Barbara seemed capable and Richard had promised to come down whenever he was needed. If objections had to be made to protect him, Richard would carry a lot more weight than an associate, however smart she was. He wondered how he would pass the time and he worried about not being at the Court in Hartford. He hadn't told Burkhardt he'd be away. Maybe his testimony would be over and he'd get back before it became a problem. He couldn't get Caruso out of his mind. This was not going to be a secret proceeding. As he was falling asleep, David wondered how much Caruso knew about his pilgrimage to Ramadi.

80

David had his answer first thing in the morning. Barbara called to report that Caruso had mentioned his visit to Ramadi in an online story with *Slate*, which was picked up in a few other online media sources. "He specifically used your name. He apparently talked to the family about your visit, about your apologizing. I think atonement is one of his themes. That was the headline. He'll be nosing around trying to get the investigation report. He'll want to compare your testimony with what you said at the hearing. I'll talk to Richard about this although I don't see what we can do about it."

This was disturbing news. Obviously, David's ill-fated mission to Ramadi had backfired with unanticipated consequences. This story would hit the national press. The next two days dragged interminably, leaving him too much time to worry about every detail of his testimony. The monotony was broken only by brief excursions in the city. He began every day with a vigorous workout in the hotel gym after the gym rats had left, followed by a jog through a nearby park or a swim in the hotel pool. He stopped into a different deli each day for a light breakfast. He visited the National Constitution Center, where he had participated in programs over the years.

He was conscious of keeping a low profile and avoiding restaurants used by the courthouse crowd. Although anxious to get this ordeal over with, the chance to slow his pace down was welcome. He could not remember the last time he had been free of the clutter and contention of everyday life. Time stood still while he waited his turn on the witness stand. He had to exercise mind control to prevent occupying himself with futile worry over what the reporter might do with his testimony. Maybe he should meet with Caruso and try to win him over, trying to influence the stories. Bad idea, he decided. Reporters like Caruso can't be conned.

Sitting over a third cup of coffee in a deli one morning, he sketched out two books. One was a futuristic endless-war novel. The other was a novel exploring the psychology of terrorists, focusing on home-grown ones. Americans had obsessed about this problem for a decade now and no one had come up with answers. He made notes as the rush of ideas flowed. There was no good time to start a novel. Actually, there was no bad time either.

He called Dana daily, Dana's voicemail, that is. She responded after the third call. Her voice revealed little about her feelings and she was always in a hurry to end the call. She seemed glad to talk about what she had done on recent trips to North Africa, where the team was trying to mop up trouble spots without military intervention. She mentioned Jake.

"Jake popped in on me in New York without warning again," she said one time. "I was afraid he would be loud and argumentative but he wasn't. He seemed contrite actually and asked if we could give it another try. I said I didn't know, and we should keep things the way they are. I need to be alone, to do my work. He didn't press too hard and we ended up having lunch together."

David said simply, "I'm surprised. I guess he deserves that much. But this doesn't sound like ending the relationship." He felt jealous, tempered only by his realization that, since meeting Ruth, his thoughts had been more about her than Dana.

Dana replied harshly. "It isn't your business to judge me. I can do what I like and that goes for my relationship with Jake or anybody else. You'll be glad to know that I asked him if he had talked with you and he said, no, he hadn't. He knew all about the trial. He tensed up at the mention of your name though."

Dana surprised him. "I did get a call from a staffer at the White House. I knew her when the President was at GCN. The President brought her to the White House. The staffer was asking me a lot of questions about you and obviously didn't know that our relationship was close."

"What kind of questions?"

"Questions I wouldn't expect if the President is not seriously interested in you. I can't go beyond that," she said. "She didn't say her call was confidential, but she would expect me not to repeat the conversation. I didn't mention the trial and she didn't ask. That leads me to believe that no one there knows about it yet. I guess they will soon enough and I don't know what the reaction will be. When do you intend to let the President in on your big surprise, the main event?"

"Not yet," David said. "When the dust settles it will either be disastrous and I'll be out the door or it will go well and it won't matter. I don't see that any good could come of raising it now. Maybe I won't even have to testify and it would be nothing but an unnecessary alarm. There's a reporter covering the trial who knows about the Ramadi incident and me," David said.

"You know best about telling the President, I guess. I would hate to think of the President being blindsided. Can you dismiss your obligation to her so easily? You're deciding on your own what she needs to know and doesn't need to know. That doesn't seem fair," Dana said with a sharp edge.

"Those are fair questions, but I think I can hold off for a while longer. I'm going to allow myself some slack and let it play out right now."

Dana was silent, which David took to be disapproval. David reached her two days later and the conversation was less confrontational. She wanted to hear what David expected to testify about and whether the trial was getting a lot of press coverage. The answer to that was negative so far. The daily story was brief and buried in the city news section of the newspaper. It was not prominent on the website.

Barbara gave him a list of questions that Myron was likely to ask. She had acquired the information from Myron's associate, Lenny, who apparently was interested in her. Although she was not particularly attractive, David thought, she had an engaging nature and strong personal appeal. He found the time with her enjoyable and he supposed that other men would as well. It was obvious that she had made a hit with both the DA's team as well as the defense team.

Despite earlier predictions, the defense was taking longer than anticipated. Myron had a number of witnesses who would counter the prosecution's witnesses on the status of Nick's relationship with his girlfriend, on the domestic violence incidents, and on the events leading up to the death. He probably wouldn't get through this phase before Friday afternoon of week three. On Monday, there'd be several veterans, laying the foundation for David's testimony. Larry would be one. The others were Douglas Garvey and Albert Rodriquez, both of whom had spent time in prison. In addition, the widows of Karl Linden and Malvin Pierce, who had committed suicide, would be on the stand briefly. Myron had gotten Garvey and Rodriquez out on habeas petitions to testify. This would be the combat PTSD phase. David might be reached on Monday afternoon of the fourth week, but more likely Tuesday morning. That is, unless the prosecution demanded a voir dire before the judge with the jury excused from the courtroom.

"I tried to get the details of the whole defense lineup but Lenny wasn't sure. He promised to meet over the weekend and let me know. I assume they'll want to build up the combat and daily firefights first, then get to the killing that we've talked about plus the counter strikes against the insurgents. You know all about that one. Unfortunately, that puts you right on center stage. They're counting on you to corroborate what the others say. I'm hoping to get a look at the notorious investigation report too. That's a stretch even for Lenny to risk. There'll be expert psychiatric testimony too, of course."

"I meant to ask you," David said, "why there is no sequestration order. I'm surprised that there's nothing to prevent me or any other witness from sitting in the courtroom during other witnesses' testimony. If there was an order, it wouldn't be ethical for you to fill me in either, since I'd be sequestered."

"You're right. It is surprising but I made sure of that situation. I suppose one or the other lawyer could have asked the judge for an order barring me not to discuss trial testimony with you or any other witness, since they know you're going to be called. Neither side asked for sequestration of witnesses or any restrictions. That made it a lot simpler for me. Myron wants you to know what the testimony is. He's setting the stage for your testimony and you need to know what to expect and what is expected of you. He's asked me a few times when you'll arrive. I was vague about it, just said I wasn't sure. He may be aware by now that you're here but, if he is, he's been too busy to pay attention.

"If they finish early on Friday, I'll try to get Lenny to meet with me and fill me in. He's coming on to me, and I've tried to keep the information flowing without getting into a spot where he's going to be ticked off if I don't go out with him. I don't want to do that. It would be unprofessional and, anyway, I'm not interested. I hate to use people but I've used him. I don't want to push that, so I have to let him take the lead on filling in the details. I've told him that it's to their advantage if you're fully informed. If they catch you by surprise, anything can happen. I think he understands that. Myron will cooperate, I think, as long as you promise to back up the defense and then, of course, follow through."

Barbara had no further news on Thursday evening, but they met for dinner and talked about the DA's tactics and the judge's conduct of the trial. She thought Judge Lacey was getting somewhat bored with the trial. But he may be bored with his criminal assignments in general. Despite his attitude, she said, "he doesn't hesitate to make tough rulings when he has to."

81

David and Barbara met in the lobby at 7:00 p.m. on Friday night by pre-arrangement. After they were seated in an Italian restaurant six blocks away, Barbara said quietly, glancing around, "I met with Lenny and got an update. The plan is to put on the veterans, Larry and the others, plus the widows, on Monday morning. You may be reached on Monday afternoon. Are you okay with that? I have some information about how Myron will focus the testimony. He's planning to follow you with a psychiatrist who will pull it all together and produce, no surprise, a diagnosis of PTSD that led to Nick's reaction that night. He'll say he was incapable of any volitional mental state pertaining to the actual victims because he believed he was being attacked by insurgents in Iraq."

Barbara began to talk rapidly. "There'll be the usual general questions about your background, when you were in the service, when you served with Nick, or should I say when he served with you, in your platoon. There will be questions as to what it was like, combat, firefights, and all that. He'll ask whether Nick served well as platoon sergeant in your platoon, how often you had contact with him, all the general details."

"Okay, that's no problem," David said.

"Myron will ask you to describe the conditions, and how often you encountered insurgents and civilians who seemed threatening. He's decided to focus on Nick's own version of the Ramadi atrocity. Here's where it may get difficult for you because his version will be different from what you remember. He's going to ask all the same questions, more or less, of all the Army witnesses. He'll ask the two widows to describe what their husbands were like when they returned home and what led to their suicides. Then comes the psychiatrist, followed by Nick. He gets to wrap up any loose ends and inconsistencies, of course, and explain them away. Obviously, he is willing to say whatever is necessary to make his story fly."

"In other words, the Ramadi affair is going to be the pivotal point of his defense?"

"Sounds like it. He'll ask you whether there was a time when you became aware that Nick had established, consistent with his duties, a friendly relationship with an Iraqi family. Did he visit them and help them out financially? Did he help to protect them? He wants detail. He obviously wants this to be a family thing, with no mention of a romantic relationship with anyone in the family."

"This is problematical for me," David said.

"I know. He'll ask whether he sometimes took other members of the platoon with him when he visited. Did there come a time when a misfortune happened to this family? The story as Myron will present it is that the daughter was brutally murdered by insurgents, AQI members. Before that, you will be asked whether you were aware of this family relationship and whether you ever issued an order prohibiting it. The answer is supposed to be no. Did you indicate that he was free to do this on his own time so long as he took the usual precautions? The answer is yes, of course. Was this uncommon? The answer is that it was not encouraged but it did happen from time to time. After all we were supposed to be winning over these people at the same time we were trying to make the environment safer. So it was inevitable."

"I'm supposed to follow his script, whether it's fact or fiction?" David asked.

Barbara nodded. "That's what he expects. Then he'll ask whether you found out who was responsible. The answer is yes, local AQI operatives. Did you find out why? Your understanding is that it was because AQI did not want the civilians getting too friendly with Americans, and they thought Jasmine was spying for the Americans.

"He'll ask what happened after that. The answer is that it got reported up the chain of command and it was decided at the battalion level that AQI had to be punished, and that Jasmine's assassins had to be apprehended or killed. Whose responsibility was it to command the retaliation operation? It was yours. Did you order Nick to carry this out? The answer he wants is yes. Did he carry it out successfully? Yes, of course, with an explanation, if you wish. His squad killed the insurgents who committed the murder. Did you see any part of it or participate in it? Yes or no, depending on how you wish to handle it. You can throw in that these insurgents were constantly troublesome even aside from this, a constant threat to our troops."

"I don't know if I can go through with this," David said. "This is no less than rewriting the facts to enable Nick to escape his crime. This is all garbage."

"That's up to you, of course," Barbara said. "I'm just telling you what he's going to ask and what he expects you to say. Otherwise, according to Myron, there'll be consequences for you to pay. That's about it except for the brutality of the defense to the attack you ordered and the toll it took, with two of your platoon getting killed. He suggests you might want to reveal that you observed personally the final of three anti-insurgent operations, the one that resulted in the atrocity. If you want, you can say that you and your squad arrived near the end of it. It was a fierce firefight and you saw that Nick's squad was handling it as best he could. There was a heavy toll on your platoon. There was so much shooting that it was risky to barge in, hard to get a grasp of the situation quickly, and you didn't want to put your men in jeopardy. But two of your platoon, a man and a woman, burst in on their own and got killed by the AQI operatives."

"This is a huge lie. He wants me to commit perjury. Utter bullshit," David said.

"I understand," Barbara said. "Moving on, you observed later that Nick was deeply affected not only by the murder by the insurgents but by the fierce fighting and brutality of the insurgents in fighting and killing two of your platoon. He was never the same. He didn't complain but it was easy to see he was totally shaken. Myron says you should expand on this with your own observations as long as it's consistent with the main story."

"Does he really think I'm going to tailor the testimony to what he wants?" David asked. "This is ridiculous."

"I'm just repeating what he said and what he wants," Barbara said, losing patience with David's protests. "I know this is not the way you remember things going down," she repeated. "I told them that what he wants you to say isn't consistent with what you remember. You were neutral about this at the investigation hearing, I gather, but now he's asking you to go beyond that and adopt an embellished version that wasn't part of the picture. I'm pretty sure he's counting on a light cross by the DA. He figures Peale won't be rough on a veteran, a hero in everybody's eyes, and a possible Supreme Court nominee. He'll choose to shoot down the PTSD defense with his own psychiatric testimony on rebuttal. It stands a small chance at best as the basis for an insanity defense. He can live with the possibility that the jury might convict on a lesser offense. We're pretty sure the judge will charge on the lesser.

"Just to finish up," Barbara added, "Myron will ask briefly about the investigation. The prosecutor knows there had to be an investigation because of the two American deaths. Myron also knows there was an outcry by the local sheikh about civilians being killed. So he wants to bring this out first rather than leaving it to the prosecution. He'll ask, was there an investigation? The other witnesses will acknowledge that there was an informal, that is, non-CID, investigation because of the two deaths and, secondarily, the civilians who were killed because they were in the wrong place at the wrong time.

"Finally, he'll ask whether Nick and everyone who participated were fully cleared of any culpability pertaining to this mission or the way it was executed. I'm going to do my best to pry a copy of the report from Lenny on the basis that we need it to prepare you for your testimony. The DA hasn't seen the report but he knows it exists. Myron can't very well reveal the report without opening up the issue of how he got hold of it. Myron doesn't know that I'm aware he has the report. Only his associate knows and he wasn't supposed to reveal it to anybody, especially me. It's not really leverage. There's no way of knowing how he got it, except that his client gave it to him. The client is protected by the attorney-client privilege, of course. If Nick were pressed, pleading the Fifth would protect him, because taking it or bribing somebody to get it is a crime.

"That's a lot to digest, I know," Barbara said, "but I wanted you to know everything I know."

"Outrageous," David said angrily. "What does he think I am? That presumptuous bastard." He sat quietly, trying to assimilate all the information and to begin thinking how on earth he would come out of this unscathed.

82

'm sorry," Barbara said. "I rattled through that too fast. I'm not suggesting for a minute what you should do. I'm just telling you what Myron wants you to do. My only concern, and Richard's, is preparing you."

"I know you're just doing your job," David said. "This story they're making up is a distorted version of what happened. It's not a complete lie. But overall it's a deliberate misinterpretation of what happened. When I started down this road, to cooperate in the trial, I envisioned brief testimony that didn't involve turning the truth on its head. Before the investigation hearing, I got the word from command to say as little as possible, to go along with the plan to get this behind us. Prevent the press from blowing it up into another My Lai. What had happened was history. Nothing could change it. The fear was that the press would stir up the public. Then the opposition in Washington would feed on it. They'd portray it as an atrocity, a war crime. My testimony was incomplete, yes, but I didn't tell any lies, at least not outright lies."

"If I'm not mistaken," Barbara said, "you came here to testify when our efforts to avoid your involvement failed. Is that correct? You never agreed with Myron or his client to testify."

"Yes, that's true," David said, "but you were supposed to keep my testimony to a minimum."

"Just so you know, I am not in control of what Myron Stewart is going to do. My job, according to Richard, is to prepare you for the worst."

David said, "My understanding is that you were to persuade Stewart that he should minimize my role, that he should realize I'm an unpredictable witness. But I want you to know what this is really about. A lot of people would say I did my duty as a good soldier. I gave up nothing, except maybe a little piece of my integrity. I helped to protect Nick, whether he deserved it or not, and everyone in command positions, the Army itself, from unfair accusations that we committed a war crime. When we signed up to go to Iraq to defend our freedom, did anyone anticipate that we could be tracked down years later for doing what we were supposed to be doing? That we would be accused of committing crimes for telling a few lies that protected the military and the government? God knows I didn't understand that. I certainly didn't understand what I'd be faced with at the age of twenty-five, for that matter."

"That's fine. I get it but my job was to find out what you're going to face when you're on the stand. And that's what I've done. I can't do more. I can't recreate the situation according to what you'd prefer."

"I know this isn't your problem," David said, "but you're supposed to be preparing me. I need to see the report. I expect you to get a copy. I have to figure this out. I want to be truthful, but I don't want to go out of my way to turn this into an opportunity to put the military on trial."

"I get it," Barbara said. "But neither Richard nor I can tell you what facts you testify to. This may sound harsh, but are you going to stick to the facts or make up your own?"

"Are you so naive," David said, "that you think facts are set in stone?"

"I'd like to defer talking more about this until Richard is here," Barbara said. "I'm keeping him filled in too," Barbara added. "Frankly, you seem to expect more than I can deliver. Look, I'm tired. It's been a long day in the courtroom and negotiating with both sides to protect you."

"Okay," David said. "We have the weekend to think about this. When do you think you might get hold of the report?"

"I'm going to meet Lenny this weekend sometime," Barbara said, shrugging. "I'm not sure, but I hope by Sunday night. Richard will want to talk with Myron and then the prosecutor. He's going to make a final pitch to keep you off the stand, for the sake of the judicial system. Judges shouldn't be put in compromising adversarial situations, but don't expect Myron to respect that. Richard is a terrific negotiator and maybe he can get some plea bargaining going."

"I'm hoping for that," David said.

"One more thing," Barbara said. "There was a reporter from the *Inquirer* in court today. I overheard a conversation she was having. Seems she's doing a feature story. I guess her editor finally realized that this trial is going on under their noses. She was looking for people to interview. She specializes in veterans' issues and PTSD. I just wanted to let you know. Caruso is still there too, of course, and I've seen the two of them talking. I get the feeling that they're having a competition to see who can break the biggest story."

"Terrific," David said, "My God. I don't need that. Let's really work at keeping me off the stand. I don't want this in print, getting picked up by the wire services."

"What do you think I've been doing for weeks now?" Barbara said. "Sorry, I didn't mean that. We're both tense and tired. Forget I said that. It's just a little frustrating for me."

They ended their conversation abruptly, leaving their dinners mostly untouched. David was not the slightest bit hungry after the heated conversation. He felt pushed to the breaking point by the conflict.

Saturday was a blur. The specter of his decision about how to testify haunted him all day and night. His dark mood was relieved in the afternoon by a call from Bradley.

"Hey, David, where are you?"

"In Philadelphia, waiting for the trial to move forward and trying to figure out how to handle it."

"You've been down there for how many days now?"

"Forever," David said. "It seems like forever."

"Richard is taking good care of you, I hope."

"He's not here yet. He's coming down tomorrow or early Monday morning. He's got an associate here monitoring the courtroom but let's just say it's not easy."

"Sorry to hear that," Bradley said. "I'm calling because I have good news, very promising news. I heard from Lehman. The President wants another meeting with you. Lehman didn't give anything away but he said the President has ordered a full background check on you. This doesn't happen unless the choice is narrowed down to one or possibly two candidates."

"That's exciting," David said. "I wasn't expecting that."

"Lehman was noncommittal," Bradley said, "and I didn't press, of course, but I got the distinct impression there is a very short list. He was giving me the heads up on that because it involves contacting so many people. I thanked him and that was it. I don't know why she wants another meeting. It could be during or after the background check. The FBI will begin its routine investigation immediately I suspect. It's time to watch your step. I know there isn't a lot you can do with this trial pending, but let Richard know. I'm sure he'll press for a resolution. Now, here's the really exciting news. The White House is going to leak a story with an anonymous 'reliable source.' You know the significance of that terminology. The story will be that the President is considering a small group of candidates for the job. My understanding is that a few names will be mentioned. They know that names will leak out anyway when the FBI interviews start. They want to preempt that by leaking the news in a controlled context. That way, the President gets feedback on candidates without committing herself to anyone."

Bradley hesitated and then added, "This is confidential but I have reason to take seriously what Lehman says. He and I have, shall we say, a special relationship right now that concerns the future. That's confidential. But you can tell Richard about the background checks."

"Of course," David said. "I had no idea the nomination process would move so quickly." Along with a flush of excitement at the prospects, David could feel mounting anxiety at the risk of his testimony. It wasn't the trial itself so much as that everybody would have a chance to dissect every word he said.

David added, "I'm not optimistic about avoiding testifying. Serrano's lawyer is being very demanding. Can you hold off with a meeting date until I get back?"

"No problem with that," Bradley said. "I told Lehman next week would be best. The President goes to the Middle East this week and then to North Africa. She's due back on the weekend. But I expect the story to leak very soon, later today or tomorrow."

"I'll call you after I testify," David said. "By the way, there's a reporter from the *Inquirer* here now. Looks like she's really interested in the case and is going to do a feature. Caruso, the journalist who was embedded with my company, is working on a story too. He did a story about the Iraqi family, the ones who survived the attack."

"I hope Richard can keep you off the stand," Bradley said. "I'm not going to bring up the subject to Lehman. Since the President is away anyway, it isn't necessary. By the time you speak with her, it will be resolved one way or the other. You can tell her about it. Then it's her call."

83

Richard arrived on a flight Sunday night. Barbara and David took a cab to meet him at the Penn Club, where the firm had membership privileges for partners. Privacy would be assured. Barbara brought Richard up to date on the trial as well as Myron Stewart's plan for using David's testimony.

"What are your thoughts about this?" he asked David. "Can you handle this without compromising too much?"

"I've thought of nothing else all weekend. To testify the way Myron wants would involve stretching the truth way beyond my comfort level. That would amount to a bigger cover-up than the original investigation was. That was designed to gloss over 'inconvenient' facts, not to lie directly. We were dealing with a situation in which thirty civilians plus two of our people were killed. That was just one raid. I'm not going to lie outright. But I won't go out of my way to blow this up into a spectacle. Whatever happened is in the past so, in one sense, it doesn't matter at this point what is said, except for Serrano, of course. I'd be inclined to answer questions simply and minimally, no embellishment."

"Fair enough," Richard agreed, nodding. Turning to Barbara, he asked, "Where does the plea bargaining stand?"

"Myron's associate told me that the DA made an offer but Stewart rejected it. The DA has been hard-nosed. He wants serious jail time and nothing less than Murder Second. Myron insists on manslaughter with no jail time. There's no way that's going to happen."

"How much jail time does the DA want?" Richard asked.

"Fifteen years to serve with parole," Barbara said. "Nick might end up doing ten of hard time."

"What would Myron take?"

"I think he'd recommend a plea. If it involved five years to serve with a chance of earlier release, he'd probably talk Nick into it. Nick could be out in five years with the last two in a minimum-security prison or a halfway house. Nick's done prison time before, although not long stretches."

"What's the problem?" Richard asked. "They're not so far apart. This seems like a relationship crime, basically a rocky relationship between two people who drink a lot and maybe use drugs. The other guy, a barfly, creates a triangle and gets killed. But he's messing around with Nick's woman or at least Nick could perceive it that way. What's the big deal?"

"The big deal," Barbara said, "is that the guy who got killed was not just a barfly. His status has been unfolding from day to day. I heard in the beginning that he supposedly had underworld connections, maybe a minor player. But he was also a Vietnam veteran and he had a family. He had enemies and friends in the police department."

"Complicated," said Richard.

"Right. He had a hard life but he pulled it together, and apparently he and Dee were not having an affair. He was trying to help her out, give her a safe place. If it were the girlfriend alone who was killed, the DA might be looking for less. In this city, maybe others, it's possible to have both police and crime connections. He may have been an informant too. It all depends on who has power and influence. In any event, there's pressure on the DA from somebody not to give this case away. Besides, the DA wants to be a federal prosecutor. He wants something to show for all this, something that will help his career."

Richard took it all in. "Stewart must realize that the PTSD defense is a long shot. It's been a long time since the war. The time has passed when juries and judges were handing out 'Get Out of Jail Free' cards to veterans. Myron should lean on him to take some jail time as long as he doesn't get stuck there forever. The fact that he was a platoon sergeant and served a couple of tours in Iraq has to mean something. I'll call Myron first thing in the morning to arrange a meeting. Let's see if we can get something going."

David and Richard were alone for a few moments while Barbara left the table. "There's a lot riding on this. Bradley called and said they want me for a second White House meeting. They've started an FBI screening and my name may be floated as a possible candidate this week. Bradley is optimistic about my chances. It becomes even more urgent to avoid my testimony if we can. It could be a problem if one or both of the reporters does a story about my testimony that gets a lot of attention. There's an *Inquirer* reporter here plus the reporter who was embedded with us in Iraq. No matter what the outcome is, stirring up controversy will probably be fatal."

"I understand," Richard said. "I'll work on this with the lawyers and the judge tomorrow. Anything is possible."

84

David slept fitfully, waking around five in the morning. Turning his mind back a dozen years and envisioning himself in Ramadi had been disturbing. He hadn't expected that. His memories and the turmoil of that period of his life had long been buried. Now he felt out of control, unable to focus on how he would handle the trial.

He wondered how Nick managed to get the widows to revisit painful times in their lives. The husbands' deaths were heartbreaking but they entered the service with serious problems. Would the widows attribute the suicides to their combat experience or to their dysfunction once they were back home?

Would any of the witnesses, who no doubt would follow Myron's script, discuss the slaughter of Nick's woman and all that followed? Most trial testimony involved a scripted relationship between the interrogator and the interrogated. It was supposed to be a truth-seeking process, not scripted at all, but that was the difference between reality and fantasy. Adversarial or hostile testimony was unscripted, except for the format. The questioner might dance around trying to trap the witness in predictable ways. Juries are rarely aware of how scripted testimony is. Problems arise when more than a single story is being told. That was the case here. The prosecution had a story it was trying to sell the jury on. The defense had another and he, David, had a third. He had made no specific promises yet.

It had been cathartic to reveal to Ruth the dark story that he had carried with him since childhood. In opening it up to daylight, he had begun re-examining what were facts and what were assumptions. The power of truth was spellbinding. His burden had been lightened by the power of truth. If he were to reveal the truth about Ramadi, perhaps his life would be improved. Maybe he should follow his intuition or perhaps his soul when he was confronted with the questions.

Barbara had said he should go to the courtroom in the morning and listen to the testimony that would directly precede his. In the absence of a sequestration order, he was free to be present. Richard would be ready to intervene if he was exposing himself to a perjury charge or self-incrimination. Richard would have in mind the MEJA prosecution risk.

He felt a jolt as he remembered the context of all this, a homicide by Nick. He went after the woman and her friend. David felt sure he meant to murder them. He was a danger to society. He began to fall apart while he was in Iraq.

David felt troubled that Nick did have a lust for killing that was frightening at times.

He checked email to see if Bradley had sent word of a news story on the nomination. His name alone was in the judicial politics blog. Oh my God, he thought. There's no place to hide now.

85

David dreaded to think of telling a contrived story that would convey nothing of the horror of what happened inside the house in Ramadi. The victims were women, children, old men, even a few animals, floating in pools of blood. One glimpse inside revealed a leg, a few pieces of arm, and the severed body of a pregnant woman with the head and shoulders of a fetus, a bloody mess. He had ducked back outside. It was the evil that was evident, overpowering him. It was savagery, a killing feast. It was his momentary indecision about what to do, an agonizing calculation that took only an instant. How could he do anything to stop it? Nick was in control and it was almost over. He could see soldiers in Army fatigues rushing around firing AKs, bodies stumbling, lunging, falling, disintegrating before his eyes. There didn't appear to be any resistance. To step in the path of the indiscriminate firing seemed suicidal.

Nick probably had taken them by surprise, just burst in and started firing. No questions asked. Probably threw in some grenades first. It looked like that with all the body parts lying around. What purpose would be served by his charging in and doing what? Stopping it? Joining it? Getting killed? So he waved to his squad to back off but Walter and Roxie, and she wasn't even supposed to be in combat, understood what was happening. Before he could stop them, they charged in, yelling "hold your fire, hold your fire." David heard shouts, "Get the fuck out of here. Get the fuck out," followed by a barrage of gunfire, screaming, more firing. David had yelled to them, "No. Don't!" But it was too late. The words were swallowed up in the fury, unheard. When it was all over, their bodies, Walter's and Roxie's, lay contorted, grotesque, sprawled on the floor gushing—no, weeping—blood. When he finally entered the room and saw what was to be seen, he retched and retreated until he got control, weeping too. What happened after that was a blur. Even the days that followed ran into each other in a river of grief.

He sleepwalked through the entire investigation. He couldn't focus, feeling that he had lost his identity, or was it his soul? He felt responsible. Knew he was responsible. This had happened because he had failed. He had failed utterly to step in and do what any decent person would have done without stopping to think. He had failed from start to finish, failed to stop Nick and his girlfriend, hoping it would end on its own. He had failed to stop Nick from taking charge of the clean-up operation. He had buried his head in the sand. Then he lied to cover it up. He failed to stand up against the pressure from superiors to protect Nick, to protect the company, to protect the whole damn Army. He protected everyone except the innocent human beings who were slaughtered without mercy. They did not have the benefit of a trial. He failed to protect the truth. His weakness, his cowardice, had prevailed. He played their goddamn game and repeated all the bullshit about protecting his men. After all, collateral damage was inevitable. It was normal. These people didn't count. He fled from his own actions. He fled from the truth.

He was sitting now, too shaky to stand. His mind was reeling and his head ached. He felt sick to his stomach. This must be his *dark night of the soul*. Maybe he had lost it years ago when he deliberately led Ronnie to his death in the heaving sea and then was unable to summon it for help when he was face to face with a brutal crime. He was in the grip of panic, and he was safely in his room. How could he face sitting in the courtroom? If anyone knew about this, what he was like down to the core, no one would respect him. He would be finished. Was this the kind of thing that drove people to suicide? Despair? He had always dismissed the idea of suicide. It was never the only option.

He had to pull out of this. He had to go to the courthouse. He had always hated taking drugs, sedatives, but long ago, during his first year out of the service, he'd needed something to help him get through the difficult days. Avoidance helped but sometimes he couldn't do that. So he'd carried a plastic pill bottle in his pocket all the time. He was never without it. He never knew when he'd feel he could lose control and maybe pass out or get sick. He'd once relied on them daily but as the years had gone on, he used them once in a while. He took one of the pills. It was mild but it was usually enough. His doctor at the VA said it was okay.

David regained control of his mind although he was still shaking. Thank God he was alone in his room. He had begged off meeting Barbara and Richard for breakfast. "Got to pull myself together," he said aloud. "I can't fall apart like this." When he felt well enough to make a phone call, he called Barbara.

"Good morning. How did you sleep?" she asked.

"Not great, thanks. Have you heard from Richard this morning?" he asked.

"Yes, he called early. He had already spoken to Myron and left to meet him. So, David, are you coming to court?"

"Yes, I'm planning on it. I'm not feeling great, but I should be okay soon. It's not easy seeing all those people again after so long and reliving the past. It was a bad time, although I expect what we'll be hearing is a different story from the real one."

"We should get a cab at nine. We've arranged a room for you to wait in until the evidence begins. I don't think the reporters will come looking for you, at least not until after your testimony. I'll watch out for you."

"Good," he said. "I'll meet you in the lobby at a few minutes to nine. Has Myron or his associate said anything more about the record?"

"I've asked again," Barbara said. "Lenny said he would bring a copy or a synopsis. He promised. I'll do my best to hold him to it."

86

After arriving at the Court of Common Pleas, Criminal Division, on Filbert Street, David was curious to see the Honorable Joseph Lacey, who possessed the power to protect him or throw him to the dogs with his rulings. David had been in a state trial court on a handful of occasions. Barbara took him directly to a jury deliberation room on the third floor where he could wait, unobserved. In a few minutes, Richard entered the room.

"How did the meeting go?" David asked.

"Stewart isn't opposed to a deal that would get his client five years to serve with a chance of parole sooner, but he's not optimistic about the DA agreeing. Peale is convinced he's got a strong case. He thinks any kind of PTSD defense has no chance. He's willing to meet with the judge, but he thinks it's better if I'm not there. There's still a chance that the DA may ask the judge to order a preliminary hearing on your testimony. I don't know if that's good or bad, frankly. The jury wouldn't be there during the preliminary hearing but the press would. The questioning might go farther afield. We should know in a half hour if there's a chance for a plea deal. I'm going back downstairs in case the judge is willing to let me sit in. Just so you know, the talk of the courthouse is that the leading U.S. Supreme Court candidate will be on the witness stand. Sorry. I know that's not the good news it should be under other circumstances."

"The background investigation is beginning soon I think. It's not a done deal," David said, subdued.

"I'm doing my best," Richard said. He returned in a half hour, looking discouraged, and said, "No deal. The prosecutor insists on ten years to serve, with a chance of parole after six and nothing less. The judge is laying back at this point, not putting pressure on, although I suppose he'd be glad to avoid having to give a complicated charge on multiple criminal counts plus a PTSD defense. He may like the publicity though. He's running for re-election next year. The DA is running for re-election next year too so that's another wild card. This case can blow up badly or it can make him a hero. The question is whether it helps or hurts to convict a veteran under these circumstances. The DA isn't going to ask for a preliminary hearing, so you can come down with Barbara just before eleven to listen to the proceedings, if you want. The jury was told to report then."

David entered the courtroom with Barbara at a few minutes before eleven.

Time and anemic maintenance budgets had taken their toll over the years. It had high ceilings, with ornate large tiles, walnut wood panels on the walls and threadbare brown carpeting on the floor. The room was large with poor acoustics. The judge was not on the bench but the bailiff was poised, standing in his box, ready to pound the gavel and announce the opening of court. David was surprised to see that the seats, probably as many as 150, were nearly full. He supposed that this was the kind of trial that drew all the regulars, the criminal court-watchers, lawyers waiting for calendar calls in other court-rooms, plus a few street people who sought refuge in the building during the daytime. This was, in the public perception, a love triangle murder by a war veteran. It provided good fodder for the watchers and the lawyers. Barbara directed David's attention to a young woman sitting in the third row with a clear view of the judge's bench, jury, counsel table, and the witness box.

"That's the reporter for the *Inquirer*," she said. "She'll probably be looking to spot you. I think she gets inside information from the DA. Doesn't she look unpleasant?"

She added, "There's Myron. Have you met him?"

David shook his head no. She pointed to a large man in his late fifties, well over six feet, and considerably overweight. His face had a serious look accentuated by a slight smirk, which was probably a permanent part of his physical appearance. His face was marked by the jutting chin of a Marine sergeant, not unlike his client's chin, David noticed.

The DA, by contrast, was in his early forties, lean, with an angular face and a slightly hooked nose. He had the look of a bird of prey, a fierce hawk, in contrast to Myron, who resembled a giant grizzly poised to attack. Together they presented a portrait of gladiators with contrasting strengths, readying for battle to the death. Curious, David thought, death is stalking this trial. The question is: who is the predator and who is the prey?

87

The bailiff slammed his gavel on the block as he roared, "All Rise!" Judge Lacey, a slightly overweight African American man in his mid-sixties, with a studied demeanor reflecting the gravity of the proceedings, entered briskly and sat down in a large chair behind the bench. He acknowledged the court staff and the lawyers. David found it a curious experience to jump to his feet for another judge. He assumed the judge probably knew what he looked like. Judge Lacey's face was inscrutable, the result of years of concealing his emotional reactions on the bench. David often prided himself on having an instinct for character and personality. Some took longer to read than others. A quick study of this judge gave him a few clues. The judge was a decent person who was comfortable and confident in his ability to preside. He was in charge. Those observations were borne out as the trial progressed.

Once everyone was seated, the judge asked whether the lawyers were ready for the jury to be summoned. The prosecutor, Gerald Peale, got to his feet and said in an aggressive tone, "Your Honor, I understand the defense is going to call as many as six witnesses who will testify to the combat experiences of the defendant and the effect on his mental health. Apparently, the defense continues to pursue the spurious PTSD defense strategy that we heard about before. We understand that all of these witnesses are present, including the featured witness, Justice David Lawson of the Connecticut Supreme Court, who apparently has taken leave of his judicial duties to observe proceedings this morning."

Peale said David's name and position with a haughty voice. "Although I have never met him, I am informed that Justice Lawson is seated in the back row. The Commonwealth moves for an order of sequestration. We deem this essential to protect the integrity of the court. I understand that other defense witnesses are also present. It is obvious that the defense wishes to educate its witnesses before they take the stand and deliver their coordinated narratives in support of the defendant."

"Objection, Your Honor," Myron shouted in a loud voice that seemed more suitable for an alleyway than the solemn space of the courtroom.

"I can hear you, Counsel. You don't need to shout," Judge Lacey said sternly. Clearly, the judge was not about to be bullied in his own courtroom. David later observed that Myron always spoke loudly no matter where he was. He usually got away with bullying his way through court proceedings and negotiations. He was unabashed when reprimanded for his behavior. Myron was shrewd as to how far he could push. He was accustomed to doing whatever he pleased in or out of a courtroom.

"Neither the Commonwealth nor the defense moved for a sequestration order at the beginning of the trial," Myron began. "My brother, the District Attorney, presented his case through a series of witnesses who artfully conformed their stories because they were free to listen to the other witnesses in the courtroom or had the testimony summarized for them. Apparently the Commonwealth had no concern for the integrity of the court until this moment when we are about to begin our case. My brother is far too late. We object strenuously. The Commonwealth has waived its right to sequestration of the defense witnesses by failing to raise the issue at the start of trial. Our rules have been consistently interpreted to require that such a motion be made at the outset of the trial, not to allow any side to pick and choose which witnesses it will exclude by selectively seeking sequestration after it has benefited from the absence of any order."

Obviously, David observed, this trial is a battle of two titans of the courtroom. David resigned himself to be provoked, attacked, and pushed to his limits. There would be no free pass with either lawyer. How the judge would view him was another story. He didn't expect any more than a superficial showing of respect from the three of them. Better to be prepared and girded for battle than be surprised and caught defenseless. He had faced worse situations and at least here he knew what he meant to accomplish. He would have a battle to give up as little ground as possible, thereby advancing his agenda. His goal was to distance himself from the investigation, avoid exposure under MEJA, and prepare clear sailing toward the Supreme Court nomination.

The DA argued that there was no such thing as waiver of this right, and the motion could be made at any point in the trial. Lacey barely hesitated before sustaining the defense challenge. "The court has discretion to order sequestration at any point. However, I feel that what's sauce for the goose is sauce for the gander. I will exercise my discretion to deny the prosecution's motion. You made your choice and you're stuck with it, Mr. Peale. There's no more reason to think that the defense witnesses would conform their stories than that the prosecution's would conform theirs. Denied!"

"Exception," the prosecutor said, pretending to be outraged. "Thank you, Your Honor," Myron said obsequiously.

"How many witnesses will you be calling for the defense, Counsel?" the judge asked.

"Judge, I expect to call six or seven witnesses, not including my client, who may or may not testify. Five or six witnesses will testify about what my client experienced during his deployments to Iraq and what he suffered as a result. One or possibly two will be experts to explain his PTSD condition, which caused him to react the way he did on the night in question."

"Skip the argument, Counsel," the judge said dismissively. "Stick to the facts."

Myron went on. "Yes, Your Honor. These witnesses will establish what happened on one particular night and why it happened. This evidence will prevail even if, by some stretch of the imagination, the jury believes the Commonwealth's witnesses. Obviously, we don't agree with what those witnesses testified, but it is of little significance in view of the defense."

David listened, reflecting on what he knew of the prosecution case from Barbara. The prosecutor had called several witnesses to the shooting, Nick's girlfriend being the main one. Barbara said that Dee was very emotional on the stand and appeared fragile. Although mostly recovered from her physical injuries, her mental injuries were another story. She had taken one bullet to the head and obviously suffered some mental impairment. She spoke slowly, Barbara said, and appeared confused at times, losing her train of thought. She had to be reminded of pending questions frequently during her two hours on the stand. Direct examination had taken only a half hour, but Myron made her go over her story dozens of times, trying to catch her in inconsistencies and outright contradictions. Myron, with his ruthless skill, wore her down to some extent, but how the jury took this remained to be seen. His strategy might backfire in an outpouring of sympathy for the woman.

Another eyewitness was a kitchen worker, Carlos Perez, a long-time employee at the bar where Nick's girlfriend worked. Perez testified with the help of an interpreter. He came outside to the dumpster and saw the drama unfold. He was obviously nervous about being the center of attention in the courtroom and his testimony had to be filtered through the Spanish interpreter. The interpreter, though, was clear and forceful as she spoke for Perez.

The two other eyewitnesses testified that they were standing by their car talking after leaving the bar. They were on the far side of the lot but had a clear view of both vehicles and the action. Their testimony corroborated the other witnesses. On cross, which was nearly as lengthy and demanding as Dee's, they had to acknowledge having three or four drinks each during the evening. They also admitted that they were "socializing," in their words, before heading home to their spouses. Their first impulse was to leave the scene before the police identified them as witnesses, but, because they were regulars and knew Dee, they put in the 911 call and remained with her until emergency help arrived.

The various pieces of testimony added up to a story in which Dee and the deceased, Harold, were sitting in his car for a half hour in the well-lit parking lot. They remained in the car when Nick's pickup entered the lot and parked about ten car widths away from Harold's car. He sat in the car briefly before going inside the building. He returned to his car and sat for five or ten minutes, scanning the lot. He appeared to spot Dee and Harold. He got out and crossed the lot to Dee's side of the car, yelling at her to "get the fuck out now. You'll get what's coming to you, bitch." She moved abruptly in the car, probably trying to lock her door, but Nick smashed the window with his gun, yanked the door open, and reached in, grabbing her arm. At that point,

Harold got out of the driver's door and started around the front of the car toward Nick, yelling at him to stop. Nick let go of Dee's arm and moved toward Harold, who did not reach into his pocket. In fact, police witnesses testified that no weapon of any kind was found on his person, in the car, or in the area. He had a valid gun permit on record, as he had since his military service.

Harold was saying loudly, "Take it easy, Nick. Everything's okay. We were just talking. Take it slow." When the two of them were about three feet apart, Nick began firing and got off five, maybe six, rounds. Harold was hit in the face and chest and went down. At that, Nick turned toward the car and fired at least six rounds into the windshield, yelling, "Bitch, you fucking whore. I'm gonna blow you away. You've had it coming for a long time."

Dee screamed and slumped out of sight of the witnesses. Nick abruptly walked back to his truck without looking around. He left the lot in a hurry, speeding through a red light at the intersection. Perez ran to the bar. The couple ran toward Dee in the car and called 911. The police and the emergency team arrived within ten minutes.

88

Given that testimony, David thought, it seems certain the jury would find that Nick was the shooter. Myron will have an uphill battle convincing the jury that a flashback caused the shootings. David felt angry at the prospect of jeopardizing his opportunity of a lifetime in order to play a role in Nick's fatuous scheme to avoid punishment for his crimes. His outrage was fueled by a brief confrontation that happened the day before. David got a call from Nick. He was taken by surprise since there had been no contact up to that point.

"Hey Davey boy, I'm glad you're here," Nick began in a mocking tone. "I was afraid you wouldn't show up. I thought your legal team would advise you to run for cover. That's your style, right? Remember, all you gotta do is back up the story. Just stick to what you said at the hearing in Iraq. Got that, pal?"

"Not really," David said. "It's been a long time. Give my lawyer a copy of the report if you want me to remember what I said. Why the hell are you calling me, anyway?"

"What, I'm not supposed to call my old friend? It's up to my lawyer to handle that," Nick said. "Just do what your lawyer says, and I don't mean the broad. I mean your real lawyer."

"I don't need you to tell me what to do," David said.

"I think maybe you need help too," Nick replied. "Maybe you don't fucking know what's at stake for you. Which reminds me, I read an interesting news item this morning. It seems like you have a big future, my friend, maybe—that is, if you're smart, if you watch your step."

"Stay out of my life," David said, holding back a wave of anger.

"My lawyer will fucking crucify you on the witness stand and in the press if you don't act smart. You got your story to follow, man. Anything you change will reveal your lies, one time or the other. If your conscience tells you to confess everything, you're going to be charged with conspiracy according to my lawyer. If I go down, you go down. It's already in the works anyway, but, if you act smart, maybe it won't happen. Got it? Clear enough for you?"

"I came down here, didn't I," David said. "Don't push me. You're in no position to push. You're in deep shit."

"I'll push all I want. Don't fuck with me."

David hung up seething with rage, fear, and the agony of indecision.

"You've got to put everything going on outside this courtroom totally out of your mind," Richard said. "Concentrate on showing the jury that you are being absolutely truthful. But just be truthful enough to answer the specific question. Don't go beyond the question. Think minimizing. No surprises. No sweeping statements. No volunteering anything beyond the specific question. I think the judge will let you do that. Expert witnesses do that all the time. This is not a time to relieve yourself of guilt feelings. I doubt that the threat of a MEJA prosecution means anything. I don't see anyone having the steam to take that on once this trial is over. Stay alert so you don't get caught in inconsistencies with the hearing testimony. Keep it simple, brief, understated and to the point. If you can't answer the question, ask to have it rephrased. You'll be fine. Barbara was given a quick look at the report. She'll show you her notes about that as soon as she sees you."

Now, sitting in the courtroom, while these thoughts swirling in his head, David forced himself to listen to Myron's argument. "As I said earlier, Judge, I'll call two enlisted members of the platoon, two widows of deceased soldiers in the platoon. Those soldiers tragically committed suicide. I have one or two mental health professionals and, finally, the commanding officer of the platoon who is a state Supreme Court justice on his way to bigger and better things." David observed the two journalists whom Barbara had identified pivot their heads simultaneously to see his reaction. They knew who he was and would be checking for his reactions as the day went on.

"Okay, Counsel, are you ready for the jury?" the judge asked.

"Yes, judge," Myron responded, echoed by Peale.

"Bailiff, bring in the jury," the judge commanded. David watched as the fifteen people filed into the jury box, six men and six women who composed the jury and two women and one man who served as alternates. Some of them looked around curiously to see who was in the courtroom today, probably wondering what had gone on while they waited in the jury room. Others looked bored and a few looked ill at ease.

After remarks to the jury by the judge, Myron called Douglas Garvey to the stand. Garvey entered the rear door of the courtroom accompanied by Myron's associate, Lenny. David hadn't seen Garvey since his final day in Iraq. He had not weathered well during the intervening years. He was a short man who had always looked out of shape, even when he was in fighting condition. Now he was forty pounds heavier, most of it concentrated in his belly. His florid face confirmed that most of the extra weight was produced by beer drinking. He had the look of a habitual smoker as well. He moved unsteadily toward the witness stand. He stood and took the oath unconvincingly. David supposed that Garvey had been selected to lead off because he had been Nick's subordinate, a corporal, loyal and compliant no matter what Nick asked him to do. Garvey had been with Nick during the raid in Ramadi.

Myron began, "Tell the jury your name and your service rank at the time you separated from the Army." That was followed by a series of preliminary questions about Garvey's life since the discharge. He had been a career soldier and, since getting out, had worked mainly as an auto mechanic. He acknowledged being in alcohol rehab a couple of times, being married and divorced, and working as a volunteer at the VA for a short time, before going to prison for attempted robbery.

Myron turned to the Iraq experience with a series of routine questions about deployments and assignments. Then he honed in on the crucial matters.

"Mr. Garvey, for what period of time did you serve as a corporal in Sergeant Serrano's platoon, as part of Bravo Company?"

The answer was, "One year, sir."

"You recognize Sergeant Serrano, correct?" Garvey nodded. "You have to answer out loud for the record," Myron said.

"Oh. Yes."

"Point him out for the ladies and gentlemen of the jury." He did.

"Was Larry Cutter also assigned with you?"

"Yessir."

"How about Lieutenant Lawson, seated in the back of the courtroom?"

Garvey searched David out, seemed surprised to see him then lapsed back into his dull, guarded expression. "What about him?" Garvey asked.

"Do you recognize him? Did you serve with him?" Myron struggled to conceal his impatience.

Garvey nodded, then said, "Sorry. Yes. To both questions."

After routine answers, Myron dug in more deeply, always careful to stay on the safe side of a leading question, confident that the prosecutor was not likely to object at this stage.

"Would you describe your experience as peaceful or perilous?"

"Perilous, sir."

"How often did you engage in firefights on the average?"

"I'd say four or five times a week during that period, sir."

David would have said twice a week was average. Despite his deteriorated condition and disheveled appearance, Garvey managed to punctuate each answer with a neat "sir" at the end of the response.

"How often did your platoon have check point responsibility where you had to do a quick visual inspection of each vehicle passing the point?"

"Well, sir, we were frequently given that assignment, I'd say nearly half of each month." David thought Garvey had doubled that estimate too.

"Were there times when you felt in danger during that assignment?"

"Yes, sir. All the time. You never knew what you'd find."

"Did you often find weapons?"

"Yes sir."

"And did you ever get fired on or have to fire at occupants yourself to stop them."

"Yes sir, frequently."

"Ever get injured in those situations?"

"Not me, personally, but I saw others in the platoon get killed or injured."

"Did you feel that the civilians in your area were friendly or hostile to you?"

"You never could tell. Many of them had relatives who were in AQI and some would be friendly but you always suspected they'd kill you if they got the chance."

"Could you tell civilians from combatants?" Myron asked.

"Not usually sir. You had to have somebody watch your back all the time."

"Were there any occasions when you encountered someone whom you thought was a non-combatant who turned out to be a combatant?"

"Yes, sir, that was often the case. It was impossible to tell. Any man, woman, or child might attack you or blow themselves up."

"Did you do patrol duty?"

"Yes, just about every day?"

"Was that on foot or mounted patrol?"

"Both, sir. About equal depending on where we were."

"You mean half were on foot and the other half mounted, that is, by vehicle?"

"Yessir."

"And did you ever get shot at during patrol?"

"Almost every time, sir," Garvey responded.

"How often did you engage in actual firefights during your patrol duty? I mean where it was more than just a shot or two?"

"Very often."

"Every day? Every week?"

"It's hard to say sir, but it probably happened three or four times a week."

The testimony, David thought, was exaggerated. He supposed it didn't exceed the way most veterans embellish their stories when they get back home.

"How did you sleep?"

"Not well, sir. It was touch and go. Somebody always had to stay on guard. You might get an RPG in the barracks at any time, and on mounted patrol. There were IEDs everywhere. I saw lots of guys, women too, get hands blown off or worse."

"Would you say it was stressful over there?"

Garvey laughed. "That's quite an understatement, sir. It's the most stressful thing I ever did in my life. We felt like we were sitting on a powder keg day and night."

89

Did you ever have occasion to observe Sergeant Serrano when you were in Iraq?"

"Yes sir. Every day. I was in his platoon for the better part of two years. We were very close. He depended on me to have his back all the time," Garvey said, puffing himself up in the chair. "And he had mine, of course. We were a team. We worked together perfectly. I had great respect for—"

"Objection," Peale said loudly.

"Sustained. Just answer the question," the judge said.

"Sorry, Your Honor," Garvey said.

"Tell the ladies and gentlemen of the jury what you observed about how the sergeant discharged his duties as an officer."

"What does this have to do with the case? Objection," Peale said, leaping to his feet.

"Overruled."

"Yes sir, well there's a lot to that, a lot to say. I was with him all the time like I said. He was the best sergeant I ever saw. He knew what he was doing and he was committed to his men. He'd do anything for his men. Why, one time—"

Myron cut him off and launched the next question.

"And women?"

"Yes, and women," Garvey said. "We had a few females assigned to our unit from time to time in various capacities, you know, under us." He stammered in response to muffled laughter in the courtroom. The bailiff pounded his gavel and glared. "I mean they worked for us. They couldn't go into combat so we had to do the dirty work. But, you know, they were okay, considering—"

Again, Myron cut off a troublesome answer with a quick question.

"Thank you Mr. Garvey. Did you ever see the sergeant upset or under stress? You said it was stressful? Did he appear to be under stress?"

"Well not usually but there was one time when I was worried about him."

"When was that?"

"Well, sir I'd say it was in 2008. I don't recall exactly when. He had befriended a family, a large family. Iraqis, you know. Arabs, I mean, locals. They had a good relationship."

"Why was that? Was that allowed, that is, being friendly with the locals?"

"Oh yes sir. It was part of our job to win over the locals. We were supposed to do that, but of course not to get too close. We always had to take care of our own first. It was their country of course. We were doing our best to protect them, to build democracy and all that. This family was important. The sheikh was a big man in the Sons of Iraq in this area. He had a bunch of kids, grown kids that is. The sheikh was in his sixties I would say."

"So the sergeant got to know that family? How often would he see them, if you know?"

"Well, fairly often, sir, maybe once a week. We were supposed to get to know the sheikhs and do what we could to keep them on our side. So they could come to the base and tell the commanding officers about any problems they were having with the troops and, you know, stuff like that. After all they were getting paid to do that. We paid them a lot of money, even gave them a name. The Sons of Iraq fought alongside us."

"Did other people on the base know about his acquaintance with the family?"

"Yeah, uh, yes sir. That's right. Sure everyone knew. And sometimes the sheikh's kids. They'd come to the base too, you know hang out and everything."

"Are you saying that they were well known to the troops? Just your platoon or the whole company?"

"Yeah, the company too, I'd say. We were a COP, that's a Combat Outpost. The sheikh, he'd give the sergeant a lot of useful information."

"Did something unusual happen to this family that caused Sergeant Serrano some distress?"

"Objection, Your Honor," the prosecutor said, jumping to his feet. "We've been patiently listening to all this irrelevant detail. But this is too much. What is the relevance of this unusual happening?"

"Overruled," barked the judge.

"Do you remember the question, Mr. Garvey?"

"Yes, I do. Something did happen and the sergeant, he sure took care of their butts."

"Objection, Your Honor," Peale shouted. "I move to strike that answer. That kind of language is an insult to the court and the jury."

"Stricken. Sustained," the judge ruled, clearly riled. "The jury is ordered to disregard that answer," he said, glaring at the witness. "Mr. Garvey, confine yourself to the question and don't use street language in my courtroom. Do you understand?"

Garvey looked chagrined, like a small boy scolded in front of an entire classroom. "Sorry, Your Honor. It won't happen again."

Myron was not fazed. He followed up without breaking stride. "What happened, and tell us when it was?"

"I don't recall the date but it was late in 2008, I think, maybe October. I'm not sure exactly."

"What happened?"

"The sergeant—and his squad, me included because no one ever went off the base alone, you know—left the base early in a Humvee. He wanted to meet the sheikh at a park near his house. It was just a social thing, as I recall. The sheikh owned a big house about a mile or so from our post. We got there first. We found the sheikh's daughter, the oldest daughter, Jasmine her name was, hanging upside down from a soccer goalpost. I mean from the crossbar that goes across the top. She was dead obviously. There was a pool of blood on the ground. She had a lot of stab wounds. Whoever killed her had gutted her the way you do with an animal so it bleeds to death. Her body was gutted from head to toe. I've seen a lot, but this was the worst thing I ever saw. She was a very pretty girl and very nice and, well, this was something else."

The faces of several members of the jury had turned ashen and several sank down in their chairs as if to protect them from the horror of the scene.

"What did the sergeant do?"

"He looked like he was in shock. He got sick, you know, threw up. Someone grabbed hold of him and helped him to a place where he could sit down. Sat him down, so he wouldn't fall."

"What about the family? Were they there too?"

"The sheikh arrived in a few minutes. A couple of his sons were with him. He collapsed. One of his sons caught him and helped him to a bench. He was wailing. I'd never heard anything like it. It was eerie. The medics came and they cut her down. They took her away soon after, and we took the sergeant back to the base hospital. He was really shaken. I was afraid for him."

"Did anyone speak to the sergeant?"

"The sheikh did, but I'm not sure what he said ... something like 'I told her to stop. I told you to stop.' I didn't know what that was all about. The sheikh looked angry though when he spoke to the sergeant. The sergeant was just sitting there. He took it pretty hard."

"What happened after that?"

"Word got out that it was the local Al Qaeda that did this, and people said it was because they didn't like the locals getting friendly with Americans. It was against their religion or something. There was some talk about which ones. We knew who some of them were who did this. We knew there'd be an order to retaliate. It was payback time. They couldn't get away with that."

"What happened after? Was there retaliation?"

"You bet. Less than a week later, the sergeant was put in charge of the operation. He wasn't in very good shape yet, but he was the logical one so he put a strike team together, just half a dozen of us. And we had a list of insurgents to go after. We were ordered to take prisoners or terminate them. It was up to us."

"Who gave the order?"

"The lieutenant, the lieutenant sitting over there," pointing to David. "He wasn't a captain yet. Lieutenant Lawson ordered the sergeant to put a strike team together."

"Okay, so what did you do?"

"We went out three or four times, and we cut them down. It went pretty smoothly although it was a little messy because they fought back of course and there was quite a bit of killing necessary on the last mission. It was a viper's nest all right. It was a real firefight. I remember it was hard as hell, sorry, to tell who was who. A lot of people were killed, all of them and two of our own guys. They were our only casualties."

"Who got killed from your unit?"

"Walter somebody, I don't remember his last name now, and a female. I don't remember her name. They followed us in, I guess, and they were mowed down, but the whole operation was a big success. We killed all those mothers, uh, sorry, insurgents who killed the sheikh's daughter and we wasn't as brutal as they were either. We did it civilized like, you know."

"I take it that the company commander and the battalion and brigade commanders approved the whole operation?"

"Yes sir. They looked into it after and concluded that we carried out our mission, and it was difficult. Killing is not easy but it had to be done."

"Did the sergeant go on as before after all this?"

"No sir. Not really. He was never the same. He seemed different, subdued, quiet you know. This hit him hard and he got sent back home. I heard he had some PTSD treatments."

"Objection. This witness is not a medical expert and he is testifying to hearsay. I move to strike."

"Sustained," said the judge, slapping his hand on the bench.

"So he was sent back to the States, right? And, did you see him after that?"

"Yes sir. Back in the States."

"What were your observations about him?"

"I went home after my tour was up in another couple of months, and I saw him there at the base. He ran some training operations but he was never the same. He was jumpy and short-fused. He'd get a sort of spaced out look and seemed to forget where he was. He'd go into long silences too, and he didn't hang around with us anymore. I heard he got divorced too. I didn't see him much after that but I heard he had a tough time and did a lot of drinking, you know, self-medicating."

"Would you say that Sergeant Serrano was traumatized by what happened in the course of that week, including—"

The DA leapt to his feet, shouting, "Objection! Objection! Is the witness a psychiatrist now? That is highly improper."

"Sustained," the judge said loudly, glaring at Myron. "No more of that," he said.

"No further questions, Your Honor," Myron said, grinning and winking at the jury as he walked to his seat.

90

The DA stood and strode briskly toward the witness, savoring the prospect of surgically cutting Garvey's testimony to shreds as a warning to the other witnesses. "Mr. Garvey," he began quietly, "was your rank Corporal Garvey while you were in the service?"

"Yes, sir, that's correct. That was my rank," Garvey said with an air of defiance.

"How long were you in the service?"

"I was career originally, but I retired early on a disability after twelve years."

"What was your disability if I may ask? Just the general category will do. You don't have to reveal private medical information."

"I don't mind sir. I was diagnosed with DBI."

"You mean TBI, Traumatic Brain Injury, don't you Mr. Garvey?"

"What?" Garvey asked with a confused look on his face.

"Never mind," Peale said. "So you had TBI. You got some kind of head injury, right?"

"Yeah."

"What was that diagnosis based on, the specific incident, that is?"

"I got a head injury in 2009. I was in a BFV. After infantry, I was assigned to the Mechanized Unit. We were hit by several RPGs after we were stopped by an IED. I was the gunner. I was standing at the top of the vehicle."

"Mr. Garvey. May I ask you to talk in words rather than acronyms for the benefit of the jury? Explain BFV, RGP, and IED. Don't use letters. Use words."

"Okay. Yes sir. BFV. That's a Bradley Fighting Vehicle. Sort of like a tank but different. RPG is a rocket-propelled grenade. It's like a bomb that you throw or you know blast off like a rocket. Everybody knows what that is. An IED is like a bomb too. I don't know what the letters stand for but it's like a homemade bomb that gets planted just about anywhere along the roads or in the fields, anywhere they thought we might go."

"Does Improvised Explosive Device ring a bell?"

"Oh, yeah. That sounds right."

"Did you have a diagnosis of PTSD also as a result of that brain injury?" Peale asked.

"Objection," Myron interrupted. "Outside the scope of direct. The witness wasn't called to testify about his own conditions. This is not relevant."

"Overruled," the judge literally shouted over Myron's loud, rasping voice.

"What's the basis your honor?" Myron asked.

"Counselor, I don't answer your questions. You heard the ruling. It was on your objection. It is not outside the scope of direct." Myron grudgingly sat down but was getting impatient and sat poised ready to spring with the next objection.

"You can answer the question, Mr. Garvey," the judge said.

"Oh. Well, no. I wasn't diagnosed with PTSD."

"Oh, I see. Did you have basically the same exposure to combat, firefights, anxiety about RPGs and IEDs as the defendant?" The prosecutor glanced at the jury, checking to be sure they weren't confused about the military jargon.

"Well, yes," Garvey said. "Basically we spent the first deployment, about a year, together in the same platoon. After the incident with the sheikh's family, Sergeant Serrano was sent back to the States. He finished his service there."

"And you were deployed one more time, right?"

"Actually, twice, once to Iraq and then to Djibouti for about six months after that."

"And you didn't get PTSD?"

"Where is this going?" Myron bellowed.

"Is that an objection, counsel?" the judge snapped back. "I'm not ruling on your questions."

"Yes, Your Honor. I object. Whether this witness was diagnosed with PTSD as my client was is neither here nor there. Irrelevant."

"I agree," the judge snapped back. "Sustained. Move on counsel."

"Is the purpose of diagnosis to find the best way to get a disability pension?"

"That's one purpose. Yeah, it can be," Garvey said.

"Tell me, Mr. Garvey, were you a tougher soldier than the defendant?"

"No sir. I was tough but he was tough too, a top sergeant. He did everything we did. He never ordered us to do anything that he wasn't ready to do, himself."

"So why do you think he got PTSD when you didn't?"

"Objection!" Myron roared, bolting to his feet. "Is the prosecutor calling this witness as an expert? I'll stipulate that the witness can answer opinion questions on combat injuries including PTSD and TBI. Otherwise, that question is outside the scope of direct."

"Sustained," the judge said impatiently. "That's enough of that."

"Mr. Garvey, you testified that you saw the defendant again after Iraq when you returned to your base. Was that at Fort Benning?"

"Yes."

"Had he been diagnosed with PTSD at that time?"

"I don't believe so but I don't know for sure. He was still on active duty so I guess not."

"Move to strike," Myron said, then added, "Withdrawn, never mind."

"And how long after he was sent home was that?"

"A year after, I think."

"So did the defendant's PTSD suddenly appear just in time for this trial?"

"That is highly improper and he knows that. Objection!" Myron was again on his feet roaring at the DA. "That insinuation has no place in a courtroom. Your Honor, I ask that you strike that question and inform the jury to disregard it and that you reprimand the prosecutor. And I move for a mistrial."

"That's enough from both of you," the judge said, raising his voice over Myron's. He turned toward the jury. "Ladies and gentlemen, I'm going to excuse you so I can have a talk with these lawyers. You are free until two o'clock." The jury, wide-eyed and amused at the last exchange, stood and left the jury box, glancing back at both lawyers and the judge.

In his limited courtroom experience, David had never seen lawyers engage in combat on this primal level. He had already developed respect for the way the judge managed to control the lawyers without himself being combative. With the jury out of earshot, the judge warned the lawyers that he would not tolerate any more misconduct. He would not hesitate to hold either or both of them in contempt. Despite the warning, David realized that he should expect relentless direct and cross-examination.

During the lunch recess, he joined Richard and Barbara. Richard observed, "These guys are classic. The DA is a tough bird. Every prosecution is a life and death battle for him. He can't stand to lose. He hates all defendants and their lawyers. He's not fond of judges either. As for Myron, he's a street fighter. Beneath the rough exterior, you'll find skill and meticulous preparation. The judge will keep control but maybe not before you get roughed up a bit. He won't crack down on the lawyers except to let them know he's in charge. He's seen it all before. A lot of what he says is for the record and the benefit of the jury.

"I don't know what's so special about the prosecution itself," Richard continued. "Nick Serrano is just another thug charged with a domestic violence murder. It happens all the time. I hope the lawyers show a little respect for you, but there'll be more action than you've seen in any courtroom. You'll take a few body blows before it's over. Just keep cool and composed. Be sure you understand the questions. Make them be crystal clear. Don't answer open-ended questions or statements that try to draw you into an argument with them. Remember that the judge will probably let you reshape the questions to some extent. Unfortunately, I can't jump in. As counsel for a witness, I have no right to intervene unless a Fifth Amendment issue arises. That's a different story."

David begged off from staying for lunch, saying he needed to take a walk to get some fresh air. He would find his way back to the courthouse. It looked now as though he wouldn't be called until tomorrow at the earliest, maybe even the day after.

When court resumed in the afternoon, Garvey took more pummeling but the DA stayed within bounds. His approach was to undermine testimony that Nick reported suffering PTSD symptoms. Then he turned to the sheikh's family. He dug into Nick's relationship with Jasmine, suggesting it was an illicit relationship and they were running a dating service for officers and enlisted men. Garvey stuck to his story. It was apparent the DA had no ammunition supporting an attack on Garvey's story. His questioning about the authority to conduct the raids gained him little ground.

In David's view, the defense story was a carefully contrived bundle of half-truths and outright lies. The problem was that it was probably consistent with his testimony at the investigation hearing. He seethed at the trap that he'd set for himself by his own failure tell the truth. He went along with the military conspiracy before. What could he do now but go along again with the defense conspiracy to exculpate Nick from another murder. In Iraq, at least, it had happened within the context of war, where killing was the norm rather than the exception.

The next witness, Albert Rodriquez, was essentially a repeat of Garvey's testimony. Both lawyers followed the same strategies in questioning him, although as with Garvey, Peale was able to cast doubt on his credibility with pointed questions about his felony convictions and prison time. Myron's tactical disclosure, on direct, of the prior felony convictions of both witnesses had softened, but not entirely eliminated, the damage to their credibility. Myron built his case for a PTSD flashback excuse, which would be climaxed by psychiatric testimony. He laid groundwork for the claim that combat PTSD could lead to violence in a non-combat setting. He continued working in the term "PTSD's rebound effect," which anyone who knew realized had no scientific significance. The jury had no clue.

91

Threading he widows of Karl and Malvin, the suicides, testified next. Both men had been close allies of Nick, deferring to his wishes over David's. Both of them had enlisted with personal baggage not bargained for by the Army, including addiction and other mental health problems. Nick exploited their problems for his own benefit. It was well known that Nick had access to any contraband that was marketable, including a smorgasbord of drugs.

Myron had seen to it that the two women were on display throughout the trial in hopes that the jury would sympathize, affording him a few more building blocks for his PTSD defense. David couldn't figure out how Myron planned to admit their testimony. What could they say that would be helpful that wasn't inadmissible hearsay?

David remembered details about their suicides. Larry Cutter had called him both times to fill him in. Karl had shot himself and Malvin had hung himself, both within six years of coming back. Both men had been high school dropouts with marginal employment history and minor criminal records before entering the service. They had not learned any marketable skills in the service. If anything, they were deeper into addiction when they left. They were destined to have difficulty readjusting when they transitioned home. Their wives seemed decent enough but it was obvious they had not had an easy time.

Myron could argue that the wives' testimony would not be hearsay because it was not offered to prove the truth of the matter asserted, the classic definition of inadmissible hearsay. Then they'd testify how their husbands cited various combat incidents as the cause of their mental problems that resulted in their suicides. Peale would probably go easy on them. No jury would want to see them manhandled the way Peale treated the other witnesses. He'd discount their husbands' stories by asking questions about the Ramadi incident that they wouldn't be able to answer. That would show the jury how shallow their testimony was and that it was contrived just to play on their sympathies.

Both women testified with little effort to conceal that they were merely reciting a script that had been carefully rehearsed. They attributed the suicides to their husbands' inability to readjust to civilian life because of their combat experiences. They testified about the sleeplessness, the nightmares, the drinking and drugs, the inability to hold jobs and the obsession with guns.

There was domestic violence as well and, on the stand, the women softened the condemnation of their husbands' violence, attributing it to being abandoned by the Army and the VA. The jury listened attentively and respectfully. The widows were sympathetic figures who had known no end of suffering.

David assumed they probably had convinced themselves that combat stress explained their suicides. The alternative was to face a dizzying array of possible factors including their own roles. Suicides were always attributed to prior issues or external events. No one in the military hierarchy wanted to open the door to speculation about deeper causes that might point the finger at military life.

The DA changed his standard approach and used kid gloves on the two women, confining himself to questions posed in quiet tones, somber tones, about details that the women had to acknowledge they did not know. In the end, the jury was not likely to give much weight to their testimony. The whole day had been consumed with four witnesses for the defense. Richard predicted that Larry would be the leadoff witness tomorrow, followed by the psychiatrist or, possibly, David. Myron might prefer to pin down the PTSD testimony before David testified as additional insurance against his upsetting the defense agenda. David could not envision light at the end of the tunnel if he departed from the prescribed plan.

It was one thing to finesse the truth, which he had done at the military tribunal in Iraq. It had been set in motion with that in mind. It was war after all, and no one wanted to embarrass a dedicated soldier for killing a bunch of insurgents even though it resulted in unfortunate collateral damage by the killing of the civilians. After all, they were living in the same house with the insurgents. It was his own failure to take action and stop the rampage that had caused the two poor souls, Walter and Roxie, to try and stop the bloodshed. David was the key. Just as he had led Ronnie, the lamb, to slaughter, he had as much as led innocents to slaughter in Ramadi. There was no escaping it.

It was quite another thing to lie in a criminal trial in the United States. There was not only a record of the hearing testimony in Myron's hands. There were two journalists who could be counted on to write their stories about the State Supreme Court justice about-to-be-United States Supreme Court justice, the go-along guy who followed the flock of other witnesses, pretending that Nick, suffering helplessly from his PTSD so many years later, had imagined, hallucinated, that he was back in Iraq. Going along with the story would not be secret as it had been in Iraq. There would be sensational press stories, and a firestorm that would scuttle the Supreme Court nomination, at least.

Since his testimony was a key to an acquittal, or at least conviction of a less serious offense, the lawyers would have no choice but to beat him up on the witness stand. Which time were you telling the truth and which time, lying? Are you lying now, or did you lie to your brigade commander? Although Peale might be pleased in the short run, he might well instigate a federal MEJA prosecution of David if he did not get the conviction. David felt that the strategy of evading consequences by walking a fine line in his testimony was precarious and probably futile. He might even have to resign from the Connecticut court. Burkhardt's enmity had no bounds.

92

After leaving the courthouse, Richard suggested a light dinner in a small restaurant that was a taxi ride away so they could ensure privacy for their conversation. Richard speculated that Larry would confirm what the other witnesses had said.

"Larry knows the truth," David said. "He was there right by my side, literally. He also knows I refused to authorize Nick to carry out this mission. I'd like to think he won't put me in jeopardy."

"Don't count on it," Richard said in a skeptical tone. "Myron has probably threatened him. He'll lead Larry through the story. The judge will let him get away with it even if Peale objects. Peale has to rely on a ruling by the judge eliminating a PTSD defense as a matter of law or convincing the jury in final argument that it was conjured up for the trial. Myron doesn't need Larry's testimony, but he thinks it will box you in more completely. Are you able to go along with the story? It is consistent with what you said at the investigation, right? I understand why you did that. No one ever wants to rock the boat and risk having CID get involved. It could embarrass the whole company, the battalion and the brigade commander too. There would be a court martial and, no matter what happened, it would look bad for the whole outfit. No one would blame you for going along at the time."

"It depends on how sick it makes me feel to know that I'll be helping Nick get away with murder. I know the safest course is to go along with the playbook. There's no official story out there to trip me up. The report would stay hidden, and Myron would ensure that it never reappears. Even if I tell the whole truth, it won't wipe out the PTSD defense. The jury could still feel that his experience caused PTSD. I suppose the psychiatrist will bring up moral injury. Maybe it was moral injury even if Nick was at fault."

"If you upset the plan," Richard said, "the jury might still believe that he has PTSD. There's no guarantee of a conviction if you tell the truth. What is guaranteed is that you'll be stuck explaining away two very different stories, one that you told then and one that you tell now. Myron will crucify you and will make you a liar then or now, one or the other.

"Which version is true? How does the jury know whether you're telling the truth now? Why are you changing your story so many years later? He may trot out that report or work it into questions. Peale might turn on you too. We don't know what's going on in his head. For all we know, he might be ready to make a deal, feeling that it's his best route out of this case. He might want to go after you, seeing you as easier prey and set things up for MEJA. What will serve his re-election best or his ambition to become a federal prosecutor? He's difficult to read. This is unknown territory."

"What about my conscience, my self-respect? Doesn't that count for something?" David asked.

Richard's impatience was written on his face. "I'm not saying you shouldn't do what your conscience tells you to do. I want you to know what's at stake. I understand you don't want a bunch of lies on the record. You should have thought of that before. That's the trouble with lies or even half-truths. They don't go away. They're like IEDs, planted, waiting to explode. They are patient. They remain there forever, deadly. No further action necessary. Landmines have been in use for years. They blow people apart decades after the conflict is over, innocent people just walking through a field or along a road."

"What's the answer, then?" David started to say.

"There is no good answer except whatever makes the least controversy now and doesn't derail your nomination. Remember. If you get nominated and confirmed, you're virtually immune. No one is going to impeach you over this."

"Right," David said. "As an appointee, I'm invulnerable. As a potential appointee, I'm highly vulnerable. Should that be the sole governing factor in what I do? That seems so unbelievably wrong. I feel as though this is a malignancy inside me that will metastasize if I perpetuate these lies. What if, someday, the villagers, the families, tell their stories to that reporter and the truth comes out about what happened plus the cover-up?"

Barbara interjected. "That's not so far-fetched. Both reporters have been asking a lot of questions, especially Caruso. He talks to the witnesses after they testify, and he came to me too, asking how he could get hold of the investigation report. He's written a couple of pieces that go far beyond the trial. I think he smells something here, another My Lai maybe or an Abu Ghraib, a big story. But I agree basically with Richard. This is no time to get cold feet."

"Sounds like my defense team's deserting me, in favor of the easy way out."

"I don't see it that way," Barbara said, "but can you blame us if we get impatient with the indecisive approach, back and forth but no decision?" She continued despite the furious look on David's face, as he turned away from her.

"The guy Nick killed is part of a big clan," Barbara said. "Some of them have been in the courtroom since day one. He was some sort of hero to them, a veteran himself, and they're steamed about this. If Nick walks away from this, it may not rest there. Caruso has been hanging out with them. They know that this PTSD story is a fake. It's a no-brainer. Years after the war, this guy suddenly has PTSD after he's nailed with this murder? There are four eyewitnesses. He has a history of abusing Dee and threatening to kill her. Then he tries to kill her. How she survived is a miracle. But he does kill the guy who's trying to protect her."

David looked gloomy and felt bitter at their attitudes. Richard was nodding in agreement with Barbara, who added, "If David tells the truth, the story about what really happened, he may be in the middle of controversy and bad publicity but at least this clan won't come after him." Richard looked troubled.

"I hear you, Barbara," Richard said, "but the truth could take a turn toward putting the Army on trial, and I can envision headlines about a big cover-up. That is going to reach the White House for sure. A single reporter can do tremendous damage. At this point, the public doesn't care about truth concerning a war that's long since over and has turned into an endless war against one terrorist network after another. Who cares? Everybody just wants it to go away. If it's a sleeping dog, I say let it lie. No pun intended."

"This is not getting easier," David said. "I don't think what I testify to should be driven by weighing the consequences of this or that story. I don't know what I'll do, but I will trust my instincts tomorrow when I face the questions. Lies—and death—have stalked me all these years. Tomorrow I may stop running and turn to face the grim reaper. When I turn to face it, I may see my own reflection."

With that, he rose and, without a word, walked out of the restaurant. It was a long walk back to the hotel but he could find his way. He longed for fresh, cool, air and the temporary peace of being a man in motion. Walking briskly, he turned his thoughts loose, leaving himself to be carried wherever destiny took him.

93

When David got back to the hotel, he had an urge to call Dana whether or not it was a wise move. Days had gone by without talking to her. He reached her on the second ring. "David," she said after a pause, "What's going on? Is the trial over?"

"No," he said, "tomorrow I testify. I've been sitting in the courtroom listening to the defense witnesses. Their testimony has boxed me in. Frankly, I don't know what I'm going to do."

"Just a minute," she said, "let me close the door in case Jake comes in the room."

"Jake? Jake is there? Where are you?"

"I'm at my apartment," she said. "Oh, I guess you don't know. We talked a couple of times, and I agreed that he could stay here. He needed a place to stay for a few days. It's not necessarily permanent."

"Not necessarily permanent?" David was stunned into silence. He felt derailed, unable to continue talking to the person whom he hoped he could still count on.

"I know how that sounds," she resumed. "I'm not abandoning you. I felt I had to do this so he and I can resolve things one way or the other."

"One way or the other? What does that mean? Are you still on the fence? I thought that was over."

"I never said that," Dana said defensively. "I'm me, my own person. Get it? You haven't even communicated with me for a week. I didn't know what was going on. You certainly didn't seem to need my advice or support."

"That's not true," he snapped. "I've been in limbo, drifting, unable to focus on how to handle this. I was afraid to bother you just to tell you about my indecision."

"Good thinking," she said. "It does wear thin."

"Thanks," David said. "Does Jake know I'm in Philadelphia waiting to testify? What does he say?"

"Yes, he knows. I believe he's been in touch with the lawyer, Nick's lawyer, and with the prosecutor too. I'm tired of hearing about your indecision. Isn't it time that you grew up?"

"Thanks for your reaction," David said. "Terrific. I suppose Jake is helping both sides trip me up. Why the hell is he doing that? Has he given them any information? I suppose he'd like to see me tried for conspiracy to commit murder. How the hell did he get all the information anyway?"

"Am I supposed to answer all those questions? You're talking to the wrong person. I have no idea," she said. "I'm not asking questions, and I'm not giving answers. Anyway, he's leaving tomorrow for a while, I expect. His business in the city will be over for now anyway."

"Oh, right, I'll count on that. I presume you're sleeping together?"

"Look, David, you don't own me. Nobody owns me. Not him. Not you. I decide what I'm going to do and not do. So just leave me alone."

"Thanks for the moral support. Tomorrow I face a hostile situation in the courtroom." He slammed the phone down, surprising himself at the force of his rage and the sense of hopelessness that swept over him.

David had a sense of being a warrior again, this time in a battle for his soul. It hadn't hit home quite that way until now. His personal moment of truth was near. He called Bradley.

"David, I was just thinking of you. I'm thinking that you testify tomorrow, right?"

"Right you are. How did you know?"

"The timing was right. Besides, Richard called me last Friday morning, and he was thinking that would be the day. How are you?"

"Not great. I feel like I'm locked in mortal combat with Satan. The trouble is I can't figure out who Satan is—Nick, his lawyer, the District Attorney, or myself."

"What do you think will happen?

"I'm boxed in by the other defense witnesses. They've built a strong case for Nick's PTSD. Everything was beyond his control without a hint of any wrongdoing on his part. As they might say on the street, he's Captain America personified. The story is that he became a friend of the sheikh's family. No mention of his relationship with the sheikh's daughter, of course. Then he gets an order from me to wipe out the insurgents who killed the girl. Some inconvenient collateral damage happens. The insurgents must have killed Walter and Roxie. The truth is they went in to stop the slaughter and got wasted by Nick and his guys. It's a redo of the cover-up that took place in the brigade investigation. The worst part of it is that it's probably consistent with the investigation. It makes me sick to think of helping to get Nick off from two shootings that I believe were intentional. He took his weapon of choice with him when he went looking for his girlfriend."

"I had no idea it could be this bad," Bradley said. "You didn't tell me about all this. Did you know about all this before the trial? I don't even know myself what I'd do. The nomination is on track but not if this blows up into a big media splash that makes you look bad. I can't guarantee anything if that happens."

"I have to tell you," David said, "there are two reporters here who look like they are planning to break big stories. They've been nosing around about the investigation. If they get their hands on the report that Myron has it could be trouble, especially if they dig deeper and find out what really happened. If anyone started interviewing the people who were there, the Iraqis or even some of our troops, they'd find out about everything. Do you hear anything from Jake or the White House?"

"No, nothing. No change," Bradley said. "I know you've got a tough decision to make. There's no question the President has exposed herself by floating your name. Good luck tomorrow. You've got to protect the President, you know. That's best for you too, and for me. She's gone out on a limb for you. Don't let us down. I know you'll do the right thing."

94

David felt nothing but added pressure from the phone conversations. He decided to call Ruth, in hopes that she would reassure him, as Willard would have done. The pain of losing Willard was especially acute at this time of crisis. Since his college years, Willard had been his moral compass and a friend who cared deeply about him. He did not compromise his morality, but he recognized the need for clear thinking about how it applied in the ambiguous circumstances of human lives.

When Ruth answered, he filled her in on the trial. He went on to explain what he was inclined to do at trial. "I have this overwhelming feeling that it's time to stop hiding from my own moral failures. I've been running away from myself and everyone else since Ronnie's death. Right now, I want to tell the truth about war, what happens in war when people are pushed beyond their limits. Although he brought it on himself, Nick ended up being pushed beyond his limit. He went on a rampage of killing. I was pushed too, pushed beyond my capacity to take a moral stand that would have saved innocent lives. This is my failing but it's also the reality of war."

Ruth listened patiently. "I do wish Willard were here," she said, "so the three of us could talk. I miss his good judgment and his moral strength at a time like this."

"Willard and I talked many times about problems like this, not always of the same magnitude. But I value your judgment."

"I come at issues several ways, similar to Willard's approach but with the addition of a psychological one," Ruth said. "Willard looked at issues from both a Christian and a pragmatic approach. I see issues from those perspectives too but also from the perspective of my training in clinical psychology."

"So you also see the psychology behind people's reactions," David said. "That's important. What does that tell you about my drive to stop running away from the truth?"

"I understand how appealing, how simple and straightforward, it seems to get the whole truth as you see it out in the open. It would relieve you, as some people would say 'get it off your chest.' But I have to ask why? What's the pay-off for you? It's important to know why you want to do this when you're asking whether it's the right thing to do. There seems to be a serious downside to doing that as opposed to dealing with the ambiguities. I understand that you don't want to protect Nick again as you did before and you certainly don't want to lie under oath. But is the situation as simple and clear as you are now saying it is?"

"That's a lot to think about," David said. "I don't know where to begin."

"I have another question. What is the impact on everyone else who will be affected by your actions now? A great many people are affected, such as the President, all of your supporters, and everyone in the military involved with the original investigation. The consequences are huge. Is spilling out the truth in public fair to all these people? It may make you feel better, although there's a steep downside for you. You may lose a lot. But if you do it mainly to relieve yourself of a burden, is it worth it when you think about the cost to all the people who are likely to be damaged?"

"I wasn't thinking about all this," David said. "I certainly thought about the impact on the President, although it isn't as though she's nominated me. And I realize that I'd be undercutting my friends and supporters."

"I'm wondering also," Ruth added, "about the clarity of the facts, the truth, as you call it, that you want to tell. How clear is it that you did not authorize Nick to do the retaliation? Is it possible that you left that issue in an ambiguous state because of your own uncertainty? Might he have stepped into the breach and assumed he had at least tacit approval? Or that he could get away with doing it even without explicit authority? Is it clear that he acted contrary to authority or was it just without formal authority? Why didn't you order someone else to do it? Why did you leave it in limbo, almost inviting him to take it on? You were perfectly aware that he felt strongly about it. Are you sure that you're not trying to repay a grudge that you've held against Nick for taking advantage of your own ambivalence?"

"You're right," David said. "I left it as unfinished business, in a state of ambiguity, but in the Army, if you're acting without a specific order, you have no right whatsoever to act. Nick acted without authority. He had no right to step into a void and take it on himself regardless of how I left it."

"Aren't you relying on a technical argument when you say that? I thought we were talking about the need to tell the truth on a moral basis. You are sidestepping that in favor of an argument about official authority."

"I think you're being technical," David said, starting to feel irritated at Ruth's persistence in challenging him. "I have a right to take the position that Nick did not have authority because I did not issue an order to do it."

"It seems to me," Ruth said, unshaken by his resistance to her arguments, "that you don't have to reveal the whole story of Ramadi by focusing on the worst case scenario of wrongdoing in order to relieve your guilt and punish yourself. It seems to me that's what you're trying to do. What happened in Ramadi, as well as what happened with your brother, which for the record is a world apart, can be explained by the confluence of all the circumstances that existed at the time. You don't need to shoulder more blame—or hand out more blame—than is appropriate. It does you no good and it will do you serious harm. More importantly, it will cause serious harm to lots of other people, who have no control over what you've decided is your moral duty. The President, for instance, doesn't know anything about this grand revelation. You've deliberately kept the information from her. You have precluded her from taking protective action."

David found Ruth's reaction troubling. "She takes some risk by putting my name out there, doesn't she? That's her responsibility. She didn't wait to see the investigation report either." David was aware of his own petulance. "Aren't you undervaluing the importance of being truthful about what happens in war, that is, what are the real reasons why bad things happen? Isn't it a higher value to have the facts speak for themselves, rather than a contrived version designed to protect the soldiers, their superiors, the political leaders, the country itself? Are you being fair to me for wanting to present the truth? I don't think Willard would agree with your arguments."

"I hope I'm being fair," Ruth said. "I'm just posing questions to help you think about what to do, understanding the reasons. Will you be serving a higher value, which is now called a *sacred value*, one that overrides everything else, even reason? Or are you seeking absolution? I'm not sure who you expect to provide the absolution for what you did wrong. The jury? The judge? The journalists? The President? You have to realize that you are sacrificing other people to your interest in being faithful to your sacred value, telling the truth period or telling the truth about war. Just be clear about why you're doing this. The question to ask yourself is: 'Is serving my sacred value so important that I'm justified in bringing down other people in the process, in addition to myself?'

"But if you're doing it," Ruth said, "primarily to get this monkey off your back, to free yourself of the bondage of your own pain, the question is whether that goal warrants sacrificing other people who have trusted you. I think that's a harder question, but both are hard actually because you are pitting your self-interest against a cost that will be borne by other people."

"You ask hard questions," David said, angry at being challenged, but subdued at the same time. "I'm beginning to doubt myself and my motives."

"That's what you should be doing," Ruth said. "We all need to look closely at our own motives and put ourselves to the test. You know, I'm seeing a parallel with suicide in some ways. Maybe that's extreme, but in suicide people try to relieve themselves of unbearable pain, the existential pain of living. But it's also an incredibly selfish act. It brings unbearable pain on other people, especially family members and friends. What you want to do is a little like suicide. Your distress at bearing this burden makes you want to end your suffering, which in this case is telling the truth or what you believe is the truth. But you already know that you are not likely to feel relief. You'll feel pain from the consequences, and you will inflict pain on others. And, you'll be here to see the pain that it inflicts on other people, some innocent and some not so innocent. Are you prepared for that?"

"I don't know," David said. "But I don't agree with some of your premises. I see the need to give the President a chance to protect herself, but it's too late for that. I owe loyalty to my friends, but I never promised anyone I'd lie."

"But did you warn them of this great secret from your past before they gave you their loyalty?"

"No, I didn't. As far as my superiors in the Army are concerned, if they didn't seek the truth, why do they need protecting? I don't owe them anything if they compromised the truth to protect themselves."

"I don't see you actually despairing, and yet you're considering virtual suicide, permanent damage, to everything you're achieved and your future. It's a kind of self-extinction. You've already faced the past. Aren't you shifting the responsibility to others, challenging them to inflict the cost on you rather than doing it by yourself? Is this essentially what psychologists call *suicide by police?* You can withdraw your name now. You can resign from the Connecticut court. You can refuse to testify. You will suffer from these actions, but you will reduce the pain and the damage, to everyone else. Then you can tell your story, or not, as you choose and bear the consequences more or less alone. That will take a great deal of courage, and it will not be as dramatic."

"But," David responded, "If I do that, I won't be making a statement about the horror of war and the damage that war does to everyone."

"True," she said, "but I'm not convinced that this issue is primarily about war. Why now? You've had years to do that. You told me that once you were on the Connecticut court, you began soft-pedaling your anti-war position. Why did you do that? Why choose a career that necessitated downplaying those important sacred values. And why now in a dramatic moment, involving so many others, do you choose to take your stand for no gain that I can see except maybe stopping Nick in his tracks and releasing yourself from carrying around the baggage of guilt? Isn't it a little late?"

"Ruth. You're a challenge. I think you outmatch Willard. I don't have answers for all those questions. But I have a few responses. It's true that I compromised the truth during the investigation, but there was a lot at stake. What purpose would have been served by causing the killings to be blown up into a major story, a story that could have seriously damaged the standing of the military, the entire government? It would have overshadowed all the good things that we had accomplished."

"But why worry about that war effort when you believed it was a contrived and unjust war? Weren't you really just protecting yourself?"

"You have a point, but that's in the past," David said. "Now," he went on, "a big blowup is less likely and Nick is trying to use that incident and others as a way of avoiding justice for his murder and attempted murder. He's turning what he did on its head to avoid punishment for another crime. By not telling the truth, I will help him do that. I will be hurting other people now, but are you saying that lies should be told to avoid hurting people? Who says they have a right to expect protection from whatever the truth brings with it?"

"Those are good arguments," Ruth conceded, "but I still question your real motive in wanting to spill out the truth now. I think your primary motive is to atone and be redeemed, to unburden yourself of guilt, possibly as payback to Nick. Maybe you should continue to suffer from that guilt, whatever it is, and not expect to get it off your back. Certainly, if your role in Ronnie's death is at all involved, that is your burden to carry, no one else's, and you shouldn't be trying to seek redemption for that—not now, not this way. That is your burden to carry throughout your life until God forgives you. No one else can. Whatever you say in the trial will not relieve you of the burden of guilt for causing or contributing to Ronnie's death. Don't delude yourself on that score."

David suddenly felt exhausted, so exhausted that he was unable to continue the conversation. His body felt heavy. The weariness infected his very soul. "I appreciate your listening and telling me what you think. I hope I'll know what to do when I wake up in the morning. I have to get some sleep. I wish I could be confident that there is a God who will guide me. Please say a prayer for me, will you? That would mean a lot."

"I will, David. Trust God to give you courage."

95

Larry's testimony was routine. Myron was more cautious with him than the others, taking care not to push him to the point where he might refuse to follow the script. He had been closer to David than to Nick.

Still, Larry was intimidated by Myron and was unlikely to resist going along. Myron's skill at interrogation was evident once again. Larry did not flinch at the suggestion that Nick's main connection with the family was the sheikh himself or at the idea that Nick was authorized to conduct the raids. Larry was not skilled at grasping the implications of questions, where they were leading.

Myron led Larry through a number of RPG attacks and two incidents when suicide bombers attacked the COP, the Combat Outpost. David remembered that they were horrendous experiences with substantial casualties. When the questioning turned to what happened in the retaliatory raid on Jasmine's murderers, Larry followed the script precisely. It portrayed Nick as a hero, someone who suffered a painful loss when a member of the sheikh's family was brutally murdered, but who then stepped into the breach when no one else did. In carrying out that dangerous mission, he led his men into an enemy stronghold and held off a powerful defense, emerging victorious. Through it all, he sustained a terrible toll on his psyche that virtually disabled him for the duration of his deployment. Whether the jury bought that neatly packaged story was another question. If the judge picked up on the scripted testimony of all three veterans, he gave no hint of disapproval.

The stage appeared to be set for David by the time the judge declared the morning recess at 11:30 a.m. Judge Lacey excused the jury and asked Myron who his next witness was. David was surprised to hear that it would be the psychiatrist, Dr. Raphael Garza. Myron's strategy was not entirely clear. Evidently, he decided to complete the story narrated by the military witnesses with expert opinion evidence on PTSD. Apparently he was confident of his factual foundation for an opinion that Nick was suffering from PTSD. This strategy would make it even more difficult for David to come up with testimony that would undermine not only the five witnesses, but the expert as well. He wondered what other surprises Myron had in store.

"The defense calls Dr. Raphael Garza," Myron announced in his sonorous voice, dialed up to its usual excessive volume. With an eye on the jury, he followed with forty-five minutes of questioning, allowing the expert witness to recite his credentials, education, professional training, practice experience, specialties and, finally, his courtroom experience. No doubt about it, Garza was impressive. He had testified dozens of times on behalf of veterans going back to the Vietnam War. He had also provided evidence to appeal boards for veterans' disability claims. His specialty was mental illnesses experienced by veterans. He had collaborated on hundreds of articles on the subject.

At Myron's request, he launched next into the preliminaries of his professional relationship with Nick.

"Do you know Sergeant Serrano, Doctor?"

"Yes, certainly, he's seated with you at counsel table."

"When and where did you meet him?"

"I met him about a year ago when I was spending some of my time at the Philadelphia VA Hospital, one of the finest in the country. I was seeing patients one or two days a week, and the sergeant came into the mental health clinic. He became my patient."

"What were his complaints, his symptoms, at the time?"

"May I refer to my notes?"

"Yes, certainly Doctor, as you need to."

"He complained of headaches, sleeplessness, relationship difficulties caused by his memories of combat experiences in Iraq, and severe flashbacks to horrific scenes of combat and violence in Iraq. He also suffered from rather longstanding addiction problems, alcohol mainly. That went all the way back to his teenage years, as I recall."

"Did you take a complete history, including his deployments to Iraq?"

"Yes."

"I'll ask you more about that in a few minutes. And did you ultimately diagnose his problems?"

"Yes, I did. I diagnosed him with PTSD, and major depressive disorder. I also felt that he probably had suffered some form of TBI. There was also the addiction, of course."

"What's that doctor, TBI?"

"Traumatic Brain Injury. I couldn't be absolutely sure about that. It was some time after his combat deployments, but based on his history it seemed likely that he had TBI."

"Did he ultimately receive veterans benefits based on his PTSD?"

"It's a long process and it isn't complete yet. If often takes two years or more depending on circumstances. I believe it will be approved after going through the whole VB, that's the Veterans Benefits Administration."

"Objection," Peale stated. "Speculative and not within this witness's knowledge."

"Sustained," the judge ruled.

"Is the VB part of the VA, Doctor?"

"No, it's separate from VA services, related but separate."

"How long did you continue to treat him?"

"For about six months, then there was a gap until about a month before the present incident happened. Since then, I've seen him once a week. He's still under treatment."

"Did he continue to experience symptoms, particularly flashbacks?"

"Yes, he complained of having flashbacks and the other symptoms when he was under stress, especially. Whenever he felt threatened or confronted, he told me that he had flashbacks to combat scenes in Iraq and afterwards he really had very little memory of what had happened during them."

"Is that a common occurrence, the loss of memory of those situations?"

"Very common."

"When was the last time you saw him?"

"About a week ago."

"Did he tell you what happened in the incident for which he is on trial?"

"Yes. He told me he had been arrested for serious charges, shooting two people, one of whom died."

"Did he say anything else about that incident?"

"Yes, he said—"

"Objection." Peale was on his feet. "I want to know whether the defendant is going to take the witness stand. If not, I object to any backdoor testimony from the defendant. If he wants his version in evidence, he has to take the stand. It can't come in through another witness, without being subject to cross-examination."

"That's nonsense," Myron said disparagingly. "The doctor can testify what he was told for purpose of diagnosis and treatment. It's not offered for the truth but merely as the patient's history for purposes of the doctor's medical opinion. The doctor's testimony based on that history is for the jury to evaluate, but it's based on what he was told, subject to the jury finding of what actually happened. This is admissible as a basis for the doctor's hypothetical opinion."

"Overruled. The witness may testify."

"I take exception to that," Peale argued. "And I move that the Court instruct the jury right now that what the witness says about the shooting incident is not to be taken as the truth. It is merely what the defendant told the doctor."

"That's correct, ladies and gentlemen," the judge said. "This version is offered because it what we call the patient's history told to the doctor."

"Okay, Doctor, go ahead," Stewart said. "What did Sergeant Serrano say as additional history of his condition on that night?"

"He said he went to find his girlfriend when she didn't come home. It was late and in a dangerous area, so he took his pistol with him. When he didn't find her in the bar, he went to look in the parking lot. He saw her in a vehicle with a man and when he approached the car, a large man got out of the vehicle and came at him, drawing what looked like a pistol out of his pocket. There was a flash of light behind the man, two other men approaching him, a sudden loud blast, and he felt that he was in an open terrace of a house in Iraq, where he had been deployed, and was being attacked by armed insurgents who were going to kill him. He heard noise and saw more flashes and doesn't remember anything after that, until police came to arrest him in New York City."

"Thank you, Doctor. Now I'd like to ask you to tell the jury what some of his combat experiences were and how they contributed to his PTSD. Obviously, in order to diagnose PTSD, you must have determined that the requisite trauma had occurred."

"Objection." Peale was on his feet, arms waving. "Is counsel a witness now?"

Myron rolled his eyes in the direction of the jury, which seemed to respond to him like a well-trained chamber orchestra following the conductor's movements.

"Objection sustained. Confine yourself to asking questions, Counsel." Myron shrugged, glancing at the jury for approval.

"Did you, Doctor, determine that Sergeant Serrano had suffered any traumas while on combat deployment in Iraq?"

"Yes, I did. Numerous."

"Please tell us what you determined. Take all the time you need. This is very important."

"Objection to counsel editorializing to the jury. Is counsel a witness?"

"Sustained. Questions, Counsel, questions," the judge barked. "We don't want your value judgments."

"Yes, Your Honor," he said, as he grinned at the jury, out of sight by the judge.

"Go ahead, Doctor."

The witness recited, with frequent reference to his notes, which he had in a large manila file, at least three incidents of RPG attacks, two suicide bombing runs at the COP, and finally with excruciating detail, the discovery of Jasmine, described as the sheikh's eldest daughter, and the retaliatory strike in three phases at the Al Qaeda operatives who supposedly carried it out.

In answer to a question about Serrano's mission, the psychiatrist testified that "Sergeant Serrano was on a mission ordered by his command to root out the operatives who brutally murdered the sheikh's daughter. As I understand it, the sheikh was a crucial figure for the American forces because he—"

"Objection" rang out with Peale advancing toward the witness, shaking his fist. "I object, Your Honor, to the witness bolstering the defense claims completely beyond any possible medical evidence. The reason for the murder of the Iraqi girl or the importance to the armed forces, while interesting, is totally irrelevant to the PTSD claims."

"Your Honor," shouted Myron, "this is a vital part of my case. Everything that was riding on this mission, these missions, contributed to the traumatic injury, the moral injury, suffered by my client, all of which led to his flashbacks. This is highly relevant."

"Overruled," the judge said forcefully, cutting off Peale's further attempt to argue.

"Go on, Doctor. You heard the judge. You can tell the jury what the trauma consisted of, the whole trauma."

"I was saying that the sheikh's support was a vital motivating factor behind the retaliatory strikes. The sheikh was a leader in the Sons of Iraq movement that was helping to combat Al Qaeda during the surge. That was what I understood from the sergeant and why the raid was so vital. According to Sergeant Serrano, the third raid turned into a firefight with civilians within the large house, more than twenty of them, producing weapons and firing at the small unit with Sergeant Serrano. Death stalked everyone who entered including two American soldiers, a man and a woman, who were the only American casualties. But virtually all of the insurgents were killed in the process."

"This is outrageous, Judge. I move to strike the entire answer," Peale shouted.

"I don't remember reading about 'outrageous' as an objection in my evidence book, Counsel. Overruled," the judge said.

"What happened to Sergeant Serrano, according to the history you took?"

"He was devastated, first, by the horrible murder and mutilation of the sheikh's daughter and then by the severity of the attack against his unit when they entered the dwelling. He was distraught over the two American deaths at the hands of the insurgents and virtually incapacitated for the remainder of his time in Iraq."

"Did he receive treatment, mental health treatment, there?"

"My understanding is that he did not. He even had to go through an investigation, which I understand cleared him. Then he was sent back to base, Fort Benning, where he finished his service."

The jury was spellbound by the doctor's testimony, which consisted largely of a monologue punctuated by occasional questions. The doctor continued to detail Serrano's symptoms after he returned to base and after discharge up to the time when he sought help from the local VA. Myron capped off the testimony about history, symptoms, diagnosis, and prognosis with questions calling for the doctor's opinions about what had happened, with reasonable medical probability, the accepted standard for opinion questions, on the night when the killing and attempted killing had taken place. Myron preceded that by recounting the testimony of the girlfriend and the eyewitnesses as to the sequence of events in the parking lot. The doctor testified that Serrano had told him about flashbacks for years prior during times of extreme stress when circumstances brought to mind combat experiences.

"Doctor," Myron asked, "Assuming the facts in the history that you took from Sergeant Serrano, including his PTSD symptoms and the nature of the trauma that produced his PTSD, and assuming the events in the parking lot as narrated by the eye witnesses—all of them prosecution witnesses by the way—do you have an opinion with reasonable medical certainty as to the causative effect of the sergeant's PTSD in the two shootings that took place?"

"Yes, I do."

"What is that opinion, Doctor?"

"Objection," said Peale. "The hypothetical is incomplete. There's no mention in the hypothetical of his bringing his gun with him that night or his deliberate decision to go to the parking lot adjacent to the bar where his girlfriend worked."

"Those facts are not necessary," Myron argued, "although I have no problem with including them. My hypothetical is based on all the facts that are known, including that he went there intentionally to look for his girlfriend. What is crucial is the sergeant's reaction at the moment when he was approached by her boyfriend in a threatening manner. That's the point at which a flashback occurred that drove his conduct thereafter."

"I'll sustain the objection. Add those facts to your hypothetical," the judge ordered.

Myron repeated the hypothetical with those facts. "Now, Doctor, tell us your opinion."

"My opinion is that his PTSD could, with reasonable medical certainty, be a causative factor in the shooting of one person and the attempted killing of the other in that parking lot because his related history of flashbacks continued regularly up to and during the incident in question."

"Then, Doctor, based on the history that the sergeant gave you, including that he suffered regularly from flashbacks ever since his deployments in Iraq and that when he did experience them, he believed he was in Iraq being threatened by an enemy soldier, is it your opinion that a flashback probably caused the shootings in the present case?"

"Yes. Of course, there are some jury questions of fact here. The jury will hear what happened from various points of view. What I am saying is that the nature of PTSD as suffered by this man could with reasonable certainty cause a flashback leading to these shootings."

"One more question, Doctor. Adding to the hypothetical the additional history given to you by Sergeant Serrano when he saw you after the incident, that is, he remembers only having a large man charge at him, appearing to draw a weapon, and that he felt threatened and in Iraq in an open terrace, do you have an opinion as to whether he was having a flashback which was a causative factor in the shootings that took place?"

"Yes, I have an opinion."

"And what is that opinion, Doctor?"

"Objection," Peale, standing, said in a loud voice. "This is preposterous. I ask that the jury be excused."

"The jury is excused. Ladies and gentlemen, I have to hear arguments about this from the lawyers."

Once the jury was gone, the judge turned to Peale. "Go ahead, Counsel."

Peale stood, angry, his face crimson. "This turns the law on its head. Defense counsel got testimony in from the defendant, self-serving testimony, through the doctor's mouth. And now the doctor is asked to give his opinion about whether a flashback, never testified to by the defendant, caused him to commit murder and attempted murder. If defense counsel wants to get this evidence in before the jury as a basis for the expert opinion, for whatever it's worth, which is not much, he has to put his client on the witness stand first.

Let him be subjected to cross-examination. He can't get this in by the back door as a basis for this ridiculous opinion by the charlatan on the witness stand. The whole thing is sleight of hand, bootstrapping at its most egregious."

"I move to strike the prosecutor's inflammatory and insulting remarks," Myron argued. "They are out of order. They stand our system on its head. The doctor can give his opinion on a hypothetical based on the history he's told. It's simply an expert testifying based on assumed evidence. It's perfectly proper. And I don't have to put my client on the stand unless I want to and he wants to."

"Overruled. The doctor may answer, but in my jury charge I'm going to tell the jury this is a hypothetical and they have to find that the facts support the hypothetical before they can find a flashback was the cause. But he doesn't have to put his client on at this point. The defendant still has the right not to testify."

"This is outrageous, Judge. I will appeal this ruling," Peale said angrily.

"You're out of order, Mr. Peale. Remember where you are."

"I'm beginning to wonder where I am," Peale muttered as he walked back to his seat.

"What was that, Mr. Peale?" the judge asked sternly. "Did you say something?"

"Nothing, Your Honor," Peale said, without turning to face the judge.

"Watch yourself, Counsel," the judge said.

With the jury back in the courtroom, Myron resumed his examination.

"Doctor, now that we've straightened out the law for counsel, tell the jury your opinion as to whether the sergeant's actions that night, firing his weapon at the two people, was, with reasonable medical certainty, caused by a flashback to his time in Iraq, based on the history given to you."

"I believe it is medically probable that the shootings resulted from the sergeant having a flashback. I base this on the history given by the sergeant plus the testimony as to the events in the parking lot."

"Finally, Doctor, in view of your answers to the previous questions, I ask you whether, in the course of having a flashback, which you said was a causative factor in the shootings, was the sergeant capable of forming and acting with intent, either general to do the acts charged or specific, to do the acts pursuant to a deliberate plan?"

"No, he wasn't."

"Now I'll go one step further. Under those circumstances, given his mental disease, PTSD, was he capable of understanding the nature or quality of his actions at the moment he shot or, if he was, was he capable of knowing that it was wrong?"

"I would say that he was not capable of knowing the nature or quality of his actions and not capable of knowing that those actions were wrong."

"Thank you, Doctor. Your witness."

Cross-examination began about three o'clock and continued for two hours. Peale hammered and slashed at the doctor's neatly-packaged story, but, given the unusual latitude extended to the witness by the judge to answer as he chose, departing at will from the questions to offer explanations, he made minimal headway in undermining the testimony linking combat experiences with PTSD and PTSD with the homicide and attempted homicide on trial.

Peale drove home the point that the psychiatrist had no personal knowledge of the history that Nick related to him, including his claims about his combat experiences, in an effort to undermine the foundation for the PTSD diagnosis. Peale repeated multiple times that the doctor's opinions were all based on the stories that had been told to him and, therefore, they were only as true as the stories themselves.

Next, he attacked the flashback theory on the basis that Nick had deliberately tracked his girlfriend down armed with his Glock. He argued with the witness about the lack of a situation in Iraq similar enough to the parking lot scenario to justify the claim of a flashback. He attacked the use of PTSD as a mental disease capable of producing legal insanity. He then attempted to undermine the claim that a flashback could vitiate responsibility for the shooting of the girlfriend because she had made no threatening gestures even if her friend had. With regard to the male victim, he argued that there was no evidence that he had a weapon and that there was no evidence of any other men in the area who could have been mistakenly perceived as insurgents.

Peale finally attacked the timing of Nick's seeking of treatment as a pretext for a later claim of insanity that he planned to make after he murdered his girlfriend.

The witness refused to concede any part of his testimony connecting the Iraq combat experiences with the murder in the parking lot. Peale's confident demeanor, however, suggested that he believed he had convinced the jury of his position. The jury seemed to be as spell-bound by the cross-examination as they were by the direct testimony. As to whether the cross had seriously weakened the defense, David's careful study of the jurors' faces revealed no discernible sign of whether they were impressed by the outrageous claim, in his view, of a flashback. When the final question had been asked, the judge adjourned the trial for the day, admonishing the jury to avoid news reports and not to discuss the case with anyone.

How, David wondered, would these people off the streets of Philadelphia go about making a decision concerning a situation that they had never faced, much less imagined? How would they evaluate the merits in the context of the crude jousting of the two gladiators in the legal arena? For that matter, how would they react to him, Ivy Leaguer turned soldier turned judge, when he took the stand in the morning?

96

The defense calls Justice David Lawson," Myron announced, watching the jurors' reaction closely. Their curiosity was palpable. As David rose from his seat, he caught a glimpse of both reporters poised to record and put their spin on whatever he said. David was sure they would order daily transcripts to supplement their observations. This was the story they had been waiting for.

David strode to the stand trying to exude confidence and authority, though he felt just the opposite. "I do," he answered to the clerk who administered the oath. Yes, David thought, here comes the truth, the whole truth, and nothing but the truth, so help me God, *maybe*. He wouldn't look for trouble, but if it stalked him, truth would be his ultimate weapon in the battle.

The DA was leaning forward, on the edge of his chair. David's gaze took in Nick as well, whose face displayed wariness driven by his natural suspicion and hostility. He did not look concerned, just curious to see what David would do. He gave the impression of being confident in his ability to prevail in any confrontation. The first round of questions was routine, pertaining to David's background, service record, deployment, and present position. Myron stayed clear of any reference to media speculation about his future. The next round dealt with Nick's performance as a platoon sergeant. He worked at painting a portrait of the two as close allies, if not friends. David had no quarrel with supporting the fact that Nick was an able non-com officer and that his performance was satisfactory. He was wary of tripping on answers that would preclude condemning Nick if the questioning turned to the Ramadi massacre.

He answered "No" to the question whether he had ever disciplined or reprimanded Serrano. He knew that Myron was seeking to lay a trap for him in this legal war game. He had to stay at least one move ahead at all times. David omitted mentioning the fact that Nick, like nearly every other non-com officer and most male soldiers, regardless of how well they performed, had been warned about treating women soldiers prejudicially. He could mention that later.

The next set of questions was troublesome as Myron ventured into the incident or series of incidents leading to the three raids to punish AQI following the brutal murder of the sheikh's daughter. To this point, Myron had thrown only a few punches while staying out of range of any counterattack by Peale or resistance by David. After the first few questions on this line, however, he took more risk.

"Did there come a time when you became aware that Sergeant Serrano had developed a close friendship with an Iraqi family?"

"You'll have to be more specific about that, Counselor. I don't know what you're referring to." David was not going to be led like a lamb to slaughter by vague and suggestive questions, leading no doubt to an expansive and misleading argument to the jury about what he had said. He would press Myron to be specific and he would answer in the narrowest terms.

"Certainly, Justice Lawson," Myron said, mocking the term *Justice*. "Did you come to be aware that the sergeant was a close friend of a local sheikh and his large family?"

"Does the sheikh have a name?"

"Yes, I am referring to Sheikh Abdul Farad," Myron said obsequiously. "Do you understand the question now?"

"Sheikh Farad was very friendly with the commander of our company and, in fact, with the battalion commander, and with me, as well. He was very helpful as a leader of the Sons of Iraq. All of us were solicitous of his welfare."

"Are you working your way toward answering my question, Judge?"

"Yes. I don't know of any special relationship that Sergeant Serrano had with the sheikh personally."

"Ah, all right, Judge. But isn't it true that Sergeant Serrano was friendly and helpful to his entire family, including his children?"

"I can't speak about the whole family, but he certainly seemed to have a close relationship with one daughter."

"My turn now, Justice Lawson. Does that daughter have a name?"

"Yes, as I recall it was Jasmine."

"Was she an adult or a child?"

"I guess that depends on her age. I'm not sure, but I'd say she was around seventeen or eighteen. I don't know specifically. Do you?"

"I assume you are aware that your job is to answer, not ask, the questions? But then, perhaps you have not been in a trial court before. I'm asking the questions here," Myron said with a sharp edge. "Did something tragic happen to this young woman?"

"Yes, she was murdered, brutally murdered."

"Can you tell us when that happened and the circumstances?"

"I don't know the date. I can only estimate that it was late summer or early fall of 2008. You would know better than I do. I was alerted very early one morning that an Iraqi citizen had been brutally murdered out in the village near her family home. I learned that it was the daughter of Sheikh Farad, who came to the base frequently. I went immediately to the site and found a half dozen people surrounding the body of this girl. She was hanging upside down from a rope tied to the crossbar of a soccer goalpost in a park not far from the family's home. She was hanging by her feet. Her body, her abdomen, chest, right down to the pelvis, was gutted, just like an animal would be gutted, I suppose, although I've never seen that firsthand. There was still a large pool of blood that hadn't yet dissipated, seeped into the ground. It was horrible, one of the worst things I encountered during the war or anywhere else for that matter."

"Who else was there when you arrived?"

"I saw the sheikh, two of his sons, the defendant, the two witnesses who testified the day before yesterday, a few other squad members, and, oh yes, a local policeman and one or two of our MPs. We called for one of our medics to examine the body before it was cut down."

"Can you describe Sergeant Serrano's demeanor, his condition?"

"Yes. He was sitting on a bench with his head in his hands. He was sobbing and it looked as though he had vomited. He was saying, 'Oh my God, Oh my God, I'm so sorry. I didn't know that would happen. I didn't know.' I remember those words."

Myron looked startled. Obviously, he hadn't expected to hear those words attributed to his client. David wasn't sure where that precise recollection had come from, but it had come to him with clarity as he was describing the scene. He was surprised that he had remembered and said it out loud. Myron followed up without missing a beat.

"Besides expressing his condolences to the sheikh and his sons, did Sergeant Serrano say anything else?"

"You didn't ask me if he expressed condolences. I don't know whether he did or not. I can say that he was clearly shaken, shaken to the core."

"Were you able to speak with him?"

"I didn't try at that point. I told his men to bring him back to the base."

"Did anyone else speak besides your own troops?"

"Yes, I remember now that the sheikh spoke to the defendant."

"What did the sheikh say to comfort Sergeant Serrano?"

"He was wailing. Iraqis are much more expressive about grief than we Americans are. The sheikh was saying over and over, 'I told her. I warned her.' He seemed angry as well as grief-stricken. His sons were trying to restrain him and quiet him down. He shook his finger at the defendant and added, 'It's your fault.'"

"I move to strike the last remark," Myron said angrily to the judge.

"You asked him what he said and you got your answer," the judge retorted. "Denied."

Myron moved on without comment. "Would you say, just from your own observation, that the scene the sergeant encountered was traumatic for him?"

"Objection," Peale said without hesitation. "This witness is not a mental health expert or a mind reader."

"Sustained," the judge ruled.

"Would you describe the scene as unusual even for wartime?"

"Yes, I suppose I would. We see horrible things but this was not even ordinary horror."

"Would you say it was especially difficult for Sergeant Serrano because of his relationship with the sheikh and his family?"

"Objection," Peale started to say, then muttered, "oh never mind. Withdrawn."

"No."

"No?" Myron asked. "Did you say No? You are saying it was not difficult for him?"

"No. I didn't say that. It was especially difficult because of his special relationship with the victim, not with the sheikh and his family. That's what I would say."

"You're saying that he had a special relationship with the victim? Isn't that so because he was the sheikh's eldest daughter and a favorite of the sheikh, isn't that correct?"

"No. Because she was his girlfriend and because she was his contact person to fix other soldiers up for dates with Iraqi girls."

Myron was not able to conceal his surprise at this blow. He looked as though he had been struck. David, who had blurted out the answer out of irritation with the suggestive question rather than after careful thought about the consequences, could sense the jurors and the judge reacting. Myron recovered quickly and angrily at being blindsided.

"Judge. I move to strike the answer. That was a blatant attempt by this witness to injure my client's case by volunteering that false allegation. I move that you instruct the jury to disregard the answer and to instruct this witness, who should know better, to limit himself to answering the questions yes or no."

"Counsel," the judge interjected without breaking stride, "you asked for that one. You asked a leading question and an argumentative one at that. Denied," he said emphatically. Peale was struggling to control his glee, waiting his turn to capitalize on that exchange. The judge turned to David and said, "Justice Lawson, just answer the questions in the most direct way. Don't volunteer information."

"Moving on, did there come a time when you learned who did this horrendous criminal act?"

"Yes. We gathered information from all our sources, including civilians, and determined that a small group of insurgents, probably three, affiliated with AQI and living in Ramadi, were responsible. In fact, they did not keep it a secret. AQI claimed responsibility although not naming individuals."

"What did you decide to do in response?"

"After consulting with the battalion and company commanders, I decided that we would have a small mission to search and capture or kill the insurgents. We found out that they might have fled from Ramadi, possibly across the Syrian border, which wasn't all that far away. They had lots of relatives living in Ramadi and they might go back and forth."

Myron looked stymied at this, as though he hadn't planned on how to incorporate that information in his trial narrative. But he kept on with his planned line of questions.

"When was it that you designated Sergeant Serrano to conduct the retaliatory actions?"

"I never got that far because of the information we had that they might have gone over the border."

"But there was a time when you ordered Sergeant Serrano to lead a squad to retaliate, isn't that correct?"

"No, I didn't."

"Isn't it so, Justice Lawson," Myron said, raising his voice in intensity and pitch, "that the good sergeant volunteered to take on that difficult and dangerous assignment?"

"Yes, more or less. He asked me if he could take a squad and wipe them out."

"And you gave that the go-ahead, didn't you? You authorized him to do that, didn't you? I remind you that you are under oath. Your position does not entitle you to lie."

"Objection," Peale roared. "That remark is uncalled for. I'm tired of all the leading questions, Your Honor. Objection."

"Sustained. The statements by defense counsel are stricken, and the jury is instructed to disregard them," the judge snapped. "I warn both of you not to make statements to the jury. Your job is to ask questions and make proper objections, if necessary. The witness may answer the question."

"No, I did not. I told him he was too personally involved and that he should not do that. Besides, there was no one to retaliate against anyway, not at the moment, not until we knew they had returned."

David could see out of the corner of his eye that the prosecutor was virtually salivating at this line of questions and answers. His assistant was writing furiously. He knew he was onto something productive, a chink in the wall of the PTSD defense. David had gotten caught up in the verbal sparring with Myron and was determined not to be putty in his hands. But he had gotten carried away with the challenge and had entered into combat with Nick and his lawyer, and given the journalists a juicy story.

"Your honor," Myron said, turning to face the judge, his frustration palpable, "it's nearly time for our mid-day recess. May we break a few minutes early?"

The judge agreed and gave the jury the usual warning. "Don't talk about the case. Don't let anyone talk to you. Stay with the marshals the whole time."

David could see that Myron was furious and Nick looked ready to attack him physically. As he stepped down from the witness box, Nick approached him, putting his face into David's, and whispered in his ear. "You son of a bitch. What are you trying to do? Fuck with me? I'll bury you. I'll bury you, you son of a bitch. You'd better get your act—"

At that moment, a court officer stationed across the room noticed what was happening. Just as Richard was heading David's way to rescue him, the officer grabbed Nick by the arm and said, "Back off. Back off. Get out of the courtroom. Leave. I don't want to have to report this to the judge. But I will if I have to." Nick, glaring at the officer, pulled away and stalked out of the courtroom.

97

When court resumed, Myron had regained his composure and resumed questioning with customary bravado. The street fighter was not intimidated.

"Justice Lawson, did you report to your superior officer that Sergeant Serrano had volunteered to conduct a raid on the AQI insurgents who murdered the sheikh's daughter?"

"No, I did not. There was no reason to. It was not protocol."

"Just answer the question. So you were willing to let them remain at large and unpunished?"

"Certainly not. I intended to order a capable unit to neutralize the threat they posed."

"But you didn't do anything immediately, correct?"

"That's correct."

"There came a time when Sergeant Serrano conducted three separate strikes on the insurgents and the people who were harboring them. Correct?"

"I heard that he conducted three raids."

"And your story is that you authorized none of them?"

"Correct."

"Did you order him not to conduct the second raid after he had accomplished his mission in the first?"

"I did not, but I'm not sure I knew about it before the second."

"Are you suggesting that a raid took place and you knew nothing about it?"

"I learned about it at some point. I'm not sure when."

"Did you order him not to conduct a third raid after he had accomplished the second?"

"No. Again, I'm not sure when exactly I found out. It's been a long time. I remember investigating the two raids and finding out the number of casualties, about a half dozen in each, none of them insurgents. I asked for a meeting with my battalion commander and told him about the raids and that I had not authorized them. I told him the results. He brushed it off and said, 'What's the problem? They deserve it. Seems to me he's doing what he ought to do.'"

"So you implicitly authorized the third raid?"

"I wouldn't say that. I did nothing one way or the other in light of the commander's response."

"Did you report the response higher up the chain of command?"

"No. That would not have been appropriate."

"Then the third raid took place. What period of time are we talking about for the three raids, by the way?"

"About a week, I think, no more than a week."

"You implicitly allowed these raids because you were in command and you did nothing to stop them, and you did nothing to support them either, did you?"

"I regret not stopping them."

"Oh you regret that. A bit late isn't it, Your Honor."

"Is that a rhetorical question?"

"Rhetorical question? I don't ask rhetorical questions."

"All I can say is that I regret it."

"What happened on the third raid? Isn't it so that when Sergeant Serrano entered the house where the militants lived, along with twenty or thirty other people who were harboring them, he and his men were immediately engaged in a horrendous firefight, with a dozen or more so-called civilians joining in the battle?"

"That's a lie."

"Move to strike, Your Honor. Nonresponsive, and I request the jury be instructed to disregard that impudent and improper answer," Myron said heatedly.

"Granted," the judge said. "It's not your job to comment on the questions. Just answer them yes or no, as simply as you can. The lawyers ask the questions. You answer them. That's the way we do things here in the trial court. Do you understand that?"

"I do, Your Honor."

"Answer the question."

"I can't answer it. It includes a bundle of assumptions. Ask your question again."

"Isn't it so that the third raid encountered resistance from militants and civilians?"

"Not according to the information I received and my personal observations as well."

"Oh, so, you did finally get information about something. Explain that," Myron spat out.

"No insurgents were there. No shots were fired besides those fired by the defendant and his squad. There were no insurgents and no weapons, and all the civilians were killed as a result."

"How do you know this?"

"I conducted an investigation and reported that to my commander. There were no weapons found and no evidence of shots fired by any combatants."

"You went there and you did nothing to stop the raid, is that correct?"

"That is correct, and I regret that very much."

Myron turned toward the jury and gave a long, lingering look at them, nodding in the affirmative in their direction as if gaining their understanding.

"Ah, another regret, one of many apparently. But two of your men, that is, a male and a female, joined the raid. Correct?"

"Not correct. They rushed in to stop it, screaming, 'Stop firing! Stop firing!' It was obvious that there was no resistance and that old men, women, and children were being slaughtered by the defendant and his storm troops."

"Objection," Myron shouted. "Move that answer be stricken. It's an insult to my client and to the whole Army, and to the jury and this Court. The witness should be held in contempt. And I move for a mistrial."

"'The jury is excused," the judge said loudly. "Now! Marshal." The jury exited, glancing back over their shoulders at the participants in this ongoing verbal jousting.

"I've had enough of this," said the judge. "This has to stop. I'll hold you in contempt, Counsel, and you too, Mr. Lawson, even if you are a judge. That was uncalled for. I'll have no more of that."

"I apologize, Your Honor," David murmured, chagrined at his last answer and his own lack of control. But he was incensed at the outlandish questions that had been thrown at him and the lies he was being asked to support.

The judge allowed nearly a half hour for the recess, probably hoping it would cool things down. He was soon to be disappointed when Myron resumed questioning.

"Justice Lawson, did you report your observations about the raid, the one you just testified about, to your commanding officer?"

"Yes."

"Orally or in writing?"

"As I recall, it was orally reported."

"What precisely did you say? Did you use the language that you just used in front of the jury?"

"I don't recall exactly what I said, and it probably was not in those words."

"Take your time and tell the jury exactly what you said."

"It's too long ago. I have no written record of it, but I believe I reported who was there, how many people were killed, and whether the incident was now closed."

"Did you report that there was no firefight? That no one fought back?"

"I don't believe so but I might have."

"Do you have a memory problem, Judge? Never mind. Withdrawn. Isn't it so that you reported nothing of the kind and, when you testified in the investigation hearing, you said everything had gone well, and Sergeant Serrano did a fine job?"

"I don't recall saying that."

"Think again, Justice Lawson. You said everything had gone according to plan, isn't that right?"

"I may have."

"May have? Think hard, sir. You are under oath."

"I don't remember exactly what I said at the hearing. It's been a long time. I do recall not making a big issue about the defendant's culpability. That was not what the Army wanted at the time. To the Army, it was just another incident with civilian complaints about excessive force or excessive civilian casualties. The Army preferred to downplay this, and I didn't swim against the tide, so to speak. I went along. But I know what I saw. The fact that I may not have explained the detail back then doesn't change the truth."

"Are you saying, then, sir, that you are telling the truth now, right now, about what you saw and that you didn't tell the truth at the hearing held right after the incident?"

"I'm saying that this is the complete story. This is what happened. I'm not sure exactly what I said then."

"I ask you again, did you tell the truth, the whole truth, and nothing but the truth at the Army investigative hearing in 2008? Yes or no."

"This is a more complete version."

"Did you tell the whole truth then? Yes or no, I repeat, and Your Honor, will you please direct the witness to answer directly yes or no without covering up and without arguing with me?"

The judge responded by excusing the jury and warning David that the question called for an answer that could incriminate himself. "Do you wish to consult with your lawyer before answering? You may do so." David answered that he did not.

"Do you wish to invoke your privilege under the Fifth Amendment of the U.S. Constitution?"

"No, I do not, Your Honor. I'll answer this question and those that follow."

With the jury back in the courtroom, the questioning continued.

"I repeat the question. Did you tell the whole truth then?"

"I did not."

"Ah, so then you want the jury to believe you now, when you have admitted that you didn't tell the truth. You lied under oath at the hearing, is that right?" To emphasize his point, Myron pounded his fist on the witness box.

"I did not tell the entire version, all the details because—"

Myron interrupted with "That's enough. You've answered. No further questions." With that, he slammed his fist down again on the witness box, looked triumphantly at the jury and strode to his seat at counsel table.

98

Without pausing for an instant, the DA rose for his cross-examination, hurling the first question from counsel table and then proceeding deliberately toward the witness box.

"Justice Lawson, what was the prior hearing? Explain that to the jury."

"The Army, the commanding officer of the brigade actually, had an obligation to investigate what happened in Ramadi that led to the raid that took quite a few civilian casualties."

"How many, exactly?"

"What I recall is that it was between twenty and thirty, closer to thirty."

"Were there any young men in that number?"

"No. They were all women, children and old men."

"Do you mean there were no AQI combatants?"

"That's correct."

"What were the commander's choices once the details of the raid came to light?"

"He could turn the whole matter over to the CID. That's the Criminal Investigation Division. CID would decide whether to prosecute any of the participants. The alternative was the informal investigation that actually took place."

"A prosecution would amount to a court martial, right?"

"Exactly."

"But the commander decided not to go that route, right?"

"Correct. He kept it to the informal procedure; there could be discipline but not prosecution. No court martial."

"Do you know why he made this decision?"

"Objection. Hearsay," Myron said, leaping to his feet.

The judge quickly responded, "Overruled, he can answer this question, whether he knows or not."

"Yes. The Army didn't want to make a big deal of this because it could get overblown into a big scandal."

"Objection, move to strike," Myron burst out. "He's speculating again and volunteering whatever he wants to say, and it's hearsay."

"Overruled."

"You're saying, Judge, that you went along with this, as a good military officer, right?"

"Objection, leading," said Myron.

"Overruled. He can lead. This is cross-examination, counsel. You know that," the judge said smartly.

"I believe I did," David said.

"Did you lie?"

"Not directly. I gave the information that was asked for. I didn't volunteer information that was not asked for and which the Army was not interested in pursuing at that time. That's more or less the story."

"Did you tell everything you knew? I warn you that this is a serious question and that you don't have to answer. In fact, I ask for a recess, Your Honor."

The judge excused the jury. "Go ahead, Counsel," he said to the DA.

"Justice Lawson, I want to advise you that you have a right to remain silent and that anything you say can be used against you. If you admit lying under oath, you could be prosecuted for perjury and you could be subject, based on what you say plus your role in this matter, to a prosecution under the Military Extraterritorial Justice Act, MEJA for short. That would involve prosecution in civilian federal court for crimes committed while serving in the military. Do you understand that?"

"Yes," David replied without hesitation.

"Do you understand that I am bound to turn over the transcript of your testimony to a federal prosecutor if I believe that MEJA applies?"

"I don't know about your being bound to do that."

"In any event, you have the right to talk with a lawyer. Do you want to talk with your lawyer before proceeding? I know your lawyer is in the courtroom," Peale said.

"No, I don't. I'll answer your questions. We've discussed the Fifth Amendment option and I'm aware of MEJA prosecutions. I don't wish to exercise the privilege. I want the truth to be on the record."

"Okay, Your Honor. I'm ready for the jury."

The jury returned and was admonished by the judge that they should not speculate about what was being discussed during recesses. The DA resumed. "Do you remember the question?"

"I do. No, I didn't tell everything that I knew. I felt the pressure. I was a young officer. I didn't feel able to stand up against the whole brigade, frankly. I let it go. But I regret it."

"Never mind that. What did you hold back out of deference to the Army?"

"I didn't explain that the defendant was responsible for creating the whole situation by maintaining a relationship, a sexual relationship and a business relationship of sorts, with the Iraqi girl. I didn't explain that I did not order him to retaliate, to lead the strike. I'm not sure I specifically said that I told him not to do it. He did it anyway."

"Anything else?"

"I didn't explain that when I got there, I could see that there were no enemy combatants, only civilians, and that he and his squad killed them all, in the absence of any resistance."

"Did you hold back anything else?"

"I didn't explain that the sergeant seemed shaken and devastated by this whole incident, but when I asked him, he said, and excuse me for repeating his exact words, that 'he didn't give a shit about the fucking hajis. It was losing the girl and that he was afraid that the sheikh, her father, would retaliate. He was afraid of getting blown away,' he said."

Before David finished, Myron was on his feet, yelling, waving his arms. "Your Honor, this is outrageous. This is a pack of lies. The witness thinks this trial is about events that happened in wartime more than fifteen years ago. This witness should be held in contempt. The answer should be stricken. I move for a mistrial."

"Ladies and gentlemen, I'm going to ask you to step outside again. I have to take up this motion." The jury dutifully got up and followed the marshal out, shaking their heads.

"You're out of order, Mr. Stewart. I'm going to have a contempt hearing when this trial ends. I'll get a transcript and send it to another judge. And you, Justice Lawson, you had better be able to support that answer, or I'll order you to be charged as well. This trial is not about what happened in combat a long time ago. I'm not letting this trial get out of hand. I want to know whether those were the defendant's exact words," the judge asked David.

"Very close to those, Your Honor. I've never had occasion to say them out loud before, but I've never forgotten them. He did say he didn't give a shit about the 'effing hajis' and that his fear was the sheikh would have him killed. That sheikh, after all, headed up a section of the Sons of Iraq and he had plenty of his own combatants at his disposal."

"All right," the judge said firmly. "I'm not ordering a mistrial. That would be rewarding defense counsel for his own words that are the main disruption in this trial. Mr. Stewart, you opened up this Pandora's box in your direct examination. Now you're stuck with it."

"Bring the jury back, officer," the judge ordered.

The DA continued. "Let me get this right. Are you saying, Judge Lawson, that you did not order the defendant to do a retaliatory strike based on the murder of the woman but that, in fact, you ordered him not to?"

"I did not order him to conduct that mission. I told him I'd find someone else to do it."

"Did you leave the issue up in the air, uncertain?"

"I don't know what was in the defendant's head at the time. He was adamant and excited. But, no, I don't believe that's a fair statement."

"Did you suggest to the defendant that he wouldn't be punished if he went ahead with the raid?

"No I don't believe so."

"Did you ever say to him that the whole bunch of them, the militants and the people who were sheltering them, should be wiped off the face of the earth?"

"We all were incensed this had happened, and there was a lot of heated conversation as you could imagine, but no I don't recall saying that in so many words."

"Could the sergeant have left with the impression that he had authority from you to retaliate?"

"Could he have? I can't answer that. I don't know. But that would have been mistaken, and there was no provocation for the strike against a house full of civilians."

"Isn't it so that the defendant undertook this raid on his own without authority in order to carry out his personal vendetta?"

"Objection," Myron shouted, slamming his fist down. "Calls for a conclusion."

"Overruled," the judge replied.

"Correct. I believe that is correct."

"No further cross," Peale announced, glancing smugly at the jury. Myron stood, the anger and frustration darkening his thick features, as he charged toward the witness box.

"You never ordered anyone else to conduct the assault on the militants, did you?"

"That's correct. I didn't get a chance because the defendant did it before I could."

"Oh come now, Justice Lawson, how long after your conversation with the sergeant did the raid occur?"

"I don't recall exactly, a couple of days maybe."

"Two days wasn't enough time?"

"Correct. There was a lot going on."

"Isn't it so that the sergeant and his squad were met with powerful resistance when they carried out your orders, in light of your failure to take action yourself?"

"I've already told you what my orders were, and were not. There was no resistance and no weapons found in the house. The only weapons were what the defendant's squad was carrying. Those were innocent people who were killed."

"Isn't it so that my client was upset and shaken because of the death and that death represented an attack on a family member of the sheikh, who was a supporter of the American mission in Iraq?"

"I can't tell you what was in his mind, but it was clear that the defendant had blood lust to revenge what he saw was an attack on himself."

"I move to strike that answer. Argumentative answer. Not asked. I move for a mistrial," Myron said.

"I'll strike the answer. Mistrial denied. Ignore that answer, ladies and gentlemen of the jury."

"Do you claim that you have told the truth, the whole truth, and nothing but the truth today?"

"Yes."

"And did you tell the truth, the whole truth, and nothing but the truth at the investigation hearing? Remember the cautions to you. They apply here."

"I have them in mind and will answer. Basically, yes."

"Basically? Basically means the whole truth to you?"

"Objection," Peale said. "Argumentative."

"Never mind," Myron spat out. "No further questions. Nothing further with this witness," he said, spitting out the words with disgust, glaring in the direction of the jury.

"Mr. Peale," the judge said, "any further questions?"

"No questions," the DA said, walking confidently back to counsel table.

"Ladies and gentlemen," the judge said solicitously to the jury. "It's been a long and difficult day. You're excused until tomorrow morning at ten o'clock. The usual warnings apply."

As David headed quickly for Richard and Barbara, the two reporters converged on him, launching a barrage of questions. He walked on, ignoring their attempt to corner him, "I said everything I had to say on the witness stand. Nothing more." As they followed him down the aisle, Richard stepped in their path.

"Please," he said, "let the Justice alone. This is a difficult time. He's spoken fully on the witness stand. You have plenty to report I'm sure. He's not going to make any additional comments."

They backed off. David was already apprehensive about how these stories would appear in the online and print editions. He could just imagine how his words would be taken out of context and sensationalized. This was going to be a big blowout. As the three of them left the courtroom, David was compiling a mental list of everyone he should warn.

PART FOUR

"Ah, love, let us be true
To one another! for the world, which seems
To lie before us like a land of dreams
So various, so beautiful, so new
Hath really neither joy, nor love, nor light
Nor certitude, nor peace, nor help for pain;
And we are here as on a darkling plain
Swept with confused alarms of struggle and flight,
Where ignorant armies clash by night."

—Matthew Arnold, "Dover Beach," *New Poems,* 1867

99

David, Richard and Barbara headed back to the hotel on foot, glad for the chance to walk briskly in the fresh air. They stopped at a coffee shop to do a damage assessment of the day in court.

"You went way out on a limb," Richard said with a disapproving look at David. "You took me by surprise. I hope you're ready for the headlines. There'll be a lot of fallout, I'm afraid. Once the press puts its spin on this, it will have the appearance of a scandal in the making, an atrocity sealed with an official cover-up. This won't go away soon."

"I realize that," David said. "I spent time soul-searching during the past few days. I knew that telling the truth was my only hope. But I thought I'd have some maneuvering room to avoid direct confrontation with Myron Stewart's story. I thought he'd dance around the facts, you know, try to avoid a direct clash. But he didn't. When we started, I didn't know that I'd react the way I did to his questions. They were confrontational, all black and white questions. There was no room for tactical moves around the hot issues. I just let the answers fly. It was time to get this off my back. I couldn't whitewash what that son of a bitch did during the war. Worse yet, I couldn't stomach letting him get away with another murder by riding on the backs of the innocent people he killed in Ramadi. I don't know whether Myron can recover and rebuild a credible defense. I suppose he'll stop at nothing to discredit me. What do you think? Do you think Serrano will take the stand?"

"How can he?" Barbara interjected. "The prosecutor will crucify him based on your testimony. I think he may recall a couple of witnesses to refute your version. Did you notice Myron didn't pull out the report? He doesn't want to have to explain how he got it. Anyway, you basically admitted what was in it so he didn't have to."

"That's right," Richard added. "No matter how skillful Myron can be, I think Serrano would have a serious problem rebutting what you said without suffering fatal injury at Peale's hands. I'd guess that Serrano is a stubborn guy though, and he might insist on testifying. He can't take the stand without opening up everything that supports his defense. He might like to come up with a story explaining away the murder he's on trial for but, if he does, he's fair game for Peale on the whole thing, start to finish."

"I'll take a train back tonight unless you think there's some reason to stay," David said. "I've been away from work for so long now I can hardly remember."

"It's a good idea for you to leave, actually. If you stay here, you might get recalled by one of the lawyers. You'll call Bradley, right?" Richard said. "What about Lehman? You'd better let the White House know about the tsunami that'll be rolling in tonight and tomorrow. I have a feeling it's likely to swamp the White House."

"I do regret the fallout," David said. "Yes, right away, Bradley first. I appreciate all you've done for me, both of you. I realize that I messed things up a long time ago. I've put the President in a tough spot now. I'm dead meat, I suppose. I'm going to check in at work and then do what I can to avoid the press until the trial is over. I'll probably go to Nantucket after I check in at work."

"Good idea," Richard said. "We'll give you daily reports. Barbara will stay on until the end of the trial. My guess is the evidence will end tomorrow. Then there'll be a full day of closing arguments plus the jury charge. Who knows how long the jury will deliberate. They have a lot to think about. I hope they're up to it. You never know with juries."

After checking out, David took a cab to the station. Bradley called before David had a chance to call him.

"Did you get my texts?" Bradley asked. "The President sent your name to the Senate, you know. I must have texted four times and left voicemail. How's the trial going?"

"Oh my God," David said, feeling a sinking sensation in his stomach. "Are you saying she nominated me? I haven't seen anything in the past day and a half—texts, emails, or messages. I've been in deep water over my head in the trial. I was on the stand for the whole day today. The jury will probably get the case late tomorrow. I was just about to call you to warn that you should expect some sensational stories in the media tonight and tomorrow, based on my testimony."

"Was it bad?" Bradley asked. "What on earth did you say?"

"I told the truth about Serrano, about myself, and about the Army investigation too. I pretty well shot to pieces the PTSD defense . . . but I took some, shall we say, collateral damage—serious collateral damage. I told the truth and I admitted that I hadn't told the whole truth at the investigation hearing. There was more, too."

"You're kidding," Bradley said. "You admitted perjury on the record? After we got you the nomination? You threw it away? I can't believe it," he said with incredulity giving way to anger. "How could you do that? Why didn't you talk to me first? You've double-crossed me. You've double-crossed the President. This will be devastating for her at a very sensitive time. She went out on a limb for you. We all did."

"I'm sorry. I did a lot of soul-searching. I reached a point where I had to get this off my back. I've carried it for a long time. I know it impacts other people. Frankly, I didn't know for sure what I'd do until I was sitting in the witness box. I answered the way I had to."

"You act like it's nothing," Bradley said. "Let me tell you this has serious repercussions for a lot of people. You should have let me know before you did that. Why didn't you call me? Did you think of anyone else besides yourself? You may see it as therapeutic, but the way I see it, it was simply selfish and stupid. It happens to be bad timing for me too. I've had a good relationship with the President. I'm sure that will be in the past tense now, thanks to you. My relationship with the White House is crucial for my clients and my firm. What do you think this does for my credibility? I live on my credibility. Do you realize that? It's nice that you feel better with the load off your back, but what did you accomplish? Sure, you may have prevented your sergeant from relying on a trauma plea when he didn't deserve to do that, but what about loyalty to him too? What about loyalty to me? To the President? To anybody else, for that matter? It's just about you, right? I predict you'll go from purging to perjury. Count on it."

"Bradley, listen. I'm truly sorry. I called to ask whether I should call Lehman, or would you prefer to? I don't want to mess things up any more."

"You do it. I'm not going to. There's nothing left to mess up. It's up to you to break the news to him and the President. They're not going to be happy. They went out on a limb for you. They trusted you. I trusted your word and your judgment. Look, I have to go now."

Bradley hung up abruptly. David could hardly blame Bradley for being upset. But his mind was filled with questions. Why did the President submit the nomination without talking to him, especially with the unresolved controversy about the investigation report? Did she rely solely on Lehman to do that? Did Lehman talk only to Bradley? Why didn't Bradley hold off? Nominations were important enough to wait for assurance all the way around.

David dialed the private cell number that Lehman had given him.

"Andrew. This is David Lawson. I have—"

Lehman interrupted him. "You're all over the news. Every news service is carrying the story of the massacre and the cover-up. Your friggin' face is everywhere. I understand you created a firestorm at the trial. I let the President know as soon as I heard. We can't believe that you testified about an atrocity and a military cover-up without warning us. Frankly, I'm totally shocked. You blindsided us. The President is very upset about this, as you might imagine."

"I wanted to tell you right away. . . ."

"Right away? How about before? Your right away is, what, about twelve hours after the fact. Didn't you know the President sent the nomination to the Senate?"

"No. I knew nothing about that. Bradley just told me he tried to reach me, but we didn't talk until just a few minutes ago. We were out of touch for a couple of days. I was on the witness stand all day today. That was when my testimony . . . uh . . . happened."

"Happened, like some kind of spontaneous combustion? Like you had nothing to do with it? Did somebody force you to open up a wound that had healed over a long time ago? Were you forced to testify under duress? Some sort of Star Chamber procedure?"

"No, that's not what I mean. Of course not. But I had to tell the truth."

"Right. How many tries did it take you to tell the truth? One? Two? Three? From what I hear, you've teed yourself up for a perjury charge and a MEJA prosecution too. It's your word, which isn't worth much, against Serrano and his crew. Frankly, I'm pissed and the President is too. I don't know what she intends to do. My advice to the President was to withdraw your name immediately, denounce you, and protect herself. She does not need to be in the middle of this mess. You sandbagged both Bradley and me too. Thanks to you, she isn't listening to me anymore. Bradley either."

"I'm sorry. I understand," David said. "Whatever she does, I understand that she has to protect herself."

"The press is going to have a field day. This is going to open up earlier phases of the war again, all the raw wounds. There'll be an investigation. They'll be looking to crucify you."

100

David sat in the Amtrak quiet car on the way back, stepping out only to make two phone calls, one to Dana and one to Ruth, the latter to see whether she could find a place for him to stay on Nantucket. He felt the need to find a refuge until the trial was over and the media chatter had died down. The press would be after him. They would have difficulty finding him on Nantucket.

"Dana. This is David."

"I've been hearing about you. You went for the brass ring, right? Let me guess. You're not finding any sympathetic ears for your heroic unburdening yourself of your sins and crimes and you're wondering when you'll be prosecuted?"

"That's about right."

"I forgot to add that you think I'll be sympathetic? Is that right? Wrong. Don't expect any sympathy from me," she said bitterly. "I warned you, didn't I? What a selfish thing to do. You're bringing down a half dozen people. You blindsided them. This was a stupid thing to do. You should have lived with your own shortcomings and failures."

"I'm not surprised you feel that way. I just wanted to touch base, to give you the courtesy of an explanation."

"Thanks. You did. Anything else on your mind?"

"No. See you later," David said, ending the conversation abruptly before she could. He had burned all his bridges. He couldn't blame them. But so far the condemnation was harsher than he expected. No point in calling Jake. He'd better go to the courthouse tomorrow. He'd stop in Hartford on the way to the Nantucket ferry, if that worked out for Ruth. He'd come and go quietly at the courthouse. Burkhardt might file a judicial complaint against him based on his admission of perjury. He'd avoid him if he could. There'd be a blowup if they met face to face. He'd lose that one because Burkhardt would stop at nothing to humiliate him.

He left voicemail for Ruth. "Ruth. It's David. I'd like to come to Nantucket for a few days until the trial ends and the publicity dies down. The press will be after me and I need to find a safe haven. Is there a chance of using Willard's place? If not, do you think you could find room for me in one of the inns? Thanks. Just leave a message please if you don't get me. I'm on my way home now from Philadelphia. I'll be in Connecticut tonight and tomorrow. I'll tell you about it. Thanks." He felt like a man without a home, actually without a country.

He settled back in the quiet car, glad to have a few hours to think and plan, and rest. He didn't stay awake long. He was exhausted, waking only when the conductor announced Penn Station. He got off and boarded Metro North for the final leg of the trip. In New Haven, he took a cab home, found the house dark and fell asleep in his office. He was not looking forward to seeing Lucille in the morning. Perhaps he'd be off before she appeared. He missed the boys, now that he thought of them, which he had to admit wasn't very often.

As it turned out, he left the house before anyone was up. He checked his phone on the way to Hartford and discovered that Ruth had left voicemail. "Just come on out here. We'll find a place. No problem. You'll be safe here." That was good news. There was more good news at the court. Burkhardt was away for the day at a conference. David talked with his law clerks and saw Jeffrey Webster, offering him a brief explanation. Jeff was sympathetic about his predicament, if mystified as to why David had gone so far as to box himself in. Then it was on to the ferry and away from everything that reminded him of the consequences that were pursuing him.

He called Ruth from the ferry. She would be at the church. He should come directly. She had a series of meetings that would last all afternoon. He could settle in her office and she'd join him when she could. After arriving, he checked email, read, and dozed off.

Richard called in mid-afternoon to tell him that Nick had taken the stand after all. According to what Myron's associate Lenny told Barbara, Myron decided that he had to have Nick's testimony to support the history that the psychiatrist relied on. He was afraid the judge would charge PTSD out, holding that the word of the three veterans was not enough. Further, if Nick didn't take the stand to validate their testimony, the jury could reject everything the psychiatrist said Nick had told him. He also had to do damage control because of the charge that Nick conducted the raid on his own.

"Nick testified point blank," Richard said, "that you ordered him to do the retaliatory raids and said, 'Kill anyone who gets in your way. Kill them all.' He testified that you said they all deserve to die including whoever is sheltering the militants. He testified that you said in so many words, 'You know what U.S. policy is about harboring terrorists. If you harbor them, you're our enemy. You're a terrorist too.' He said he had never undertaken a mission unless he was ordered to do it. He had never disobeyed an order and never acted without one. That is enough to expose you to a MEJA prosecution if some hotshot federal prosecutor wants to make headlines. There's enough for a conspiracy to commit murder charge. Voilà. MEJA steps up to the plate. Just calling a grand jury would be enough for a U.S. Attorney to get publicity and to expose you to a huge risk.

"Peale slammed Serrano on cross about the shootings," Richard said, "mostly about bringing a gun with him and then shooting his girlfriend after killing the guy. But he held his own pretty well. He's a bull, difficult to push around. I'm not sure who the jury believes at this point or whether they'll focus on Philadelphia or Ramadi, or both. Then Myron recalled a few earlier witnesses including the psychiatrist to try and repair the damage you did to the PTSD defense. Nick's buddies said basically that they remembered hostile fire in the house. The psychiatrist testified that, even if what you testified to was accurate, his opinion was the same. Nick suffered from PTSD and his flashback was legitimate. The traumas of the war and the trauma of going on a strike against AQI was the cause. His case was severe enough to produce lasting flashbacks at stressful times of life."

Richard recounted the lawyers' closing arguments, with each attempting to eviscerate the other's case. "They were explosive," Richard said. "As expected, Myron attacked you for your duplicity, for failing to tell the truth. He argued that you lied under oath at one time or another—or both—and your testimony couldn't be trusted. The jury should disregard, totally disregard, your testimony as worthless.

"There's more," Richard said. "Stewart argued that Nick had a devastating flashback in the parking lot when he was confronted by the large menacing figure approaching him from the car—the car in which the person was probably having sex with Nick's treacherous girlfriend. Nick perceived the figure reaching for a weapon, and in his own mind he was back in Iraq, facing death at the hands of a ruthless enemy. He had to act quickly and decisively. It didn't matter whether the approaching figure was actually armed or not. What counted was what Nick saw and believed. His PTSD was a product of combat, fighting to make our country strong, doing the dirty work for the college boys who served as, technically, their superior officers, and whose loyalty was suspect. That's you, I guess. Just telling you what Serrano argued," Richard assured. "He came on strong."

The major media outlets up and down the East Coast were carrying the trial story now in vivid detail and with various spins. David was the featured player in the drama. It was not a pretty picture. He looked bad and he knew it. Richard reported that the judge would instruct the jury in the morning and they would begin deliberations. Since it would be a Friday morning when the jury got the case, the lawyers were betting on a late Friday verdict so the jury could go home for the weekend with this bizarre trial behind them, this trial with its backdrop of war and politics. Not only was a defendant on trial with his innocence at stake, a potential Supreme Court nominee was on trial for his deception and lies. The military was on trial for a cover-up, and the war itself was on trial—the war that would never end.

101

David, still asleep on the sofa in the office, awoke when Ruth entered the room. She motioned that he should take his time coming around and pulled a chair over closer to him.

"You must be exhausted," she said. "I can't imagine what you've been through these past few weeks. I'm dying to hear about the trial when you feel like talking about it. But there's no rush on that. It's over, right?"

"Everything but the court's instruction and the jury's decision," David said quietly. "I don't know what will happen. I took a beating in the final arguments, not to mention on the witness stand and in the news reports. It looks as though I'm the one on trial, but I'm responsible for that. I put myself in that position. Maybe they'll find me guilty," he said managing a sardonic smile. "Actually, my lawyer kept warning me that I might be put on trial for perjury or for a criminal prosecution under a statute called MEJA. I was so obsessed with getting the truth out, I didn't take it seriously."

"I'd like to hear about that. But first, are you hungry? Shall we go out for a bite?" she asked. "Or we could get take-out if you're exhausted. By the way, Willard's apartment is still available for you, but the rectory has plenty of rooms, even a private suite. You're welcome to stay here if you don't feel like being alone."

"I would worry about compromising your reputation, Pastor," he said, managing a smile. A little humor relieved the stress. Humor had been absent from his life for ages, it seemed. "I'd feel more comfortable at Willard's, though I appreciate your offer. I feel as though I'm in my safe place away from the chaos, my refuge. Willard's apartment will do nicely. You, at least, still have a reputation."

David felt refreshed by the cool evening breeze, and inspired by the muted sunset reflected in the thick clouds that blanketed the island. The small seafood restaurant was not crowded so conversation was comfortable and private.

"Do you feel like talking now? I'm ready if you are," she said gently, leaning closer. "Do you feel a sense of relief that you told the story that was burning inside you? I'm wondering whether you feel that you atoned for whatever wrongs you feel you committed. Have you gotten any reaction from your friends and colleagues, and your political allies?"

"Where to begin?" David said. "As for the reaction, it's been overwhelming. Overwhelmingly bad, that is. Everyone is disappointed in me and furious too.

My main political ally, my point man on the nomination, Bradley Thompson, feels betrayed. We've been friends since college, but I doubt that our friendship will survive this. I haven't talked to the other friends who supported me, Tim O'Leary, for one. He didn't return my phone call so I assume he feels the same way as Bradley.

"Bradley got feedback from the White House that the President feels betrayed. She did not bargain for this. She committed herself to me publicly, and I pulled the rug out without warning. You may not know yet that she actually submitted my nomination to the Senate. Bradley learned of her intention to submit it from Lehman and gave the go-ahead even though he couldn't reach me. I can't figure that out. You always make sure a nominee is ready and available before taking action. But I don't blame Bradley for that. He was doing his best for me. I don't know why Lehman would give the okay either, unless Bradley didn't fill him in, which is inconceivable to me. The President wants to talk to me. I have to go there on Monday morning. I don't know what she'll say, but my guess is that she will tell me she's pulling the nomination or that she wants me to withdraw."

"You've been expecting that all along, I think," Ruth said.

"Yes. As for Dana, you'll remember we were developing a relationship. She condemned me outright. That relationship is over for good. She made clear beforehand that I should be diplomatic and non-confrontational on the witness stand. Jake, her boyfriend or former boyfriend—not sure which—and my college roommate, is furious because he thinks I betrayed him. He's right. Beyond that, I'm sure he thinks I should have backed up Nick and the military, you know, the whole loyalty and honor thing. What I did would be dishonorable in his eyes."

"That is overwhelming. Is there more?" Ruth asked. "What about the prosecutions that you said could happen?"

"Richard, my lawyer, doesn't approve of what I did, for my own sake, but he's not upset. After all, he's just a lawyer. It's just a legal matter. I don't mean that quite the way it sounds. The lawyer has to accept the person and do the best job possible. Otherwise, it could prevent him from representing the client properly. I don't think Richard was surprised. I did give some advance signals, after all. Richard said Nick's lawyer is angry and bent on revenge because I sandbagged his client. The DA apparently is likely to notify a federal prosecutor because it may help his career. Both of them probably believe that I messed up the stories they wanted to present. Lawyers, judges too, want nice neat stories that fit this or that stereotype. They look for the story that leads to the result they want," David said. "If somebody messes up the story, they don't know what to do. I ruined their plans. We won't know the outcome until the jury comes back with a verdict. If the DA turns the file over to a federal prosecutor, the claim will be that I actually authorized the killing of the civilians and then covered all that up by lying at the investigation hearing. Everybody wants my head."

"That's amazing," Ruth said, shaking her head. "I can't believe they're all blaming you. At least you have your job on the state court."

"That's uncertain too. I heard from Jeff, my friend on the court, that the Chief Justice, who considers himself my mortal enemy, is threatening to get the legislature to impeach me. He told Jeff that he's suspending me from sitting because I lied under oath on one occasion or another. Of course, the controversy adds fuel to the fire for Lucille's divorce action. I expect she'll capitalize on that to crucify me.

"There's something I want to add," David said. "I want you to know that I did a lot of soul-searching about all you said regarding my motivation for telling the truth at the trial. I realized that part of me sought release from the burdens that I've carried for so long. That alone would not justify causing damage to all the people who would suffer damage. But I also felt that perpetuating the cover-up of the Ramadi affair was intolerable on moral grounds. I think Willard would have approved. And lying in my own self-interest and contributing to a false defense to help Serrano escape a conviction was also indefensible. My consolation, if you can call it that, is that I will suffer more personal loss than anyone else. I deserve that."

"I understand," Ruth said. "It's a closed matter, as far as I'm concerned. I don't doubt your integrity."

Early on Friday evening, David got a call from Richard. "Wait 'til you hear this. I just got a call from Barbara. The jury sent the judge a note about four o'clock saying that it had reached a verdict. It took a while to get everyone assembled in the courtroom. They found Serrano guilty of manslaughter first degree with a firearm, as to Wickes, and attempted murder second with a firearm as to Dee. How do you figure that out? They obviously rejected the PTSD defense as to both shootings, although of course it could have been a compromise to reach a unanimous verdict. The result would indicate that they believed your testimony and didn't credit his testimony about a flashback. But they gave him a break, maybe because of the love triangle aspect and because he's a veteran. He did not get a complete pass, though. He faces a hefty sentence but, regardless, five years can't be suspended or reduced so he'll serve that as a minimum."

"Did the judge accept the verdict? What about Myron Stewart? Did he raise any legal objections to the verdicts because of the factual differences in the two crimes? Did he claim they were legally inconsistent?"

"Both lawyers asked for a recess right away," Richard said, "before the judge acted on the verdict. The judge sent the jury out. Peale asked the judge to accept the verdict but Myron objected on quite a few grounds. He argued that the court should reject the entire verdict and send the jury back because it was legally inconsistent. He argued that his client couldn't have known that he'd find his girlfriend and certainly couldn't have known she'd be accompanied by anyone. He argued that the jury couldn't rationally find manslaughter on one and attempted murder on the other because his client was having a flashback the whole time. He argued that PTSD and self-defense should apply to both. That was his theory at trial. The flashback didn't end halfway through the episode. Of course, he said there would be an appeal."

"What did the judge do?"

"He accepted the verdict. He said it was not legally inconsistent. The jury had the right to believe whichever witnesses they chose to believe and they could logically find a different mental state for each victim. There were two different acts in sequence and the facts were different for each one, but it was within the jury's province to accept or discredit testimony. He said he would not ask the jury to reconsider the facts or the verdicts. In any event, he wouldn't consider directing the jury to deliberate further. There was no way he would prolong this trial. Peale seemed fairly satisfied, although he thought both should have been murder. Myron was angry. I think you may have an enemy there. I think you can count on Peale to go forward with MEJA as we suspected."

"I can't figure out whether the jury believed me or not," David said.

"I interpret the verdict to mean that they believed your testimony," Richard said. "They gave him no break on the crimes. There'll be post-trial motions, and an appeal."

"I guess this is just the beginning, isn't it?" David said.

"I'm afraid so. How are you feeling?" Richard asked. "What's happening on the political front?"

"Everybody feels betrayed. Everybody condemns me. I'm persona non grata. But I have to see the President on Monday. I believe she'll pull the nomination, but she may want me to withdraw my name. If she leaves the choice to me, which I doubt, I could persist and bring my story to the Judiciary Committee. That's not likely. I don't think the result of the trial will have any impact on the President. If she perceives that my telling the truth was the right thing to do, she'll still dump me. After all, I admitted that I perjured myself at the hearing and raised questions about my credibility at trial.

"Then there's MEJA. What matters for her is that my testimony will discredit the Army command and incite members of Congress to demand an investigation. That phase of the war is now out in the open again—fair game. The controversy will heat up again. A new massacre is on the table, plus a cover-up. Her actions to escalate the U.S. presence once again in Iraq and Syria will put her on the spot again. She can't be happy about a sideshow that threatens to derail the rest of her agenda, even her domestic agenda."

"Do what you need to in order to salvage your career. Be careful. If you want to talk, call me evenings, weekend, anytime. Don't make any hasty decisions. Come and talk it over first."

"I will. I'm grateful for your advice—even when I don't follow it."

102

David stayed on the island through Monday morning. He drove directly to Logan Airport for a flight to Washington. Since he was staying only for the day, he passed up a rental car in favor of a taxi to the White House. This visit was worlds apart from the last. The uncertainty that he felt on that occasion was at least tinged with hope and potential. Now he was gripped by nothing but discouragement and pessimism. Hope was no longer part of the equation. Once again, he was retrieved from the foyer by one of Lehman's aides. She did not even try to make conversation as she walked him to Lehman's office. Lehman kept him waiting twenty minutes before summoning him.

"Justice Lawson," he said with an amused smile that was a mockery, a mere facial reflex lacking all sincerity. "You surprised everyone. But this matter no longer concerns me. This is my last day. I'm returning to private practice as counsel with Bradley's firm. Your nomination is in the President's hands entirely. I have no idea what she will do. I know what I'd advise her to do, but she's not seeking my advice. You took care of that. One of the consequences of your surprise testimony. Do you understand what happened?"

"I have no idea," David said.

Lehman stared coldly at him for a moment. "I can see that you don't. The President had a window of opportunity to submit your nomination. How that came about, a deal with the opposition, is another story. I was charged with checking with you before she submitted it. I checked with Bradley and he gave the green light. We both wanted to snatch the opportunity while it existed. I reported the go-ahead to the President. We both trusted you and acted to protect your interest. Little did we know, you ignited a national conflagration without telling anyone in advance, even Bradley. You sandbagged us all and, what's more, you destroyed my relationship with the President. You also destroyed your relationship with Bradley. You're on your own. I'll have a staffer take you to the President."

David was silent. He felt regret at what he had brought about but he felt anger as well to be blamed for the stupid mistakes on the part of Lehman and Bradley, sensing that their self-interest played a role. Good riddance to Lehman, he thought. But he felt deep regret at failing to live up to Bradley's trust. He left with the staffer without further conversation. Lehman had already gone back to his office.

David was deposited abruptly into the Roosevelt Room opposite the Oval

Office. After a half hour, the President appeared with two staff people. She motioned for him to take his seat. "I'll get right to the point, Justice Lawson. Your failure to be fully forthcoming about your situation, that is, what you planned to testify to, has caught us all by surprise. I realize that the predicament in which I find myself is not entirely because of your doings. A series of circumstances—mistakes, misjudgments, and misrepresentations—by others within my sphere of trust, has contributed to a political dilemma for me. You had every right to testify according to your oath and your conscience, but you had an obligation to let me know what you intended. I have to deal with the consequences. This affects, not just the Supreme Court nomination, but my entire legislative agenda and my foreign policy objectives. I've lost the advantage that I had within my grasp. You know there have been constant battles over executive versus legislative power for two decades now. This is an embarrassment for me and it hurts my position. I am personally disappointed as well. I thought you could be a positive force on the Court."

"Madame President," David began, "I'm so very—"

Before he could get the words out, the President raised her hand and said, "Let me finish please. Apologies are too late. They will not help you or me. Your remarks about the Ramadi affair have touched off a furious fight on Capitol Hill. Members of the opposition party are threatening to hold hearings, not to discredit the military, but to discredit you and vindicate the military. Members of my party threaten to discredit the military as well as you personally. They perceive the need to expose what looks like a cover-up of an atrocity. With the endless wars against extremist networks in the Middle East, one after the other, the military has a lot at stake. I'm not opposed to a close examination of these ongoing wars, past and present. Perhaps that will come to pass. If that happens, and we have a study like the Vietnam Readjustment Study, it will be a good thing. But I don't foresee that this will lead to constructive action.

"You will be at the center of the firestorm that will consume valuable time and resources and derail other important issues. You wouldn't be able to hide behind a black robe even if you were to be confirmed. On that score, my sources assure me the votes we once had for you are no longer there to confirm you. If I were to support your nomination at this point, the result of months of hearings would be further damage to the White House, not to mention further damage to you.

"Personally," President Madison continued, "I can't help but admire, on some level, your decision to speak the truth against your own self-interest, even though it comes very late in the game—many years too late. Lord knows, the truth is in short supply these days, especially in this city, where you'd think truth with a capital T would be honored. But you failed to warn me of the situation. Even if I wanted to continue with your nomination, which I don't, my political resources to manage it are depleted. I hear there's a likely grand jury investigation into MEJA crimes too. I have no idea what will happen on that score. Perhaps you will be prosecuted. But whatever the result, it's bound to generate more controversy and more distraction. Frankly, it would be best at this point, and maybe less embarrassing for you, if you formally request that I withdraw your name. I say that regretfully, but realistically. This is a loss all the way around."

"Madame President," David said, "I came prepared to do that. I'll sign whatever statement you'd like. I'm deeply sorry for the trouble I've caused and, of course, I'm personally disappointed. But that's minor compared to the damage I've caused. I can only hope that some good will come of all this." The meeting ended shortly and David returned directly to Connecticut.

103

During the following week, the cascade of consequences following David's trial testimony continued. When he returned to the house, Lucille announced summarily that she had instructed Morehead to start a divorce action. "I'm not waiting any longer; I'm moving forward. I don't want to be associated with you. It's bad for the boys too. They come home upset every day. The other kids are calling you a liar and a war criminal. It's not fair to them. Oh, and your lawyer said he'll advise you to make yourself available to accept service of the complaint. That would avoid awkwardness for you. You'd better get in touch with Herb right away because John is not going to wait. Don't try to delay this. I want you out of the house. I can't put up with the tension here. That's not good for the boys either. The sooner you separate from us, the better."

"You've got it all arranged then," David said. "You know it will just be a drain on money that we don't have if I have to get an apartment."

"Deal with it," she said. "You have until the end of the week to move out. I'm willing to let you see the boys, of course, but only with proper supervision. Just so you know, the story of your testimony and your sergeant's about your authorizing the killing of civilians has been carried in all the Connecticut newspapers. It's no secret, in case you had some illusions about that."

"Thanks," he said. "Very kind of you. I knew you'd take advantage of any opportunity to get the upper hand. You're true to form. Kick me when I'm down. All the war criminal stuff, that's bullshit. You're just exploiting that to get what you want."

David decided it was wise not to attempt to remain in the house. It could lead to false accusations by Lucille and make matters worse. He'd make arrangements to rent a condo just outside of New Haven, which would be convenient and, hopefully, not too depressing. He authorized Herb to arrange for service of the complaint. Herb assured him he'd be able to hold off crucial aspects of the divorce orders to give him time to deal with all the problems that he was facing. Delay was easy. If anything characterized the divorce process, it was delay.

Richard agreed to handle the deluge of inquiries that followed the trial proceedings. Journalists from all over the East Coast called for interviews. Several requests came from radio and television talk shows for David to appear and explain more about the Ramadi affair. The political news cycle was quiet, enabling the war atrocity story to occupy a conspicuous position in the news. Richard advised David to avoid making any comments, given the strong possibility of a MEJA grand jury proceeding, which had been announced by the Justice Department. Justice would handle the matter until a decision was made to refer it to a U.S. Attorney to implement. A possible perjury prosecution took second place in the news to MEJA, which made a far more intriguing story.

Richard also would be the point man for any requests or subpoenas from Congressional committees that had threatened to hold hearings after the first of the year to investigate the Ramadi incident. The House Committee on Military Affairs was the likely leading force, although demands were being made for a special prosecutor to be appointed. The committee might appoint a special subcommittee to look into the Ramadi massacre, which some sources were calling the affair. Nothing much would happen until after the first of the year but the publicity engines were in full gear.

David made his first trip to the Supreme Court in Hartford after the first term cases had been argued. Burkhardt had decided not to assign him to any cases in the next term. David learned this only by seeing his copy of the assignment calendar. When he saw that his name did not appear, he decided to confront Burkhardt. In early October, he drove to Hartford, alerting only his own secretary in advance. He knocked on Burkhardt's door without an appointment.

"What's going on? Why haven't you assigned me to cases?"

"I'm not assigning you indefinitely," Burkhardt said, "and I've consulted with the Governor and the co-chairs of the Judiciary Committee. With all that's hanging over your head, you shouldn't be hearing cases. Some legislators are considering an impeachment. The Governor may ask you to resign. The other alternative is that Judicial Complaints will act on a complaint that I'm preparing."

"This is ridiculous," David responded. "I won't stand for this. You try any of those moves and I'll be all over you. You have no right to remove me. Neither does the Governor. And you have no cause for a complaint. If the legislature tries to impeach me, I'll fight that to the end. I demand to be assigned to cases immediately."

"I have nothing more to discuss, Lawson. You're through, one way or the other. The decent thing for you to do is to resign. I'm working on having your pay suspended too, by the way. The sooner you resign the better. You have no place here. You're on record as a liar. You're not bringing this court down with you."

"You'll be the one to suffer a fall if you try any of these moves. You've tried to get rid of me since I joined the court."

"We're finished, I think. You know your way out," Burkhardt said with a sneer. "Or shall I call a court officer to escort you?"

David left, slamming the door behind him. He went to his chambers and called Jeff to let him know about the conversation. Jeff promised to keep him informed and to support him. "I'll call my contacts at the legislature," Jeff said. David stayed on to make phone calls from his office and to let his clerks know what had happened. The clerks told him that they had been reassigned by Burkhardt to work for judges who would be filling out en banc panels. Despite his outrage, David saw no point to forbidding them not to do that. They were, after all, employees of the court itself, and the Chief Justice had the authority to reassign them.

David had never felt so abandoned and cornered at the same time. Every avenue of support was blocked. He felt defenseless against attacks from every direction—the divorce, his job, his friends, his future career, and topping it off, a possible federal prosecution that could jeopardize not only his freedom, but his life. Any crimes prosecuted would be capital crimes. Aside from a few lawyers, Richard, Herb and Jeff, his support system was eviscerated. He could deal with the divorce. That was familiar territory with fairly predictable results. But suspending his work on the court and the tactics to remove him were in uncharted territory. He knew that Burkhardt was exceeding his authority, but how to combat it was not clear. Financial pressures would close in soon, as well. And he had no idea what would emerge from a federal grand jury—or Congressional proceedings—and how he would defend himself. Storm clouds were gathering.

104

Several weeks passed without new developments. Each day presented David with a challenge to maintaining his emotional equilibrium. In an effort to ward off depression, he plunged nearly full time into writing, whether in his New Haven office or the modest condo he had rented on Long Island Sound twenty minutes east of New Haven. Not only did writing occupy his mind, it was valuable as a way to chronicle the events that occurred during his Iraq deployment through the present. Whether or not he ever published the narrative, it would serve to prepare him for the ordeals that would come soon enough.

Ruth called toward the end of September to let him know a few tentative mid-October dates for Willard's memorial service on Nantucket. They had been in touch every few days since his return to Connecticut. Ruth urged him to come immediately to Nantucket, which she promised would raise his spirits. No urging was necessary. "You can stay with me here at the rectory or stay over at Willard's place. Nothing has been changed there. It's yours for the asking. Please consider staying on for as long as you want."

David said he would pack all he'd need and be on the ferry tomorrow or the next day. Ruth's closing words were: "I'd like to be with you during this time. I think I can help. You need a safe and loving environment. It will nourish your soul. And you'll gain your strength and stamina back. What you've been through has been an assault on your body, mind, and most of all your soul. We can go running or swimming every day. The water will stay warm enough well into October. We just have to find the right tide and the right beach each day."

In addition to outdoor exercise—running, biking and swimming—and writing and talking, they spent time each day planning the memorial service, to be held the following week, on a Saturday morning. Willard's children and grandchildren chose not to speak at the service. Ruth would conduct the service, but at her suggestion, David would deliver the homily. They expected well over a hundred people to attend. There would be services in other venues as well, including New Haven, Washington, and Boston. David's idea was to shape the service in a way that reflected Willard's interests and ideas, to celebrate what he believed and the way he carried out those beliefs.

In the hopeful moments that David began to experience each day, as his physical, mental, and spiritual health gained dominance over discouragement about the difficulties that lay ahead, David looked forward to the service as the vehicle for regaining his own spiritual footing as well as honoring Willard. He felt the beginning of hope that he might survive the loss of nearly everything he had achieved.

He advanced beyond feeling regret at telling the truth and accepting the consequences. His immobilizing guilt over Ronnie's death was less crippling than before. He would never be free of that, nor should he be. His deep regret at mishandling the Ramadi affair, and the needless loss of innocent lives, remained but became more proportionate to his actual role. His remaining sadness was due mainly, he felt, to the alienation from his friends and family. While he was under attack from all quarters, he could not complain that the consequences were unjust or disproportionate to what he had done and failed to do. He had no moral right to cry out against unfair treatment.

From this vantage point, he began shaping his homily. He focused on what Willard would have thought and said under similar circumstances. Willard relied on reason as well as spiritual insight. For him, faith was trust, based on a long-range view of human life and experience. He did not expect magical solutions or redemption-on-demand.

David believed that Willard would have supported what he had done: simply spilling out the truth, the raw and honest truth with all its rough edges and scratched surfaces. That gave him confidence, day by day, that what happened in the short term was too limited a perspective. The point was to envision what the impact of all his actions and all his reactions would be in the long run, beyond his own life. He had revealed without shame his failings, his fears, and his doubts. He had willingly paid a price for that disclosure in serving truth. The point was not that loss occurred. The point was did it count for something. Did it produce some gain, some value?

His remarks would be about Willard's spirituality and his humanity. As one of the many beneficiaries of Willard's spiritual guidance and search for justice, David conceived of himself as a voice and, with humility, an interpreter for Willard's ideas. David browsed nearly all of Willard's books and sermons. One week before the service, he felt he had captured as much as he could of Willard's message. He hoped that he might find himself as well.

He felt hopeful for the first time in months, despite news that the impaneling of a grand jury had begun in federal court in Philadelphia. He and Ruth embraced each day as if it were the last day, the only day. He felt inspired by her warmth, her confidence, and what he imagined to be a nascent love that would flower over the years. What that love might become was as uncertain as all the other events of his life. He felt happier that he had in years.

When the moment came for David to take his position in the pulpit before the community of Willard's family and close friends overflowing the spacious church, he was ready. With a final meeting of his eyes with Ruth's, he turned to face the congregation.

105

I begin," David said, "by asking you not to dismiss the message because of the messenger." He paused, searching the faces of the congregation for signs of acknowledgement. "I want to offer a few words about the universal ideals that guided Willard's lifelong pursuit of justice—legal justice, social justice, moral justice. I visualize these ideals existing within the contours of the infinity symbol, signifying unity. They are faith, hope, love and courage.

"These ideals find their source in Paul's letter to the Romans. As you know, Willard admired Paul, whose letters constitute nearly half the books of the New Testament. Willard saw Paul's *conversion* from Saul, the cruel and cynical persecutor, to Paul, the idealistic and courageous missionary, as a pivotal event. He also believed that Paul's interpretations of Christ's teaching provided the means for Christianity to flourish. We can relate easily to Paul because of his human experience and especially because of his conversion, which is personally inspiring to me. Some of you may feel the same way." David paused for emphasis, hoping that his personal message was clear.

"In our intense focus on justice, we may overlook the spiritual source of justice. It is not a relativistic concept, and certainly not a human creation. Justice has its birth in faith. Willard liked to say that faith springs from trust, hope springs from faith, and courage springs from hope. The closest translation of 'to have courage' is, in the French, 'to take heart,' especially when facing formidable obstacles. Courage is companion to hope.

"Paul's letter tells us that God is a God of hope, as well as love. Hope is found not by our physical senses, but rather by our spiritual nature. When faith and hope are activated by courage and love, they lead us to justice. Willard said 'without truth, there is no justice,' and that truth requires more than marshaling convenient facts or opinions. It requires *soul-searching*—in a literal sense. Souls are pathways to the infinite, seeing beyond what we can comprehend.

"As Willard wrote, our souls emanate from God, are of God, and return to God when our earthly lives are over. Our souls are the means by which we are open to God's messages, which surpass any of our individual senses.

"Willard's idea of praying was to stand on a beach, in a meadow, or in the desert, in a place where his relationship with God could flourish, in one of the *thin places*. He would say that, in the deepest part of night, he would experience the voice of God. It would come from within because it comes to us through the soul.

"The mystery of the soul is the great enigma. We cannot comprehend what happens when time and the future no longer exist for us. But Willard loved to quote his famous theologian friend, William Sloan Coffin, in his book, *Credo:* 'If we are essentially spirit, not flesh; if what is substantial is intangible; if we are spirits that have bodies and not the other way around, then it makes sense that just as musicians can abandon their instruments to find others elsewhere, so at death our spirits can leave our bodies and find other forms in which to make new music.' Play on, immortal soul. Take heart. Have courage. Do not lose hope."

When David finished, he took his seat next to Ruth. Before resuming the service, she placed her hand on his, giving him an approving smile. Their eyes held the gaze for a moment. David leaned slightly toward Ruth, whispering, "I see the promise of *Paradise Regained*." She laughed almost imperceptibly.

106

The remainder of the day was devoted to Willard's children and family, along with the friends and colleagues who remained for the reception on the back lawn of the church. That was followed by another gathering in the parish hall, in preparation for the expedition to the Old North Cemetery, to place an urn in the Coleman plot. A smaller group of close friends and Nantucket natives joined for the scattering of ashes in the surf off Jetties and Brant Point, two of Willard's favorite beaches. Ruth and David would do a bike ride to Dionis Beach the next day. By evening, only the family remained to meet in the church library following a final tour of Willard's apartment and preparation for their departure the next morning.

Ruth and David were alone at last after the Sunday morning service, weary but satisfied they had carried out Willard's wishes. After a bike ride to Dionis Beach, their one remaining task was to bring Willard's ashes to Tuckernuck Island for scattering in the surf off the beach below the Coleman cottage in the East Pond area. They decided not to wait for Monday morning but to make the trip out later in the afternoon, despite the storm forecast. Ruth had arranged with the Jensen brothers to borrow one of their small fishing boats. She was a skilled pilot and navigator. Although the small island was only a short trip west from Madaket Harbour, beyond Smith's Point on Nantucket, the passage was often rough because of the big tidal rip, wind, and strong currents, and ever-changing shoals. They packed overnight duffels and brought raingear, food, and extra clothes.

Ruth guided the boat through the passage safely despite the downpour and the wind that stirred up unusually high waves that pounded against the boat, tossing it about. David felt some growing anxiety about their safety, and could not help but be aware of the irony. He, who had put Ronnie's life in jeopardy by teasing him to go out in a storm and causing him to be washed overboard, was now in jeopardy and distress. He who showed no mercy was at the mercy of the storm, the high seas, and the pilot. Where was the divine justice that would cause him to be thrown overboard?

After several close calls, they landed safely at the dock in the lagoon formed by Whale Island, now a sandspit connected to Tuckernuck. Drenched to the skin, but relieved and exhilarated from the adventurous crossing, they walked the sandy road leading to the northeast corner of the island and the Coleman house, standing in a cluster of houses belonging to related families. The Coleman house customarily remained open through the end of the month when it would be closed up for the winter. They spent the evening, with heavy rain pummeling the house, exploring the cottage and enjoying a simple candlelight meal. They stayed up talking until ten o'clock, before climbing the stairs to the master bedroom where they had mutually agreed to spend their first night together. They undressed in the semi-darkness illuminated only by candles. After disrobing, they laughed about the natural state in which they found themselves.

"I feel as though we're Adam and Eve in the garden," Ruth said, "but I'm not innocent, I guess, because I'm perfectly aware that you are naked and I'm enjoying every minute of it."

"I am, too," David said. "I am aware, and I feel no shame. What does this say about the Garden of Eden story, after all?"

"I've always had mixed feelings about the story, especially all the blame placed on Eve. I will say that they certainly knew what to do. As a psychologist, I think their behavior was completely predictable."

David approached Ruth slowly and they met halfway across the bedroom. He reached out to enclose her in his arms. "This is amazing. I'm not tired anymore and I was half asleep," David said.

"Same here," Ruth said, as she embraced him. "I've been waiting for this moment. But I'm a little scared too. It's been a long time since I allowed myself to be physically intimate with another person. That takes trust."

"I feel vulnerable too," David said, "and I understand what you went through when your marriage ended. You can trust me. I've wanted this since the moment I first saw you on the ferry. I wondered about destiny then. Now I believe in it. I believe in us. I want you, Ruth, more than I've ever wanted anyone." They moved to the bed. Passion triumphed over the last vestiges of reserve and fear. After making love, they fell asleep in each other's arms, oblivious to the storm raging outside.

They awoke to the first rays of morning sunlight streaming in the windows and beckoning them outside. David arose to make coffee and returned to bed where they talked quietly about their future together. When they could no longer resist the smell of fresh coffee, they stepped outside barefoot on the lawn with their cups. Looking out over the glittering water toward the east, they gazed in awe at the spectacular sunrise, a glorious display with a dozen different colors stretching across the horizon and reaching upward to the azure sky. They thrilled at the brilliant celebration in honor of their awakening to newly discovered love.

After taking their time to savor the light breakfast food they had brought, they hiked to the beach below for a swim, later spending the morning hiking the trails at that end of the island. In their happiness, it was easy for David to dismiss from his mind the troubles that threatened to envelop him in the coming months. After lunch, it was time to carry out their final ceremonial mission for Willard. Heading back to the beach that he had loved so much, they walked in the soft, cool sand until they found the perfect spot. Wading back into the water, they dipped their hands into the urn and flung the remaining ashes into the breeze. A sudden burst of wind lifted the ashes upward, carrying them, accompanied by Ruth's prayers, far across the water. The surprise gust inspired laughter, then tears, and finally an impulsive swim out into the deep water, taking care to guard against the powerful currents that coursed around the island and threatened to wash unaware swimmers away from safety.

As the afternoon passed timelessly, they sat on the terrace gazing out at the spectacular view and remarking on the rapidly changing cloud formations and the streaks of vivid colors in the sky as twilight lingered until darkness prevailed. Ruth spoke expectantly about the days, weeks, and months they could spend together while their relationship grew. David could take over Willard's small apartment, spending his time writing as well as staying in touch with his lawyers by phone and email. They could tolerate the short trips to the mainland when he had to attend court or hearings. Ruth felt confident that he would prevail in all the legal matters. Surely the government would not prevail in a MEJA prosecution or convict him of perjury, given the difficult circumstances he had faced. David was simply doing his job in an ambiguous and pressurized situation.

David nodded in agreement although he felt the uneasy stirrings of doubt growing. He began to question the wisdom of trying to manage his legal problems while hiding out at a place of refuge. But not wanting to mar their precious time together, and falling more deeply in love with Ruth with each hour that passed, he held back his concerns about remaining on the island while the legal matters brewed.

They made love again in the early evening, this time more freely and unselfconsciously. David was even more convinced that, once he put his legal problems behind him, they could move forward with their life together. In the morning over breakfast, as they were nearly ready to depart, he finally spoke cautiously about his thoughts, anticipating her disappointment.

"I want more than anything to stay with you on Nantucket, to escape from the world, never to leave. I'm happier than I have ever been. I'm growing more in love with you day by day. I feel confident that we will have a life together."

"I feel the same way, David. I want you to be here, and when Christmas is over, we can go away to a warm place for a couple of months. I feel sure that, by then, you will have won all your battles and you'll be free."

"That's my hope too," David said. "But I've been doing a lot of soul-searching, literal searching of my soul, as I mentioned in my remarks at the memorial service. I feel as though I've been running from everything since Ronnie's death—from my betrayal of him, my failures during the war, my guilt over that, and the web of lies that I wove. It feels as though I've been running from myself. I can't run any longer. I have challenges, trials of all sorts, waiting for me on the mainland—the MEJA grand jury, the divorce, possible perjury charges, and a subpoena to testify before a Congressional committee. Then there's my responsibility for the damage I've caused to the people who believed in me, who put themselves out to support me. I want to stand up to those challenges and, hopefully, regain some of the trust that I've lost. It's time for me to stop running and hiding. I need to go back and face the world. I take seriously all that I said about courage. I'm praying for the courage to face all my trials and survive them."

"You're saying that you want to leave now?" Ruth asked. "Isn't that like some sort of throwback to warrior days?" she asked. "As though you have to prove yourself again in some sort of traditional manhood test? What would that accomplish? And what do you risk losing?"

"I need to stay there until I have faced these demons or I'll never be a whole person. Willard's words and ideas that I used in the homily convinced me that I can't keep running. The truth is out. I believe I made the right decision to tell the truth at the trial. Now I have to pursue truth wherever it carries me. As Willard said, it can't be contained and it can't be controlled. Lies are manipulated but not the truth. I have to value courage and, for me now, courage involves facing all the consequences of my actions.

"I will come back to you. I don't know how long it will take but we can have a life together once I confront my past and put it behind me. That's where faith, love and hope come in. I am hopeful—I believe—that I can get over these obstacles. Courage requires that I face up to what I've done and failed to do."

"The demons are not in Connecticut or Washington or Philadelphia," Ruth said. "The demons that you've faced down were inside you. There will always be people in the outside world who will produce demons for you. The important thing is how you react to them. The strength has to come from within. You don't need to run off somewhere to deal with them. What's more, you've taken all these things that Willard said and used them out of context, as though they are independent ideas, not the unity that you professed to believe in. You've given them your own context, to serve some pre-conceived primitive idea that you have to face the challenges alone. That's not required by Willard's type of courage. He believed in people acting together too to bring about justice. He never said that the old male idea of going to war to prove himself—alone—had to be the way. You've taken Willard's ideas and stuck them onto what you decided you want to do."

"You don't understand, Ruth. It means something in the world I come from, that I have lived in, not to run from your fears, not to run from the fight. I'll be perceived as a weakling, a coward. I did these wrongs by myself, and I've got to face the consequences by myself. I'm not the same person I was before all that has happened, before owning up to the truth about myself. In a sense, I've undergone a conversion, not as dramatic as Paul's of course, but a conversion nonetheless. I can't go back to what I was, what I stood for. There's no way back."

"Oh, I'm so sorry to hear you say this. When you were silent last night, I was afraid you were having misgivings about something. I thought it was our relationship. In a way it is our relationship that you doubt. You've just decided that the relationship doesn't encompass our facing the troubles of life together. I was right in a way, sad to say," Ruth said. "I hoped it wasn't so. I'm afraid of what will happen if you leave me now. We've just found each other. I've just felt myself awakening after a long sleep. The thought of being separated terrifies me. I know you may face criminal punishment, maybe even more time away from me. If you stay here, and go back only when you have to appear in court, we can keep our hearts open to each other."

"We can still do that," David said. "My being away doesn't change that."

"But it does. Don't you see? It makes all the difference. I want us to have a life together now, not later. If you stay here, while you fight your demons, I can help you. But if you return to that hostile environment, you may be caught up in the problems and never return. What if you decide to reconcile with Lucille to avoid the divorce and losing the right to live with your children? What if you are tempted to sell out your principles because of the pressure you face alone? What if you become swept away with your ambitions again and choose to resume your career. What will happen to me? Does it matter to you? I can't leave myself so vulnerable. I don't think you understand how I felt for all those years, closed up. Now, I feel so open and vulnerable to rejection, to abandonment, to pain."

"Of course it matters. I understand how you feel," David said. "But I have to face my trials, my temptations, on my own, like Christ in the desert, though it seems pretentious to make the comparison out loud. I can't run or hide from them. I can't hide behind someone else, even you. We can talk often and I can come back on some weekends, but I need to face the people who accuse me. I can't have them also accusing me of being afraid and hiding out. That's like creeping back to what I was—a denier of the truth, a coward. I have to deal with the consequences of what I've done and what I've failed to do. I need help to maintain the courage to do this and keep alive the hope that we'll have the rest of our lives together. That's all I ask of you."

"What is it that you expect of me, in particular I mean?" Ruth asked. "Do you expect me to put my life on hold while you leave to face these battles, as you call them, on your own? And, then after what, months, maybe years, you will return in a triumphal procession to reclaim your woman? Is that realistic? I don't see the world that way. Our relationship has started to flourish based on a new set of values for you. Pain and loss has given you new insight into what is important. If we lose what we have now, will our relationship be relevant? Can it survive?"

"I don't expect anything of you, except waiting," David said. "But I hope you can bear with me on this and not give up on me until we're together with all this behind us. I told you that my determination—my conversion—came about as a result of soul-searching and this is what I believe deeply I have to do."

"I'd say this is the opposite of soul-searching. You're afraid of what people—what people, I'm not sure—will think and say about you: you, the man in our society. That's a false standard and certainly not the result of soul-searching. I'm not saying I won't try," Ruth said. "I'll do my best. But separation changes relationships. You'll change and I'll change over the months. If you've undergone a conversion to the truth, to standing up for what is right, you have the free choice of what to do in the future. It has nothing to do with the conversion or with courage. The courage is to accept who you are and go on living with that acceptance. Yes, you have to face trials but nothing dictates that you must separate from me to do that. I can see that you don't understand this. I can't make that happen but I'll hold onto hope now for our future. I'll pray that you find the courage to confront the trials you face. I'll pray too that neither of us loses our love or our hope that we'll be together again to resume a new life. But we know that life makes no promises and offers no guarantees. We have to go on with our separate lives and keep hope alive as long as we can."

An hour later, after closing the cottage and walking back to the dinghy, Ruth navigated the return passage to Madaket Harbour on Nantucket in silence. Two hours later, after tearful goodbyes at the rectory, David walked alone down the hill to the ferry and took a seat outside on the back deck. As the ferry pulled away, he fixed his gaze at the island receding in the distance until it disappeared at the horizon. As the ferry carried him back to the mainland, his mind went to the events of the past few weeks, to the ache of regret at leaving Ruth, and finally to the uncertainty that lay ahead.

David had no illusions about the obstacles that lay in his path, the wrongs that demanded his atonement, before he would deserve the life he longed to have. Silently, as doubt crept into his mind about the wisdom of his choice, he prayed for courage, as yet untested, and for hope, as yet unseen.

Acknowledgments

I am very much indebted to the people who provided help in research and editing. Dennis Carnelli, an Iraq war veteran, was a valuable resource in helping me understand the dynamics and details of the war in Iraq. In reading earlier versions of the manuscript, he guided me through the complexities of combat as well as the military justice system. Colleen Barnett provided outstanding help in the crucial final editing process, with her close reading of the manuscript. I am grateful that they offered me their expertise and knowledge; any errors in substance or form are my own.

I offer my profound thanks to my daughter, Donna Colburn, for creating the exquisite original painting that graces the covers of this book. In reading the manuscript and understanding the mood as well as the nuances of the story, she brought it to life in color and form as only such a talented artist could do.

Malcolm Feeley, as always, was a source of guidance and advice in locating a publisher. I offer thanks to my publisher, Alan Childress, and to Danielle McClellan for her fine editing of an earlier version.

My wife, Carol V.C. Schaller, above all, deserves my heartfelt thanks for her love and support throughout the adventure of writing my first novel and for providing me always with valuable insights into human emotions and behavior.

I want to add special thanks to the veterans of the Iraq and Vietnam wars who candidly shared their stories with me in connection with my previous book, *Veterans on Trial*. Their stories equipped me with valuable insights into the nature of war, its moral dilemmas, and its consequences.

B.R.S.
January 2016

About the Author

BARRY R. SCHALLER is a former Associate Justice of the Connecticut Supreme Court and a Clinical Visiting Lecturer at the Yale Law School, where he earned his law degree. He also received his B.A. from Yale College and an Honorary Doctor of Laws from Quinnipiac University School of Law. Since retiring from the Connecticut Supreme Court, he has continued his judicial service at the Connecticut Appellate Court and the Superior Court, where he is developing a judicial mediation program. He is the author of *A Vision of American Law: Judging Law, Literature, and the Stories We Tell* (1997), *Understanding Bioethics and the Law: The Promises and Perils of the Brave New World of Biotechnology* (2008), and *Veterans on Trial: The Coming Court Battles over PTSD* (2012).

Justice Schaller teaches an advanced degree literature course at the University of Nevada as well as serving as a Visiting Lecturer at Trinity College in Hartford. He has been a faculty member at the Florida Advanced Judicial Studies program and at the MacArthur Foundation Law and Neuroscience Project. Prior to becoming a judge in 1974, he served as Chair of the Connecticut Board of Pardons and as Counsel to the Minority Leader, Connecticut General Assembly. He has served in all three branches of state government and on all of Connecticut's statewide courts.

Schaller serves on the Middlesex Hospital Bioethics Committee and is active with the Connecticut Bar Foundation, where he is a Cooper Sustaining Life Fellow. He has been a featured speaker at the American Judicature Society's judicial ethics college and served two terms as Chair of the Committee on Judicial Ethics in Connecticut. He teaches business ethics to disabled war veterans for the EBV program at the UConn Graduate Business Learning Center. He lives with his wife, Carol, in Guilford, Connecticut.

Visit us at *www.qpbooks.com.*

Made in the USA
Lexington, KY
03 October 2016